BEWARE GREEKS BEARING GIFTS

GARETH LUSH

Copyright © 2021 Gareth Lush

All rights reserved.
ISBN: 9798709624351

The characters and events portrayed in this book are fictitious. Any similarity to real persons, living or dead, is coincidental and not intended by the author.

No part of this book may be reproduced, or stored in a retrieval system, or transmitted in any form or by any means, electronic, mechanical, photocopying, recording, or otherwise, without express written permission of the publisher.

Cover design by: canva.com
Printed in the UK. Independently published.

DEDICATION

To my partner, Helena, for always pushing me forward.

To my family, who were the first to jump into this new world of mine and experience it right along with me.

This one was for me: to distract from a year (2020) unlike any other.

CONTENTS

1	Prologue	5
2	Shield & Snake	11
3	The Alliance	39
4	Remembrance	79
5	The Sun, The Moon, and The Blade	129
6	Beware Greeks Bearing Gifts	147
7	The Labyrinth	186
8	Trials in the Deep I-IV	244
9	Achilles' Heel	284
10	Ascension	339

PROLOGUE

1

Everything was dark.

The rain swept through the streets, rattling the rooftops of the weak wooden houses of the city. Flimsy signposts bent under the pressure. Planted trees screeched as their roots tore and branches fought against the winds. Puddles formed, and water flowed freely from the tops of buildings to the streets below. The city was loud and silent at the same time. The city cried that night.

In the lower part of the city, an above ground labyrinth lay sheltered from the wind, but open to the watery downpour.

A boot glanced off the top of a solitary puddle. The puddle resonated, rippling in numerous directions. The second boot glanced off another. And another. Furious in their canter. The towering buildings loomed over the maze of alleyways; its darkness hiding twist after turn. The towering wooden walls, jutting upwards in poorly constructed manner, led to dead end after dead end. Those inside sheltering from the rain dared not speak a word. Dared not appear at their dilapidated windows.

But the figure in the night knew the way forward and was frantically heading for the familiarity of safety.

A heavy breath escaped an aching mouth. The breath was hard. Short. Gasping. The figure was running for his life. But he was not alone. He clutched the hand of a child. A child not equipped for this weather, let alone the furious pace that his father was keeping. But they drove ever forward into the night, hurtling down alleyway after alleyway. Heading for what, only the father knew.

He was frantic, furious, and calm all at the same time. He could not, and would not, let his child see his fear. His uncertainty. He was everything to this child and knew that any lapse in his stoic front would be met by a child's worry. Which they could both ill afford.

The father picked up his pace further still, aware that they were now almost at the end of the seemingly endless catacombs of the lower City. Light blared into view, creeping around the corner of this final corridor. He glanced back at the small child feverishly trying to catch his steps and threw a wink in the night. He hoped his son would catch it, and fortunately the son strained a tiny smile back at his father. He was relieved. They both were. Heartbreak and loss would follow once this was all over, but for now they were through the worst of it.

The father shifted his son around the final corner, clutched ever tighter in his grasp, before he glanced back quickly into the darkness of the alleyways they were about to emerge from. Good, he thought to himself. Nearly there now.

He turned sharply, as a crash of lightning flooded the streets behind and before them. The thunder was instant. And deafening.

A figure stood before them, standing tall in the centre of the open courtyard.

Adorned with a long black leather coat draped down to the floor, stroking side to side across the surface of the road as the wind continued to stream through the city. A tilted umbrella was held aloft above the figure's head, obscuring its face from above the jaw. A noticeably thick breath emanated from beneath the lower edge of the umbrella. Rhythmic almost, and undeniably calm. Heavy. But calm. White against the dark night. The figure's right arm was concealed in their coat pocket, whilst the left hand held the umbrella aloft with a strong white clawed grip.

The father's eyes slowly adjusted to the darkness

again as the figure came back into view. His eyes never once leave the figure. He knew that any lapse in concentration at this point would be fatal. Not only for him but for the small boy at his side, clutched desperately at his father's cloak.

The umbrella tilted upwards slightly and a wry grin stretched across the figure's face. He slowly opened his mouth to speak but the father impatiently interrupted.

"It seems I've misplaced my trust!" the father barked into the night. "We end this. Tonight. But whatever becomes of me, allow my son his chance at life. You owe me at least that." He paused. The fresh rage he felt now bubbled inside of him before slowly boiling over.

"You have attacked everything I hold dear tonight, and I intend to kill you for that, but come what may my son lives. I need your word."

The coated figure considered this request briefly before he tilted the umbrella upwards slightly further and nodded his approval. A loud click was audible through the clatter of storm, as the assailants' umbrella shot upwards and away from its handle, revealing the shape of a sword in the night. The umbrella floated lazily down through the air, left to right. Right to left. Left to Right.

"So that confirms it…" the father breathed to himself as he crouched next to the son at his side – keeping a view of his adversary's drawn sword, always. Rain streamed endlessly down his son's face. He feared the rainfall concealed heavy tears on the poor child's face. But it would soon be over. He needed to reassure his suffering child as much as he could in light of the already tragic evening.

Sadly, his son's future was sure to be filled with many such instances of suffering. Very much as his father's was. And his parents before him. The nature of their lineage demanded it. The curse of their family, forever targeted. It would pass to his kin sooner or later, and although he truly wished it weren't so, it would inevitably come to be. He hoped that his offspring would finally be the ones to end it. He prayed to the gods each and every night.

The father spoke as softly as the evening would allow.

"We will have time for tears when this is all over, but for now you need to be strong for me. For us. I have, and always will protect you with my life. I will do the same tonight. Your old man is the best there is. As much as he hates to admit it. Sit tight and I will be as quick as I can be."

He winked for the final time that evening. His son smiled for the final time that evening and nodded to his dad, as he wiped his face with his father's even wetter coat.

2

Thunder roared and lightning crashed through the air again, illuminating the sky. But this time was different. The lightning was emanating from the father. He was controlling it. Bathed in it. He *was* the lightning. He stood tall in the night.

The light flooded the streets, blinding the little boy's eyes. He squinted to keep his eyes set firmly on his father, as he threw his right arm up to block the light and sneak a peek through the brightness.

He blinked against the light, and as his eyes opened again, his father was no longer stood beside him. He was unbelievably fast as he flew towards the courtyard assailant.

They clashed. Sparks of red and gold flickered and raged into the air as steel crashed against steel. It was mesmeric, and as the son watched through peeking eyes he marvelled at his dad's skill and grace, mixed with a level of ferocity he had not seen before. His attacks were swift and all at once the man with the umbrella was on the back foot, floundering against a flurry of calculated and measured attacks.

Furious blows rained down on the assailant. His father was simply too fast, and too skilled.

The boy's father swung his sword, laced with wondrous light, high from above and down against the attacker's sword, causing a mix of piercing red and gold light to circulate wildly out of the area of contact. The son was bowled over by the strength of the impact, its gust mighty, but managed to gather his bearings quickly enough to see the assailant's sword spin rapidly out of his hand and into the sky, before slicing deep into the courtyard floor beside the both of them.

It was over before he knew it, and the night turned quiet. When the boy's eyes refocussed, he found his father walking back to him and smiling sweetly. The attacker left motionless and slumped over behind him. Defeated. Dead.

The father reached his son, crouched in front of him and dropped his sword neatly back into its sheath.

He placed his hands either side of his son's face. The son felt warmth, fighting against the piercing cold of the rain. His father kissed his forehead. Sweetly.

He watched on as his father opened his mouth to speak only to stop in his tracks, a look of morbid uncertainty on his face.

An overwhelming pain was emanating from the boy's chest now. He looked down to see a sword pierced into his body, the rest of the blade running straight through his father and into him. He coughed thick dark blood onto the sword. It almost seemed to meld with the black blade piercing him.

His father looked bewildered as he uttered his final words into the night. The son only caught part of it, as he felt his lungs slowly fill with blood, but it sounded like his father couldn't quite believe his killer was alive.

The father slumped to the ground beside him. He

caught one last look at his son, and his eyes closed for the final time.

As the lights also drained from the son's eyes and as his body went limp, he looked up into the eyes of the man who had ended his father's life. His face was pale as the moon above them. It was passive now. Unfeeling.

The boy felt the sword sluggishly pulled from his body. The man then leaned in close to the boy's face, settling just to the right of his ear and almost hissed at him.

"For me, death is only temporary."

All went dark and silent.

CHAPTER I
SHIELD & SNAKE

1

Heracles awoke in a cold sweat. His breath heavy. The hairs on his neck and arms stood neatly to attention. As he sat up, he felt a bead of sweat trickle down the small of his lower back.

He had stirred from the same recurring dream. The same dream he had always had when stressed. Or lonely. Or basically feeling anything other than *normal*. This time the stress concerned The Alliance's annual 'Ranking' ceremony.

He hated this time of year.

A huge part of that lay with the need for him to pretend he loved it. His colleagues and friends all enjoyed this day more than any other and waiting all year for it was part of the fun for them. That was not the case for Heracles.

He couldn't think of anything worse. Ranking all the soldiers in The Alliance in order of strength? Missions accomplished? Status? Whatever the criteria were this year. It was always such a brutal process. Progressing up and through the ranks was not a matter of time. Not a matter of age. It was a test of strength, endurance, and ultimately godly resilience. Those that progressed needed to be striving for that progression at all times. It broke people. The stress they placed upon themselves was immense.

Heracles had always hated it as he felt that the constant up and downs those within The Alliance faced on a daily basis, coupled with the desperation of latching on to any and all opportunities to prove their worth, was counterintuitive. He felt it was the wrong way to go about creating a healthy mindset. The stress was paramount. A carrot dangling desperately out of reach.

Further still, those who even came close to being considered for promotion into the Stratigos (the highest rank within The Alliance) often fell far short due to the sheer leap in terms of the responsibility, strength, and skill, needed for the role.

The whole business was ferocious and unfortunately for those aiming for the ultimate heights, the five members of the Stratigos were leagues above everyone else. A change in their ranks was an uncommon occurrence.

This year, however, was different. The retirement of Ares, the undisputed number one Stratigos of The Alliance, and one of the finest Generals The Alliance had ever seen, had come as a huge shock to everyone.

Ares Angelis was due to speak at the Ranking Ceremony today, as he had done annually for the past thirty odd years, and would be announcing the promotion of one of the Taxiarhos (the second officer rank within the Alliance) to the Stratigos. The thought of the announcement had changed the atmosphere immensely, and had The Alliance fired up. The furore in the courtyards as teams headed to their respective destinations had been paramount.

Still, he absolutely loathed this day.

The real reason being that he knew, in his heart of hearts, that he could be out there on the front lines as one of those vying for the elite spots of The Alliance. Recognised among his peers as equal, finally.

He didn't really hate the competition. He hated that he couldn't be a part of it all.

But the simple truth was that he wasn't one of the elites of The Alliance. And he never would be. He would never be anywhere above captain level (he hated calling it the official title of 'Lokhagos'), let alone anywhere near the top rankings.

It was too dangerous to even consider. No-one could ever know what he was capable of. All he could do, as he always had, was lie low and continue his role in The Alliance: keeping the training grounds stocked, clean and ready for the daily sessions, and assisting the new recruits in their first year of training and embedding.

He trained all the same. Night in, night out he trained. And trained *hard.* He was cautious about the bruises. The scars. The blood he shed. He couldn't afford not to be careful. He was meticulous in his cleaning of every piece of equipment he used in the Panathenon. Raking up his footwork in the dust. No tracks or marks left behind. He saw to that each and every night without fail.

At least his role within The Alliance allowed him access to the training facility without anyone batting an eyelid. As long as he was careful of course. Educating new recruits on The Alliance, whilst being their go to advisor for their first year, wasn't the most acclaimed role but it was perfect for him and his situation. Just the right amount of responsibility to be known across the academy for general greetings and conversations, whilst never being considered for further promotion.

Heracles pondered this whilst he dressed into his uniform – the staple dress he had worn for many, many years now.

He threw his white linen shirt over his head, and it dropped neatly down above his knees on to his slightly baggy white trousers. Clipping his black leather belt at the middle of his waist just over the tunic, he grabbed his black boots from beneath his desk and slid them on to each leg, sitting just under his knees, before he checked himself in the mirror. He wasn't a vain man by any means, but he did want to ensure he was always presentable, especially given the new recruits would be inducted today. He always felt the need to project the right attitude, the right presentation.

Heracles wondered why they never updated the old, formal staple uniform. He much preferred it when he could wear his casual clothes and remove all that official clothing.

He would always opt for his brown baggy linen trousers, tucked messily into his combat boots, when he could, coupled with his sleeveless white shirt open at the collar. It was simple, and he much preferred training in his casual clothes. He kept his golden hair a medium length to be somewhat presentable but he had always longed to grow it out.

He did envy the uniform of those of a higher rank, especially those that were permitted to wear a flowing cape, draped across their shoulders in a wondrous fashion, but was resigned to the fact that this was reserved for only those in the higher echelons of The Alliance. A shame, but understandable given the symbolism of the cape and the respect it drew from the peers around you. The higher ranks were also allowed to tailor their uniform to their personality and Heracles hated that he couldn't do just that.

Heracles finished by grabbing all of the things he would need for the day, gathering his parchments and items necessary for work, and trotted off to the Panathenon: The Alliance's ever impressive training grounds.

2

Prometheus was of course present at the training grounds already, ready to greet Heracles. He was itching for his new recruits to arrive and thankfully, Heracles' arrival coincided nicely with the rest of Prometheus' team as they steadily entered the Panathenon.

"Morning Alcaeus!" Promo (Heracles' affectionate nickname for his mentor) bellowed as he punched Heracles square in the chest, rocking him slightly.

Alcaeus was the name that Heracles went by following that fateful night 19 odd years ago. Promo's idea. A way of distancing him from his past and keeping it hidden from those that may wish to use it against him. Although Heracles had, in the early days, responded to people many times with a part of his actual name before quickly correcting himself, Prometheus had never slipped up. It was too important to him, and once Heracles realised that he had never slipped up again.

"Morning sir." Heracles coughed, rubbing his chest with one hand to feign injury, and raising the other up to his temple in salute.

"A fine morning for it, don't you think?" Promo said as he looked around the whole of his staff.

A few of the team piped up and shouted back to him. The majority of the team were clearly as excited as he was and why shouldn't they be? New recruits to mould into fierce warriors was always something to look forward to.

"Absolutely! Think we'll see anything special today? My money is on one or two surprises at least." one of the chirpier team members spoke in return, over the level of the others.

"Right you are Cleon. I've poured over the list personally, of course, and there'll undoubtedly be some surprises," Promo winked at this. He had clearly thought he knew something the team did not. "Lets' prep up. Busy day ahead of us. We've only got the morning with the recruits before the ceremony and this place looks like a fat bastard of a Cyclops had its guts shaved by some overenthusiastic sword swinging."

Thirty odd minutes later, with the Panathenon looking much more presentable, twelve young adults entered the training grounds. Some bullish in their stance.

Some more reserved but still radiating a sense of confidence and a right to be there. That was good. Those who didn't have a sense of something about them were never going to survive the next year. And even those who did would find it harder than anything they had faced in life so far. It was good that they had confidence in themselves. They were going to need it. And whatever they had done in the build up to arriving here was a solid indication that they were gifted enough to fight, given The Alliance was not an easy establishment to join. Quality was paramount above all else at The Alliance.

A deafening gong rang across the stadium, breaking any stance the recruits might've been holding, and causing the majority to cringe at the sound. Promo was ready.

"Good Morning to you all and welcome to The Alliance's infamous Panathenon," he bellowed, as the noise carried to all parts of the stadium. He could be impressive when he wanted to be. "Where the best of the best raw minds and bodies come to be moulded into something a little more spectacular. To spill their blood and sweat on to this hallowed ground. To become what they were meant to become." Promo paused to great effect. A skill he had honed over many years of public speaking.

"A BIG day today of course. Not just for you new recruits, but for all of us. Use today as the inspiration for your time here. Let it be your fuel. Those you see paraded in front of you at the upcoming Ranking Ceremony are what you should aspire to be. And of course, we are celebrating the successes of one of the greats of The Alliance – Ares."

He looked at the twelve bright faces staring back at him to gauge their reaction to him mentioning a Stratigos. Their faces, as he had suspected, glowed with passion, layered with some hesitance, which was to be expected.

"Down to business then. Alcaeus will take you through your inductions and show you the ropes, but be ready for tomorrow, where the real work begins. The team, and I, will be teaching you how to think. How to act. And ultimately, how to fight. Some of you might make it all the way, but you will *all* have a role to play in The Alliance. We will always find something for those who are ready to commit fully to the cause." Promo looked out, pausing for what he imagined would be an eternity for the new cadets, before nodding and continuing.

"Alcaeus, over to you."

Promo turned away from the cadets, walking purposefully back towards the rest of his training staff. As he passed Heracles, he laid a hand firmly onto his shoulder. He turned his face to him, his stoic visage turning to a grin now that he was facing away from the cadets, and winked. Promo was in his element. He knew he was going to break every single one of the fresh faces behind him. And he *lived* for it. Because he might see someone here today make it all the way into the Stratigos. That feeling gave him the most exhilaration of all, and Heracles genuinely wished right along with him, hoping his old friend would see it happen again before he retired.

Heracles walked over to where Promo had been standing, surveying the recruits in front of him carefully, before addressing them.

3

Heracles waited until the others were out of earshot and continued.

"Welcome to the Panathenon. As you will see before you, this training ground is the greatest in the world: its circular shape allowing a three hundred and sixty degree view of the training floor, ready for when you'll need to show off your skills come the end of the year. Plenty of seats to watch you toil, sweat and train."

Heracles took a more serious tone.

"I warn you now, this isn't a settling in year. You will be pushed to your limits, and you will be better for it. You will falter, but you will learn from every fall. Everything we do here is for the simple purpose of bettering The Alliance and honing your contribution. My role is to keep you all on track and be here to kick your arse if you step out of line. The role of your teachers is to break you, and then mould you into your future selves. It will not be easy."

Heracles paused for effect and to look around at the faces staring desperately back at him.

"However, everyone here is here for a reason. You all have what it takes to succeed. In what capacity that will be is yet to be seen but know this – all of you are now a part of The Alliance and from now on, everything you do is to better yourselves as a member of this great establishment. We all fight for The Alliance, and against those that aim to harm our lands. So, let's make it count."

Some of the recruits moved to clap, but Heracles swiftly waved them away. He motioned to the centre of the Panathenon and all of the eyes before him followed the length of his arm to the spot he was pointing to.

Heracles nodded to Prometheus who was now standing ready by a long wooden pole, stuck firmly into a part of the outer wall of the Panathenon. He placed his hand on it and slammed it downwards.

Where it had been relatively quiet before, there was now a muffled rumble of earth, growing in volume as the centre of the arena moved away from itself, revealing a slowly rising circular platform. Dust crumbled and rolled off as it rose. Nestled on top of the platform was a large bed of stone and rock, jutting upwards in an arch, and on top of that still sat a colossal shield. Its sheen radiated in the light rushing in through the open ceiling of the

Panathenon.

As the recruits approached, fascinated murmurings began. Heracles had always thought the shield incredibly detailed, every inch of its surface covered by intricate designs and patterns. Runs of meandros designs, The Alliance's classic decorative borders, ambled in a straight line, repeating multiple times across the shield. The recruits marvelled at it.

Heracles had always enjoyed being in its presence. He would often draw it out in the dead of night just to marvel at it, as centred on the shield was an elaborate circular tapestry of countless warriors, all posing in various battle stances. Some victorious. Some stoic. Some waiting and ready to strike.

Hopefully the recruits had understood that this was a depiction of great heroes that had come before, captured on this wondrous shield for all time. Those who had been a part of The Alliance in some shape or form over the years, many of whom had sacrificed themselves for the good of the world, cementing their place in the halls of history.

A recruit next to Heracles moved her hand closer to the shield before Heracles lightly caught her mid movement. He shook his head sharply and moved her hand back towards her side.

"Eager?" he said with a grin as he walked up to a set of stairs that had appeared to one side of the shield, nimbly climbing them with a skip in his step. He asked the class to follow suit, and one by one they ascended and gathered around the shield's tapestry.

"This is the Shield of Aegis. A shield of unbridled beauty and history, the Aegis has been a part of the Panathenon since its conception nearing thirty years ago. Little is known of the origins of it before it came into our possession, but it is thought to be timeless. An artefact of a bygone era."

"You will find on the rich tapestry depictions of

current and fallen heroes of The Alliance, added to its fascia by the Aegis itself. It transforms and contorts when it deems a hero has done something of great worth. This is the ultimate achievement." Heracles paused at this to allow the recruits to survey the shield and wonder at those that had gone before.

He picked up. "You will also notice that centred on the shield is an interesting attraction. May I introduce you to the snaked head of Medusa."

As if summoned into life, the snakes aroused and began to weave around their mother's head, coming in and out of view as they disappeared and reappeared from behind her. Medusa's eyes remained closed, and she merely bobbed slightly, breathing silently.

"She assists us in assessing the potential of our new recruits. As you will be aware, you are here today because you carry the 'Mark of the Gods'. A mark that identifies you as someone who can call on the power of the gods and draw a weapon from the Shield of Aegis. This is a privilege and honour that only a limited amount of people are afforded, so don't forget that."

As Heracles talked about the mark, the recruits' eyes wandered. Heracles recognised this as them looking to the position of the marks on their bodies. Some looked to their torso. Some looked to their shoulders. Some had the marks in view on their necks and wrists.

It was thought that before the shield came into The Alliance's possession, those with the Mark of the Gods embarked on great pilgrimages, searching for the shield wherever it lay to gain the strength of the Gods. Fortunately for those born in the city of Athenaeus, the shield now lay here. Those with the mark were invited to an entry test into The Alliance on their eighteenth birthday. A lot failed, heading back to their normal lives, as if those with the mark hadn't drawn a weapon by their thirtieth birthday, they would lose the mark forever. A shame, and there were many who tried year after year to gain acceptance into The Alliance, just to fall short. The test was notoriously gruelling, testing many facets of those who entered: strength; speed; strategy; knowledge; bravery.

Those before him today had all succeeded, and he could see a few that were older in age that had clearly stuck with it and persevered through disappointment. Good for them, Heracles thought to himself.

"The weapon you will receive is bound to you and for life and lost to you in death. Every member of The Alliance has been a part of this ritual and you are no different. This is the time to see what weapon you will receive. There are no second chances with your drawn weapon. Your blade is a part of you, an extension of you. There can only be one drawn. Finally, remember that the weapon chooses you. And you will gratefully receive its power."

Heracles smiled at this final part of his well-rehearsed speech. It always made the recruits light up in a way that he had never tired of. Excitement bloomed around him.

"Now. Form a line. Decide amongst yourselves the order."

Nervous shuffling commenced before him.

"It is time for 'The Rite' to commence."

4

Heracles placed his hand in the air and hovered it in the space above Medusa.

"The drawing process is unique to you," he proposed. "Be prepared for that. Not all weapons are created equal, and don't be deterred if your weapon appears less special than any other. I know several high ranking members of The Alliance who have done exceptional things with their perceived 'less powerful' weapons. *You* determine *your* strength and skill through hard work and dedication." He paused to try and drive the point home.

He didn't want to deter them too much at this early stage, but what he would say next may well do just that.

"However…there may yet be some of you here given *exceptional* power."

A few murmurs rang across the group. Heracles ignored it and continued on.

"We will teach you all how to fight with your newly acquired weapons. How to block, parry, and ultimately, how to survive. We will teach you to control any power your new weapon possesses. And know that we will not treat any of you any differently. Be humble. Be thankful that you have been given this precious gift. And know that any slack given to your training will allow those with the passion and drive to be better than you."

Heracles had given this speech plenty of times before, but today felt extra special for some reason. An underlying niggle in the back of his mind that today's speech would be somewhat more poignant. Heracles waved it off as the anticipation of Ares' retirement. It was a nice feeling, and he felt good about this group of recruits. Even without hearing a single word from them, barring some inaudible murmurs. They were attentive. They were respectful. That wasn't always the case, but those important traits made for excellent soldiers. In any case, it was now time for them to start their journey.

Heracles grabbed a small parchment from the back of his belt. One that had been neatly rolled into a cylinder shape, tied, and tucked since his walk over to the Panathenon. An important document for all of those in attendance as it detailed each and every recruit present, with some notes for Heracles on their strengths, weaknesses, and general points about them that Prometheus had jotted down for him.

Heracles looked over at Promo, who was now waiting patiently to the left hand side of the orderly formed recruits, and nodded for him to take his place at the front of the queue. This role was Prometheus' to perform, as the highest ranking member of the team but to Heracles' surprise, Promo shook his head, and pointed back at him. Heracles, a little shocked but aware of the faith Promo had in him - and revelling in this opportunity - nodded back in acceptance and turned back to the recruits.

5

The first in line, slightly shrugging off some jostling behind him as he stared back at Heracles, was clearly quietly confident. For a young lad, he was holding himself in pristine pose – his back arched slightly forward, accentuating his powerful chest. He was clearly in exceptional shape, and Heracles would've bet a lot of coin on him having received high levels of basic training prior to his arrival here.

"Name?" Heracles asked, hands firmly on the outstretched parchment, and ready to locate the cadet.

"Achilles, sir. Achilles Elias Junior".

He spoke strongly and clearly. Drilled to perfection, and as Heracles had thought, named after a past member of The Alliance. But he hadn't anticipated just how great a member. A famous former Stratigos, Achilles Elias Senior. An ex-Strat unfortunately, due to his untimely death some years ago.

The question now was, would Achilles draw his father's sword in The Rite ceremony?

"Welcome Achilles. Step forward, slowly, and hold your lead hand over the head of Medusa as I am now." Achilles complied, quickly and efficiently as expected. Heracles glanced at the training team, who were now slowly gathering around Promo.

"Repeat the following words, but only when I have moved back from the centre. This needs to be all you Achilles."

Heracles moved backwards out of the centre to allow Achilles his time in the spotlight.

"Make sure you look Medusa directly in the eye…yes, that's it…she will be opening hers shortly. Now repeat after me, with all the force of the gods."

Medusa, Queen of Gorgons. Mother of Serpents.
The one who Watches, the one who Protects.
Turn me not to stone.
Grant me gift to protect the weak and help my kin.
Medusa. Grant me my golden arms.

Achilles studied Heracles with great attention. He nodded at various points, and once Heracles had finished, he breathed deeply and repeated the prose perfectly.

Heracles watched on. He had always wondered whether any of the recruits would actually turn to stone during the ritual, but none of them ever did. Those with The Mark were worthy. Those without The Mark, would be stone where they stood. You couldn't fake The Rite, and that was what Heracles loved about the process. Those that were picked, were worthy by gift of the Gods.

As Achilles uttered the last word of the passage, the snakes floating around Medusa's head began to animate, toiling furiously around their mother. Heracles had never gotten over how hypnotic the ritual was, and for those directly in front of Medusa it was simply mesmeric. Achilles was lost in the snakes and their movement.

Medusa's eyes suddenly flew open, shining blood red and piercingly bright.

Achilles became instantly lost in Medusa's piercing gaze. And that was good. It showed that he was completely at one with Medusa, and ready to receive his arms from her.

As the serpents swirled and snaked, Medusa's eyes fixed on Achilles. He looked on, almost dumbfounded as Medusa's mouth opened and gaped. The handle of a sword came clearly into view, vomited forth from deep with the Shield.

Heracles shouted out to Achilles again, after his first call went unheard, breaking his hypnosis. "Grab it now Achilles! Take it. It's yours!"

Achilles, refocussed now, reached down to the handle, grabbing it firmly, and pulled strongly upwards. Sound reverberated around the walls of the stadium. Rubble cracked and creaked against the old, worn stone faces.

The recruits watched on as Achilles withdrew a glorious sword. Achilles held it high above his head, panting heavily after the sheer amount of stress The Rite had caused him, but he was clearly enamoured with his catch as he stared deeply at it.

A darkly golden handle, decorated with bright red diamond gems, led into a long and lightly golden spear styled blade. Clearly sharper and straighter than any blade in the training centre, and probably across the majority of The Alliance. Heracles recognised it instantly. Achilles had indeed drawn his father's blade as he had suspected. He recognised it from one of the book's in the library, but could not recall mention of the power it held within.

It was known that a blade could pass down through a family following the death of a parent, and Heracles felt his chest tighten slightly at this thought.

"Achilles Senior's sword." Heracles whispered into the air, as he stepped towards Achilles and placed his hand onto the small of Achilles' back – ushering him down and away from Medusa's perch and back onto the training ground floor.

"Congrats Achilles. Your father's sword I presume?" Heracles muttered to Achilles under his breath.

Achilles looked initially taken aback, before gathering himself and nodding with a somewhat bittersweet smile. Heracles nodded in return, to confirm he would press no further, and climbed back up towards Medusa. Heracles knew all too well the tales of Achilles' father's sword being cursed. Maybe the boy was apprehensive about that given the fate that befell his father.

Heracles turned back to the recruits and addressed them.

"Ok, you've seen how it works. One by one, I want to you to step forward and engage with Medusa."

The recruits readily complied and one by one they took their turn to climb up onto the perch and greet Medusa, clearly reciting the chant.

6

Whilst Heracles hated the day of the Ranking, he loved the process of The Rite and the new recruits drawing their arms.

Those post Achilles weren't especially unique weapons for the most part. It was quite rare to see several unique weapons per annum. Still, there were varying shapes, sizes, and styles that were drawn. Some swords. Some spears. Some daggers. One large mallet styled hammer. It was a beautiful thing to behold and the look of elation on the recruit's faces made it all the sweeter.

Even though none of the ones drawn were anything to write home about here this morning barring Achilles so far, Heracles was always quick to remind himself that it was the skill of the fighter that was of the upmost importance. That was why he had always stressed this to all of his recruits. They would see some examples of Alliance members up close and personal today who had made a name for themselves, and in turn for their weapons, without them ever being considered special initially.

Heracles felt the same feeling course through him, as he had several times this morning. He suspected that the drawing of special arms wasn't over today. There were still over half of the recruits left to complete The Rite ritual, and he had his bets placed firmly on some of those before him.

One recruit, in particular was of great interest to Heracles. Strangely, she had been silent throughout the whole process so far. Stoic. Composed. At the very least the others had interacted with each other (whilst always cautious of the training team's eyes). But not her. Heracles scanned the parchment again, and no female names jumped out at him that he might recognise from previous, or current, members of The Alliance. Strange. But fascinating none the less.

7

Before her turn in the queue though was a slightly older recruit. Less imposing than the others in stature, even with his taller frame, and also much more jittery. His short, black curls shook slightly as he darted his head left and right to see whether everyone was looking at him. He was still of an athletic build, as one needed to be to get anywhere near this stage, but he was slimmer and more toned in contrast to Achilles' muscular frame.

He wore the general recruits' uniform slightly baggy, where the others had clearly chosen their sizing appropriately, perhaps where his muscles were less developed than the others. His brown linen tunic was tied tightly around his waist by a belt he had clearly added another notch to, and his brown boots were scruffy from where he had shuffled nervously in the dirt.

He had been mingling well with the others, although it was clear the rest of the recruits had held some contempt towards him for his lack of stance, composure, and poise. He was deathly anxious. Heracles assumed there had been some failure in his attempts to join The Alliance previously, and that had kept him back somewhat given his older age. But through that, here he was, standing before Medusa in The Alliance HQ.

Heracles wondered what had changed this year to help him pass. Perhaps he had got lucky. Perhaps his persistence had paid off. Heracles was keen to explore that further if he could.

Heracles called him up to take his place.

"Name?" Heracles asked, slightly stern to force a reaction out of the kid.

"Apollo…Helios, sir!" he stuttered, before stepping meekly forward. Heracles supposed that the kid must've had something about him, and Promo was absolute in those he picked to join the programme. There just felt something off about him and Heracles could not quite put his finger on it.

"You know what to do." Heracles said. He felt the need to try and toughen the kid up a bit, so was forceful with his delivery. Heracles had serious doubts just from looking at him.

Apollo climbed forward and held his hand aloft. The amber skin of his hand reflected the light streaming down upon the shield as it trembled. His nerves in plain sight for all to see. He tried to compose himself, breathing in heavily, before exhaling downwards towards his feet. He raised his head up straight, took one last deep breath, and began the prose.

Almost immediately, the temperature rose across the stadium. It swept through like a warm wind, circulating around all of them. Heracles hadn't experienced heat like it before, even with Prometheus as his mentor, and it continued to rise in intensity. It was almost contradictory. Immensely hot, but at the same time comforting. Safe somehow. Powerful, undeniably, but safe.

Apollo continued to chant.

The snakes around Medusa's head swirled and weaved frantically, as if attempting to hide behind the head of their mother, safe in her shade. Audible hissing sounded from Medusa's vicinity.

Heracles reached down and swept his hand across the surface of the shield before recoiling back. Red-hot to the touch. His gaze never left Apollo. He was slightly concerned for the boy at this juncture but Apollo seemed completely calm. At complete odds against the jittery character of a moment ago.

At last, he uttered the final word of the prose.

A wave of circular flame raged upwards from beneath him, blowing Heracles backwards off the shield and obscuring his sight of Apollo and Medusa. The flames engulfed Apollo.

Prometheus sprinted past Heracles, who was now getting up from the floor, with sword in hand and slightly out of its sheath. Promo touched the flame with his other outstretched hand. The look of concern changed to confusion as he washed his hand back and forth within the fire.

Heracles joined Promo in touching the fire. A cool, empowering feeling oozed from it. The fire was astronomically hot but was not affecting him in the way that he had assumed it would. It was pleasant, inviting, as if those who were of no danger to the flames were safe from it. Heracles had experienced similar powers before in the past, whereby they were designed to hurt only those who aimed to hurt them.

It was undeniably powerful. The colour of the fire was both red and white, radiating heat. Promo eased beside Heracles, turned, and walked back to where he had been standing, patting Heracles on the shoulder as he passed, his hand now off of his blade, satisfied that the boy was not in any danger.

Heracles returned to where he had been standing

also, brushing his uniform as he went, and watched as the flame spewed high into the sky above the arena.

The flames stood for a second as Apollo emerged from within them, before bursting upwards for a final time and dissipating, small particles of ash floating down through the air around them. The lack of confidence he had displayed before was now visibility reduced.

Heracles looked to Apollo's hand and saw a captivating blade. One he had not seen before. Apollo looked equally shocked as he looked at the sword he held, and the flames still radiating from it.

Heracles glanced over at Promo, who was now beaming. Promo was an expert in fire swords, owning one himself, and he seemed wildly impressed. It was more raw power than Heracles had ever seen come from Promo's sword, even after years of seeing it in action during sparring sessions, although he highly doubted Prometheus had ever wanted to use anywhere near his full power during training.

The exceptionally long hilt of the sword was black, as if to magnify the beauty of the blade itself, and laced periodically with tiny silver circlets down the handle. The hilt's guard was that of a silver bow, arching left and right. The pummel was the shape of a flame, jutting out of the base of the handle – almost as if the flame were alive, and swaying in the air. The blade itself was edged and lined with a shining silver, with a core of pure red. The colour of the brightest sun.

It truly was a magnificent sword. Heracles had only seen a handful of swords that could surpass this one, and they were the rarest, owned generally by those destined for the Stratigos.

This was a memorable Rite.

Heracles noticed movement and moved his gaze to Medusa. Apollo did the same, sensing her addressing him. Heracles knew this part all too well.

Medusa, her snakes once more in full view to the

sides of her, opened her mouth and almost spewed forth the confirmation that Apollo had drawn something quite special.

"Apollo." She hissed. "The Burning Sun."

8

Apollo stumbled on his feet, and Heracles was quick to flash towards him, grabbing his arm as he steadied him.

The kid had bulked noticeably since his part in The Rite. The power that Apollo now drew from the sword was having an effect on his body. He also seemed more assured and confident now.

Heracles mentally noted to speak to him later on about his nervousness before the ceremony. He had clearly had something weighing firmly on his mind. For now, though, Heracles simply needed to make sure the rookie was ok.

"You ok kid?" he said, straightening him upwards.

"Yes, sir." Apollo offered, no longer stumbling over his words, the colour in his cheeks quickly returning as he regained his balance.

"That was…I feel amazing." Apollo said, marvelling at what had just occurred and looking over his body.

"Medusa only speaks when something truly special has been drawn Apollo. Congratulations, you're the standout so far. Head over to Prometheus and he'll sort you out."

The rookie nodded, his newly acquired sword clutched tightly in his hand. He cautiously headed to Promo, looking at the rest of his body as walked, aware of the transformation.

'A fire sword, and one hell of a power at that.'

Heracles thought to himself before re-addressing the recruits.

"That'll do." He growled, as the recruits all coughed and halted their murmuring, clearly excited by what they had just witnessed.

Heracles continued through the list of recruits and one by one they stepped up to Medusa to repeat the prose. Some forgot as they went, and Medusa got highly impatient at their transgressions.

Iris drew a long whip, cracking it backwards and forwards as she tested its strength.

Sophia drew a short sword, clearly built for speed and stealth. The right training could allow her to fit nicely into the Reconnaissance Corps.

Kyril drew a long thin spear that he dropped shortly after extracting it, to the audible jeers of his fellow cadets, and to the annoyance of Prometheus who took him to one side to reprimand him.

They were then down to the last cadet. Namely, the stoic young lady Heracles had noted earlier.

9

"Selene. Selene Cassia, sir." she replied as Heracles called her forward. It was reassuring to Heracles to know that she could actually speak.

"Selene. Step forward and place your hands...yes like that and speak the words, clearly and precisely." He was badly impersonating Promo today he thought. Heracles very rarely spoke this officially in any situation.

Selene complied and began to recite the prose. Speaking calmly, and concisely as Heracles had asked.

About three quarters of the way though, Heracles was kicking himself for thinking that she would draw a special weapon. It had just felt like something was coming earlier, and he was always bitterly disappointed when he was wrong about things. A toxic trait of his. He always liked to be right in his assumptions and had an uncanny knack for sensing things.

As Heracles pondered this, he abruptly felt a calm wash over him. His body relaxed. His mind wandered. A complete calm enveloped him.

He was also acutely aware that the Panathenon had become darker, with a blueish hue washing over the floor and up onto the stone wall perimeter in a wispy haze.

A pale moonlight had descended over Selene. The calm was emanating from her drawing. Of course it was. That was clear to Heracles now. Selene was the epitome of calm, in stark contrast to both Achilles and Apollo, whose drawings felt like a gathering of fearsome energy.

She reached down and began to draw her weapon from the open mouth of Medusa. Heracles recognised the moment instantly as another special weapon being drawn. He had been completely wrong about Selene. He felt the usual pang of shame he felt after he had incorrectly judged someone.

Selene finished drawing her sword and held it in front of her face, examining it thoroughly.

The handle of the newly forming sword was topped with a fantastic crescent moon, radiating a pale light, and pulsing with tranquil emotion. It was stunning. A pale blue blade emanated from the hilt, straight as an arrow, and somewhat thin compared to some of the other swords drawn today. More akin to that of a fencer's blade, albeit slightly wider. Light to hold and built for speed and style. There was a hue radiating from around the blade. One that seemed sharp to the touch.

Selene rested the tip of the blade in the palm of her left hand to examine it further. A grin spread across her face.

The stadium had reverted to its previous state almost immediately post the drawing, but Selene was still emitting the sword's power. Heracles could feel it washing back and forth across his body and making him feel at total ease.

Medusa, as she had done so with Apollo, opened her jaws and spoke, although this time in a more elegant manner. A manner in which to match the person she spoke of.

"Selene. Goddess of the Moon."

10

"Another fine drawing. Congratulations to you Selene. A simply stunning sword." Promo had stepped up to congratulate her personally on this occasion, clearly taken in by the sword and the influence she had emitted.

Heracles drew his attention to the past hour or so of activity. What a morning it had been. Especially for all of the recruits. Such was the occasion of experiencing The Rite for the first time. It had been an incredible showing.

The stand-outs of course were Selene, with her blade of the Moon; Apollo and his blade of the Sun, a seemingly endlessly powerful blade; and Achilles, with his father's sword. Heracles was keen to see each and every sword drawn today in action, but none more than those three.

11

Heracles looked over at Promo and gave him the nod to conclude The Rite. The closing should and would be conducted by Prometheus as the highest ranking officer here. It wasn't Heracles' place to do so, and he was already out of place by conducting The Rite this time – had it not been for Promo's influence within The Alliance he would never had been allowed to do so. This was not lost on

Heracles, and he noted to thank Promo heavily later on over several ales.

Promo nodded in return and addressed the cadets.

"Right. Your first Rite completed, and a memorable one at that. Congratulations to you all, and I mean that. It is no mean feat that you are here before today, and to draw such fine looking weapons this morning suggests great things are to come. Put in the work and you will be rewarded and repaid down the line," he paused, studying each and every cadet with a sudden intensity. "And remember: those who put themselves first, shall become last!"

Promo let the final sentence hang in the air for a few seconds before he continued.

"Right, there is now one short hour until the annual Ranking ceremony. I want you all to head back to your dorms, compose yourselves, change into your ceremony attire and return to this spot no later than ten minutes prior to the ceremony. We will then head over to the Amphitheatre together. Good luck to you all. From here on out it will be hell for you, but know that the journey is well worth it."

Promo turned away, but before getting half way in his turn he seemed to remember a final point. He spun back with his finger raised in the air, pointed upwards.

"Oh, and one final thing to remind you of. The Rite is a onetime deal. The weapon you all possess chose you. You don't get a second chance. That's it. It is impossible to draw again. Accepting that fact will be key for you all. Some have gone quite mad over obtaining more power, and I would hate to see it happen to any of you. Don't disappoint me. Dismissed."

The recruits saluted, turned, and headed back to their dorms, patting, and jostling one another as they went.

"Alcaeus, a word please."

Promo turned to the rest of the team before addressing Heracles again.

"The rest of you get ready for the ceremony." He said before turning back to Heracles.

"Walk with me." Promo said before beginning to walk away and out of the Panathenon.

"I think this year is going to be interesting. With Ares stepping down, and a new Alliance member taking his place, things will be different. Ares has been the undisputed number one Stratigos for some time and I can see a 'friendly' power struggle developing in the ranks," Promo adjusted his uniform as he spoke, realising that there was remnants of rubble on his chest, and brushing them lightly away from his uniform. "Stay close to Atlas, and you'll be fine. He will keep an eye on you."

Atlas was a close friend to Heracles within The Alliance, much as Promo had been over the many years since his parent's death. One whom he had bonded with over their time together, having joined The Alliance at the same time. Going through the intense training and constant strive for improvement was enough to make anyone close.

Prometheus continued.

"Three exceptionally powerfully arms drawn in one sitting as well."

"I can't wait to see them in action." Heracles concurred.

"I would've put money on Achilles drawing his father's sword. I actually know the kid fairly well following my time with his father some years ago, and he should grow into a fine warrior, although he holds an immense amount of pride, and it has gotten him into many a scrap. I hope that doesn't bite him in the ass. The opposite of Selene really. Got my money on her becoming a key tactician and strategist in the future."

He paused at this, his face falling surly.

"This Apollo kid though. I assume you had some doubts about him also?" Heracles nodded. "I just…sensed something about him, but he made the list none the less.

I've been watching him for a few years now. He always failed the entry tests due to his complete lack of confidence in himself. He would always fall at the last hurdle as a result," Prometheus looked saddened by this. It had always hurt him to see those fail when they were clearly good enough to succeed. "He also had no one there at the exams to support him. Not out of the ordinary of course, but he seemed a bit lost. He managed to summon that little bit extra this year and we passed him but keep an eye on him for me will ya? He's definitely hiding something from us."

As Heracles and Promo approached the intersection to their respective quarters, Promo stepped slightly ahead of Heracles and placed his arm in front of him. He looked around the concourse for anyone close by, before returning his gaze to Heracles and speaking quietly enough for Heracles to have to lean in closer.

"Be extra careful this year."

Promo wasn't about to talk about that in the open, was he? He was always so careful. They only ever discussed this over an ale or two within the privacy of Promo's quarters.

Heracles tried to wave him away but Promo held firm.

"Listen to me will ya? I'll be quick. Just be extra careful from here on out. I can see the way you look during the past few Rite rituals. Don't think I haven't noticed these last few years. I can see you wanting more from all of this," he waved his arms left and right whilst looking around at The Alliance HQ, "And trust me, I get it. I really do. But you need to remember why you can't. They *will* come for you if they find out you're not dead. They failed that night in killing you. You gotta keep 'em thinking you're just run of the mill. So just remember why we're doing this ok?"

Promo looked genuinely upset at the last point and Heracles understood why, but that still didn't make it ok. He was doing the best he could with this situation, and he was fine. He was in control. He knew why they were doing this.

"Promo…I…look, I appreciate everything you've done for me. You know I do. But I've got this ok?" Heracles growled, before catching himself.

"…sorry. It's frustrating as hell ok? But I am fine. I've got this." Heracles repeated.

Promo held his gaze for a second, seemingly to check Heracles' resilience to the matter, before closing his eyes and sighing in agreement.

"Ok, ok. Just step back slightly this year though. Not to make it too shit for you of course, but just step back a little. Don't get carried away. I wanted to give you control of The Rite today so you could have something bigger but…you know."

Heracles held his anger. "Fine, consider it done. Let's just get going ok?" Heracles brushed past Promo and headed back to his quarters, hand in the air in a wave as he went.

He didn't look back. It wasn't worth arguing with Prometheus when he was like this. Heracles knew he was right. As always. But just once he'd love to show everyone what he could do. He wasn't a kid anymore.

He could handle it.

CHAPTER II
THE ALLIANCE

1

Heracles considered skipping a return to the Panathenon, opting instead for Promo to pick up the task of escorting the recruits to the Amphitheatre, before reluctantly trudging off anyway. It wasn't worth the hassle it would cause, and deep down Heracles knew Promo was only doing right by him.

The conversation with Promo had still riled him though, even though he knew it shouldn't have.

Heracles thought about it all on a daily basis. Of course he did. He knew the importance of prudence, and Promo reminding him of it wasn't necessary. But he was undeniably right. He was in the perfect position as he was: a mid-level member of The Alliance, being not high enough to draw too much attention but not low enough to be questioned all the time in what he was doing.

He was older now, soon turning thirty this year, and better versed in all the secrecy. Still, he ached for battle as much as any of the new recruits he had seen initiated this morning.

In light of the seminal anniversary of his parents' death, Heracles was *more* careful if anything but the dreams were more frequent now than ever. Coming up to twenty years since that night. That was a hell of a long time to keep a secret.

But keep it he would.

2

Heracles was jogged back from his thoughts by intuition, sensing something coming towards him from behind. He briefly considered anticipating this but felt it preferable to let it happen. He was not known for his speed of reaction within The Alliance, even though it was secretly one of his greatest strengths.

As suspected, a hard open palmed slap struck him on his back. He rocked forward before catching himself.

He addressed his assailant before he even needed to confirm who it was.

"You've got to stop doing that to me Deme. I'll have a heart attack one of these days!" he coughed as he turned to face his aggressor.

Stood before him was a scruffily uniformed woman, no older than Heracles. Her hair was at least relatively neat today, wrapped in a simple plait that hung down to just above her lower back - often her hair was left flowing and natural. Her spear jutted out the top of her shoulder, nestled in its holder, and Demeter was clearly opting for a less ceremonial style than The Alliance would've hoped for on an occasion such as today. She was quickly adjusting her clothes to be a bit more presentable as she laughed.

"Come on, just trying to toughen you up a bit. That crappy sword you carry around wouldn't slice an apple in half!" she jested at Heracles, calling fact to the sword hanging neatly at his upper waist. Of course, it was just a regular sword that Prometheus had swiped from Hephaestus' workshop years ago. The fact that Prometheus had managed to fake Heracles' public Rite passage still amazed him. He was highly adept at smoke and mirror trickery given the fire powers of his sword. Heracles' actual drawing had happened in secret later in the dead of night. And what a drawing it had been.

"Look, I've told y..." he began before she hastily cut him off.

"What do you think Ares will go into after he steps down from the Strats then?" Demeter often cut Heracles off mid-sentence and it infuriated him as much as it made him feel closer to her. Deme had always been a bit odd, sometimes loud and obnoxious, but oozing self-confidence more so than anyone he had ever met. She knew who she was and was stronger for it.

"He'll probably step into a tactical or advisory role, like some of the other ex-Strats. If you can survive your time at the top of The Alliance without dying, you're set for life." he replied.

Deme considered this for a second, then nodded. "Good call. At least there's some brains in there." she said, smiling whilst tapping on his forehead. That smile that Heracles adored. She was just magical when she wanted to be.

"Righto, time to get going then dumbass."

Deme was moving Heracles forward before he had chance to reply and as he walked beside her, they chatted generally about their respective mornings: Heracles discussing the new recruits in light touch, and Deme regaling him with news of her morning's preparation with the other Taxiarhos.

All of the Taxiarhos were especially interested in the upcoming ceremony and were preparing particularly rigorously. None more so than the three candidates vying for ascent into the soon to be vacated final seat of the Stratigos.

Heracles' money was firmly placed on Demeter Floros.

3

Belying the surface façade, Deme (which she had

implored Heracles to call her as she hated her full name for some reason) was an incredibly talented and formidable member of The Alliance.

Over her time in the organisation she had climbed the ranks with relative ease, outshining those she had trained with at the academy, holding the top spot at each of the lower ranks of The Alliance's hierarchical structure; before finally settling into the Taxiarhos for the past two years.

Her ascent within the Taxi had been comparatively slow by her standards, but by The Alliance's standards it was exceptional. She was currently third seat in the Taxi, and would undoubtedly be fighting for first given more time, but given Ares' sudden announcement it was an opportunity she simply couldn't avoid putting herself forward for. Of course with the support of her senior officer Hermes, who she had maintained a close relationship with across her time here. The two were very similar in their approach, which of course helped. Light-hearted the majority of the time, but serious when the moment called for it.

The Alliance prided itself on having complete order and clarity when it came to its rankings, and its word was law. The annual Ranking ceremony was primarily handled by the Polemarch, the single most senior rank.

The Polemarch was the Supreme Commander of The Alliance, and as a result its overall figurehead. The current and long standing Polemarch was Gaia Galanis, and one of the founding members of The Alliance. A formidable leader and tactician, she preferred to operate from the shadows. Ares was her front facing figure, empowered to deliver her strategy to the wider team and allowing him his much craved limelight. His charisma was unparalleled, making him the perfect person for the job.

The individual positions within the ranks changed relatively frequently year on year.

Members either demonstrated increased value

over the course of the year, enabling them to push up the rankings, or the opposite if one had a particularly poor year, dropping down ranks. This was far more regular within the lower ranks, especially with the Hoplites, The Alliance's foot soldiers, being given opportunity to step up the ranks, only to struggle with the increased responsibility. The only caveat was that The Alliance would rarely punish you if you hadn't had an eventful year due to opportunities not presenting themselves, but if the opportunity was there and you hadn't seized it, it counted heavily against you.

Heracles was always careful to keep himself away from such opportunities, or at the very least doing an ok enough job to get a 'tick' next to his name, whilst not performing well enough for anyone to be noticeably impressed. An exhausting approach and one of the reasons he had gotten so frustrated at Promo earlier today. It took a lot of effort to be perfectly average.

The only rank that rarely changed was the Stratigos. The five members were quite content with their positioning generally. It was commendable. Of course, behind closed doors it could be a very different story, but they were the models of excellence in The Alliance and acted as such. They were also without doubt the strongest five warriors, exceptionally strong in their own individual rights.

Heracles had created a one pager for the new recruits, taking into consideration all of this, and would give them a quick run through upon his arrival at the training centre. It was also a good exercise to refresh his memory. Of course, it would all alter after today's ceremony but it was important for the cadets to understand the hierarchy, as they would need to quickly acclimatise to it.

Deme wrapped up her morning round-up as Heracles finished his last thought. She got a quick punch in on his chest, before she sprinted off towards the ceremony hall with left hand raised high in the air, waving left and right frantically. She very rarely let him get a word in edgeways, as much as he would've liked to, but that was just Demeter.

He waved back to her without her turning back and sighed, before finishing off his walk to the Panathenon.

He leaned heavily against the large oak doors, pushing them open, before stepping in.

4

Prometheus was again waiting to greet him, as punctual as he always had been.

Heracles also saw two other members of the team, the twins Cleon and Anstice, just finishing tidying up a few bits around the place. They were so swift with their duties that they were done in only an hour after the recruits had messed it all up with their Rite rituals. Heracles wasn't at all surprised to see them both here. They had always been inseparable and Anstice was a woman of great detail. She would want everything in place before leaving, and Cleon was happy to join her to keep her happy. It saved him much grief.

"Alcaeus, you ready?" Promo offered to Heracles, and he nodded. Heracles passed him the sheet of paper he had scribbled The Alliance rankings on for reference. Promo accepted it gratefully and thanked him.

Within minutes, the new recruits were all present. They were exceptionally punctual and Heracles was glad that Demeter hadn't delayed him overly with her ramblings.

They all looked exceedingly sharp in their uniforms, wearing the traditional white ceremony uniform: complete with black boots up to just below the knee; tight fitting white trousers buckled at the waist over the snuggly fitting white tunic top, complete with black trim on the long sleeves and down the front of the tunic. Similar to Heracles' uniform, although he had bronze trim on his uniform due to his more senior rank as a Captain.

Heracles and Promo both had a good look over them to just double check they were indeed squeaky clean before either of them spoke. All of them were clearly very well drilled prior to their arrival at The Alliance.

"Right, let's be quick about this as we need to head off to the ceremony," Promo began. "I want to go over a few ground rules and get you up to speed so you're not all sat there gawking at the Stratigos, or not understanding a lick of what anyone is saying."

Promo unrolled the parchment Heracles had handed him.

"Firstly, an overview of The Alliance for you. This tell you who to look out for at the ceremony and ensure you are up to speed on ranks and naming. Listen carefully, as I *hate* repeating myself." said Promo, almost spitting the word hate at the students. Heracles knew from experience just how much he hated it.

"If you remember nothing else of what I am about to say, remember this. There will be two key people to know at the ceremony. Firstly, our Polemarch Gaia, who presides over the entire Alliance. You won't see her often during your initial time here but know that she will be keeping a very close eye on you all." Promo glanced at Achilles quickly who was slightly startled at the 'out of the blue' look towards him.

"Gaia will introduce the man of the hour to you all at the ceremony, Ares. As you may have heard, Ares will be stepping down as the number one Stratigos today. Aside from those two key players, I would like to call out the remaining four Stratigos in order of their rank as they are extremely important figures within The Alliance."

"Athena, the next in line to be the top ranking Stratigos and known as 'The Great Tactician'. Her knowledge and intellect are unrivalled, saving countless lives with her calm and calculated forethought."

"Hermes, the 'Demon of Speed'. The fastest man at The Alliance," Promo threw a sly glance at Heracles and Heracles nodded knowingly back, "and our master of sabotage."

"Atlas, 'The Man Mountain'. Undisputedly the strongest man at The Alliance in terms of brute strength. His foes would attest to that if they hadn't already been crushed into bloody pulps by his mighty fists."

"Finally Artemis, 'The Huntress'. Master of resourcefulness, she is the newest Stratigos, but none the less respected. Hot headed and deadly."

Heracles saw Apollo shift uneasily to his right at the mention of Artemis. The boy was growing more curious as the day continued.

Promo handed the parchment over to Achilles and asked him to have a scan, before then passing on to his colleagues.

The parchment was laid out thus:

Polemarch (Commander)
Gaia Galanis

Stratigos (General)
Ares Angelis
Athena Aegean
Hermes Herodes
Atlas Asker
Artemis Barberis

Taxiarhos (Brigadier)
Pontus Pavilis
Nyx Rella
Demeter Floros

Syntagmatarkhis (Colonel)
Prometheus Pollaris

Tagmatakhis (Battalion Lead)

Lokhagos (Captain)

Hoplite (Foot Soldier)

Prometheus continued as he watched the recruits pass the parchment between one another.

"Outside of that, please pay close attention during the ceremony. One day you could all be involved in the ranking selection, and I look forward to seeing that happen with great anticipation. Until then, keep your mouths shut, listen, and learn. That is all. Let's be off."

5

Promo, Anstice and Cleon led the recruits from the front towards the Amphitheatre, with Heracles holding up the rear.

The Headquarters was awash with people as they hurried across the cobbled stone flooring of the central courtyard. It looked to Heracles as if they had opened up the ceremony this year to citizens of Athenaeus, the city that stood below The Alliance Headquarters at the base of Mount Olympus. They would no doubt all be here for Ares' retirement.

Achilles was of course at the front of the group, just behind Prometheus, Cleon and Anstice. It seemed as if he had gained even greater confidence after drawing his sword, and his leadership qualities would surely be a key component during his time at The Alliance, albeit with a need to learn a little humility. He clearly had something to prove.

Heracles was holding up the back of the group, walking slightly to the right to get a good look at all of those in front of him, much like a teacher with a young group of students.

His focus turned to the back of the group, where he realised that walking slightly ahead of him, with head down at the ground, was Apollo. He was a few feet off the pace of the recruit in front and sluggishly dragging his feet, clipping cobbles as he walked. Heracles seized on the opportunity to find out a little bit more about 'The Sun'.

"Apollo," Heracles spoke with a slightly hushed voice, as not to catch the attention of the other recruits. "Walk back here with me for a moment."

Apollo jumped with the mention of his name.

"Yes, sir…" Apollo said, dropping his speed to match that of Heracles.

"Big day for you. Got some serious nerves, haven't you?" Heracles said.

"…Yes, sir, big day…sorry if I come across as a bit nervous. Well, a *lot* nervous. I know everyone can tell. I…I have had a few knockback, and I can't really believe that I made it here." Sincerity ran through his voice as he spoke, reassuring Heracles somewhat. He eased.

"I won't lie to you Apollo, it has been very noticeable but you're here now, and you deserve to be. The entry exams are gruelling and you clearly did something right this year. Be proud of that fact."

Apollo smiled at this affirmation.

"Be conscious of your nerves and conquer them. People will soon forget about your first day here. It's what you do next that's important. You've been given a hell of a power. Don't waste it. It'll be up to you to show us what you can do. Do that, and you'll be just fine." Heracles smiled as he finished to reassure Apollo further.

Apollo was maybe early twenties, so sat

somewhere in between Heracles and that of the regular age of the new recruits. It sounded like Apollo had made a few attempts at gaining entry to The Alliance, and the fact that he had persisted was of note. A hell of a lot of people took the easy route out and gave up after the first set-back.

Apollo markedly calmed. He smiled back and bowed slightly, before becoming highly embarrassed that he had tried to bow to Heracles. He looked out to the recruits ahead of him to see if they had been watching but they were somewhat oblivious; caught up in the furore of the noise now rising as they neared the Amphitheatre.

"Thank you, sir, I appreciate it massively.... I..."

Apollo went to speak and then halted. Heracles needed to coax whatever was on his mind out of him. Now.

"Don't mention it, but we'll have a hell of a lot more trust in each other if you're honest with me."

Apollo paused to gather himself.

"You're right. The reason I am so unsure of myself...it's complicated. You see, Artemis, from the Stratigos...she's...she's my half-sister."

Heracles was slightly taken aback by this revelation but quickly adjusted his mind to what he had gathered from Apollo so far. His nervousness and lack of confidence must've stemmed from the success of Artemis, the youngest and newest Stratigos and an exceptionally powerful warrior, hugely confident in herself and her abilities.

Apollo continued to explain as they neared the Amphitheatre.

"My father, and not to speak ill of him, just doesn't see me at all. I've lived with him since an early age, since my mother passed, along with Artemis and her mother. Artemis has always had everything come to her naturally. I saw the way he looked at her growing up. So full of pride. Love. He wouldn't talk to me for weeks on end. I lived with them, but I spent the days by myself away from the house, just sleeping there mostly."

Heracles felt the kids' pain all too well. The loss of a parent was a terrible thing for a child to go through and Apollo's steely determination was really something given what he was telling Heracles.

"So I've never had that confidence in myself, but I just keep going somehow. It's taken me so long to get here. But I can promise you this: I will give it *everything*."

No wonder he appeared so downtrodden.

Apollo put out his hand to Heracles as a sign of thanks. Heracles took it gladly and shook it firmly.

"Well you've got my vote Apollo. We'll do this together. And know that I have rarely seen raw power like yours. Now's your chance. Take it." Heracles instantly felt better about Apollo, his honesty and candour alleviating Heracles initial concerns.

"Catch up and interact with the rest of the recruits. That'll help your confidence. Remember that everyone here is as petrified as you. You'll be spending a hell of a lot more time with all of them over the next few years so get to know them well."

Heracles didn't realise how wrong he was.

6

Heracles watched on as the recruits took in the sight of the Amphitheatre. They would have seen it on the way into the HQ but with the whole Alliance congregating upon it, and the atmosphere around it, it was fully realised.

The Amphitheatre sat directly at the centre of The Alliance's Head Quarters as its most wonderous attraction.

It was surrounded by four large courtyards, where members would train, eat, and interact. Each was connected by several pathways, leading to a different zone of the HQ. The Alliance was walled in with a circle of stone, and the roof was left bare. Not ideal for a rainy season, but they were few and far between in the climate of the area.

The bottom right zone contained the ever impressive House of Hephaestus: a large and imposing building, adorned with painted weaponry in gold and silver on its walls, and with two large statues of anvils at the entrance holding the roof aloft. Smoke continuously bellowed out of the large chimney on its roof, pushing out the immensely hot air of the workshop. It housed all of the blacksmithing and masonry conducted for The Alliance. Shields, swords, and armour were their speciality and Hephaestus himself made a lion's share of everything, or at the very least checked it over in minute detail before it left the building. Ever the perfectionist, Hephaestus was a giant of a man who had helped Poseidon, one of the founders of The Alliance, build this workshop some thirty years ago. Poseidon being a part of the 'five founders', namely: Gaia, Poseidon, Hemera, Zeus, and Ares. The workshop was frequented by Poseidon before his disappearance some years ago. Word has it, he had always been one for disobeying orders and for theatrics. Word also had it that his visits to the workshop were mainly centred around long sessions of drinking with Hephaestus.

At the bottom left zone sat the War Room. This building was more akin to a temple than a room, coloured red and gold, in homage to Ares. It was where all of the tactical operations and strategy were discussed, dissected, and deployed. Large columns at its four corners set the building, with two further columns framing the door and entrance, holding aloft the triangular roof. The columns were made of the finest marble and Heracles often stroked them whenever he happened past. He loved the texture, smooth to the touch. Heracles hadn't had the opportunity to go inside the building unfortunately, but he often thought about what took place inside as he passed.

The top right zone housed the living quarters for The Alliance. This area was dedicated to Hemera, another of the five founders. She truly believed in the wellbeing of everyone at The Alliance, and her passing was hugely untimely. Still, her legacy lived on within the living quarters, with the rooms as comfortable as could be afforded given the number of Alliance members bunking inside.

The top left zone was the Panathenon, Heracles' daily haunt and a building very close to his heart. It was the legacy of Zeus – paying homage to the greatest warrior The Alliance had ever seen. The Panathenon was open topped, fronted with two large oak doors, with a run of tiered stone seating in a grand arch from one side of the entrance to the other. The entrance was as grand as any of the other zones, if not more so. Several large columns marked the entrance, with lightning bolts jutting out of the pillars in various forms. The columns, and tiered seating, were laced with blue and gold, the colours of Zeus. Heracles had fought hard to become a member of the team there, helped in no small part by the influence of Prometheus.

And right at the centre of it all was The Amphitheatre.

The Amphitheatre was stunning to look at. It was similar in size to the Panathenon, but where the Panathenon had a grand entrance as it's focal point, the Amphitheatre had a sizable stage at its back from which it conducted its addresses. The back of the stage held a fantastic banner of The Alliance, right at the heart of it all. The tiered seating of the Amphitheatre ran nearly all around in an arch, before breaking at the stage on either side

The design of the Alliance was hugely unique and totally different to that of Athenaeus, and, Heracles guessed, the wider world. It was well designed, well-fortified and built for practicality whilst retaining a beautiful appearance. It was all held together by the Alliance's logo, resting on any flat surface it could.

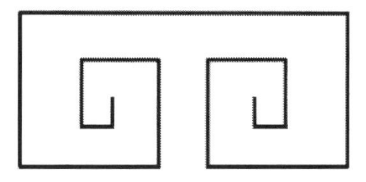

The Amphitheatre had been designed by Gaia herself. Ironically, it was the place that provided the most exposure, designed by a person that despised public addresses.

The recruits were rightly stunned. The level of detail that had been given to the crafting of such an iconic build was remarkable. A plethora of foliage layered the exterior walls, hugging them tightly. Heracles dreaded to think of the number of hours necessary to create something of its calibre, let alone the number of people necessary to build it. He had been in awe of it since the day he had set foot in The Alliance.

7

The Amphitheatre was awash with noise.

It appeared that the whole Alliance was present, and as a mandatory event for the annum that was to be expected. But there also looked to be a great deal of civilians in the stands this year. It was all likely an exercise in maintaining strong relations with the city of Athenaeus.

The Alliance itself sat tall on top of a steep incline, stretching up from the city below with hundreds of stone steps embedded into the hillside. These steps were known as the 'climb to Olympus', with the patch of ground the HQ sat on often referred to as Mount Olympus by a large majority of the city's population - a nod to those who had founded the establishment. For the protection and support The Alliance provided to the city of Athenaeus, there was often reverence directed towards the hillside and its inhabitants, and those that made the steep climb up to 'Olympus' felt rewarded by any interaction they had with those that dwelled there. Gaia had always waved away any such attention, but some of the population even went as far as calling the five founders 'The Five Gods of Olympus'.

Ares of course revelled in the adoration, and Heracles supposed it was natural for those that felt protected by someone else to have that level of faith in them.

The city had seen its share of hardship. Prior to the creation of The Alliance thirty years ago, the city was a hot bed of bloodshed, at constant war with the rest of the land. The Alliance's founders were originally denizens of the city and sought to improve the life for all the inhabitants, and protect the city from outside threats, and ultimately, itself. They built sentry posts, barracks, hospitals. They provided jobs, and general support throughout the city. Steadily, over many years, it grew to be prosperous. It was a beacon of hope and protection for many years, until that tragic night twenty years ago rocked The Alliance to its very core.

Since then, The Alliance had been on eternal alert for fear of another attack from that night's assailants.

Tartarus.

Strangely though, the past few years had been relatively quiet, with Gaia convinced that they had finally driven Tartarus back to the hole they had crawled out of. Heracles hoped that peace would persist, but he was always acutely aware that the danger was never fully gone.

The citizens that had made the climb up to The Alliance HQ were assisted by a ropeway that stretched from the base of the hill to the top, providing a much more efficient and speedy way of getting up and down. The stairs were long and steep, and many members of The Alliance used it as a training opportunity, running up and down the steps of a morning.

8

Heracles took his seat next to the training team towards the upper rows of the left hand side of the stage. It provided an excellent view of the stage and the acoustics resonated within the area superbly. The perfect spot to watch an historic event such as this.

The new recruits lined the row below them.

A bellowing gong resonated from the stage, hit hard and true by a member of Gaia's personal team, sending the Amphitheatre deathly silent.

The show was about to begin.

9

The crowd in the Amphitheatre erupted as the curtains at the back of the stage opened, revealing an immaculately dressed Syntagmatarkhis (or Colonel), with her black cape draped wavily over her shoulders and twin daggers resting at her hips. Heracles always loved it when an Alliance member used both their drawn weapon coupled with a similarly fashioned weapon crafted in Hephaestus' workshop. Twin daggers were a popular choice when it came to doubling up, and Persephone was better than most with hers, known now to be an ex-member of the Assassination division of The Alliance, identified only as 'The Episkopos', before joining Gaia on her personal staff.

She studied the crowd intently for a moment. Persephone had always been very intense, learning well from her superior Gaia and being by her side for many, many years. She held a quiet authority. Few crossed her and not just for her position at Gaia's side, and her history with the Episkopos, but for her own fierce character. She had been the inaugural speaker at the annual ceremony since she became Colonel rank.

Persephone addressed the audience.

"Welcome one and all, especially to our esteemed guests from the city of Athenaeus, to the annual Ranking of The Alliance ceremony." Rapturous applause erupted once more, until Persephone impatiently waved it off.

"Today we celebrate. Today we celebrate all of you. The members of our great Alliance. Those who have worked tirelessly over the past year. Shed blood, sweat and tears for The Alliance, and those of you worthy will today be rewarded for your toil. Today we celebrate greatness, and in turn celebrate the commitment, the ferocity, and the unwavering loyalty of one of the greatest warriors The Alliance has seen. I am of course referring to our current number one Stratigos, Ares."

More rapturous applause and cheering at the mention of Ares, a firm favourite of many an Alliance member.

"Before all of that however, it will be my pleasure to preside over this wondrous ceremony and in turn introduce the spearhead of The Alliance, Gaia."

More applause, deafening in its thunder. Gaia was a popular figure who held much mystery. Heracles had heard tales of her powerful speeches prior to the attack on The Alliance twenty years ago, but since then she had become more and more reclusive. People longed for even a glimpse of her, and the annual ceremony was as good a time as any.

Persephone, with her back turned to the audience now and her right arm held up in a bowing motion, stepped back from the podium to allow Gaia to emerge from the back of the stage and out into view.

She took her place at the podium, slowly rapping her notes before raising her hand swiftly into the air to call for silence. The Amphitheatre once again turned silent at her request. Her influence was immeasurable. She held the audience at her first word.

"Thank you, Persephone, and once again a warm welcome to you all. I will be brief in my address, but today I find a moment of reflection. A day to reflect on the year behind us. Have we achieved our goals? Have we excelled in our endeavours? Or have we allowed ourselves to become complacent?"

Gaia held herself at the last question. The crowd remained silent and attentive.

"I mention this because the individual we celebrate today has never wavered from the cause. He has always stood for what is right about our great Alliance. His fiery sprit and hunger for success are what drive him, and those around him, forward. He has sacrificed and bled for us countless times and today we honour him. A lesson to us all, and I hope we can all take something from this message. Be true to yourselves, be true to your passions and use them to guide you and others around you. This could make the difference in the fine margin between life, and death."

Gaia held the audience in the palm of her hand, and she knew when the best moment to close was. She had made her point succinctly.

"That's quite enough from me. We will now commence the Ranking of The Alliance ceremony, and for the final time as a Stratigos, please join me in welcoming 'The God of War' himself, Ares."

10

Electricity shot through the audience. Everyone was on their feet and cheering. This was the moment they had all waited for. Heracles felt it fully, and as much as he loathed the day itself, he couldn't deny how close it brought everyone together. There would be jubilation. There would be tears. And after the ranking had taken place, those in attendance would go back to their day to day lives and fall into their usual routines.

But for today. Everyone was one.

11

Ares stepped out on to the stage and bathed in the adoration. Where Gaia was stoic and non-plussed by the applause, Ares lived for it. Heracles wondered what life would be like without 'The God of War'. He wouldn't have long to wait of course, but it was an interesting thought.

Gaia met Ares at the podium, Ares bowing low to her as she walked past him towards the side of the stage. Her place to watch the ceremony. A hawk on her perch.

Ares greeted the crowd with a roar.

"Hello!" He said, using the incredible acoustics of the Amphitheatre to carry his sound impressively. "You've had enough welcomes to last a lifetime so I won't welcome you all again. You're here for one thing. And that of course, is me!"

He laughed heartily, placing his hands on his stomach, and arching back in an exaggerated movement.

More applause rang round the Amphitheatre.

"I jest, I jest. We are of course all here for the rankings, and to celebrate all of you. The Stratigos and I have been pouring over all of the observations we've made this year, and all of the data from your superiors, and we feel pretty damn confident that we are in the best place to deliver, to you, the new rankings and put you all out of your misery."

Ares smiled. It was a dry smile often with Ares.

Promo had called him paranoid every time he mentioned it but the smile failed to convince in Heracles' eyes. Ares was at his best when he was fire and brimstone, barking orders and calculating strategy. That was his true calling. Not throwing a smile that Heracles really felt he didn't mean.

"First though, a quick treat for our esteemed guests from Athenaeus. I give you, The Alliance's Stratigos!"

From the back of the stage emerged four figures, with Ares walking over to join them at their centre.

You could feel the atmosphere change somewhat. There was a rumble of murmuring and excitement at the marvel of all of the Stratigos gathering in one place. A rare occurrence as, with one of or many members of the rank out on various missions at any one time, it was hard to gather them all together. Often it was reserved for exceptionally important strategic meetings but even then, there was often one member missing due to important commitments. The life of a Stratigos.

Even Heracles was excited for this one.

12

The furthest left member of the Stratigos was another stoic character, holding herself in the most superior of postures. A light blue helmet rested snuggly on her head, slightly obscuring her face, Corinthian in style. Her uniform was cut off at the arms, and more dress like in appearance, with the front of the dress hanging down the middle of her body, front and back, exposing her legs on either side, with folded pleats. She had blue plated bracelets on either arm up to her elbow, the crest of the alliance on her left breast and above that the single star of the Stratigos rank. She opted not to wear the red cape of the Stratigos, as Heracles had heard tell she hated how it clashed with her blue attire.

Athena was proud. She was smart. Ultimately, she was the voice of reason for the Stratigos and soon to be the top of the order, preferring reason and calm over bullish arrogance and pride, in stark contrast to Ares. Heracles placed her in her late forties. She was one of two older Strats, second behind only Ares. Stratigos often either left before they felt the hand of age soften their skills or didn't make it to see their later years, but Athena was still as powerful as ever. She would always question the need for war and would be the last to sign off on it, only agreeing to it if it were an absolute must and was often heard rowing with Ares about matters of war.

To the right of Athena, was a shorter, and slimmer in stature man. Heracles suspected the showing of posture he was portraying was killing him, as Demeter had mentioned he was not fond of the serious nature of these events. Hermes was akin to Demeter in all of those aspects. They were the perfect mentor and mentee pair.

Hermes was known as the 'Demon of Speed', and his attire reflected that. Everything he wore was minimal and built for speed. He wore no upper part of his uniform, instead opting for two gold straps meeting and crossing at the centre of his chest. Either side of the point at which the straps met were silver wings. He wore nothing on his arms or head to weigh him down, even avoiding his Stratigos helmet in battle. He preferred to kill swiftly before the enemy ever had a chance, perfect for his role as leader of the Episkopos. He had an elaborate pair of golden shoes that were each topped with a pair of silver wings. Hermes held his weapon in hand, always. It was a short golden staff, topped with two golden wings, acting as an assassination tool when combined with his speed of movement. It contorted when he was about to attack into a sharp two sided axe, swift and true in its movements. Heracles was probably one of the few people to see this in action, due to his sharp reflexes, as Hermes moved at frightening speeds even in training.

At the centre was Ares. He was a powerfully built man, his uniform tight against his muscular form. He wore his large golden shield flush against his back, and his crimson red blade on his hip. His attire was a dynamic contrast between red and gold. Ares wore the deep red cape of the Stratigos with pride, being longer and with more of a flourish when compared to the regular Stratigos' capes. A trimmed brown beard hung on his chiselled chin, matching his short cut spikey brown hair. High topped golden boots sprung up from his feet to just below the knee. Everything about him was of immaculate detail, and nothing but the finest of quality of materials. He was a monster of a man.

However, the man to his left towered over him still. Atlas remained the largest human Heracles had ever encountered barring Hephaestus (who was half-giant). Atlas was a tower of strength and endurance. All muscle, but when Heracles had sparred with him in secret, he was surprisingly graceful and swift. He had grown steadily over years of training and showed no sign of stopping. Atlas, as with Hermes, opted for a bare chest but Atlas's choice was not one of vanity, but of practicality. No uniform could hold him, and as such he opted for shorts over the usual trouser, his bulging thighs barely contained. His cape hung from a small clasp on his neck, and the cape looked in proportion to his body but had Hermes cause to wear it, it would drown him. Atlas had placed on the floor next to him what would look like a boulder to those not familiar with him, but Heracles and the rest of the academy knew this was actually Atlas' weapon: a heavy boulder attached to an iron chain that Atlas would swing with great ease and to devastating effect.

Atlas was the same age as Heracles, and they had been best friends growing up at the academy. When Atlas had begun to progress without Heracles they had begun to interact less and less, and even more so now that Atlas was a Stratigos, but they still maintained a firm friendship. Heracles and Atlas made sure to catch up over an ale or two whenever they got the chance and they would do anything for each other. Outside of Prometheus, Atlas was the only one who knew of Heracles' past and his true strengths, which had thankfully only made them closer.

Finally, to the far right was Artemis, half-sister to Apollo. Artemis was nicknamed 'The Huntress', and her apparel reflected that. She had a bow draped over her right shoulder, and a quiver of arrows strapped to her back, visible just out of the top of her left shoulder. She was Ares' favourite because she lusted after battle as much as he did. Artemis had long black hair, shining under the bright lights of the Amphitheatre, and neatly tied up. She wore a tight leather girdle around her torso, and a small leather skirt, frilled at the edges. Long leather boots reached her knees. Everything she wore, barring her flowing red cape, was brown and was often caked in mud, so made some sense why she wore it. She held a wry smile on her face throughout the applause for the Stratigos.

Atlas abruptly clasped his hands together, sending out a huge boom of wind into the crowd, and breaking Heracles's concentration. The whole Amphitheatre shook and a large selection of the attendees, although sitting down, fell sideways into one another. Artemis joined in, kicking a basket of apples now placed next to her, high into the air above the crowd before shooting them all in quick succession with her arrows, slicing them all neatly into small chunks that rained down onto the audience.

A female member of the audience screamed audibly, making the rest of the audience turn to her. Hermes now sat beside her, chatting nonchalantly with a few chunks of apple in his hands, offering her to join him in the snack that Artemis had kindly prepared for him. Heracles hadn't even seen him move from the stage; his eyes occupied with Artemis' skill.

Athena stood still on the stage, clearly not eager

to join in the show, her arms folded over her chest and her face neutral. Ares shrugged at her and turned to the crowd. He took his sword from his hip and drove it into the stone stage. A blast of pure power radiated from the sword, hurtling out in an arch into the bodies of the audience. People toppled and yelped. Others turned away from the overwhelming power emanating from Ares' blade. Silence hung over the stadium at Ares' show of incredible power. Heracles felt a pang of fear resonate through him.

Once the audience had gotten back to their feet, they erupted once more, cheering, and applauding the Stratigos' hint at their real power.

Ares bellowed an almighty laugh and cried "We hope you enjoyed the show!" He cleared his throat. "Right. Let's begin the rankings shall we!"

13

The display of strength and skill was swift, but hugely impressive.

The Stratigos waved to the crowd as they stepped off the stage, taking their seats at the front of the Amphitheatre audience, ready to join them in watching the Ranking unfold. Ares was left alone on stage, about to commence the main attraction of the ceremony.

"Right, let's get this show on the road. As per usual, we will start with those that have been promoted into the lowest ranked position in The Alliance, the Lokhagos, and then rank the Lokhagos in ascending order to the number one spot. Let us begin."

Ares began with those that had made it up into the Lokhagos this year from the foot soldiers' level, or Hoplites as they were officially referred to.

One of the promotions came from the pool of recruits that graduated from the academy last year, which was highly rare. Heracles knew her well as he had recommended her himself. She was a gifted warrior and had been given permission to complete several higher ranking missions already due to her quick progression. Heracles was glad to see Cyrene accepted into the Lokhagos, and she was now Heracles' rank already, having skipped two levels altogether due to her potential. All went to showcase Heracles' stunted progression in The Alliance.

"So, with those newly promoted members making up the lowest five positions of the ranks, there will naturally be those that will lose their rank."

Ares reeled off those that were leaving the Lokhagos. Heracles recognised the majority, and he was unsurprised. The leap to Captain rank may have been perceived as insignificant compared to the other ranks but it was still a ranked position, and as such the responsibilities grew significantly.

"And here is the new ranking of the Lokhagos for this year." Ares continued.

Ares started from the tenth position and ascended through the ranks. Heracles listened intently, as he did every year. This was important to him. Important for his position. Last year he had been ranked number two, which was too close for comfort. He really couldn't afford to be promoted. It might cause more eyes upon him, making his secrecy all the more difficult.

Ares arrived at the announcement of the top two Lokhagos, all without mentioning Heracles, which was concerning. He hadn't been on the list leaving, so it couldn't be that he was being demoted. Unless Ares was making a real point of it as Heracles was a long standing member?

Ares continued on. And read the final top two positions without a mention of Heracles' name.

"Unfortunately, this year, as you probably will have gathered, there will only be one promotion to the Tagmatakhis, our Battalion Lead rank for all of those new to The Alliance. We felt that this Alliance member was due a step up in responsibility after his long service. So please allow me to congratulate Alcaeus Demos on his promotion!"

Ares scanned the crowd for Heracles. He found him surprisingly fast, Heracles noted to himself. Ares turned to his attention to the first row of seats by the stage and nodded slightly. As Heracles watched on, he was all of a sudden hit with a wind sharply in his face and, before he knew it, his body was moving through the air.

He was on the stage in front of Ares in an instant, with Hermes stood smiling next him.

14

Heracles was a little overwhelmed. Standing in-front of this volume of people wasn't something he was used to and was certainly not something he wanted. What was strange was that he couldn't remember anyone coming up for any rank announcements lower than the Taxiarhos in the past, yet here he was.

Heracles felt a sharp nudge in his back as he was jostled closer to Ares. Heracles glanced back to catch Hermes retracting his arm, and past that at Atlas who looked as confused as Heracles did. Atlas simply shrugged. As Heracles looked back to Hermes, he was already gone, sat back in his seat at the front once more.

Heracles could barely hear the noise of the crowd over his own thoughts now. This was exactly what he, and by extension Promo, hadn't wanted – any large scale attention drawn to him.

Heracles had stood on the stage, when nobody else was present, and had looked out to the seating before him. That had felt overwhelming in itself, but this was a different beast altogether.

"Alcaeus, don't be shy. Come over here and shake

my hand."

Heracles needed to pretend that this was the best moment of his life. He strained a smile onto his face and stepped forwards. He took Ares' outstretched hand and he shook it firmly. Heracles attempted to return the pressure somewhat but he could feel Ares' strength radiating through him even without Ares trying.

Ares, with Heracles' hand still firmly grasped in his, turned his face towards the audience.

"Ladies and gentlemen, a warm applause please. Our newly promoted Tagmatakhis, Alcaeus Demos!"

On the announcement of his name, a crash echoed from backstage and there was instant loud murmurings from the crowd. The sun above him seemed to be covered momentarily, as the Amphitheatre grew instantly dark. Heracles turned to the backstage to see what the noise was and, as he did, he felt a familiar rush of air fly past him and away again in an instant. He kept his gaze on the backstage for only a second, but the darkness prevented him from seeing anything.

It was the tiniest moment in time. Another second passed before there was a sound, and the darkness suddenly lifted, raining light all around the Amphitheatre.

And then there was screaming.

Heracles turned his face back to Ares to find him staring back at him with a look of stupor across his face.

More screaming from the audience and those around him rang through Heracles' ears. It was deafening.

Heracles was aware he was still holding Ares' hand firmly.

He continued to look at Ares, now with a look of confusion on his own face as Ares wavered slightly. His knees buckling, his body swaying. Heracles let his eyes fall in realisation.

He looked down at the sword he was now gripping, replacing what he thought was still Ares' outstretched hand.

The sword was as black as night and was pierced deep into Ares's chest. Dark blood was now seeping out of the wound, congealing quickly. It looked to be pierced through Ares' golden armour, and straight into his heart.

Ares grabbed Heracles by both shoulders firmly, but as he held them there the initial strength faded swiftly and his hands loosened before falling back to his sides. His eyes rolled in their sockets.

15

Heracles drew his hand back sharply, leaving the sword protruding from Ares' body. Ares sank to his knees, before landing face first onto the hard stone of the stage, crashing firmly against it. Limp. Lifeless.

Heracles turned his head just in time to see Athena strike him, hard. He landed in a lump against one of the corners of the stage. His head throbbed and ached from the collision with the pillar. His vision blurred. Time slowed.

He attempted to look out to the audience and saw chaos before him now, inaudible to him under the ringing of his ears but he could see that blades were drawn.

Heracles assumed they were drawn for him, but it almost looked as if the blades were clashing with one another across the audience members, sparking in their collisions. Several bodies lay hunched over the back of the seats in front of them.

As his vision settled, it was clear that there was fighting taking place all around him. Furious and panicked. Clouds of dust sprayed up from the earth and the stone of the Amphitheatre crumbled under the impact of the fighting. The wonderful building was being torn apart by blasts from unknown powers. Screaming pierced the air.

They were under attack.

Heracles looked back to the stage and found three

figures standing around Ares' still body, guarding him. It was Athena, Gaia, and Artemis. Weapons drawn. Their eyes focussed on something.

Then Heracles saw them.

Emerging from the back of the stage were three figures, shrouded beneath black hooded cloaks: the hoods obstructing their faces completely.

Heracles went to move but his body held still. He felt a wealth of power wash across the stage. Whoever the three figures were, Heracles could sense that they were immensely powerful. They were emitting such an intent to kill that it held him back momentarily.

At this thought, Heracles was jerked back into the darkness of the side of the stage. Heracles turned, his body finally reactive again.

It was Atlas, leaning over him with a stoic look on his face and cupping his hands around Heracles' mouth. He was looking from Heracles to the stage, desperate to go and assist his fellow Stratigos.

"Listen to me closely Heracles." Atlas spoke, softly enough for their cover but loud enough for Heracles to hear.

Heracles went to protest that he didn't have the slightest idea what was going on and Atlas grabbed him firmly by both shoulders.

"Shut it will ya!?" Atlas rasped at Heracles, silencing him instantly.

"I know you didn't kill Ares. That clearly wasn't your sword. And that little rat bastard Hermes is missing. Gaia will know that too. She knows everything about you Heracles. She's been helping Promo and I keep you safe all these years." Atlas was flitting his eyes from the stage to Heracles face, and back again. Alert to everything happening around them.

"You need to keep away from everyone else though. They will attack if they see you. It was pretty damning what the audience saw just now and they will be scared out their minds with Ares dead. And it very much looked like you killed him. You've been set-up."

Atlas dropped his hand to Heracles' weapon, Heracles grabbing his hand as he touched it.

"Relax. Where is your actual sword?"

Heracles studied Atlas briefly. He had never seen his old friend so stern before. He was in complete control of himself and the situation. A true confirmation of his place in the Stratigos.

Heracles was cautious though, his mind conscious of the recent attempt at framing him.

"It's where it always is Atlas."

Atlas smiled slightly.

"Good. Not trusting me is wise, but we're wasting time. I am with you, always. Nothing has changed, but you'd better get to your sword *now*. Use it to protect yourself, but make damn sure whoever attacks you doesn't live to breathe a word to another soul. I fear the ones attacking us are Tartarus. And they may well be after you," He rose to his feet. "Good luck old friend."

With that, Atlas jumped away from Heracles and back out on to the stage to join Athena, Artemis, and Gaia in confronting the three hooded figures. Neither parties had moved as Atlas and Heracles had talked. Both were just studying each other's movement and conversing.

Heracles looked on from the shadows, intent on watching the confrontation unfold, before replaying Atlas's words in his mind. He took one last look at his friend, before retreating out of the side entrance from the stage and into the wider Headquarters concourse.

16

Heracles emerged from the side hatch to find chaos around him.

The noise was thunderous. Everywhere he looked

there was fighting and violence, bodies lying on the concourses, blood spilled into the dust of the floor. It was hard to tell who was who. It looked as if some of those Heracles had suspected to be denizens of the city were in fact a part of the attacking force. Clever.

He quickly surveyed the scene for anyone he knew but struggled to identify anyone in the midst of the heated battle. There appeared to be way more attackers present than those originally present at the Amphitheatre. They must've snuck in during the ceremony when all of the team were preoccupied.

He began to move, his training sword drawn in preparation. He knew that the best place route to the Panathenon was around the outside of the walling surrounding the HQ, but that would be far too slow. The quickest way to his sword was directly through the action. He would need to be sharp and ready but that would ensure he made it to the Panathenon as quickly as he could.

Heracles was swift in his movements, no longer shackled by the worry of others noticing his abilities. Everyone around him was otherwise engaged.

He longed to help those engaged in battle as he passed, but he could help more with his drawn sword. He needed to trust his comrades and their training.

There was, on the face of it, a hundred more assailants that had entered the Headquarters during the ceremony. The fact that it had spilled out into the pavilions was good. Heracles assumed the assailants would have wanted to attack quickly whilst everyone was pinned in to the Amphitheatre, but The Alliance's drills had paid off. They had managed to force them out into the open, and that allowed space for a counterattack and for people to go all out. A lesson Athena had drilled into the team on more than one occasion.

Those that were present from the unknown assailants were clearly powerful though, and there would be severe casualties after this was over. What were they after?

Heracles pressed on, head down and driving his legs forward. There were several swipes and attacks aimed at him as he shot through, low and fast, but even with a training sword he was very well trained and easily dodged the oncoming strikes, hitting back hard with his sword and driving them off enough to turn on his heels and continue onwards.

As he neared the Panathenon he finally eyed some familiar faces, and his heart rose. With their backs against the large oak doors of the Panathenon stood Achilles and Apollo, engaged with several attackers, holding them back as best they could and preventing them from entering the Panathenon.

They had clearly returned to the Panathenon as a familiar and potentially safe place. Clever lads.

Heracles stole in to get the drop on their attackers and succeeded in immobilizing two of those towards the back of the small group attacking Apollo and Achilles, without the others noticing. He sliced his sword across one set of legs, and then the other, immobilising the attackers.

He then sliced across the backs of two further attackers in two quick motions, felling them both with powerful slices. He wasn't one for the dishonourable back attack, but the situation necessitated this.

Apollo, seeing Heracles' arrival, was noticeably buoyed. He drew his sword around his head several times, drawing a small pocket of fire around himself. The kid was a natural with his newly drawn weapon.

Apollo swiftly purged the flames from his body, expelling it against two of the attackers near him, propelling them back as their charred bodies landed and slid across the courtyard floor.

Achilles, seizing the moment in the confusion, ran his sword through one of his foes, turning to face the other as he did. There was not a moment of hesitation in his attacks. The final foe turned and fled, unwilling to tackle multiple opponents on his own.

Achilles went to follow him when Heracles approached him. "Leave him Achilles. It's over."

He rounded on Heracles instantly, raising his weapon towards him.

"Traitor!" he cried, his face a scarlet red. Ready to strike if it came down to it. Ready to lay it all on the line for The Alliance already.

Apollo walked to the side of Achilles and placed his hand on his sword, nodding at Achilles and pushing it downwards.

"He helped us Achilles. Let's hear him out."

Achilles was reluctant, and forcefully resisted Apollo's push of his sword, keeping it raised at Heracles, but he stilled, nonetheless.

Apollo turned to Heracles, still stone faced and clearly as angry as Achilles but with a calm reason about him. He motioned to Heracles to explain.

"Thank you, Apollo. There's little time to explain, but I am here to help. I didn't kill Ares. I can't prove that to you right now but given the current situation you need to either kill me or trust me. What'll it be?"

Achilles and Apollo turned to each other, assessed one another's face for a moment and then both nodded, with Achilles lowering his weapon to his side.

"For now, we'll trust you…but one wrong move and I will cut you down myself." Achilles said. The boy had seen too much too quickly Heracles feared and his adrenaline was flying through his veins.

This wasn't the way it should've gone. They shouldn't have seen action for at least a few months of training and nothing close to this level.

"Some of the recruits are dead Heracles, and the rest of them are inside the Panathenon," Apollo began. "It seemed like the safest place for everyone. We've been moving some of the civilians in there also. By Hermes' suggestion. Selene is inside looking over them."

Heracles baulked at the mention of Hermes.

"Hermes? He was here?" he said, shaking with a building rage.

Apollo nodded. "He gave orders to lead the team to the training centre at the start of the attack."

Heracles, knowing that Hermes was not to be trusted now, was instantly concerned.

"Both of you, inside with me now. I fear that Hermes is no longer an ally of The Alliance. Those inside are in danger."

17

Heracles pushed open the large, heavy doors of the Panathenon and entered alongside Apollo and Achilles.

Heracles swayed at what he saw.

Lifeless bodies of the remaining recruits, and dozens of civilians, lay motionless, littering the floor around the centre of the Panathenon. The dirt was soaked in a clotted red.

It was a massacre.

Heracles scanned his eyes further forward and saw that the Shield of Aegis had been raised, and a hooded figure was standing at its centre. To the right of him was Hermes, grinning feverishly.

The figure looked to be attempting to draw a weapon from Medusa, his voice audibly reciting the passage to the snaked woman, as guided by Hermes.

The hooded figure hadn't noticed their presence, being fully engrossed in The Rite. Hermes however was slowly turning towards them, still wearing his devilish grin.

"Hermes!" Heracles cried out, as he began to walk towards him, training sword raised. As he drew closer, he felt a hand clasp his ankle.

He looked down to find Selene. Blood stained. But alive. He bent down to her.

"Selene...oh Gods." He whispered softly, not wanting to draw any more attention to the poor girl.

Selene coughed dark blood. "He's too powerful...I couldn't...don't engage with them. You have to run. All of you." She rasped at the three of them, with what little strength she had left.

Heracles surveyed Selene carefully as she spoke. She was on the verge of death and if she wasn't treated soon, she wouldn't be long for this world. She had been brutally attacked, and the wounds seemed deep and precise. The clear work of a master assassin.

"Selene, you're going to be ok. Don't speak." Heracles turned to Apollo and Achilles. "Look after her, both of you and then get the hell out of here."

Apollo went to protest.

"No, Apollo. Get out of here. I'll handle this. Do *not* try to back me up. Your lives, and Selene's life, are your utmost concern right now. Understand?" Heracles said sharply at them both. Achilles and Apollo had a look of huge reservation at this. Heracles supposed his status and rank didn't carry much confidence.

"Trust me, both of you. Now go!"

Achilles took one further look at Heracles, and then shook Apollo into concentration. Achilles scooped up Selene in his arms carefully and, remaining low, started to move towards the door of the Panathenon.

Heracles watched them both for a second before turning back to Hermes.

Hermes smiled at Heracles dryly before he was gone, disappeared into thin air, only a faint mirage of his body remaining in place on the shield.

Heracles moved, as swiftly as his body was capable, towards Apollo, Achilles, and Selene.

He turned as he ran and caught Hermes' blade with his own as Hermes drove it towards Apollo's back.

Heracles held his sword in place, grabbing Hermes with his left hand and holding him firm. Hermes slight body was no match for Heracles strength, and Hermes had clearly not been caught many times before.

The look of astonishment on Hermes' face was paramount as he watched Apollo and Achilles continue forward, picking up the pace with Selene, and flying out through the oak doors of the Panathenon, slamming them closed behind them.

"Your fight is with me Hermes." Heracles said, his training sword lying on the floor many yards away now, and a new sword firmly in his hand.

18

Hermes audibly gulped as he shot back and away from Heracles, skidding in the ground to a halt as he slowed his speed.

In Heracles' hand now was his drawn sword, one which he could summon when near using the connection he had honed with the sword over the past ten years. The lightning power of the sword allowing it to be summoned to him.

The sword was astonishingly golden. Its handle was black, but only to amplify the beauty of the rest of the sword, and it grew up into the face of a golden lion, immaculately carved, with lightning bolts protruding from either ear. The blade itself was long and dipped in thickness three times on the way to its end. A thin slit ran down the middle of the sword, with gold trim surrounding its edges.

"How the hell did you do that?" Hermes snarled, as he stared directly into Heracles eyes. "You are *nothing*. You're only a captain! No one can match my speed!" He looked to Heracles like a stubborn child throwing a tantrum.

"This is my true power you treacherous little shit."

Hermes turned back to the Shield, before disappearing and then reappearing at the hooded figures' side, causing dust to kick up around him.

He placed his hand on the figures' shoulder and the figure grabbed his hand, throwing it back off again. Hermes said something along the lines of '…got to go.' to the assailant, who snapped back at him inaudibly.

"Forget this." Heracles heard Hermes say before he turned back to Heracles. He smiled a final time, tipping an imaginary cap, before he was gone, flying across the Panathenon floor, up through the seating and over and out of the open roof. Heracles struggled to keep a track on him as he went. He was moving even faster than he had before.

And then he was gone.

19

Heracles turned to the hooded figure, now confident that the coward Hermes had made a swift exit.

The hooded figure was reaching down into Medusa's mouth. Heracles's heart dropped; his intuition peaked. Was this the reason for all of this bloodshed? All just for a distraction and to assist in conducting a Rite ceremony for this unknown character? Did they have the Mark of the Gods?

Heracles needed to strike now and prevent the figure from drawing a weapon. He could feel an immense power emanating from the shield. They were clearly drawing something exceptionally powerful.

It was time to end this quickly.

20

Heracles ducked low, placed all of his power into his legs and flew forward through the air, putting as much speed into his movement as he could to ensure he prevented the finishing of the hooded figures' Rite ritual.

He drew his sword in front of him, intending to pierce it straight into the hooded figure. No fear of the kill now. He would do what he must. He couldn't afford to let this moment pass and approach cautiously, or attempt to reason with the figure. Heracles' rage was already consuming him at the thought of the recruits around him and their untimely deaths.

He had to act. Now.

He threw his sword downwards as he reached the hooded figure just in time to meet the oncoming steel flying upwards towards him. The impact was strong and hard, and Heracles could feel the power radiating between the two blades.

It was familiar somehow.

Electricity emanated from Heracles' blade, almost growling at the assailants own weapon, as they reverberated against one another. The dust around them, kicked up from Heracles movement, hung motionless in the air. Locked still in time.

The figure was facing him directly now, a deep grin smiling from beneath his hood.

21

Heracles felt his sword waver slightly under the immense pressure against its edge. His feet were firmly gripping the surface of the Shield of Aegis but they were slipping. He hadn't clashed with power like it before. The assailant was nonchalant but exerting immense pressure upon him effortlessly.

Heracles looked down to the weapon locking him in place. It was a sight to behold, and again something seemed oddly familiar about it all.

It was a sword not too dissimilar to his own. It was almost blinding to look at, with its radiant golden colour beamed with light. It looked deathly sharp.

Its golden handle was topped with a half circle, adorned with three clear gems. The blade itself was wide at the base, slimming somewhat in the middle and then widening towards the edge in an arc, with a razor sharp tip.

It was the same for Heracles' sword. A majestic, but simple design that contained immense power. Power that Heracles had only been able to scratch at the surface of over his time with it. It granted him the power to wield lightning. Speed. Electricity. The potential of it was frightening and Heracles often worried he wouldn't be able to control it fully, as it had threatened to boil over in many a training session with Prometheus.

Heracles felt the exact same potential from this sister blade. He couldn't hold back here. No matter the cost. Or he would surely be dead.

He drew back, creating space between himself and his assailant before driving powerfully forward, landing face to face with his attacker as their swords clashed once more.

Heracles sent a powerful spark through himself and out from the tip of his sword. It ricocheted off of his assailant's blade and up into the air above them, forcing the hooded cloak off of the man's face as it flew upwards.

The hood fell almost in slow motion, revealing a somewhat familiar face.

Heracles felt his mind fall into darkness.

CHAPTER III
REMEMBRANCE
--Twenty years ago--

1

Hera cuddled Heracles close to her as she crouched.

Silent in the night, listening intently for the slightest sound. Her breathing slowed. Her hand nestled lightly atop her son's head.

Her husband had created a big enough distraction at The Alliance, with him and Perseus drawing the assailants towards the city. This had allowed Hera and Heracles to escape outside, hidden under cover of darkness, dispatching any small fry assailants in their way.

Hera and Zeus had quickly agreed that the best chance of both of their son's survival tonight was to separate and regroup at the small camp outside of Minos when it was safe to do so. Zeus would be first to arrive and ensure it was safe, and Hera would follow later when, hopefully, the attack had quelled somewhat. Perseus was to go with Zeus as the younger of the brothers, far safer in Zeus protection in the heat of the attack, and Heracles was to remain with Hera.

Hera had been waiting patiently for the right moment to make their move, when not a person could be heard against the raging storm around them. A storm that had suspiciously crept in during the assault on The Alliance HQ.

Her ears were sensitive to the night, and she possessed a keen perception. She felt calm and focussed, lightened slightly from the ease of impending danger.

She slipped out from underneath the gap in the stairs leading up to The Alliance HQ. It was a secret safe place that Zeus and Hera had purposely built into the architecture of the stairs when the build was being finished, with only a small number of confidants knowing of its existence. It was a well-kept secret, and no doubt that without it they would be dead already. The Alliance was crawling with people apparently targeting them.

Hera motioned for Heracles to remain hidden within the confines of the stairs as she crept through the overgrowth for a better look out into the night. She found no sign of life around her, so stepped out, albeit cautiously.

The storm raged on. She had not seen anything like it. It was unrelenting in its attack. Gales swept around Mount Olympus and the city below, upturning loosely embedded trees and leaving rubble scattered in its wake.

Hera looked towards the city, and then back up to the HQ. Where fire and desolation had raged, the storm was quelling the flames somewhat whilst doing exponential damage of its own. The rebuilding was going to be hard. Long. Years they had held the HQ as a fortress. A safe haven for all that dwelled inside. Until tonight.

But rebuild they would. Rebuild they must.

If they got the chance to do so of course. She had little knowledge of how the battle was unfolding, having spent her recent time tucked away inside the underbelly of the stairs, but the sound around them had dampened and that could well be a sign of the easing of battle.

Hera went to move back towards the growth and stopped dead in her tracks. The storm around her vicinity seemed to stop in time. Particles of dust and rubble hung in the air in front of her. The winds howled against an invisible circle around them, stopping them from entering the eye of the storm she was now in.

A voice slithered through the night.

"A strange time to go for a stroll Hera."

The voice was deep, thunderous, and seemingly echoing in the storm itself. Bathed in it.

Hera turned to confront the voice.

Stood before her was a man with not a drop of water on him. The storm seemed to be radiating from him, writhing around him, but never quite touching him. They were indeed in the eye of the storm as Hera had sensed. Nestled under his left elbow, was a grizzly dragon-headed helmet. His clothes appeared to be dark flowing robes, with his hood pulled back to reveal his face, which was haggard. Tired. A thick scar ran from just below his hairline, down through his right eye and through his nose, settling just above his lip. An unkempt beard covered most of his lower face, barring the line of the scar. His eyes were unavoidable, bright white in colour and wild. He held a small staff in his right hand, one that was vibrating furiously. Hera assumed this to be controlling the storm surrounding them. A drawn weapon. But this was no Alliance member. How had he come by this weapon?

"Thank you for marvelling at it all," The figure said as he watched Hera looking at him and then the storm. "My creation. My power. My *art*. It's really doing some damage to your beloved Alliance…and a wonderful job of tracking that bastard husband of yours. *He* is out finding them, though so I can concentrate on you."

Hera's whole body seized at the mention of Zeus. Her thoughts drifted to Heracles. She hoped she had got through to him when she told him to remain hidden.

"Not in a talking mood I see." The assailant seemed somewhat disappointed at this but continued his monologue regardless.

"*He* told me that you'd be somewhere around here. That there was a cosy little hiding spot along these stairs and for me to wait for any scurrying rats to pop out. *He* knows you both so, so well."

Hera felt a smile through his voice now. Had someone been compromised? Surely none of the friends she held so dear at The Alliance would ever endanger them. Perhaps Poseidon had been right…

The assailant barked into the night, grizzled laugher emanating from him.

"The look on your face says it all! You poor saps really had no idea!"

He began slowly walking towards Hera. She tried to lower her hand to the sword at her hip but felt weight at her arm. A wind was pressed against either side of her body now, focussed entirely on her and restricting her movement.

A pointed finger wagged in the air back at her.

"We'll have none of that thank you. As fun as this might be Hera, I can't be wasting any further time with you. Tell me where the other rat is and I will make it quick for you both."

He knew. His information was solid and true. Somebody had indeed been compromised and had spilled all of the information the enemy needed. They had complete strategic advantage. But Hera would die here to protect her son at all costs, just as Zeus would do with Perseus.

"Fuck you." Hera said into the night.

"At last, she speaks! I prefer it when my prey screams and begs for mercy," he said, sighing audibly. "But a simple response from you is enough for me."

He was almost sadistic, sexual in his lust for torturing Hera verbally.

"No matter. I will level this whole place as soon as I am done with you. A rat can only hide for so long."

He slammed his staff into the ground and attacked, swift and fast. His hand disappeared, contorting into a large claw as he drove at Hera, her movement still gripped by the storm around her. He was unbelievably strong, and completely in control of his power. A high ranking member of Tartarus she presumed.

Hera managed to touch the tip of her sword and

the wind turned to ice around her. She summoned her strength and broke away from it, smashing it into dust as she moved to avoid the attack. He caught her regardless, ripping into the flesh of her stomach with his outstretched claw.

"Got you, rat!" she heard him shout into the storm, maniacal in his pleasure. "What fun!"

Hera rolled and drew her sword in swift motion. She lunged her sword back at him, but was thrown back by powerful winds, sharp to the touch, circulating through the air in a concentrated arch.

Steadying herself, and ignoring the laughter bellowing from her attacker, she flew back at him, halting the wind around her with a thick layer of ice. But Hera could not keep up with the sheer amount of wind and hail the assailant was conjuring. The gash in her belly moaned as she moved. She was blinded slightly by the storm.

He drew his claw once more, moving the storm out of his own way, but Hera was nimble. She swiped her sword hard and fast, catching and dismembering one of his clawed fingers in the process. For the first time he cried something other than laughter.

The storm raged further on, heightened in its fury in that moment.

Hera's body again froze, and he was upon her, easily batting her sword out of her hand. It clanged heavily to the ground. He had been toying with her. He grasped his claw around her neck, tightening, squeezing the life out of her. She felt them dig into her neck and warm blood escaped into the harsh cold storm. She tried to numb the pain with what little power she could muster.

She felt the world swim and go dark. Images of Perseus and Heracles came clearly into her mind's eye. Her husband Zeus by her side. Happier times.

She had been completely bested. As skilled as she was with her power, her assailant's raw power, and his control over it, was staggering. His control of the storm outside, whilst still fighting her in this confined space, was commendable.

She felt her neck crushed under the weight of his grip, and the end drew closer. Her breath was thin as she tried desperately to draw it into her lungs. Her mind turned to Heracles.

At the thought of her eldest child, she abruptly felt an immense heat rush around her, driving the storm up and away from her body, and the claws around her neck retreated, ripping into her as they moved away.

She forced a view through slitted eyes and saw a figure driving off her assailant. She would recognise the figure anywhere.

It was Prometheus.

He had clearly gotten the drop on her attacker, who was flailing and writhing against Prometheus' attack. Fire bellowed and raged against the storm, the wind amplifying it, feeding its radiant heat. Prometheus was direct and skilled, the fire raging in furious whips at Hera's executioner. She blinked in and out of consciousness, fighting against the darkness as it fell upon her.

The assailant shrieked, and his robes flew off into the wind around them, flying up and high into the air and then out of sight, revealing an armoured body, with an unrecognised crest on the front of the chest plate. He changed his clawed hand back to a staff, and slammed it into the ground once more, releasing a strong wind which toppled Hera's head back in her weakened state. Prometheus held firm, fire raging around him and protecting Hera from further damage.

The assailant stepped back to the edge of the storm before he uttered his final words of the evening.

"The damage is done." He said before stepping back into the storm. He was gone, cackling as he went.

Hera heard Prometheus breathe something under his breath as she swam once more. 'Typhon.'

She swam back into consciousness as Prometheus

addressed her, great worry in his voice. She heard her own voice as she tried desperately to talk and wondered whether Prometheus would be able to make her out. Her neck felt like it was no longer there.

"Promo stop... There's no time. Get Heracles to Zeus. Go to…Mi…Minos."

Hera coughed deeply, dark blood escaping her chest. She could now feel her neck again, as the pain of the injuries rushed her, and blood to fill her lungs. Breathing had become impossible.

Promo went to interrupt but Hera stopped him. Her voice was hushed. Promo leaned in closer to hear her against the noise of the storm.

"As his godfather…he is yours to protect now. Thank you for everythi…"

Hera coughed a final time and heard the 'everything' only in her mind as she slipped completely. The darkness taking her for the final time.

2

Prometheus held his dear friend tightly in his arms. He cried hard into the storm.

Gaia had sent him to this spot to see if he could find any of the Olympus family, knowing that this attack was potentially meant for them, for an as yet unknown reason. But he didn't expect to find his friend fighting for her life. And ultimately losing.

They had been betrayed.

"Typhon. That bastard." Promo muttered under his breath.

It was undeniably Tartarus that had attacked them after seeing Typhon, whom The Alliance had cause to believe was one of their generals. Poseidon's intel. Prometheus had gotten lucky. If he hadn't gotten the drop on Typhon, he'd also be dead now. He was an immensely powerful foe by the looks of things.

A full scale attack, directly on The Alliance Headquarters no less. It was unthinkable. They had some intel on Tartarus' strength, but tonight proved that they had underestimated them, at a huge cost. They were growing in power, and with the death of Hera they had succeeded in weakening The Alliance mightily. Zeus was going to unleash hell when he found out.

Promo slowly closed Hera's eyes, and watched as her sword faded and dissolved into the ether. Back to where it came from.

Prometheus thoughts were interrupted by movement to the left of him. He raised his sword and drove his arm deep into the overgrowth, drawing out a child from beneath it. It was Hera's first born, Heracles.

"Heracles, you idiot! You could've been killed if it hadn't been me!"

"Sorry uncle Prom…" Heracles stopped mid-sentence as he saw his mother, motionless on the ground. He went to dive towards her, his face bursting into tears, and Prometheus stopped him, placing his hand as gently as he could over the kids' mouth.

Once he was sure that he wasn't going to scream, he grabbed the boy by both shoulders and stared at him, hard.

"Heracles, your mother…she's dead, kid. And if we don't get you out of here right now, there's a damn good chance that you will be too. We're in a war here. You need to understand that."

The kid held one last look at his mother, and then turned back to Prometheus and nodded. Tough kid. Trained well Prometheus thought, knowing full well that he had been the one to train him, alongside his father. He scooped the boy into his arms, Heracles now deathly silent with the death of his mother seeping into his whole being.

Prometheus pushed forward into the night.

3

He knew the quickest way to Minos and its labyrinth of alleyways. He was rapid, even with the added load of Heracles in his arms. He maneuvered through the city, his feet powered by his flames which propelled him swiftly forward.

He arrived at the Labyrinth of Minos, not slowing an ounce as he entered. This was his second home. He lived and breathed it, frequenting it regularly. He passed no one. It was deathly quiet in the alleyways, barring the thunderous mess Typhon had rained down onto the city. Prometheus imagined the citizens of Minos were holed up tight in their poorly constructed houses, deathly afraid of what was happening around them.

Heracles was silent still. Utterly withdrawn, the thoughts of his mother surely tearing the poor kid apart.

Prometheus reached the end of Minos and burst forth into the pavilion before the entrance to the military camp. He stopped dead. Surveying the scene quickly, sword drawn. He lowered his sword once he was sure that they were alone.

Alone. But only to the living.

Ahead of him, lifeless on the floor was Zeus. The strongest member of The Alliance, and by some way. Hero. Best friend. An untouchable, previously undefeated warrior. Seemingly no more. How the hell had this happened? It would take an inordinate amount of power to defeat the 'God of Olympus'.

Prometheus felt dead weight in his arms, and he jerked slightly downwards. Heracles had passed out. The boy had seen too much this evening. They both had. He carried the boy over to his father and lay him down beside him.

He looked hard at Zeus, desperate to find any sign of his killer. He was caked in blood, his chest awash with a deep dark red. There had been some sort of struggle here, an almighty battle. Scorch marks and small depressions in the ground littered the floor, undoubtedly caused by Zeus' lightning attacks. He could smell ash and burning in the air, but it was faint on the wind now. A lighter wind Prometheus thought, with the storm around them dissipating further as he assessed the scene.

The attack had all been planned to perfection. But why? To kill Zeus and Hera? Perhaps. If that was their aim, they had delivered a devastating blow to The Alliance, one that would leave them wounded beyond measure.

A spark ran through his mind at that thought.

Perseus.

He surveyed the scene again but found no sign of the younger Olympus boy. Likely dead also.

He checked Zeus over once more, and found his hand clutched tightly in death. He prised it open gently, if only to honour his fallen friend, and it slowly opened, revealing a small timepiece. A gift from Hera and Zeus to Perseus at birth. Now clutched in his father's hand. That likely confirmed Perseus' death.

A great tragedy had befallen the Olympus family tonight. The mother and father dead. The youngest son missing, and most likely dead. And the eldest child scarred at what he had witnessed. Heracles was thankfully alive, but Prometheus feared that death had gripped Perseus as well as his parents, and he wept again, holding the unconscious Heracles tightly in his arms.

He needed to keep the boy safe above all else. Not just for tonight, but for the future too. He was convinced Tartarus had targeted the Olympus family this evening and they would surely come after the boy if they knew him alive. The rest of The Alliance would either fall tonight or drive off the attack. Prometheus had only eyes for this boy and his survival now. He felt the attack was mostly over now though, the storm quelling around them, only the darkness of the night remaining. Prometheus felt sure that The Alliance would be successful in its defence, albeit with a heavy cost.

He would report back to Ares and Gaia with his news once the dust had settled. He feared how Ares would take the news of both of his close friends', and his godson Perseus', death. His wrath would be absolute.

Prometheus scooped up Heracles into his arms and took him deep into the Labyrinth of Minos.

CHAPTER IV
AFTERMATH

1

"Perseus?"

Heracles swam back to reality. Memories of a time past rushing his mind.

"Hello brother." Perseus said as he ran the fingers of his right hand through his long blonde mane; his voice laced with bitterness. He was now standing several paces back, having swiftly avoided the lightning Heracles had thrown upwards at him.

Heracles was shell-shocked. It wasn't often that he couldn't regain his composure quickly but finding out your younger brother had been alive these past 19 years would be enough to rock anyone. He felt his eyes swell. He made no attempt to stop the tears as several escaped his eyes. He let them sit on his face, trailing downwards slowly.

"Oh?" Perseus said as he watched Heracles bare his emotions before him. "Tears for your dead brother. Really?"

Heracles studied his sibling closely. Having not seen him for nineteen years, his memory of him was hazy – having no memorabilia of his family left in his possession, on Promo's instructions. Any photos of Hera, Zeus, and the two brothers together could have tied everything back to Heracles in his adult life. Promo had been very careful to monitor that side of things and ensure everything had been destroyed across The Alliance. Any who knew of the family were told that all of them had died that night. A tragedy of The Alliance, and anytime Heracles had heard mention of himself, and his family, it had been with mention of a heroic and tragic death of two truly great Alliance heroes and the heart-breaking passing of their two sons.

Heracles had been devastated at the destruction of his memories but it had been for the good of his life and had ultimately toughened him. Hardened him. But perhaps seeing his brother alive and well was a step to far for that strong façade to handle.

His brother was wearing the same robes as the assailants at the Amphitheatre. His hooded robe was open at the front, revealing what seemed to be a dark grey chest plate, long armoured boots on top of dark grey trousers. The rest was obscured, but Heracles could make out a crest on his chest. He had seen it only in books, but it was undoubtedly the symbol of Tartarus. It was a long black boat, sat atop a crudely rendered river. Two shadowy figures sat in the boat, coloured black. The boat was clearly the boat that ferried lost souls across the river Styx. To the Underworld.

Perseus continued to talk at Heracles, with little reply.

"So, you drew our father's sword, did you? I expected to draw that sword today myself, being far closer to father. But here you are, with sword in hand," Perseus voice and words continued to be spiked with resentment towards Heracles. "Your face screams that you thought I was dead too. Correct?"

Heracles nodded, still overwhelmed by the moment.

"Fine. Good. The two Olympus brothers alive and well! It'd be funny really, if only…"

Perseus halted at the end of the sentence, rearranging his attire neatly, before raising his newly acquired blade and pointing it directly at Heracles.

"This is how it'll go. We'll talk for a moment

longer, for as long as the chaos around us allows," Perseus paused, swinging his arms around himself left to right to support his mention of the fighting around them. "And then we'll see exactly who is better."

He smiled excitedly.

2

His brother, somewhat incongruous in his demeanour, was a lifetime away from the content, happy child Heracles remembered. Withdrawn, where he had previously been so full of life. He wanted to ask him everything all at once. Where had he been all these years? How did he survive the night of the attack? But he asked the one question he knew would benefit The Alliance, over him.

"Fine, Perseus. If that is what you want, I'll play ball. Just answer me this: Was all of this just a distraction to allow you access to a drawn weapon?"

Perseus threw his head back and laughed deeply.

"Of course! Don't act as if it's some big revelation Heracles. A child could've figured that out. Tartarus, as I am sure you've gathered that I am very much a part of, are not *quite* ready for a full scale decimation of your dear, dear Alliance. But we're *close*. Your time will come, your end is near. We have great interest in this shield of yours." He was pacing now, left and right, looking between Heracles and the Shield of Aegis, complete in his menace.

"Today was a gamble. As an Olympus born, I haven't been able to acquire a weapon through Tartarus' means unfortunately. I can make no pact with the underworld. My blood prevents it. Woe is me," Sarcasm rang through his voice. "So the only way to grant me greater power was to perform the Rite ritual, in the hope that our bloodline would pay off. And it duly delivered! Mother would be proud."

He raised his sword high into the air, and brought it slicing into the ground, the impossibly sharp edge embedding deep. Ice quickly sprang forth, releasing a wave of spikey ice towards Heracles and lacing the floor with bright blue frost, reflecting beautifully against the light streaming in through the open roof of the Panathenon.

Heracles recognised the power instantly as his mothers. For Perseus to create this amount of ice instantly was intimidatingly impressive.

Catching him slightly off guard, Heracles was still quick enough to dodge away with the assistance of his sword, using the lightning inside to teleport up and away before landing safely onto the ground a few metres away where there was solid footing. His speed was his greatest asset but still something he had yet to master completely. Using it in a real life or death fight was not something he had ever experienced before.

"Yes! I remember that power!" Perseus shouted at Heracles. "Our father's power versus our mothers'. Let's see how well you use it Heracles!"

Perseus's eyes were wild. He was now circling a vast amount of ice particles around his body, controlling large chunks of it with ease and shaping them with his mind. His younger brother was talented it seemed and had been trained well.

But Heracles was handy with his sword also. He drew it up towards the sky and instantaneously, a thick, white hot lightning bolt engulfed Heracles. He was bathed in the lightning, clenching his right fist tightly around his sword. He controlled the lightning and spread it through his body. It became his armour.

The lightning dissipated. Stood in place was Heracles, bathed in a stunning golden armour. Heracles had honed it over years of training, wrapping himself in the lightning he wielded and shaping it into this radiating armour, one that was dangerous to the touch with the volts streaming through it. It was simple in its design, but on the face of the chest place was the head of fierce Lion.

He drove his weapon forward, shooting a razor thin lightning bolt at Perseus. He had no intent to kill him but if he didn't stop him, he would undoubtedly be dead himself. Perseus reeled left and away from the bolt, impressively so with how fast Heracles' lightning could travel, and it caught him only slightly on the left arm as he turned. Even with that slight touch, Heracles could see Perseus's body tighten up, feeling the effect of thousands of volts running through his body.

Perseus was up and running again promptly, learning from every move Heracles made. He hurtled chunks of thick, sharp ice from around him. The ice was crumbling and crashing all around them, as Heracles sent bolt after bolt of lightning to combat the chunks of ice, obliterating them into tiny specks of dust.

Their powers were strangely neutral to each other. This would be decided by skill. Perseus had learned from the first bolt of lightning that had hit him and was now covering the parts of his body that Heracles was targeting with ice, to soften the effect of the lightning on his body. Neutralising it. Stopping the lightning from conducting and immobilising him, and halting Heracles' intended strategy. He was a highly intelligent fighter.

He was strong also, shaking off any attack that Heracles could throw at him, whilst wounding and impacting Heracles at a heavy rate. Sharp ice sliced and pierced through Heracles' golden armour, even before the volts could dwindle them into dust. He was learning his new weapon with ease in such a short space of time.

Heracles was already weakening considerably. He was well trained but lacked any experience in live combat with any killing intent involved. The years of training with Prometheus were keeping him alive right now, but it was worryingly apparent that Perseus was experienced in both fighting and strategy. Battle-hardened beyond belief. It seemed that he was an exceptional fighter even before drawing such a powerful sword.

And ready to kill.

Heracles was unable to use his speed and teleportation to its full potential as well now, as Perseus' attacks had covered the majority of the Panathenon in deep, thick ice rendering Heracles' footing highly unstable. He simply couldn't gather his footing enough to attack with his speed and was now resigned to hurtling lightning bolts at Perseus from a distance.

3

Perseus suddenly stopped his attacks as Heracles again slipped and fell to the deck of the Panathenon, skidding across the floor before popping back up to his feet, and heating the ice around his feet to melt it away to gain a foothold. All of the ice particles surrounding Perseus crashed to the floor around him, littering the floor of the arena.

Heracles readied himself, standing firm before Perseus.

"Well this has been fun, chief!" Heracles winced at remembering the nickname he had given his younger brother all those years ago. Hearing it again after so many years hurt him greatly. "But it seems we're out of time. We've got what we came for."

Heracles' ears focussed to outside the Panathenon now, having previously been completely engrossed in the fighting with Perseus, and he realised the noise from around them was quelling, the fighting seemingly ending.

As the final word left Perseus' mouth, Heracles felt several sharp objects pierce his back. He stumbled forward and put his hand up to his back to feel sharp blocks of the coldest ice. Perseus had distracted him long enough to get them behind him. As Heracles looked up, Perseus was stood before him.

Heracles went to react but felt his whole body immobilised, being quickly encased in a layer of thick ice now, spreading across his legs and arms before spreading up to his neck, leaving only his head free. He was stuck in a crouched bowing position. His throat was being constricted steadily by the ice; his breathing being cut off: suffocating him.

He struggled against it all but knew it was in vain. Perseus had been toying with him. He realised that now. Using the time before he needed to retreat to have some fun with his older brother. They stared intently at each other as Heracles's throat constricted further. He blinked in and out of consciousness, fighting against the lack of oxygen. He kicked and struggled. His blade had slipped out his hand and was lodged between rock and rubble at his feet.

Perseus suddenly became highly stoic. His face turning to slight unease.

"I'm not going to kill you Heracles. I could. But I won't. And don't mistake this for compassion. *He* has plans for you apparently," He paused, his face slightly breaking. "But I have to know why. Why you never searched for me. Why did you just give up on me?"

Perseus' hand was raised towards Heracles, contorting, controlling the ice as it's thickened around his brother's neck. He was clearly hurt.

Heracles went to struggle an answer through the constriction and was suddenly halted, as the ice around him melted instantly, freeing him from his prison. He dropped his hands to the floor to catch himself and gasped desperately at the air around him. He looked up to see Perseus backing away, brushing off a fiery blaze attempting to consume him, covering himself in thick ice to prevent the flames from engulfing him.

"Promo!" Heracles said as Prometheus increased his onslaught against Perseus, slashing his sword in downwards spirals, sending out fiery lacerations through the air. This was a complete mismatch with their powers, and Heracles could see that Promo was putting everything into this. The fire was vast and was steadily penetrating Perseus' ice.

Heracles went to move towards Promo and was shot back through the air by a powerful blast of heat.

"Perseus! This isn't what your parents would've wanted! You're throwing your life away, son." Prometheus said, his emotions clearly running wild at seeing Perseus alive and well.

"Don't call me *son*! You all left me to die that night! I have a new family now. One that raised me as their own. One that respects me."

Perseus was incensed but Prometheus continued his attack, driving him back. Perseus was trying desperately to get a handle on the heat but he was no match for Prometheus's fire. He slammed to the floor as a ball of fire hit him square on and he rolled over several times in the dirt, before stopping and laying still.

Prometheus used the chance to turn to Heracles. They locked eyes and Heracles could feel the pain Prometheus was going through at attacking his best friends' youngest son.

"Get out of here, you dumbass! You're no match for him as you are now." Promo yelled towards Heracles, fire brimming in his eyes.

It only took a moment, but the moment he took his eyes off of Perseus it was over. A black blade drove deep into Prometheus' back and Heracles watched as the blade emerged out of his front, right through his heart. Black mist descended across his body, engulfing him, and turning his body a dusty black. Parts of his body crumbled away, turning to dust in the air as Heracles watched on helplessly. The hooded figure that had delivered the blow was now backing away towards Perseus before settling next to him. Checking him over.

Prometheus took one last look at Heracles,

opening his mouth to speak, but only dust escaped. The hooded figure behind him turned back and clicked his finger. Prometheus's body cracked and dissolved into a cloud of dusty ash.

And he was gone.

4

Heracles screamed in silence. The world seemed to close off to him. The only thing he was able to focus on in that moment was the remains of his closest friend, slowly blowing away in the slight wind of the Panathenon. Heracles' rage was all consuming. It became him. He saw a brilliant white wash over his eyes. He was lost to himself.

He blinked in and out of consciousness. He was aware that he was up and running, raining attack after attack down on the hooded figure and Perseus before him. Perseus was no longer smiling. His face sullen at the scene before him, simply flailing under the assault and trying to catch a solid foothold, to no avail.

Heracles blinked again. Perseus had thrown himself away from Heracles and now simply watched on as Heracles' thunder roared, lightning tearing at the hooded figure.

A final blink into consciousness.

Heracles sword lay stopped in the palm of the hooded figure. Halted mid swing, with all of the power of his lightning slowly draining from his body, his strength deserting him completely. The hooded figure's body was engulfed in darkness, clouds of smoke and ash flowing slowly around his frame. The life seemed to drain out of Heracles as he dropped to his knees. All power sapped from him. He clenched his weapon tightly, but it was all he could muster. His hands were pale. His rage and anger all gone.

The hand released its grip and allowed Heracles to

fall to the floor to steady himself, his sword clashing hard against the ground before him. Heracles looked up to find the hooded figure standing over him.

Where Perseus had been talented and strong, the hooded figure before him was a monster.

"Apologies for my interruption," The voice said, with not a hint of remorse. "I felt it time to intervene. Prometheus was getting the upper hand you see."

With a tiny part of Heracles's strength returning, he looked up to see Perseus walking over to him to stand beside the hooded figure. He was breathing heavily and had a regretful look on his face that he was seemingly trying to hide from the hooded figure beside him. The hooded figure doesn't seem to notice, his face entirely focussed on Heracles, the lower part of which was covered by the shadow of his hood, showing only a hint of pale skin. White eyes pierced out from within the darkness of the hood.

"Well fought boy." he said as he surveyed Heracles hungrily. "That rage of yours makes you powerful."

"Alcaeus Demos, or rather, Heracles Olympus. All grown up, your father's power coursing through you. But by the looks of it, you can only harness a fraction of it. A shame. This place is hindering you. Squandering that wonderful rage of yours."

He was toying with Heracles. His strength depleted; Heracles could do nothing but patiently listen.

"Now, what shall we do with you Heracles? I fear you are not yet ready. But you will be…"

A thunderous crash interrupted the hooded figure as the huge oak doors on the Panathenon flew off of their hinges and slammed to the floor some metres away. Heracles turned to find several Alliance members flooding into the arena. In his depleted, slightly drunken stupor, he could just about hear the hooded figure and Perseus step back slightly and away from him.

It was a collection of power, acting as Heracles' cavalry. Atlas as the driving force of the group, and clearly the one who had broken the doors furiously off of their hinges, followed closely by Athena and Artemis of the Stratigos. Following closely behind them was Demeter, a sight for sore eyes, along with Apollo and Achilles. They had trusted Heracles and thankfully gone for help, and also, hopefully, delivered Selene to those that could aid her. Also in attendance were Nyx and Pontus of the Taxiarhos. The two other candidates in line for the single spot vacated in the Stratigos with Ares' departure.

The hooded figure laughed heartily.

"Well now. Welcome, welcome. A truly fearsome group, and just for us? How lovely of you all to join."

"Cut the shit. Surrender. Now." Atlas said as he stepped forward, his boulder firmly in hand. Atlas had always been a man of few words, but all the more impactful for it.

The hooded figure tutted audibly back at him. He held both his hands aloft, and three black waves of smoke appeared in the air above him, before descending in spirals to the floor beside him.

The smoke dissipated to reveal three further hooded figures. Heracles identified them from their frames as those at the Amphitheatre during the initial stages of the attack.

"I don't think I will be surrendering today unfortunately. We have what we came for," His voice remained calm and raspy, almost sickly in its speech. "Ah, before we go, one final thing."

One of the hooded figures beside him revealed two folded hooded robes, drawing them from beneath their own robes.

"These are for you two." The figure said, Heracles unsure of who he was addressing. Suddenly, two figures flashed past Heracles, knocking him over slightly as they do so. They stood before the figure, weapons in hand, before lowering them and placing their hands out.

"What the hell are you two doing!?" Demeter screamed at the pair as she was held back by Athena.

The two robes flew around in a circle simultaneously and lay neatly onto the shoulders of both Nyx and Pontus. They turned and both smiled sweetly at Demeter, insincerity ringing through their lips.

Atlas raced forward, intent on ending this now. Pontus visibly flinched. Atlas loomed over the hooded figure at the forefront of it all, swinging his boulder in a wide arch before crashing it down upon him. The hooded figure simply grabbed the boulder nonchalantly out of the air, sending black waves along the chains in rapid succession. The boulder dropped lazily to the floor, before Atlas followed suit, sloping to his knees. Nyx was quickly beside him, swinging her boot into Atlas's face and sending him flying back towards the other Alliance members, taking both Athena and Demeter to break his fall.

Heracles had never seen anyone able to move Atlas like that, confirming the hooded figure's status as a monster with a deadly and unknown power. Atlas looked visibly drained, as Heracles had felt when he had tangled with the figure.

The hooded figure left his sword dangling out of his sleeve long enough for Heracles to lay eyes on it, and then it was retracted. It was darker than night. And clearly it was the sword he had held briefly as it had impaled Ares's chest at the ceremony. Heracles thought he saw a visible terror run across those in attendance from The Alliance.

"A highly successful day!" the figure began as he spoke once more. "Ares's untimely death at the hands of young Heracles here, all staged of course; two new members added to our crew; a powerful new weapon for my young cohort here, and all for the cost of a few measly lives."

The hooded figure laughed uncontrollably,

coughing in a sickly way after finishing. He turned to his compatriots. He nodded towards Pontus and Nyx, who bowed low in return, content with their work in all of this.

He threw one look back towards Heracles.

"Today's your lucky day Heracles. I've had my fill, for now. But know that I will be back for you. When it is time." He said directly to Heracles, before clicking his fingers once more. A grand circle of darkness formed below the group, before flashing upwards around them and high above their heads.

And they were gone.

Leaving only The Alliance members in their wake, completely and utterly routed.

5

Heracles scrambled to his feet, before sprinting over to what little remained of Prometheus, falling, and tumbling as he tried. Tears streamed from his face. He cared not. His mind was fully focussed on his long-time friend and mentor.

He grabbed at nothing, simply snatching at dust and dirt that he desperately tried to fool himself into believing were the remains of his dear friend. He was gone of course. Faded into the darkness. Completely obliterated. Stripped of his life. Turned to dusty ash.

Heracles felt a light hand grip his shoulder. It as Demeter, lowering herself towards him. A look of horror and understanding on her face as she saw Prometheus' sword vanish from existence, fading, and returning to the Shield of Aegis.

"Alcaeus..." she whispered to him. He knew. It was all he could do to not break down there and then.

Heracles drifted. Thoughts of Promo and better times littered his mind, awash with fond memories. And an aching guilt that he would never talk to Prometheus again, never train with him, never drink with him, never laugh with him. Never.

He composed himself and walked back towards the Stratigos. Athena was over Atlas now, having helped him back to the others. Heracles imagined her struggling under his weight and frame. He was still deathly pale. Athena quickly glanced up at Heracles as he walked over, before returning to Atlas.

"The same ooze that was on Ares before we left…" She hovered over the black goop around Atlas' hand, still clinging to him post the attack by the hooded assailant. She never touched it, simply hovered over it. It was retracting slowly of its own accord, seemingly powerless now that the attacker was gone. Whatever it was, it was a powerful tool that the enemy possessed. One that could cripple a Stratigos with ease. Athena's eyes flicked back to Heracles and then to Artemis. She nodded slightly.

Artemis was behind Heracles in a flash. She grabbed both of Heracles' arms and toppled him heavily to the floor. Atlas went to pull Athena back but she shook him off easily in his weakened state and walked to Heracles, before dropping down to his level.

She was calm. Composed.

"You're going to slowly and truthfully tell me exactly what you have to do with all of this," Her eyes never once left Heracles as she spoke. Heracles felt the pressure of her words. The weight of them. "Else I have cause to kill you for your crimes."

Heracles stared back at Athena. He no longer knew who to trust. Who to turn to. He was completely lost without Prometheus here to back him up in that moment.

"Artemis, for the god's sake, let the boy go."

A voice emanated from somewhere Heracles couldn't see with his face pressed into the dirt. He could only see Athena, who turned towards the voice.

"Athena," The voice said, as calmly as Athena had addressed Heracles moments before. "I can help with the explanation later. For now we've work to do. I will vouch for him personally. And you're all going to have to get used to calling him Heracles from now on."

6

Gaia had appeared before them all.

She held her hand over the ground in front of her. A flower sprouted instantly from the dirt and grew up to meet her palm. A large hibiscus flower formed from the stem, the stigma contorting to form what looked to be a rudimentary microphone. Heracles had seen several flowers sprout across the HQ whenever Gaia needed to make an important announcement. Her form of communications equipment. A strange thought popped into Heracles head. Perhaps this was what was used at the Amphitheatre earlier today to amplify the sound of those on stage?

Gaia spoke clearly and impressively.

"This is Gaia. To all those that can hear me, I thank you all. With your valiant display, we have driven the assailants back. I understand that this has come at a great, great cost. We have lost many treasured lives today, but there will be a time for mourning in the days to come. For now, those of us able need to assist those still in need. Tend to your injured comrades. Your commanders will be issuing orders to you all in turn. Be ready, and remember that we are together as one, and we will persevere. Always. Over and out."

The microphone stigma rescinded, before the flower wilted and receded back into the dirt below. Gaia turned to the group in front of her, towards the Stratigos mainly. Heracles was returned to a standing position by Artemis, albeit with a close eye remaining on him and with a scowl resting on her face.

"Athena. Atlas. Artemis. We are weakened today with the loss of Ares, and the betrayal of Hermes, but we need you now more than ever. Atlas, I want you to find Ares' body amongst the rubble of the Amphitheatre. I wish to examine his cause of death. I have some fears which I will talk you through later."

Atlas nodded, his colour now mostly returned and the black ooze no longer across his arm. He squatted deeply into the ground and propelled himself towards the exit, bounding through and out into the concourse, his heavy legs pounding the dirt as he ran.

"Athena, The Alliance will need your calm now more than ever. Please round up all of the Taxiarhos and Syntags and issue them their orders. They can then distribute down the ranks, as necessary. We have a lot of work to do, but our main priority is tending to those in need of aid and the containment of any panic. I trust your judgement and strategy, as always."

Athena nodded in response. She walked calmly to the exit, in stark contrast to Atlas' rampaging run.

"Artemis, go to Hephaestus and ensure that we are defensively stable. Go through all the rebuilding work that needs to be done and mobilise the foot soldiers, as necessary. Take all the help you need, but don't disrupt the aid work of Athena. We must rebuild and fortify. And fast. In case of a follow up attack."

Artemis took one final look at Heracles, along with a quick glance towards Apollo, and was gone, set on the instructions given. Gaia turned to Demeter and addressed her with her full attention.

"Demeter. In light of the treachery of Pontus and Nyx, there seems little point in delaying. Congratulations. You are now a Stratigos. Your first duty is to round-up any denizens of the city and tend to any wounds. Keep them here for now, for their own safety. We also don't want news of this attack spreading too quickly. Be careful and ensure that none of those you round-up are still assailants posing as city dwellers."

Demeter, shocked but clearly brimming with pride, thanked Gaia heartily before she turned and proceeded out of the Panathenon.

"Apollo, Achilles. Go to your friend's side. She'll need to see some familiar faces when she wakes up post-surgery."

They both nodded and turned. Apollo shot a quick glance over his shoulder at Heracles before they left and smiled. Gaia turned finally to Heracles.

She was thinking, hard. Clearly working out how to address Heracles after all that had happened there today. She would undoubtedly hold back, but Heracles would press her for any information he could get. If he could just hold on to his fleeting strength. He felt close to passing out.

"Heracles. I owe you an explanation. I…"

He heard no more, only seeing the silent movement of Gaia's lips. His mind was wandering. Darkness descending. His injuries too much now. The last thing he felt was his body falling through the air towards the dirt of the Panathenon below him.

And then he was gone.

7

Heracles was swimming. His body drifting through various places from his past and current life. Lifeless. Floating.

His mind was trying to remember. Trying to recall something of interest. But it didn't feel like it was his memory he was trying to return to. Or himself leading the search.

He was climbing the stairs to The Alliance Headquarters.

He drifted through the concourse to the Panathenon, and, after flying above and into the stadium, he watched as several trainers took the new recruits through their morning drills. His heart then sank at the sight of Prometheus, sat in the stands and watching the new recruits intently. Promo had been a fierce teacher following his retirement from the Stratigos.

And a fierce friend.

It was now clear that this was not Heracles' own memory. Heracles had only known Prometheus as a Stratigos in the early years of his life. He had stepped down in the days following the attack on The Alliance twenty years ago, with Gaia unable to convince him otherwise as he wallowed in the death of his best friends. He had then regained his love for The Alliance with a training position at the Panathenon several years later, one he held until his death.

Here, he was clearly still a Stratigos. Heracles wished he could stay in this moment longer and watch his old friend in action, but he was quickly moving on past the Panathenon. His arms grabbed at nothing as he floated by.

He was racing through the Headquarters again, seemingly towards the War Room specifically. He flinched as he shot through the main doors and into the lobby, before entering further into the war room.

Whose memories were these if not his own? He had certainly never ventured into the War Room.

He drifted into a vast room. One with a large circular oak table in the middle, with a wonderfully polished gloss finish, and surrounded by high backed oak chairs, padded with a horizontal rectangle of the most marvellous black leather. Exactly ten chairs sat around the table. The Alliance's crest was carved into the backs of all of them. Ten of the chairs were filled with a silhouette of fog, not quite appearing as people yet.

His movement stopped, and he floated to the

floor. He could move again, although it was a restricted movement. He felt that if he tried to turn back towards the exit, he would be stopped. He would see what needed to be seen.

Heracles waited patiently. His mind was indeed trying to tell him something, to show him something. Several of the apparitions started to solidify and contort into a few faces he recognised, and a few he did not.

At the 'head' of the table was Gaia. She was considerably younger. She was dressed differently to the Gaia that Heracles knew. However, her uniform reflected her powers as always: a relatively earthy coloured uniform, with a dark green lapel across her chest where the jacket met, with slight flowery detail engraved into it. A pad with various scribbled notes rested on the table before her. Likely an agenda.

The seat to the left of Gaia was empty.

Two places to Gaia's left sat a slightly more petite woman. Her hair a wave of delightful blonde locks. She wore more casual attire than Gaia, having a light blue floaty dress on that attached at her neck and flowed downwards, but was still immaculate in her presentation. Heracles recognised his mother instantly. As beautiful as he remembered her. He missed her deeply in that moment. He tried to move towards her but his feet stuck firm. He was at the complete mercy of the dream. And it's owner.

He recognised many other faces around the table now as they came into focus.

Prometheus was present, Heracles assuming that the scene he had witnessed before was earlier in the day. As was a much younger Hephaestus. His beard was platted delicately, now no longer the greyish mess he wore in Heracles' time, and it dangled down to the wooden table top before him. He regularly picked it up in his right hand to stroke it from top to bottom, before letting it fall back into place.

He recognised Achilles' father after staring hard, knowing his face more for his son than for him. A towering man, stoic in his disposition much like his son. Heracles recognised Poseidon, not from meeting him in person, but from a picture he had once seen of him in the Panathenon archives. Poseidon had been missing from The Alliance for many years now, but it was comforting to see him sat there and present with the other founders.

Hemera was present and still alive at this time. It must have been a good two decades ago as she had been killed during the attack on The Alliance along with Heracles' parents.

There was one person present that he did not recognise. She sat in a different uniform to the others, a uniform Heracles was not familiar with. Perhaps a visitor to The Alliance?

Heracles tried to call his mind back to another history book he had read about the past ranks of The Alliance and saw a piece of parchment wash in front of his eyes, blurry but filled with what information he could recall:

Polemarch
Hera Olympus
Gaia Galanis

Stratigos
Zeus Olympus
Ares Angelis
Poseidon Papatonis
'Unknown'
Achilles Elias
Prometheus Pollaris

He knew that Hemera chose not to partake in any ranking system, preferring to quietly go about her business in the background. He also knew that his mother and Gaia both held the position of Polemarch and ran The Alliance together, and that his father, Ares, and Poseidon, were all not interested in the Polemarch positions.

There was one final member present, of those he recognised, and his heart leapt once more.

It was his father, Zeus. His long blonde beard sat powerfully on his chin. His large muscular form was intimidatingly commanding. He wore his hair much as Perseus did now. He was also dressed in his military uniform, and Heracles had heard that he was fond of always being prepared for battle. His preferred colour of gold rang across everything he wore. His armour was much as Heracles' manifestation appeared when he drew the powers of his sword to form around his body. He now knew the reasoning behind his armour: a subconscious manifestation of his father's.

It was both joyous and heart-breaking to see both his parents, but he welcomed the time with them, nonetheless.

He could not account for the one person present he did not recognise, still very much a blurred silhouette of smoke, or the one who should be sat in the vacant seat to the side of Gaia. As his mind worked through the possibilities, the doors of the meeting room burst open.

8

It was Ares, hurriedly entering the room and taking his place to the left hand side of Gaia. A look of embarrassment on his face that Heracles had not seen before. The only look Heracles had ever seen on Ares' face was one of a stoic nature or projecting that wry smile that Heracles had never quite trusted.

Perhaps Heracles had been wrong in assuming that Gaia was sat at the head of the table, as Ares was turning to Hera in what seemed like an attempt to apologise for his lateness, but Hera waved him away. She stood up, and leant forward on the table, her arms resting heavily on the wooden top. Some sort of remote control rested under her left hand. Heracles had only ever seen the technology in books, the most common source of his knowledge.

Hera began to address those gathered.

"Thank you all for coming, and for understanding the urgency of this meeting. It is imperative that we discuss this topic now and decide on the best course of action."

His mother was urgently serious. Heracles had seen her act a similar way as a child, on that fateful night all those years ago.

"Gaia and I have been made aware of a situation. One that could have grave consequences for us all. It concerns objects of great power. Objects that if combined, have the potential to destroy countless lives. Gaia will fill you in on the full details of what we know so far, and then we will open the floor to discussion."

Hera slid the remote to Gaia, who caught it with a downward palm slap. She nodded to Hera and continued where she had left off.

"Thank you, Hera. From Poseidon's many trips away from The Alliance Headquarters," She threw a rather indignant look at Poseidon, who smiled cannily back in return. "We have discovered that there is ancient information which speaks of a great power. This information has been gathered from various sources, such as hidden cave walls, tombs, and catacombs. It has come at a great cost and I thank all of those that gave their lives for us to be able to discuss and address this discovery."

Gaia held the remote aloft and pointed it at the centre of the table. A cylinder of wood, with a small black circle on the top of it, slid upwards and out of the table. The small black circle came alive and formed an orb of fantastic colour. The wisps of colour flew over and under each other, contorting and merging to form three separate spheres, suspended in the air. Two remained out of focus, as the first came into clarity.

It was the city of Athenaeus, a wonderfully projected model of it. Heracles had never seen technology like it and was dumbfounded in its presence. It was years ahead of anything he had witnessed in the present time, except maybe the glimpse he got of an airship visiting The Alliance a few years back. He had been just as stunned then as he was now and had thought to himself then that the wider world perhaps held far more advanced technology than they were privy to in Athenaeus.

"Athenaeus. It has come to our attention that our dear city may contain one of the powerful objects we now discuss. There are rumours that we are not the only ones aware of their whereabouts. The small military faction we have been coming into ever more frequent skirmishes with over the last few years have also come by this information somehow. Tartarus."

Heracles balked at the mention of the group who had caused such destruction to The Alliance over many years, and dramatically so the past day in his timeline.

"They are growing in size steadily, and we don't see them as a major threat to those we protect yet, being small in number and strength…"

Heracles thought back. With Gaia's choice of words, and the presence of his parents, then the attack on The Alliance HQ twenty years ago hadn't happened yet. Maybe they underestimated the level of power Tartarus held in their ranks during this time period. Or they had some poor intelligence coming through.

"There are several high ranking officers that we know about. They call themselves the Titans. We don't know who sits at the top of the organisation though, but we do know the names and potential threat of some of these Titan commanders. And if they are after these same items then we will need to quash any chance they have."

Gaia paused, looked over at Poseidon and nodded, before she sat back in her seat. Poseidon remained sitting down, somewhat lackadaisically, and began to offer a further explanation to the group.

"These are the ones from Tartarus that we need to watch out for. They could cause us problems down the line if we're not careful. The first is known as 'Typhon' and seems to be somewhat high into the ranks. All we know on top of that is that he is referred to 'The Storm'. Little is known about his powers but those we gathered information from were terrified to discuss him further."

"The second of those we know of, we know only as 'The Sky'. All accounts note that they are capable of flight."

Poseidon threw a roll of his eyes to Zeus, who coughed to hide a small laugh.

"And finally, the other person we know from the higher echelons of the organisation is named Ourea, or more commonly 'The Mountain'. Good reason for that as well, as accounts state that he is a giant of a man. Tall as a mighty oak and as wide as this very room," Poseidon sank lower into his chair. "And that's as far as we have gotten for now."

Poseidon was a stocky man, not as tall as Ares and Zeus but still powerfully built. He was clean shaven, and well-presented despite his outward demeanour. He was wearing his military uniform, and his was centred around a dark blue colour. His short brown hair was trimmed tidily and was military in nature, buzzcut short.

Poseidon sat up in his chair suddenly, leaning forward with his head down, drawing it up slowly as he spoke.

"Oh and one final thing." Poseidon said. "I have cause to believe that there is a rat amongst us."

9

There was shocked silence in the room, until Poseidon's close friend Hephaestus spoke up, speaking in his deep and booming voice whilst still retaining warmth in his address. Clearly, he felt no seriousness in Poseidon's words.

"That joke is a little too far, even for *you* pal. No need for throwaway comments like that, is there?"

Poseidon turned to Hephaestus, his serious demeanour remaining.

"This is no joke Heph. There is a leak, and I am genuinely worried about the level of information escaping from this very room. Would I get this serious if there wasn't cause for it?" He moved to make a secondary point but was interrupted.

"What do we have if not trust." Hera stole in. "All of us here have been together as group for some time, having built this wonderful Headquarters together. We've saved countless lives in the city, have lived, laughed, and lost together. What do we have if not trust, Poseidon."

Poseidon looked undeterred.

"I understand your concerns Hera, but you need to recognize that this is not false information. The enemy might know more about us than we them. One of our intel gatherers found intimate plans of our Headquarters on their, unfortunately last, reconnaissance mission. Details that no one lower than the Stratigos ranks would ever see. Intimate plans of hiding places, secret bunkers. How could they possess layouts without someone spreading information? They are not so easily obtained."

Silence in the room. A look of shock sat on some of the faces, a look of offence and betrayal at Poseidon's suggestion on others.

"I agree, in part, with Poseidon. Although not with the way he is going about it," Zeus finally joined the conversation. Everyone remained quiet as he spoke. A sense of authority and respect noticeably spread through the room. "We cannot afford to be unprepared. Even if this information proves to be unfounded, what harm is there in preparing and mobilising, strengthening our defences, pouring some passion and urgency back into the troops. If something happens, we are then ready. We will need to act against Tartarus sooner or later, so it can't hurt to explore and prepare for this potential scenario."

He paused and looked to Poseidon to confirm his support of him.

"But know this. What we need to have is solidarity. We need to all be together as one. Or not at all. I for one trust every single person here in this room with my life."

The room nodded in agreement, and Hephaestus offered a 'hear, hear' to Zeus. Poseidon sank back into his seat, the matter seemingly settled for now. Gaia rose once again.

"Fine. We will explore the possibility of a leak but there is no cause to point fingers. The leak would be coming from somewhere else if this information is to be believed," Gaia turned her focus back to the three projections in the centre of the table. "Now. Back to the discussions of the objects of power. We don't know exactly what we are looking for. All we know is that one of the items could potentially be hidden deep within a Labyrinth of the city."

"Minos? That's just a hotbed for crooks and merchants Gaia. It's just a series of long and dark alleyways, I highly doubt it holds any secrets of this importance. The object would've been found and sold by now, surely."

Hera cut Ares off before he could offer more explanation. "Just listen will you Ares?" she said, and Ares rescinded, swiftly. Gaia continued on.

"Minos isn't what I am referring to Ares. It has been long believed that *under* the city there is an actual labyrinth. Crafted untold years ago, by who or what we know not. We have no one that has seen the entrance, let alone been inside the place, so this is of course hearsay and speculation currently. But we have reason to believe it exists, and that it hides a great and powerful object."

Ares bellowed, rocking backwards in his chair. Hemera shot him an icy glance but he ignored it. He sat forward in his chair once more, becoming slightly serious again.

"This is ridiculous. If we have no information to go on, and we aren't sure that this place even exists, then what good is this to us?"

"Simply put, Ares, we have *this*."

Gaia dove into her pocket, and from it pulled a thin strand of thick golden hair. On second inspection, Heracles felt it not hair, being more akin to wool.

"We believe that the item this wool comes from is one of the three objects of power, and may well be the item that exists within the Labyrinth. Allow me a demonstration of its power. Zeus, please humour me."

Zeus rose to his feet, as instructed by Gaia now. He stood in front of her, towering over her with his height, and braced himself as she instructed. She breathed a large breath and clutched the hair tightly within a balled fist.

She hurtled her fist forward at Zeus, the most powerful and hardened of the Stratigos. The impact of her punch sent him flying across the room and hard against the wall on the other side, leaving a large concave, deep enough to stick Zeus in place for a moment. He looked shocked. And sore.

Gaia looked back towards the rest of those present and found shocked faces, some of them dumbfounded at Gaia's newly found strength.

"This is what the tiniest fraction of the wool can do. This is a strand from what we believe to be a full fleece. Imagine if it was whole. It would grant immeasurable strength. And that is why we cannot allow it to fall into the wrong hands."

Murmurs spread across the room. Hera placed a hand in the air and silenced them as Achilles Snr grabbed Zeus by the arm and pulled him out of the wall, grunting as he did so. Gaia continued.

"We will action two things following this briefing. One, we will put into motion the strengthening of The Alliance's defences given Poseidon's intelligence and Zeus's support. Ares, you are to lead the strengthening of the defence. Zeus, you, and Achilles are to investigate the leak," All three of them nodded slightly in acceptance. "Two, we will create a team who will be responsible for gathering intel on anything relating to this subterranean labyrinth. Poseidon, you will mobilise the Episkopos for this. With your teams' skills of persuasion, it should allow us to get a quick foot hold on anything concrete."

Poseidon also nodded in agreement. Gaia turned to Hera to continue but she swiftly closed the meeting.

"That is all. Dismissed."

The congregation rose and dispersed, departing the room. The figure, still shrouded in smoke and out of focus, departed just before Ares and Gaia. It seemed Heracles wasn't to know her identity. Ares hung back slightly, touching Gaia lightly on the arm as the others exit out.

"Gaia, a word please." Ares said. He was serious now, a look of fire in his eyes that was strangely hypnotic. Gaia was somewhat entranced as he spoke, her eyes never leaving his.

"There is something you should know. I think I know who the rat is, and it's the very person accusing us all."

"Poseidon? No…no. Ares he's our reconnaissance expert. If he were to be compromised…" Gaia said, a look of confusion spread across her face.

Ares' gaze intensified.

"Trust me Gaia. We need to keep tabs on him, monitor him secretly. As he says, we need to be ready but ready for *his* move above all others. My suggestion is to give this business a week to rest, hold fire on any preparations of strengthening our defences until we can investigate him further. We can't make moves that he could compromise or relay."

Gaia stared back at Ares, eyes never leaving his. She reluctantly nodded without saying a word, completely lost to Ares' persuasion. The conversation was over. They moved to the door and exited out.

Heracles desperately wanted to know more but all at once he was rushing back through the exit of the War Room, back past the Panathenon and upwards and out of his deep, deep slumber.

10

Heracles slowly opened his eyes, his vision hazy before it gradually started to come back into focus. He sensed a presence beside him and turning his head he found Gaia at his side. She looked forlorn. Deep in thought, and focussed on her hands in her lap.

"Gaia?" Heracles said, breaking Gaia out of whatever thought she was tracking. She looked down at Heracles in his bed with a warm smile, something Heracles had not seen before from Gaia. It was a welcomed gesture, but his mind was swimming with confusion, anger, and doubt now. He would allow her an explanation first. He prided himself on being nothing but rational.

"Heracles, thank goodness. You were out for a while. A full day. I was worried about you. I am glad to see you're ok. And I mean that. Sincerely."

Heracles nodded in appreciation. He wasn't ready to talk just yet.

"You must have questions. I have been wracking

my brain to come up with the right way of explaining and…it won't be perfect but let's talk everything though. What would you like to know?"

Heracles' mind filled with questions instantly. He tried to pluck out the important ones as they rotated and formed in his mind. He spotted one, grabbed at it and drew it to his lips. "Is everyone else ok?"

Gaia smiled even more sweetly.

"Dear boy. The right first question. We have tended to those that were injured as best we can. You'll be eager to know that Selene has made a recovery, as have Achilles and Apollo. Unfortunately there have been great casualties from this attack, and I am sorry to say that only Apollo, Achilles, and Selene remain of your new recruits. The others were simply not ready for the strength of both Hermes and your brother. I am so sorry about Prometheus. He was an exceptional man and he will be sorely missed."

Heracles appreciated the sentiment but was devastated by the news of the young, talented new recruits, cut short in their lives. Gaia motioned for Heracles to continue with his questions.

"Did you know my brother Perseus was alive?"

Gaia's face soured slightly.

"That I did not know. We had some doubts following the night of the attack on The Alliance Headquarters twenty years ago. Your father's body we found, Prometheus having alerted us to its location. Prometheus confided in me everything that took place that night, and only me. He was rightly convinced that The Alliance had been compromised. We had a few…trust issues around that time. But your brother's body was never recovered. We sent search parties out afterwards but found no evidence of him being alive, so it was considered a lost cause. It looks like we were very wrong."

"I have been keeping a very close eye on you ever since, mostly in honour of your parents memory, and at the behest of Prometheus. I know everything Heracles, and it was wrong of me to keep that from you. We were wrong to shelter you as we did but Prometheus and I feared you falling into the wrong hands, especially after you drew your father's sword. You could've been killed tonight and it would've been because we didn't allow you to obtain any real combat experience. I just thank the stars that didn't happen. But dear Prometheus…"

Heracles had never seen Gaia express so much emotion. Her usual stoic and closed off demeanour likely a façade, and he was witnessing her true feelings. A leader's curse. She composed herself.

"Your brother is now one of them Heracles. A member of Tartarus. You will need to accept that. He is as good as dead how he is now. I am sorry to say."

Heracles was instantly unhappy with her handling of the situation surrounding Perseus. He decided there and then that he would not abandon his younger brother. He was the only family he had left. Heracles moved the subject on swiftly to his final question before exploring the memory he had just witnessed.

"What of Ares?"

"Ares is…Atlas was unable to locate his body in the ruins of the Amphitheatre. He is either dead, or more likely missing. After everything we learned today from the reappearance of your brother, a missing body could signify their survival," Gaia leaned closer to Heracles now. "I have had my suspicions about Ares for some time now. A long held suspicion, beginning around the time of your parents untimely deaths."

Heracles was taken aback at Gaia's confirmation that she felt the same as Heracles. The wry smile. The wayward glances Heracles had noticed over the years. The number one ranking member of the Stratigos and hero of The Alliance. It seemed doubts about him stretched further than Heracles' paranoia.

"As well as keeping tabs on you, I have been

keeping tabs on Ares also. I put my faith in Hermes' to gather whatever intel he could following the departure of Poseidon. He was leaps and bounds ahead of any of his colleagues in the Episkopos, so upon his promotion I tasked him with the secret mission of keeping an eye on Ares. For over twenty years I have kept tabs on him, but he has never once given me cause to suspect further. It now seems my faith in Hermes was again misplaced. I fear Ares got to him, with his…persuasion."

She paused. She was clearly hard on herself for not only her misplaced faith in Ares it seemed, but also now in her misplaced trust in Hermes.

"I couldn't mention this to anyone and risk another leak, and again I was wrong to do so. Ares was cautious, clever, but I fear he made his move today, with Hermes along for the ride. It was he who 'killed' Ares on stage today. Surely you felt his presence as I did. Felt him drop that sword into your hand with his speed?"

Heracles nodded, remembering the familiar breeze he felt before seeing the black sword buried deep into Ares's chest.

"And with Nyx and Pontus defecting, it seems Ares had rallied more to his cause. I now believe him to be in league with Tartarus. To what degree I know not, but these are my fears. Ares has always had a way about him that simply terrified me. Haunted me. Persuaded me."

Heracles felt it time to bring up his vision.

"Ares persuaded you to delay the preparations in fortifying The Alliance before the attack twenty years ago, didn't he? Persuaded you that it was Poseidon who wasn't to be trusted? And that lead to Tartarus getting the drop on The Alliance that night, didn't it?"

Gaia sat back in her chair, shock spreading across her face. Heracles could see the cogs whirring in her brain. She was very sharp Gaia, and all of this talk had confirmed that. But this had rattled her.

"How can you possibly know that?"

She stopped, something clearly dawning on her. She smiled, then laughed sheepishly. A laugh Heracles had not heard before.

"That son of a bitch."

11

She got up and paced around the room. Composing herself. Heracles waited patiently. She would explain herself in due course, Heracles was sure of that.

After what seemed like eternity, Gaia turned to Heracles to address him.

"Tell me what you saw in the vision Heracles. It may help us in the current situation. I will then tell you my thoughts on this, and who implanted that in your mind."

Back to being as guarded as ever. Ok, he thought. He would play Gaia's game. For now.

Heracles recounted the vision he had been subjected to. Also adding that it was not his memories of course, and that he felt guided and puppeteered by someone the entire time. Seeing what they wanted him to see. Hearing what they wanted him to hear. Gaia sat silently, no doubt running through the scenario in her mind again and again. She studied Heracles once more, deciding what she would say to him and how to say it. She settled her mind and proceeded to continue the discussion.

"There is a reason he showed you this Heracles. And by he, I mean Poseidon, our missing founder, and someone I haven't seen or heard of in near twenty years."

Heracles had expected her to mention Poseidon, but he wasn't sure how he knew. Perhaps Poseidon had implanted this knowledge in his mind also.

"Poseidon always had a knack for being right. It was infuriating. He was nonchalant about everything, no matter the severity of the situation. Unmoved.

Undeterred. But under it all he really did care deeply about The Alliance, and I realised that too late. I used to chalk it up to Ares' influence over me, but really it was due to my arrogance. My pride. And it cost us a powerful ally. He was utterly loyal. Until I drove him away."

Gaia was solemn now. Looking down at the ground, away from Heracles' hard gaze.

"That meeting is as you described. Ares stopped me and asked me to delay the fortification preparations, to convince Hera to agree with my decision. It cost The Alliance deeply, and I have never forgiven myself for that. That is why over the last twenty years I have given everything to The Alliance, and ultimately been so cold and distant. It should have never been me that took sole charge of The Alliance following Hera's death. I even made Ares the face of The Alliance to ensure all eyes were on him, so that he couldn't move for fear of somebody recognising him. I couldn't afford to let him control me again. And, with that decision, my pride failed me once more as it seems I gave him exactly what he always wanted."

Gaia broke. Heracles had never seen her like this, but it was somewhat comforting to see her human side. That she was opening up to Heracles meant a great deal after all that he had lost over the years. She had made huge and terrible mistakes. But hadn't we all? Heracles could see that now. And Ares had manipulated her the entire time. He was to blame for all of this. Not Gaia.

"My apologies Heracles. You don't want to see me wallow," Gaia calmed herself. "Poseidon fortunately prepared defences without my knowledge, and that saved even greater losses. Following the meeting I was convinced Poseidon was the spy. Convinced by Ares, the puppeteer. Then, after that night I confronted Poseidon and he had finally had enough. I...I drew my weapon on him. He was mourning the loss of his close friends, and we attacked him, knowing full well he was exceptionally more powerful than me. But he merely disarmed us, and disappeared away from The Alliance forever. I had heard nothing more about him in twenty years. Until now of course."

She took a deep, sorrow filled breath.

"I was a fool Heracles, and it has cost you dearly so many times. And I fear it is going to cost you more when we are done. Following today, you can no longer stay at The Alliance."

Heracles pushed up in his bed.

"What the hell do you mean?" Heracles spat at Gaia. She did not react.

"Heracles listen to me. The reason you can't stay is that it will take time to convince people that it wasn't you who killed Ares…"

"Then tell them Gaia! Convince them. You owe me that much."

Gaia nodded.

"I know Heracles, I do. But Ares was heralded as one of the greatest heroes we have seen at The Alliance, and people will not easily forget what they think they saw. Hermes's treachery will itself take time to justify and explain, plus Nyx and Pontus defecting. Then to have Ares' on top of that. They won't easily be convinced, and you would be in grave danger whilst we tried."

Heracles went to speak some more but Gaia waved him off.

"But. This opens an opportunity for us. I am now convinced that Ares had two goals twenty years ago. One was to weaken The Alliance with your parent's death, and the other was to afford him time to locate this fabled Labyrinth. He failed in the latter pursuit but crippled us immeasurably. He then used the following years to bide his time, gathering people to his cause. I was too close to him for him to succeed, but I fear that the attack today was to finally free him from his shackles. We cannot allow Tartarus to get their hands on these three objects. And I hate to ask this of you, after everything you have been through, but I want you to lead this imperative mission."

12

Heracles sat in silence. This was a lot to take in, and so soon after all he had experienced recently. But in his heart, he knew that he had been crying out for this moment for a lifetime. An opportunity to prove himself. An opportunity to get out into the wider world and show everyone the real Heracles.

He still maybe couldn't quite trust Gaia after all he had learned today, but he felt genuine sincerity emanating from her, and what did he have to lose on top of what he had already lost.

"You know Minos as well as anyone Heracles. That could prove instrumental in locating the real Labyrinth. You may assemble a team to assist you, but no more than three additional people. And only those that don't hold a high status at The Alliance. They would be missed and noticeable in their absence. That small a team should allow you to move quickly and somewhat undetected. The rest of us will continue the rebuilding efforts and prepare for the worst, come what may. My final condition is that Demeter is off limits, as a newly promoted Stratigos. I know you are both fond of each other but that's final. What do you say?"

Heracles pondered the information laid out before him, but his mind was already made up. If he wanted to break free of the chains grounding him to The Alliance's Headquarters, he needed this. He craved it. And he felt that staying at The Alliance now would bring him greater restriction.

"Fine, Gaia. But I'm not doing this for you. I do this for The Alliance, and for those we've lost in Tartarus's pursuit of power."

She nodded, understanding Heracles reluctance to trust her fully. She continued with her briefing.

"One final thing. After you have found the item in the Labyrinth, as I now wholeheartedly believe that is possible, keep whatever it is safe with *you*. Tell no one. Don't bring it back here. No matter what you hear from anyone else who might find out about your pursuit. You must keep it secret. It is the safest way. I trust you implicitly Heracles, for whatever my words are worth to you right now. After you have the item, you must locate Poseidon. He may or may not know more about the other two items, but it's the only suggestion I have. Clearly, he calls to you. He will guide you. I now have faith in that."

Gaia rose from her seat and turned to leave. Heracles still had questions, but she was done with him.

"That is all Heracles. I can't help you any further from here. You need to assemble your team and get out of The Alliance without being seen. It's taken as much as I can influence to allow you to stay in the medical centre for as long as you have. I'm sorry for what I ask of you. I truly am. But you're on your own for now. God speed, my dear boy."

She took one look back before leaving. "Oh and keep a close eye on *those* three for me if you are planning to take *them* with you." She winked at Heracles, and she was gone, out into the light of the corridor.

It was settled.

13

Heracles sat upright in his bed and nervously played with his hands. He needed a plan, and fast. It seemed that his safety was limited, but he was so lost for what to do next. What could he possibly bring to a multiple decade long search for something that may not even exist? How was he supposed to locate Poseidon:

someone who has been missing for nearing twenty years from The Alliance, with no news about him whatsoever.

Heracles swung his legs around and hopped out of the bed. His injuries were bandaged up, and his body ached in ways he hadn't felt before. Injuries would heal, but the scars from battling his own brother would be with him for some time. He hadn't even had time to process his brother being alive, let alone Perseus being an integral part of Tartarus. It would take a while for the revelation to sink in, but the task at hand would ultimately help focus his mind.

He peeled back one of the bandages slowly, and found his body had healed quickly, as it always did. Another immeasurable benefit of his father's sword was that the current that ran through him increased his body's capacity to heal. He ripped the remaining bandages off and walked over to the chair in the corner of the room, finding his civilian clothes neatly piled on the seat. It was rare to get a chance to wear anything but official uniform at The Alliance of late with the amount of work he was involved in. Or *had* been, he guessed. Heracles feared that yesterday was the last time he would wear the uniform, and it was now civilian clothing going forward. It would at least help him to blend in as he ventured forth into the wider world. A striking and recognisable Alliance uniform could both help and hinder him, but he thought it likely to hinder him more than help given his current ostracising from The Alliance.

14

He dressed, quickly and quietly so as not to draw any unwanted attention from outside the door of his room. His sword was in its sheath under the pile of clothes, Gaia had left him that much at least. He reached for it and it sparked, a current of cool electricity radiating from it: a memory of a hard fought battle still lingering in the sword. He scooped it up and threw the black strap of the sheath over his shoulder.

He felt casual. That was good. It would help his mind to blend in with the civilians in the city. He was wearing his black tailored jeans, folded twice by the ankle, with his black leather boots snuggly on his feet, the tongue of the boots messily pulled forward and sat in front of his jean legs. His black belt, with its golden buckle, sat under his white linen vest, cut off at the sleeves in a purposely ripped fashion. He wore it open at the neck in the heat of the climate.

He slicked his blonde hair back with his hand. The quiff of his fringe sat in place excellently, due to the dirt and grime residue still present in it. It would help him fit in even more. A little bit of 'working grease' through his look.

Now to the task at hand. How was he going to find and engage with the three people he had in mind for his task force? He rubbed his hand against his chin, before having a sneaking suspicion that, given the events of yesterday, it may be easier than he had first thought.

It all rested on his current location and tracing another of those injured heavily during the battle yesterday, one who would be receiving the best treatment she could get.

It was time to locate Selene.

CHAPTER V
THE SUN, THE MOON, AND THE BLADE

1

Heracles slowly slid the door to his medical room open. Gaia had left it unlocked after their little chat thankfully, and intentionally no doubt. He was glad she hadn't expected him to climb out of the window in a bid to keep himself hidden.

He looked down the corridor of the infirmary. It was busy, with medics walking towards him up and down the corridor. Almost running actually. It wasn't surprising given the increase in workload they must be experiencing post the attack.

As medics neared, he slid his head back inside his room until they had passed as a precaution, but it was busy enough for him to not be noticed. The question was, where would Selene be? He suspected she would be close, as he seemed to be on the emergency ward. Given the severity of Selene's injuries, it was likely she was being tended to by the finest medic The Alliance had: Chrion, the 'Master of Medicine'. If Heracles thought right, Chiron would have Selene patched up after a day, given his powers of healing and his supreme knowledge of medicine, despite Selene's grave injuries.

Chrion was the Chief Medical Officer of The Alliance. He was a long standing member and was of centaur descent, having been rescued by Heracles' mother Hera on one of her missions many years ago. Chiron was exponentially skilled in medicine and although seemingly rudimentary in approach, the ingredients, and practices he had embedded had been worth their weight in gold. If it were indeed Chiron who had tended to Selene, her recovery would be swift and miraculous. Chrion was a master at his craft. And Heracles was betting that the growing friendship of two further young cadets would have them placed directly at Selene's side until fully healed. Namely Apollo and Achilles.

They would hopefully complete his ragtag team, and given their status as recruits at The Alliance, this would be an excellent chance for them to get some real life experience. A gamble, but one Heracles felt confident taking, given their heroic actions during yesterday's attack.

2

Heracles slowly progressed down the corridor. As he passed a door, he would wait for the medics in his close vicinity to clear, to gain an opportunity to peak through the glass porthole of the door into each room. He hoped that the medical team had skipped the ceremony yesterday due to their workload. This would help him remain anonymous somewhat if that were the case.

He tried the first door but didn't recognise the figure in the bed. He moved on. The second door he came across actually contained somebody he knew very well. It was Cleon of the training team. This was the first time he had seen him without Anstice by his side, and Heracles thought the worst. He was highly tempted to enter and check on him but didn't, his need to avoid further eyes on him than necessary regrettably greater than seeing Cleon.

He searched on, checking several rooms as he went. The next three doors yielded nothing, and he feared that several of the medics leaving their patient's rooms were getting suspicious of his presence. He needed to find Selene, and quickly.

He saw one of the medics stop in her tracks and look directly at him, her face tilted to one side slightly as she tried to remember the face she was looking at. Heracles grabbed for the door to his left without looking, backing up into it and landing his hand on the handle. He pushed down and entered the room, closing the door behind him.

Two imposing figures stared back at him, slowly getting up and out of their seats.

3

"What the fuck are you doing here?" Achilles said, lacking any trust in Heracles, and how could he blame him? Although his quickness to anger was an ugly trait of his.

"Achilles keep your voice down. We're in an infirmary idiot. People are trying to rest."

Selene was sat on the edge of her ward bed. She was now in the middle of lacing up her low cut boots, sat neatly below her Alliance uniform. A fresh uniform it seemed, given the injuries she had sustained and the blood she had spilled during the attack. Chiron had, as Heracles had hoped, worked wonders on her. No other medic in the HQ was capable of such a feat and as always, Heracles was mightily impressed at his craft. However, she now had a noticeable scar running from the right side of her chin, down through her neck and into the top of her shoulder blade. A nasty scar, and no doubt the wound that had ejected the most blood when he had seen her yesterday.

"Thank you, Heracles. I hear that if it weren't for you, and of course dumb and dumber here," Selene pointed from Apollo to Achilles in sequence and they looked deeply offended, "I would be dead. I had the privilege of the Polemarch stopping by for a quick chat this morning, and she kindly filled me in."

"Gaia came to see you? Why?" Apollo said, coming to life.

"To check on me you idiot. I'm kind of a big deal," She paused. "Of course, she did mention something else that I might be interested in…"

She winked at Heracles. Achilles spotted this and grunted. Apollo turned to address Heracles.

"You have my thanks also sir. If you hadn't shown up when you did, I doubt Achilles and I would have been able to hold the attackers off. And Selene…"

"We could've taken 'em." Achilles was stood with his arms crossed staring at Heracles, his face cold and unimpressed.

"That's kind of you both to say but I should be thanking you. You did wonderfully, considering yesterday was your first day and you were new to your weapons. It was highly impressive." Heracles said.

Selene hopped out of her bed and onto the floor, her boots now laced.

"So what's the plan?"

Selene was eager. Heracles liked that. Gaia had clearly hinted at the mission and Heracles could already count her in. He felt that Apollo could be swayed too, but Achilles would undoubtedly be a tougher sell.

"As Selene knows, I have been given a highly important, and confidential, mission by Gaia just now. I cannot discuss the details out in the open, or until you all have agreed to join me. That may seem counterproductive but I need your buy in first. All of this is your choice either way. No one will force you to trust me or force you to join the mission. You are free to walk away right here and now."

Heracles paused.

"But what I will say is this. This is an amazing opportunity. A hugely dangerous one naturally, but if you want to experience the real world out there around us then this is the chance to do that. I can no longer stay at The Alliance. Although I didn't kill Ares, I have little to no proof. There's no coming back for me, so I am leaving on this mission either way. If you are not at the bottom of the stairs of Mount Olympus in one hour, I will assume that this is my task to face alone. It is a great ask and it is your choice to make. And yours alone."

He lingered at the last point before smiling at them all and turning on his heels. He fielded no further questions, even though he heard Apollo move to ask one as he moved out into the corridor. He closed the door to Selene's room behind him.

4

Heracles thought an hour would be enough for them. They would need time to decide, and if they wished to join him, they would also need time to get back to their dorms to gather their things. Or time to rat him out of course. Either way, at least he'd know their answer.

He moved the thought from his mind. There was something about the three of them and he already trusted them. Their actions during the attack yesterday told him everything he needed to know. They were brave, strong, and loyal. He also felt that they would keep their mouths firmly shut.

Heracles thought about going back to his dorm also, but it was too dangerous. He couldn't afford to draw attention to himself out in the open after what had happened yesterday. He could purchase supplies and clothing in Athenaeus, as necessary. Gaia had at least left him his clothing and a heavy bag of drachma to get them started.

Now he moved to the task at hand. Namely getting himself out of The Alliance HQ without being spotted.

5

Heracles quickly vacated the medical facility.

He needed a swift exit: a tough ask when in civilian clothing, as it was not often those at The Alliance wore their casual clothes during the day, but he hoped that several civilians would have been treated within the HQ following yesterday and that would alleviate concerns.

Sure enough, the medical centre contained several people wearing casual clothes and he was able to cover his face slightly whenever anyone glanced at him, feigning a sneeze, making it to the entrance of the medical centre rather easily.

He exited out of the main doors of the medical building and tucked himself neatly behind a towering pillar to the right of the entrance. He tried to rotate around it and out of the view of the majority of the people out in courtyard of the HQ. He placed his hand on the handle of his sword, and instantly felt electricity course through him. It was empowering, as always. He loved the confidence and strength it gave him.

He poked his head out from around the pillar and searched for the nearest water source. It was of course the large fountain display at the centre of The Alliance's courtyard, dedicated to those lost over the years of its existence, with generic statues of heroic figures framed for eternity in a creamy marble. It was a long distance from him, but he felt confident in his accuracy, being one of the things he had spent years honing in the Panathenon.

He held his hand out in front of him, with his thumb pointing skywards and his index finger pointed directly at the fountain. He steadied himself and ensured nobody was in the path of the shot or looking in his general direction. He took a deep breath and exhaled, discharging some of the electricity inside of him. It was lightning quick, beaming through the air in small sharp arcs, with one central current running straight and another current snaking around it. It was thin enough to go unnoticed and was so quick that it reached its target in an instant.

Light sparked from the water of the fountain, and those that were sat on its edge, reading, and chatting, were shocked into life. The small lamps dotted in the fountains water blew into shards of small glass. One by one the lamps blew, creating loud audible bangs of smashing glass.

The final light sat in the water of the fountain went. The noise and activity had caused a great deal of commotion, mostly from the screams of those in the near vicinity at the unexpected noise. Many others were rushing over to see what was happening. Some had run in the other direction. Fear of another attack, Heracles thought. That had been, cruelly, what he had looked to use to his advantage. Not something he enjoyed doing but a necessary evil to ensure he could slip out of the Courtyard unseen.

He took his chance and bolted out from behind the pillar. He used the remainder of the current within his body to amplify his speed and he was out into the fresh air in a heartbeat. He took a few steps further into the sunshine at speed, before crashing hard into something unbelievably solid.

A shadow loomed over him, covering him in darkness and blocking the sun above him.

6

Heracles looked up. He couldn't make out the figure yet, due to the light of the sun streaming around the figures head and causing a shadow to form around their body, but Heracles knew who it was instantly and felt a huge relief.

"Atlas," Heracles said as his sight focussed. "You're a sight for sore eyes, my friend."

"Heracles!" Atlas cried, before catching himself, hushing his voice slightly. "You should be gone already. What the hell are you still doing here?"

"I am about to leave now, I promise. I assume Gaia has filled you in on everything?"

Atlas looked around him to check they were alone. They were. For now.

"Yeah, she filled me in. Seems I am one of the only ones in the know. Probably best given the attack and betrayals yesterday. The buzz around you is awful mate, sorry to say. The best place for you for now is as far away from The Alliance as you can get."

Heracles seethed at this thought.

"But I am glad to see you before you leave. Might be a while before we get to have a drink together old friend."

Atlas looked genuinely sad at this last point. Heracles felt the same way. They had known each other for a long time now and Heracles would miss Atlas deeply.

"Alright, alright, don't get too mushy on me."

They clashed hands. Hard and satisfyingly. Heracles recoiled slightly from the impact, as he always did. He needed his friend right now, but it was out of his control.

"Now get out of here," Atlas said, pushing Heracles onwards towards the stairs. "I'll see you again when you've proven yourself to everyone. I will await the return of 'The Lion'."

Atlas smiled sweetly, lingering for a second and then entered the HQ, hand in the air as he walked away.

Heracles, conscious of time now, stepped forward. He arrived at the top of the HQ steps, checked whether anyone was on to him, before taking his first step down. He hurriedly flew down the stairs, skipping steps as he went.

7

An hour passed.

Heracles had been sat off to the side of the bottom of The Alliance stairs, just outside of Athenaeus, hidden slightly but with enough view to pop out if the three he waited on arrived. There was no sign off the trio though. Heracles' heart sank as the hour passed. Although he still didn't have a concrete plan of attack for finding the location of the labyrinth, if it truly existed, he had at least felt somewhat buoyed by the possibility of having those three by his side. But it seemed it wasn't to be.

Heracles got up slowly, his legs still aching somewhat from the fight yesterday, having not rested as much as he would've liked. He checked the coast was clear before stepping out into the open. He took one last look at The Alliance high above him, his home for over a decade now, and turned away from it: turning his back on those he called friends and colleagues; those that he admired; those that he had trained; those that he had lost.

It was a difficult moment for him, but one that he couldn't avoid. The people inside wanted him dead now, barring a few that knew the truth.

He turned to the entrance to Athenaeus.

8

Although the prospect of exploring the city was a delight, as he had very rarely got to go back into the city since he'd joined The Alliance, this time felt different. As soon as he had been admitted into The Alliance, he had forfeited his previous life and was committed to the HQ full time: living there, eating there, sleeping there, and working there. It was a rigid life, but a much better life than the one he previously had in Minos.

Still, he did miss elements of the life he had left behind and felt his old haunts would be a great place to start the investigation. The 'Labyrinth' where he grew up was a hotbed of activity. A lot of shady activity mind, but the alleyways had a wonderful vigour. It wasn't the best life for those that lived there, but they were at least free. Free to do and say what they liked without the rest of the city looking down on them.

It was well known in the city that Minos was a den for thieves and outlaws, but the rest of the city was far more corrupt under its outwardly façade, given the shady deals organised by its mayor. Minos simply wore it's true colours, and proudly.

9

As he was nearing the entrance to the city, he again turned to look back at the steps, mostly to offer himself one last flicker of hope that the three recruits would be bounding down after him.

It was eerily quiet around him though. Heracles suspected that it was a case of all hands on deck at The Alliance right now following the attack and they would not want to alert the city and cause any alarm, likely getting in touch with the Mayor directly and discreetly, keeping those that had witnessed the event at HQ for the time being. Heracles wondered how long that would last given the volume of city dwellers present at the HQ yesterday, and the number of loved ones waiting on their family to return from the trip, only to find they wouldn't right away. Or some, sadly, not at all.

He turned back to the entrance of the city, despondent at the other's lack of arrival, when his hope was revived. As Heracles took some steps forward, the archway into the city getting closer now, he spotted a leg poking out from the right hand side of it. As he drew closer her saw Selene come into view, quietly sitting on a wall to the right of the entrance. Her left leg was folded over the other, her hands resting on her top knee, knotted in patience. She was as calm as ever and was in such a daze of her own that she didn't immediately acknowledge Heracles. Her long white hair was wonderfully plaited and reached far down her back, sat over her pale blue blouse, down to just above her waist. Her civilian clothes were figure hugging, and she looked slightly uncomfortable as she sat crossed legged, the trousers tightly bunched.

As he continued to walk towards her, she finally noticed him and calmly turned her head towards him.

"Took your time." she said, and Heracles laughed. He was both happy to see her, and slightly miffed at her cheeky greeting. Heracles thought it best to ignore it, but before he could, his mouth blurted back in return.

"I assume you have trouble understanding exactly where the bottom of the stairs is Selene?"

Her face remained calm, and that feeling of tranquillity rose in Heracles again, the same as it had done at her Rite ritual. She was learning quickly to control her power and assert its influence over people. Heracles calmed instantly.

"Technically I *am* at the bottom of the stairs. Just, I assume, not as close as you would like. The two lumbering idiots draw too much attention, so hiding slightly is no bad thing. Surprised you didn't see us all sneaking down the side of the hill."

She smirked slightly, knowing Heracles wasn't angry at all. She was now also calling him Heracles. Gaia must've tipped her off to his real name.

"But we're here now."

"We?" Heracles enquired. He could only see Selene, as he glanced around.

"They'll be back any minute. Achilles is still unconvinced with you. He came all the way down here, after I charmed him somewhat, before having a change of heart and heading into the city to get away from us. He'll flip flop right back in a moment. He won't want to miss this opportunity."

Selene sighed. Only a day had passed but Heracles could sense that there would be a firm friendship between Achilles, Selene, and Apollo. He just hoped to be a part of it all.

Sure enough, Heracles saw Apollo come into view on a street before them, with Achilles trudging reluctantly behind him, avoiding Heracles' gaze. Heracles felt he needed to address this. Now. Or this was going to be a long trip.

"Thanks for coming, all of you. I feared the worst after the hour passed, but here we are, and I am hugely thankful."

Heracles tried to show some humility to his juniors. Achilles, brash as ever, stepped forward.

"Right we're here. What's this mission Heracles?" He paused. "Or is it Alcaeus still? I've got some issue with the secrets you keep, and I may turn right round if your answers are not to my taste."

Apollo shot him a fiery look, but Achilles brushed it off. Achilles was such a big lad that the grey jacket he wore, sat over a lighter white vest, bulged under his arms, and sat very tightly, open somewhat at the front assumedly due to his size. His brown boots came all the way up to his knees and his tight fitting, again due to his size, trousers tucked messily into the top of them, spilling out and over the boots. His long hair was messy once more, having not tried to tidy it or wash it in his rush to leave. A sign he was keen to partake in the mission, Heracles thought to himself.

"Me being here doesn't mean that I trust you either. And it certainly doesn't mean that I like you."

Heracles felt that no matter his manner, he was still interested in all of this. And that was good, no matter what his mouth said.

"That's fair." Heracles replied. "I owe you that much. Let's go into the city a bit and get away from the HQ. I would feel a lot more comfortable out of earshot of anyone that is desperate to kill me if that's ok with you."

Achilles looked at Selene, who nodded at him. Achilles turned back to Heracles and nodded.

"Fine. Let's go." He said.

10

They walked in silence. Twenty minutes passed walking across the cobbled streets of Athenaeus, with Achilles getting visibly agitated at the lack of discussion. Heracles turned past a run of thatched roofed houses, down a side street and into a deserted park. One in desperate need of some repairs, and definitely not a place parents would want their children playing in. The first part of their walk through the city was as high wealth as the city got. Anyone with a touch of high society would gather as close to the HQ as they could. The closer you were, the more respected you were within the city. A sad but true fact. Which made it all the stranger that this park was desolate, being right on the edge of the wealthy part, but it thankfully acted as the perfect place for them to talk in peace.

The city was essentially laid out into lines. The first line of the city, and closest to The Alliance's Headquarters, was well respected and affluent - the upper class of the city. It was only a small region, mostly due to the upper echelons of society commanding the lion's share of the wealth and keeping their numbers as low as possible.

The second line of the city was home to the middle class. Those either on the periphery of wealth, or the periphery of poverty. This area grew and shrank depending on how the city was economically. Currently Heracles thought it was in a relatively good place, from what he had heard, having enjoyed a few years of peace now (doubtful to continue after the attack yesterday).

The largest line of the city was known affectionately as 'The Dump', named for both its condition and its complete lack of funding. It was awfully run down. The Alliance had tried to assist the city's mayor Sisyphus with funding over many years, to little success. They had since moved away from supporting that project, mainly due to Sisyphus and his ability to 'lose' the funding at will. He was a hugely stubborn man. A voracious man. Any money coming into the city was hoarded to make the wealthy wealthier, and the poor poorer. Sisyphus had made himself powerful in the city and he was content with doing the same thing day in day out – namely filtering any wealth into his own pockets and the pockets of anyone who could assist his climb to the top.

The Dump stretched from the middle line all the way to the entrance to the city. Not a great invitation to visitors, and something that was deterring tourism and crippling the city little by little, with Sisyphus seemingly unaware or at the very least unmoved by it all. Any visitors would usually need to go through all of the city to get to The Alliance, so that deterred visitors and new patrons that lived outside of the city. The only good thing that it offered The Alliance was a natural security measure.

Minos was the heart of 'The Dump'. It stood as its capital. And ultimately, their destination.

11

Heracles invited the assembled team to sit: Selene neatly perched on top of a seesaw that had permanently been levelled in place by two iron chains reaching deep into the ground; Apollo sat, his back resting against a small climbing wall, crumbling still as he leaned against it; Achilles sat on a tiny rocking boar, one that had also been permanently moored, but none the less hilarious to Heracles. However, he dared not laugh at this crucial moment in convincing the three to join his quest.

It was time to tell them everything. Everything he knew up until this point. And everything he didn't yet know but had a gut feeling for. This may or may not convince them. But it was all he had. He began.

Heracles detailed his family: That he was the son of Zeus and Hera Olympus – one of founders of The Alliance and one of the original Polemarchs, and for whom the hill The Alliance HQ stood upon was named; that his birth name was Heracles Olympus, and that Alcaeus Demos was a dead name now. He detailed the night of his parent's death, and that it haunted his dreams still; the death of his mother at the hands of someone from Tartarus; his rescue at the hands of Prometheus, his mentor for the next twenty years; the death of his father and the apparent death of his brother.

He referenced his childhood growing up in Minos: his change of name being due to Prometheus, his guardian as his godfather following his parent's death; his long standing fear of anyone knowing the truth about him; his growing up in poverty, knowing that one day he would escape; entering The Alliance at the age of twenty and training every day, without being able to show off his true talents.

He described the scenes of yesterday and how he was framed by Hermes, with Ares' body still missing and Gaia's suspicions therein. For how long Ares had been orchestrating the attack he knew not, but Ares was a character they could not trust and there was fear he was assisting Tartarus. He recalled the vision he had seen and the potential for Poseidon's involvement, as an ex-Alliance founder. He had their undivided attention throughout.

No questions asked. They were patient and Heracles appreciated that greatly.

He rounded out with the task at hand.

"In light of yesterday, Gaia is tasking me, and as an extension you all, with finding this fabled object in a fabled Labyrinth below Athenaeus. We don't yet know that it exists for definite but Gaia seemed convinced. We need to find the labyrinth and confirm it truly exists, before conquering it and finding the item that lies within. I hope that in doing so, we will then be able to then seek out Poseidon and hopefully the further two objects."

Heracles paused, all information now relayed and him in need of a drink to quench his thirst. He concluded.

"After all that you've heard, I'd love you all to join me on this mission. I will not beg. It is a lot that I ask for and it is wholly your decision to make."

He sat quietly with his elbow rested on his knees, holding his chin up with his fingers arched over his mouth, allowing them all the time they needed to process the large amount of information laid out before them in order to make their difficult decision.

12

They sat in silence for what felt like eternity.

Heracles had always been patient. A trait he had inherited from his mother, whom he had always been closest with. He remembered Perseus and could now see his confusion at Heracles inheriting his father's sword over him. Perseus and his father were always far closer.

The silence was torture. If they said no now, after thinking they were a shoo-in when they arrived at the bottom of the steps, then it could derail the whole mission. Not only did they know everything about him now, but they also knew exactly what he intended to go after.

He waited.

He shook his head slightly, trying to hide its movement. He had to have faith in these three cadets. Faith that their curiosity, their desire, and their passion, would push them forward.

He waited.

Finally the silence was broken. It was Apollo, shocking Heracles. If he were to give them each a defining trait as he knew them now, Apollo would be the thoughtful one, Selene the calm one, and Achilles the brash one. Heracles knew that he was always quick to judge, and it was unfair to do so, but he had always had a knack for feeling people out upon meeting them. Still, he would allow them to show him what they were made of.

Apollo stood up, sliding his back up the crumbling climbing wall. He was confident now, a glowing heat radiating from him all of a sudden. He placed his fist strongly against his left breast. The sign of The Alliance.

"I'm with you Heracles. I can't stand in my sister's shadow anymore. I am my own man. I am Apollo, the Sun, and I will light the path when we descend into the Labyrinth. I feel something special here, as I know you do."

He looked at Heracles with a fiery passion. Apollo had read him perfectly. He knew Heracles felt something about this team, and clearly Apollo felt it too.

Apollo turned to Selene and Achilles in turn. Awaiting their decision. Finally, Achilles rose from his boar, still hilarious, and stood tall. He looked Heracles in the eye, his gaze sharp.

"I'm in," He said at last, breaking slightly. "Anyone who's been through all of that and still stands tall is alright in my book. I can relate to losing people close to you."

Achilles was softer in that brief moment somehow.

It didn't last long.

"But this doesn't mean I'm gonna call you boss or

nothing. And I aint got any cheesy lines to throw at you like Apollo."

He looked at Apollo, sighed, and slammed his fist against his left breast also. The three of them turned to Selene, serene as ever. She stood, elegant and strong.

"I was in all along. I was the one who dragged your asses down here. Don't pretend like you both have your shit together."

She smiled a sweet smile. Apollo and Achilles frowned slightly. She pushed her clenched fist into her left breast in harmony.

A happiness washed over Heracles. This was it. The team was formed. Come what may, they were in this together. He followed suit and clasped his arm to his chest. Something that Prometheus used to call him growing up popped into his mind. He allowed an image to form in his head of the four of them standing strong and unified together.

Apollo, The Sun.
Selene, The Moon.
Achilles, The Blade.
And Heracles. The Lion.

CHAPTER VI
BEWARE GREEKS BEARING GIFTS

1

The newly formed group departed the playground, and headed for Minos, the destination Heracles had described as their best chance at gaining any information relating to the Labyrinth.

Heracles really couldn't believe he had managed to pull this all together so quickly but thank the gods he had, as time was of the essence now. With the attack on the HQ fresh in their minds, and with the knowledge that Tartarus could be making moves imminently, using the distraction of The Alliance to their benefit was the best course of action. They had to be quick and careful. If they ran into Tartarus before they could secure the object Gaia spoke of, it could be very bad for them.

Heracles would also need to do some on the job training with Selene, Apollo, and Achilles: reconnaissance gathering; sourcing the necessary equipment they would need if they ever did find this mythical Labyrinth; and also trying to find a way of assisting them in learning about their new found powers. A difficult task.

Heracles led the team through the city.

They passed rows of thatched roof houses, some connected, some not, all popular in this part of the city. The houses were much fancier than those of the middle and lower grounds of the city. The well-crafted roofs sat on top of black and white painted buildings. The streets were spotless, not an item of litter on the cobble stone floor. They would soon find themselves trudging through the dirt as they reached the middle grounds of the city though as the wealth decreased. Gas light lampposts ran down the sides of each street to provide firelight in the evenings when the sun descended. There were libraries, museums, banks. Everything the city could need.

Well, anything the *rich* could need.

Heracles could tell that all of them were somewhat familiar with the city, which was highly useful. Heracles was curious as to their level of knowledge so decided to delve further as they traversed the wealthier side of the city.

"Apollo, am I right in thinking that you and your sister grew up in the city? You seem pretty familiar with the area."

Heracles had remembered Atlas making an offhand comment along those lines about Artemis at some point. Apollo nodded as he explored the thought.

"That's right, although Artemis has been at The Alliance now for a number of years. I'd been down here in the city for a while without her, after my many failed attempts at getting into The Alliance. Much to the humiliation of my father and step mother…"

Apollo looked a little jaded as he spoke. Heracles motioned for him to continue.

"My family live not far from here actually. Moved in about a year ago from the middle ground of the city. Artemis made sure the first thing she could leverage as a Stratigos was keeping her family safe and prosperous. She…has been very supportive."

Achilles grunted. "Assume you're not too fond of your sister then 'Pollo?"

Apollo winced slightly, clearly called out.

"It's not the best relationship to be honest," Apollo paused, trying to not speak ill of his sister. "Artemis can be…difficult. Still, my Father and her mother adore her, whereas with me…"

Apollo broke his sentence and swiftly changed the subject.

"But I am finally in The Alliance. That's all I ever wanted - to prove myself. And I can really see this mission helping with that. Sorry to have a selfish ulterior motive Heracles."

Heracles smiled. "Not at all. Glad to hear you've got something to push you forward. You'll need that Apollo."

Heracles glanced over at Selene, who was deep in thought and miles away, admiring the row of buildings they were walking past on the long straight stretch of street. Heracles thought it rude but couldn't blame her. The buildings were fantastically crafted. They were clearly made with money and skill. Large oak doors lay open and inviting to those looking to shop, or pop round to their neighbours for tea.

Heracles thought it time to get a few more words out of the calm and collected heroine of their group.

2

"What about you Selene? Did you grow up in the city?" Heracles asked.

Selene's train of thought was broken. She slightly mistimed her step on the cobbles as she looked up at Heracles, before carrying the correction off quite well.

"I don't really talk about myself, if that's what you're digging for?"

She was as closed off as ever. Heracles, Apollo, and Achilles had their work cut out, but Heracles felt it was a trust thing. She would come to open up in time with a bit of gentle encouragement. Achilles seemed to agree.

"Come on Selene. Apollo opened up, didn't he?"

Selene grew ever more stoic.

"I don't care what Apollo did, I don't…"

"Ah come on. It'll fill the dead air at least." Achilles wasn't even looking at Selene now as he spoke to her, which seemingly annoyed her even more.

"*Fine*," She said, through gritted teeth, before sighing heavily. "I grew up around the port to the west of the city. My dad's a fisherman down there. A working man. Dad has worked hard to provide since mum…well he worked hard to give me the opportunity to get into the academy and here I am. Or rather, *was*. Let's just leave it at that."

She sped up, walking past Heracles into the lead, and the conversation was seemingly over. Apollo went to push further, but Heracles shook his head at him. It looked as if they all had some sort of family baggage.

They walked in silence again, Selene content on not discussing herself further and the other three not wanting to annoy her too much at this early stage of their time together.

After the tension ebbed slightly, Heracles felt it time to switch the attention to their brash and self-confident team member.

3

"How about you Achilles?" Heracles enquired.

Achilles prepared himself, apparently about to delve deep. This could take some time.

"Sure, sure. Well, we've always had money in our family. I'm a lucky bastard in that respect, but dad did work his arse off to give us everything we have…he ultimately gave his life for it."

Achilles paused at mentioning his father. A sore subject, on the face of it. A trait that all of them seemed to share. A family member lost to the underworld.

"We haven't struggled since he kicked it. The Alliance has looked out for us ever since. They came knocking as soon as I was of age, trying to get me to join their ranks. I wasn't sure I wanted to follow dad into this life to be brutally honest with you, even though I know I've got something about me. He was far too kind, too forgiving. It got him killed. But I trained as a kid anyway, wanting to be strong regardless of what I ended up doing. And here I am."

Heracles needed to be careful with what he said next. He still felt Achilles was the one that was closest to turning back and throwing this all away at any second. He was very proud.

"Kindness can be a great asset Achilles. It's what binds us all together, even in the darkest times."

Achilles laughed. Heartily.

"You sound just like him. I'm having none of it. I am where I am because of my strength and skill. All of which I have built by *myself*. It's all I need, thanks. It's done me pretty damn well up until now."

"Just think about it, ok Achilles? That's all I'm asking. We'll need strong teamwork to get anywhere near to fulfilling this task." Heracles said in return.

Achilles scoffed again, but his face read like he would indeed think about it. For how long Heracles was unsure, but it was good that he was, on the face of it, open to discussion and instruction, albeit with an attitude.

However, Achilles suddenly switched his approach to the conversation and the look on his face turned quickly to anger.

"Let's just get this straight Heracles," Achilles was in his face now. "You are no longer a member of The Alliance, and I am on this mission for myself, and not for you. Don't forget that when you're barking orders around the place. You know damn well that you need me here."

Apollo and Selene stared on. Likely marvelling at Achilles' staggering pride, as Heracles was.

Heracles must have shown his rage slightly, as Achilles seemed to be taken aback at the look on his face. He quickly tried to change the subject as a result and took a step back from Heracles.

"Anyway, what about you Mr Olympus? Tell us more about Minos. Seems like none of us have a great deal of experience with it."

This was a key moment for Heracles. Did he sit on the aggression Achilles had shown and let him have his moment of power? Or did he quash this. Now.

He chose the latter. Heracles took a step forward to Achilles, whilst touching the tip of the handle of his sword for just enough of a jolt. Electricity radiated through him once more, electrifying him. Filling his with confidence and radiating a thin layer of light around his body.

"Listen Achilles, if you don't want to be here, that's absolutely fine. Piss off out of here. I won't follow you. I won't beg. But if you're here, with us, you're a part of this team and you'd damn well better start acting like it or else we're going to have a serious problem."

Heracles held his ground. Firmly. He didn't expect so much conflict straight out the bat with someone so fresh into The Alliance, but if he didn't show his rank, (for what it was worth nowadays being ostracised from The Alliance), here and now it would come back to haunt him later. He was sure of it. He needed to level out this childish pride now, or let it harm them all at a later point of their mission. His anger had always had a habit of springing to just below the surface, despite his level of patience, but he rarely let it show. Now was the time to let some out.

Achilles stared back, squaring up to Heracles. The tip of his hand also hovering over his sword. They held each other's gaze for a moment, one that felt like an incredibly long time, neither backing down. Electricity sporadically sparked around Heracles' eyes. Achilles was using his height advantage over him to great effect.

Heracles noticed Apollo go to move towards them in his periphery vision, but Selene's hand darted for him and held him in place.

Seconds passed. The ground was rumbling now. Heracles was very aware that there were a few passers-by looking over. The cobbles vibrated at Heracles' feet. Achilles was letting out some of his power, as Heracles was, and it was steadily growing. This was not good. They should be drawing attention away from themselves, not to them. He needed to say something.

But the power around them quelled suddenly, the ground settled, and Achilles stepped back. His pride finally giving.

"…You're right."

Achilles loosened. His body fell into a more natural position. He continued to look at Heracles but he could feel no pain or anger now. He looked somewhat sheepish actually.

"I'm. sorry, ok? I can go a bit too far. It's not a good look on me, I know. I'm just…can we forget about it please? I do want to be here. Be a part of *this*. Whatever it is. I went too far."

Heracles studied his face and saw genuine apathy there. He was thankful for it.

"Glad to have you on board, Achilles. Forget it. It's in the past."

Heracles needed to remain tough in this moment. He didn't want to assert dominance over Achilles but there needed to be a structure to the group and it was better this way. He needed to lead these three. Guide them. Mould them. It was at the least a good breakthrough.

Selene placed her hand to her face.

"Well that was time well spent." She said as her eyes rolled deep into their sockets.

4

They marched on.

There had been a small amount of people in the area who had stopped to watch Heracles and Achilles square off, and as they walked on, they still had looks towards them. It was a worry. Was it too obvious that they were from The Alliance? That could be a hindrance for them moving into Minos. They needed a change of approach.

"Minos," Heracles began. "An interesting place. It's where I grew up, so I know it well. Well, I did many years ago. We'll see how it's changed since I left. Prometheus and I made a few trips together to the old haunt over the years but they were few and far between. He was a much more frequent visitor."

Heracles spoke as he walked, heading towards a small market he was familiar with on the border between the middle ground and the lower grounds of the city. He missed his friend deeply every time he mentioned him.

"There are a few sources we could tap up if they are still around. Which I believe they will be. Minos, on the surface, looks like a den of thieves, and gamblers…which is exactly the look they want to portray. But there's heart there. A loyalty to each other and their own. If I can find someone I know, we'll have a much easier time. If not, well..."

Heracles trailed off, as not to panic the others. They were approaching the market now. It was small in comparison to some of those in the lower ground of the city, but that was good. It was more crowded here, and they could simply blend into the sea of people and crowded close placement of the market stalls. There was also a lot of noise and action in this particular market. It was popular amongst middle classes, even with its crowded nature. Heracles couldn't recall its proper name, but the locals called it 'The Market of Muses", named for the vast number of fortune tellers and so called *seers* that littered the market place, looking for coin to buy their next meal. They had come over from the poorer region, and the middle class had taken a liking to them, enjoying the stories they sold them of the fame and fortune they were destined for.

Heracles halted the three of them before they entered.

"We'll need to split up. A group like this will draw unnecessary attention and we need to be relatively low key when we start asking questions of people. We want to achieve a few things here. One, buy some low key outfits. Hooded poncho's for example, in case we need to obscure our faces. Secondly, grab some items for your pack. Think food, drink, torches. We'll need everything we can get if we locate this Labyrinth and I have no doubt that it's going to be cold, dark and wet."

"Won't that draw more suspicion to us, wearing that type of garb?" Selene interjected.

"It's a good point but we'll blend right in to the crowd in the lower grounds, and especially so in Minos with hoods covering our faces. We'll need to rip the ponchos a bit and dirty them but it's a staple outfit around those parts, just as they are cheaper and easier to acquire."

She nodded in acceptance.

"Apollo, you'll come with me. Selene, you, and Achilles head for the other end of the market and search there. There will be plenty of clothing stalls. Sort both of you out, and we'll make sure we're sorted."

Heracles paused as a thought popped into his head.

"And don't engage with any of the seers. They only want to fill your head with lies and take your money."

Heracles turned out his pockets and handed Selene a stack of coin.

"That should sort you both out. We'll meet back at the fountain over there. It's slightly obscured at the moment but you'll see it. The one in the middle of the market. Look out for it. Be there in thirty minutes. No longer".

They all nodded in response. Achilles and Selene turned on their heels and headed for the other end of the market. In a flash they were gone, merging seamlessly with a passing crowd of people. Heracles turned to Apollo and signalled to follow.

"Let's go".

5

"Keep an eye out for anything we're after Apollo. Hopefully, we can be in and out."

"Gotcha." Apollo quickly replied. "I think I see somewhere selling ponchos over there. I'll go check it out. I'll get you one if they are any good."

Heracles threw his thumb up in agreement and off Apollo trotted. Heracles turned deeper into the market to find some necessary supplies. With Apollo on the team, fire would be easy to come by but they would need some dry wood to light, along with something sturdy to carry their supplies in.

Heracles, not wanting to stray too far from Apollo, surveyed the scene. The market was awash with people. And many stalls. Some more built up and fancy than others, but most at the very least presentable.

He was at once drawn to a shabby little stand to his right. One that looked as if it had been thrown together overnight, with a poorly constructed wooden fascia front, two wooden boards on either side to steady it and two long vertical wooden posts holding up the stand's sign. At the back of the stall hung a tatty length of brown cloth, ripped in places, and slightly open in the middle.

Heracles approached the stand for a better look, out of curiosity more than anything.

Leaning against the frame of the stall, which extended over her head and read 'Ixion's Elixirs', was an outwardly timid woman, at odds with the loud sellers in the market. She looked to be very old. Both in her appearance and by the way she carried herself. Frail. Slow. She looked up at Heracles as he approached, and all of a sudden came to life. Her whole dynamic changed. Her eyes gleaming in the sunshine.

"My boy!" She croaked. "Come over here. I am sure I can fix all that ails yah." Her accent was thick.

She motioned for Heracles to come over, and an interest in what she was selling arose in him. Perhaps she had some elixirs that would aid their cause. She grabbed for his hands and held them in hers. She surveyed them and Heracles felt slightly awkward, not wanting to offend her by drawing his hands away, but also desperately wanting to. She flipped them over, and back, and over again studying intently.

Unexpectedly, her eyes swiftly moved to meet Heracles's. They stared at each other, him with a look of puzzlement, her with a look of exploration.

"You've been through a lot already, young one." She said, finally breaking the silence. Heracles didn't react. He was desperate to head his own words and not connect with anyone looking to sell him stories or lies.

She stared on. Heracles removed his hands from hers, thanked her for her time and turned to leave and find Apollo.

"Ah ok. I see. Don't want my help do you?"

Heracles shook his head, thanked her for her time, and moved to walk away.

"But you see, I know that you, young one, seek to find the Labyrinth."

6

Heracles stopped in his tracks, slowly turning back to face the old woman. She lit up once more.

"What did you say?" Heracles said.

"I am Ixion. You probably gathered by the sign…"

"Never mind the sign. What did you just say?"

Heracles didn't want to confirm nor deny his search for the labyrinth but was keen to push the point.

"I thought us aged beasts the ones hard of hearing love. I *said*, 'you seek to find the Labyrinth'."

Heracles stood. Motionless. How the hell could she possibly know that? Her country drawl hid her sharpness. Had he been too loud when discussing with the team earlier?

"Heracles. I've found us some ponchos." Apollo was beside him now, looking from Heracles to the lady before him.

"Do you want *me* to grab the rest of the supplies as well?" He said, sarcastically.

"Better stick with me Apollo. We may have a problem." Heracles spoke to Apollo but his eyes never once left Ixion.

"What do you mean by the Labyrinth?" Play dumb. That would be the way forward.

"Don't play dumb with me young 'un. You seek the Labyrinth. Let's not waste my time, nor yours." Ixion shot back at him. She smiled, as a dark shadow stretched across her brow. Heracles felt a chill run down his spine. A power emanated suddenly from this superficially frail woman, with Heracles keen on questioning her ulterior motives.

She turned back to her potions, rummaging through them, moving all sorts of strangely shaped bottles aside and out of her way. She picked up a few colourful ones, filled with unknown liquids. Some thick. Some creamy. Some watery in appearance. Some were contained within recognisably potion shaped bottles. Some were shaped like gourds. Some shaped like animals.

She settled on an item and smiled. She turned with it, showing a small wooden box to Heracles and Apollo. They both looked on with interest. She dusted the top off with her left hand, and then brought it to her face, blowing the rest of the dust away.

"This, my dears, is a box."

Apollo audibly stifled a laugh. Heracles was less patient for jokes at that moment in time.

"I am a patient man Ixion, but you are wearing me thin. What is your point?"

"Now, now, let's be civil Heracles."

Heracles went to retort when it registered with him what she had said.

"Wha…Do we know each other?"

Ixion shook her head from side to side vigorously.

"No, no. But I see far and wide. I am no simple potions peddler. Judge me not by my appearance, boy."

Her tone had changed now. No more dearie or love. Straight to *boy*. She almost spat it out of her mouth.

"Let's cut to the chase shall we. You seek the Labyrinth and I can assist you. I know who you are Heracles, son of Zeus. And if you wish to keep that information a secret to all present here today, you will come with me."

She turned on her heels, flapped the worn curtains of her stall to the side, and headed out from behind her stall, heading into the market.

Apollo and Heracles looked at each other in a shocked daze, before darting after the mysterious woman.

7

Ixion was moving. Fast. All preconceptions of her frail nature were gone from Heracles' mind now. He and Apollo were hot on her trail though, matching her speed as she ducked and weaved through the crowded market place, breezing past stall after stall, clearly knowing the lay of the land well.

They emerged from the market and Ixion darted down an alleyway to her right, leading Heracles, and Apollo, as she went.

She halted. Apollo and Heracles skidded in the dust of the now unpaved ground to avoid crashing into her.

They are outside a small house, sandwiched by two regular sized houses. The house, more of a hut Heracles felt, seemed completely out of place and he had a sneaking suspicion that the three of them may be the only ones on this street that could see the place. He didn't understand the suspicion but those that passed seemed unperturbed by its existence, its' worn front a disaster to look at. Maybe they had seen it too many times, but Heracles felt that they just seemed unaware of it.

She turned to face them and smiled sweetly. Back to her previous façade.

"Come on in dearies." she purred as she opened the small wooden door of the hut. Both Apollo and Heracles had to duck to get through the entrance, with Ixion having no problem entering with her slight frame.

Heracles expected a small, tatty hut filled with nonsense and trickery. He was certainly not wrong about the trickery as once they were inside, the wooden door, now twice the size it previously was, slammed shut behind them. They now stood in a grand room. One adorned with a circular wall that surrounded them, filled with thousands of books and hundreds of bottles of potions and elixirs.

As Heracles wondered at the room, he felt Ixion grab his hand and guide him forward. He quickly looked back to find Apollo with him, thankfully, with the same astonished look Heracles imagined sat on his own face. She guided him to a table in the middle of the room. A relatively small table compared to the size of the space, but one which would look large in other living rooms. One that seemingly fitted no more than six people sat at it judging by the number of chairs laid out, but with plenty of space between each chair. She motioned for them to sit and they complied.

The table was magnificent.

Its marble legs held a large circular table top, decorated with wondrous things. It immediately reminded Heracles of the Shield of Aegis. He darted his eyes across it, seeing many fabled mythical beasts illustrated onto its face. He recognised a few, but some were foreign to him.

Medusa sat to the left of the centre, with a similar pose to the one she held on the Shield of Aegis. On the other side and slightly up was the mythical horse Pegasus, said to be called to those of great courage and humility in times of need. His father had once spoke of Pegasus coming to his aid and flying him out of a desperate and impossible situation. Heracles had of course dismissed it as a fairy-tale story from father to son, but stranger things had happened at sea. He spotted several Cyclops, waging war against their enemies. The Centaurs were present, Heracles having met only one Centaur in his life, The Alliance's own masterful medic Chiron. There were beasts he didn't recognise: one was similar to a dragon but with seemingly endless heads jutting out of its body. Heracles felt a chill run down his spine as he stared at it. Another was a giant scaly creature that rose out of watery depths. They were fantastic to marvel at.

"Like what you see Heracles?" Ixion broke the silence, walking slowly back to the table. Heracles hadn't even sensed her go, mesmerised by the table as he was.

"Marvellous isn't it? Everything you see on the table exists in this world. The table acts as our way of keeping tabs on the beasts that roam this land, and as entertainment when poor humans stumble upon them and are devoured."

A slightly sinister tone resonated at her last word and she chuckled. She spoke as she walked, balancing a tray of drinks awkwardly as she stepped, some of the contents spilling slightly over the edge of the poorly crafted wooden mugs and onto the tray.

She laid five drinks in total onto the table top. Heracles knew not why there were five drinks presented but felt he was about to find out.

As the thought crossed his mind, and exactly when Ixion drew herself down onto her seat, two more figures appeared at the table in a haze of smoke.

8

They were carbon copies of Ixion.

It was incredibly jarring to see them all together. Triplets. Nearing identical except for two elements. They sat in line, with Ixion at the far right of the trio now, with Apollo and Heracles across the table and facing them all. They all varied greatly in age, but their facial features identified them as sisters instantly. It made no sense but they were undoubtedly sisters, Heracles certain of what he was seeing.

Heracles also now noticed the biggest difference in the sisters. Their outfits were similar in style but each had their own unique colours and accessories. Ixion was wearing the tatty robes from their meeting in the market, draped messily over herself, but the clothing she wore was defined by the detail. Her robes were pitch black, mirroring all of the sisters, but the edges of where the robes folded over each other and bunched were finished with a bright blue. She also wore what appeared to be a small pair of scissors around her neck now, attached by a thin bit of string. The scissors were made of a sea blue handle, with sharp white blades. Her hair was greying, thinning, decaying slightly. She looked ancient, but by the way she carried herself, she could've been much younger.

The sister to Ixion's left, from Heracles view, was dressed in black robes also but her robes were lined with a light gold. A neat golden ribbon was tied around her neck, finished with a bow. She seemed to be middle aged and was beautiful. Her dress was also slightly more presentable.

The third sister, to Ixion's far right, or to the far left from Heracles' view, was dressed in the same black garb but her outfit was finished with a bright white and was more accurately fitted and was perfectly presented. Not decayed by time as the other's clothing seemed to be. A white pearl locket hung around her neck. She was simply stunning to look at, and Heracles gathered she was around Apollo's age, twenty years old or so.

Ixion stirred, ready to begin the conversation.

"Heracles. I have misled you. As you have lied about your true self for many years, I too have lied to you about mine. Ixion is very much my stage name for the market. My true name is Atropos."

Heracles must have been less shocked than she thought at this revelation as she scoffed slightly at him.

"We, the three sisters, are the sisters of past, present, and future. Some refer to us as The Fates."

Apollo muttered something under his breath. Heracles nudged him to speak up.

"The Fates," He blurted out. "My step-mother talked about them when I was growing up. She had used it to deter us from doing anything bad. She would say that the fates 'would conspire against us' if we were selfish or naughty. It…it was just an old wives' tale."

Ixion, or rather Atropos, cackled in a croaky, old

voice.

"Your step-mother is wise boy. You do well to heed her words so far, Apollo."

She winked, slowly and dustily. Apollo retreated in his seat, clearly completely uneasy. Heracles didn't blame him one bit. This was the last scenario Heracles had hoped to get into and he felt foolish to have followed Atropos as he did. But he was desperate to know more about the Labyrinth.

"These are my sisters. Lachesis," Atropos said, pointing to her right. "The Allotter. She represents the present day. To her right, Clotho, The Spinner. She represents the past. And finally myself, Atropos, The Inflexible. I represent the future. We see all. Know all. But you should know, our esteemed guests, that information doesn't come for free. You seek information about the Labyrinth that we can provide. But it will come at a cost."

Heracles joined Apollo in being uneasy. Here was the real reason they were here. Did he believe Atropos in what she was saying? He felt he did, unfortunately, and where Gaia and the Stratigos had failed for so many years in even confirming the Labyrinth existed, they could succeed here and now and gain information The Alliance could not.

He decided to play with fate.

9

The sister's waited patiently. All three sisters stared intently at Heracles, occasionally changing their gaze to Apollo's direction, continuing his unease as his eyes quickly darted away from their stares.

"We need some guarantees," Heracles began. "How can we possibly believe all of this without proof? Give us that and maybe Apollo and I will be happier to talk."

"Brash isn't he." Clotho scoffed in a young person's manner. Her voice was liquid silk. Everything about her screamed youth and vigour.

"Brash indeed." Atropos concurred.

"I beg to differ sisters," Lachesis said. "The boy is smart. Cautious. A fine trait."

She smiled sweetly at Heracles. Her smile belying a sense of cunning that Heracles was instantly wary of. Heracles had always had a sixth sense for people's feelings and motives. Something he could never put his finger on, but he had always been capable of gauging people's real intentions. He had, over the years, attributed this to his father's sword and its power. But lately, he was coming to question where the sense came from. Perhaps it was more akin to his mother.

Atropos moved her hand to the box that had been neatly sat on the table in front of her. The box she had shown Apollo and Heracles in the market. Heracles didn't remember it ever being there, but it would be impossible for her to have drawn it out and placed it on the table whilst they were speaking without him noticing. Surely.

"You seek proof boy?" Her tone and demeanour had reverted to the cold and harsh Atropos now. "Here. Take it."

Atropos slid the box across the table with a slight push. It continued to slide effortlessly, even where gravity dictated it should slow to a halt way before reaching Heracles at the slight push it received. Heracles placed his hands in front of him to buffer the speed, but he needn't have worried as the box perfectly landed in his outstretched hands. Heracles studied it, turning it over in his hands slowly.

He turned to Apollo, now aware that he had not uttered a word since the story of his step-mother. He felt the urge to involve him now.

"What do you think Apollo?"

Apollo, thankful of Heracles engagement, studied

the box as Heracles turned it in his hands. He stuttered as he tried to speak, before gathering himself, and continuing.

"If what the three sisters tell us is true, and take no offense to what I say next please," He turned to the sisters and apologised before even saying anything worth apologising for. "Then the three of them are undoubtedly powerful creatures. The item in your hands could be a literal 'Pandora's Box'. Another tale my mother told us, but one I am now also starting to believe in full."

"Another smart lad." Lachesis chimed in.

"And quite the handsome one." Clotho added.

Heracles pondered Apollo's words. It was true that the box before them could contain any number of things, but if it proved that the Labyrinth existed or pointed them in the direction of it, surely it was worth the risk. Even though they had only just started their search, Heracles was hugely aware of the pressure Tartarus posed to them and their limited time. Heracles recalled the story of Pandora, and that it was she who released the beasts from the belly of the underworld upon the land they lived on many, many years ago. Would they be doing the same when opening this box?

Heracles nodded at Apollo and thanked him. He turned to the three sisters.

"No tricks. No parlour games. If this fails to convince us of the existence of the Labyrinth, we walk out of here and we both gain nothing."

Atropos frowned further, her face darkening now.

"You try my patience, boy. We have lived for millennia. Sat and conversed with much stronger than you. Much smarter than you. Shared bread with philosophers, scholars, heroes, villains, gods." Her voice raised continuously as she talked. "And you question us? Question *The Fates?*"

Atropos rose from her seat, slamming her hands hard onto the table in front of her. She seemed taller in that moment, and far more menacing. More imposing than ever. The darkness on her face clouded like a storm. The room felt heavy in that moment. And unbelievably loud with thunder. The room darkened around them, and suddenly, the other two sisters mirrored her fury.

"Boy. Open the box now or we *kill* you where you sit for ever wasting our time."

10

Heracles laughed. Heartily. He was petrified but couldn't help but laugh. Apollo wheeled round in his seat, unbelieving of Heracles' reaction.

Atropos stormed on. Her rage growing at Heracles' pretentious act. But Heracles couldn't help it. He had measured her, in his strange sensing way, and found her wanting. Despite her face. Despite her presence. She was not going to kill him. She had too much intrigue placed in him.

"Atropos. With all due respect. We are all now here on the pretence of assisting each other. So let's cut the bullshit. I will open the box, find the clue to the Labyrinth and you can then set about telling us about the help that you desire. And Apollo and I can get the hell out of here and leave you in peace."

Silence in the room.
Nothing but silence.

11

Atropos rescinded. Somewhat reluctantly at first. She fell slowly back into her chair, her manner calming. The room brightened and the two sisters beside her rescinded also. She looked at Heracles now with a neutral face, neither pleased nor unhappy.

"You're a brave one, son of Zeus. I will give you that. Of course, I knew this was how the conversation would go. But you needed to be tested. The Labyrinth holds no place for the weak."

She motioned for Heracles to open the box, and he complied. First untying the small red ribbon looped around the clasp attaching the lid to the base before opening the lid itself. He was calm. Controlled.

He lifted the lid of the box slowly, aware that any number of things could jump out at him, given the outward appearance of this tiny hut and the inner sanctum hidden within.

Apollo leaned over next to him to see what Heracles was seeing. At first, the box held a misty grey smoke hovering at its surface, blocking any view of what was inside. It held for a moment before dissipating, snaking over the sides of the box and into nothingness.

They now saw what was in the box, but Heracles didn't recognise it. He looked to Apollo who shook his head in confusion. The item seemed to be ivory in nature. A chunk of it. With no real sense of shape. Heracles felt it might be chipped from something whole but was unclear on its relevance to their search. They both turned to face the sisters. Apollo addressed them, his confidence growing now.

"Is this a part of something? The missing piece of a whole?"

"Correct," Lachesis said, nodding slightly. "This is the confirmation you seek. This, our dear guests, was taken from the beast that dwells in the Labyrinth many years ago, at the last attempt made at exploring it. The would be adventurer spent his life trying to find the Labyrinth below the city."

Clotho interjected.

"He came to see *us* of course. He had heard tale of us from gossip and murmurs. The only way to find the

Labyrinth is to know exactly where to look, you see. We sensed his desperation and of course offered a helping hand," She cackled. "He found the Labyrinth, as he wished, but by the time he did he was older, less confident, less sure of his strength. His strength had dwindled, his eyes had blurred. He was not the man he once was. Cronos, father of time, had caught up to him."

Atropos continued the tale. It felt like a well-choreographed scene from a play, although Heracles felt an otherworld connection between the sisters, perhaps they even shared the same thoughts.

"He ventured further, using a clever technique of trailing yarn behind himself to find his way out of the Labyrinth when necessary. He did not get far into the Labyrinth before he fell upon the beast that ivory chunk belongs to. His luck ran thin. The beast attacked, mortally wounding the adventurer. He managed to escape the grasp of the beast by clashing his sword against one of its mighty horns, chipping a piece of it clean off. He scooped up the piece and using the rage of the beast to his advantage, along with the last of his strength, he made it back to the exit."

Lachesis picked up the story from there, not skipping a beat from where Atropos had stopped.

"His son waited outside for him, having followed his father in secret but being unable to go in after him due to crippling fear. He watched his father die in front of him. The adventurer paid his price for our information. With his life."

All three sisters cackled. Heracles sensed that they were getting closer to discussing what they wanted of him and Apollo.

"The son couldn't stand to hear of the Labyrinth ever again, and fortunately *happened* upon Ixion's Elixirs, where he sold this chunk of horn to us for a small fee," she smiled wickedly at this. A cruel, cruel smile.

"Now, on to what you seek. Each of us will divulge one piece of the information you require to succeed in your quest, in return for a gift of our choosing. Are you ready to begin?"

Heracles steadied himself. He saw Apollo lean forward in readiness beside him, and he followed suit, placing his elbows firmly on the table.

"Let's discuss terms." he said.

12

Clotho waved her hand over the table before them. The pictures on the surface contorted and shifted shape. Heracles quickly raised his elbows off of the table to get a clear view. The images settled into what looked like the city of Athenaeus from a bird's eye view.

"You have good insight Heracles. Your thoughts are correct," Heracles jumped at her minds touch. "This is the city of Athenaeus. I will pin point the exact entry to the Labyrinth for you in due course. But first, my terms."

She paused, and to great effect.

"The price of this information is thus: The Labyrinth is an ancient tomb, aeons old, and one which feeds on sacrifice and despair. The Labyrinth is alive. A living entity. You will heed the tale of the last adventurer and mark your way through the catacombs with a ball of thread. Follow the thread back to the exit once your quest is successful. *If* it is successful of course. Before you are able to leave the Labyrinth, it will ask for a sacrifice. Only then will the Labyrinth contort and allow you to leave it's grasp."

"A sacrifice? What kind of sacrifice?" Apollo interjected, real worry in his voice.

"A sacrifice to the Labyrinth, boy. A willing sacrifice. A loss of something crippling to one of your group, something leaving them no longer whole. The Labyrinth craves despair. It will feast on the pain and open its' doors for you. Fail in this endeavour and you will be lost to the Labyrinth forever."

The wry grin that adorned Atropos' face had now moved to Clotho's. She marched her gaze between Heracles and Apollo.

"I can't wait to see what you choose."

She laughed gleefully, awaiting their answer. Heracles turned to Apollo. His voice lowered.

"That's the one thing we can't afford Apollo. I wouldn't wish that on anyone of us."

"Agreed," Apollo considered for a second, before continuing. "But if it's going to aid The Alliance in any way and prevent this powerful item falling into the wrong hands, then it is a sacrifice I am willing to make Heracles."

"No Apollo. If a sacrifice is necessary then I will be the one to make it."

Apollo shook his head heavily. "Heracles, you're the one this mission belongs to. You're the one who is guiding us. We can't allow you to fall."

Apollo went to object further and Heracles stopped him.

"It can only be me Apollo. I won't put you through that. Promise me you won't do anything stupid."

Apollo again moved to argue and stopped as he looked deep into Heracles' eyes. Heracles hoped he could see the immovable mind that lay behind the eyes.

Apollo reluctantly nodded. "I promise."

Without allowing a further word from Apollo on the subject, Heracles turned to Clotho.

"I agree with the terms. A sacrifice will be made to the Labyrinth."

Clotho's smile deepened.

"A wise choice. So it shall be. You will find the entrance to the Labyrinth here," Clotho pointed to a section of the map, south of Minos and just outside of the walls of the city. "You will need to find a man by the name of Theseus. He is the grandson of Aegeus, the last great adventurer to gain access to the Labyrinth. He yearns to avenge his grandfather. He is the key to gaining access to the Labyrinth. Without him, you will fail."

Clotho sat back in her chair, relieved of all of the information Heracles and Apollo could expect. She became blank in her stare.

"That's it?" Heracles enquired.

Clotho remained silent with a neutral look across her face. Seemingly her side of the conversation was over. With that, Lachesis leaned forward.

13

"You seek to traverse the Labyrinth. In doing so, we have seen that you will face the beast that dwells within in a bloody and hard fought battle. In order to assist you in your quest, I will gladly tell you about the beast to better prepare you. At a cost of course." Lachesis said, picking up from her sister.

Heracles braced himself for the worst. The first request was far crueller than he had expected. Surely this couldn't be.

"All I ask is that you bring me the horns of the beast. The horns, which we have that tiny piece of, are, let's say, of great importance to us. For our *medicine*."

The familiar cackle. She glanced at Atropos as she did so, throwing a glancing wink towards her sister. Heracles felt a pang in his body, a feeling that gifting the horns to these three could empower them further. They were dastardly sisters. Twisted. Sick. Their elixirs could cause harm. This wasn't as easy a decision as it appeared on the surface. He relayed his concerns to Apollo, who nodded in return, before asking a question of Lachesis.

"What of this medicine? People are going to get hurt, aren't they?"

"Dear boy. We Fates live. Endlessly. Ever watching. Ever judging the people of this world. Creating life. Ending life. It all begins and ends with us. Who are you to question our methods? Who are *you* to question who lives and who dies? Everything comes at a price and yes, people will die, as they always do."

Lachesis removed the golden ribbon from her neck.

"This is the measurement of life, dictating how long a person has to live. Their thread of life. We control all. It shrinks and grows at my whim. A demonstration is required, perhaps?"

Lachesis motioned to Clotho, who sighed and removed her necklace from around her neck, placing it on the table in front of her. She hovered her hand over it and it opened, revealing a ball of thick thread. She removed it all, holding one end in one hand and one end in the other. She held it out to Lachesis.

"This is a citizen of Athenaeus's thread of life. This dictates how long they will live."

She took her bow and placed it against the thread, measuring the length of it.

"The person my sister has chosen is due to live a relatively long life, and they have lived a large portion of it. Eighty six years, three months and two days to be exact, having used sixty five years, four months and three days of it so far. As Atropos explained to you earlier, Clotho represents the past, namely one's birth, as the spinner. She weaves the thread of one's life. I represent the lifespan of a person and decide how long one lives. I am the present. Atropos represents death and the end of one's life, cutting the thread when their allotted time is over."

She motioned to Atropos, who removed the blue scissors from her neck.

"Atropos represents the future, and should we, with our infinite wisdom, decide to cut a life short…"

Atropos was swift. She sliced through the thread like butter. Lachesis let it drop and before it could touch the table it was gone. As it disappeared, Heracles heard an almighty cry from outside. He moved to leave his seat to check on the scream when Atropos bellowed at him.

"SIT DOWN!"

Heracles complied. Lachesis revelled in his shame.

"A demonstration of our power to you both. The cry was probably from the kin of the life you just forced us to take. I hope that serves to confirm your position in this little game?"

Heracles nodded meekly, his heart filled with regret at having toyed with the three sisters so much. It had cost someone their life. An innocent person, their life cut short because of him. He had been completely bested. Rage filled Heracles blood now. The usual rage that crept upon him suddenly during confrontations. He struggled to control it, as he always did. Fortunately for him, this time he was able to subdue it before the white mist descended. He unclenched his fist underneath the table.

"So, can we consider the horns ours Heracles?"

Heracles nodded. Emotion ran through his body still. Anger at them for their actions. Anger at himself for questioning them. "Fine, we'll get them."

Lachesis clasped her hands together and smiled sweetly. Falsely.

"Oh I am so glad. Now on to the information you so desperately seek."

She waved her hands over the table and once again it contorted and shifted in shape. It produced the form of something neither fully man, nor fully beast, but both.

"The Minotaur. It guards the sacred treasure of the Labyrinth and prowls the hallways for prey. Food. Sustenance. Its next kill."

The Minotaur, stalking around what must be the halls of the Labyrinth, lay before them as a moving image upon the table top. It was towering. Its body was that of a giant, muscular man, dauntingly powerful in its appearance and holding a large, and sharp, axe in its right hand. Its' legs and head were that of a bull. A large ring hung from its snout, and as it snorted and snarled, small grey puffs of smoke exhaled out of its nostrils and blew against the crusting phlegm around its top lip. Two large ivory horns protruded from the top of its head. The target of Lachesis' request.

"The Minotaur was once human. His name, Asterion. The ruler of this fair city many centuries ago. A strong and fearsome man. A once great hero. He was pleasantly unaware of the Labyrinth, as all who live here are. However, he sealed his fate when he angered the Father of Time, the All Father Cronos and the god we serve, by stealing one of his precious treasures. He was turned to a beast and would've decimated his own city had Cronos not been merciful. His power was too great to be left to roam these lands but perfect for forever guarding the treasure he once coveted. Cronos hid the item in the Labyrinth and The Minotaur was bequeathed the task of forever guarding it."

"And how do we go about killing this mess?" Heracles enquired.

Lachesis simply laughed back at Heracles.

"Its hide is pure leather; no ordinary sword will penetrate it. Its' fists like boulders, its' nails like knives, its' axe mighty. Its' horns sharper and harder than steel. Its' fur is resistant to fire." She said, glancing at Apollo. "It has no real weakness. But…"

She paused again, for what seemed like an eternity as they sat patiently at the table, sipping their ever warm and refilling tea.

"I have seen your little team best this foe Heracles. That will serve as your determination."

She sat back in her chair and held a now neutral face as her sister Clotho had done minutes before. Her part of the conversation over. Heracles once again tried to gather some further information but Clotho held firm.

14

Finally, the conversation turned to Atropos again.

"And now, boy, you seek to learn the nature of the treasure you hunt. Correct?"

Heracles nodded. "We do, but if it comes at a high price, we can surely do without that information."

Atropos was unmoved.

"There are many treasures in the Labyrinth. It is a nest of discarded items. We have been hiding things there for many, many years. Our very own hideaway. Traps. Treasures. Distractions. Without knowing what you search for, you could easily take something that is worthless to you. And the Labyrinth may then have cause to punish you further."

The dark smile returned.

"Fine," Heracles conceded. "Name your price so we can be done with you." Heracles was wary of angering them again but he felt a growing need to remove himself and Apollo from the situation.

"My price for information is simple Heracles. I see the future of this world. I know and see all surrounding humanity. My sisters and I know the past, present, and future. It is ours to watch over. To guide. Ours to meddle with as we see fit. We were created in Chaos to manage this task. We see the journey you embark on with your little friends beside you. I see you in the Labyrinth…face to face with the beast within…we see you victorious."

She paused. A habit Heracles was growing tired of.

"But we see no further. We do not see your tale past the Labyrinth. For the first time in a long while the future is clouded around you. Only you. The future is a haze. I know not what it holds for you Heracles."

She paused, again, studying Heracles intently.

"We can help you no further than what we tell

you today, but we hold great interest in you, boy. Not for a long time have we held interest in a human. My price is this: when you find the three items that you seek, you will face us again. But you will only face us when you have all three items. Fail in your task, and we fear darkness will fall over you all."

Heracles didn't know how to respond. Was this another trick cooked up by these dark and twisted sisters? Or was it genuine, which in itself held grave ramifications.

"If we don't succeed in gathering the three items, I'd imagine we'll all be dead anyway, so we agree to your terms."

"So be it." Atropos reached into her robes and drew out a tuft of radiant golden wool. Heracles instantly recognised it as that held by Gaia in his vision.

"That's correct Heracles. Gaia and we are acquainted. I am assuming she failed to regale you with tales of how she came by her lock of wool?"

Heracles remained silent. Gaia and he had hardly spoke in his lifetime, only really having a proper discussion before his untimely departure from The Alliance today.

"I see she did not. No matter. She sought us out nearly twenty years ago, and we chatted much as we are now in this very room. She sought what you now seek and we provided her with that lock of wool as proof of the existence of the three sacred items but…things got in the way of her finding the Labyrinth, as you know. She brought it back to us for safe keeping until she could restart the search. But she never returned."

She cackled again. It ran deep within Heracles, scraping his very bones.

"Gaia wrongly assumed that the wool was taken from the Labyrinth. She asked the wrong questions, where you ask the right questions. She initially asked where to find the Labyrinth but shied away from our price. She then changed to asking for proof the items of lore's existence. We provided the lock as proof of the items she sought."

She turned the wool over in her hands, somewhat mesmerised by it.

"This lock was taken from the 'Golden Fleece'. The wool of an immortal winged ram that grants immeasurable strength to all who wear it. Yet, the fleece lies not in the Labyrinth, and we will aid you not in your search for this particular item. What you seek in the Labyrinth is the 'Hide of the Nemean Lion'."

15

Finally, Atropos had reached the final piece of information they were going to draw from them. She stopped there, receding into her chair, and holding the same neutral face as her sisters. Heracles tried to push it a little farther.

"And what will this hide look like when we locate it?"

A simple question with a surely simple answer but one Heracles was keen to check given the crooked nature of the sisters.

Atropos remained silent. The conversation was over, and it was time for Apollo and Heracles to leave this place. Heracles motioned to Apollo and they both rose, tucking their chairs neatly under the table before them. Heracles thought it best to close the conversation with a positive.

"We thank you for your hospitality and your help." Heracles bowed deeply and Apollo was quick to copy. They turned on their heels and headed for the exit. The room darkened as they turned and, as they headed for the exit, Atropos called out at them through the darkness. Heracles turned to meet her gaze but the room in front of him was empty. The voice carried only in the air.

"Beware Heracles. The sword of Damocles hangs heavy over your head." The voice rang, and then it was gone, replaced with three distinct cackles, fading into the darkness. Heracles and Apollo removed themselves from the building as quickly as they could.

16

Apollo and Heracles sprang forth into the hustle and bustle of the market. No alleyway stood around them now, only stalls and people. Heracles turned back to find the tatty stall named Ixion's Elixirs, devoid of anyone manning it. No sign of Atropos, or either of her two sisters. No sign of the hut or the alleyway they had followed Atropos down. Only the marketplace.

No sign of the woman who screamed either whilst they were in there. Was that all a ruse?

"Apollo. Tell me you remember all of that right?"

"Like I could forget that!" Apollo exclaimed, a look of confusion on his face as he looked hurriedly around the market. "Those three will haunt me always." he said, shuddering as if an icy wind had just struck him.

Heracles suddenly recalled Achilles and Selene. It had been well over an hour since they followed Atropos into her hut. They had been conversing for a long while. The others would likely be waiting. And likely, highly concerned.

"Apollo, we need to get over to the fountain fast," Heracles said, glancing round quickly. "Let's grab a couple of supplies and high tail it over to the fountain. Achilles and Selene will have been waiting for a while now."

"Gotcha." Apollo replied in approval.

They sped off to a stall ahead of them, grabbed some items quickly, not even stopping to count the coin they threw to the vendor, before sprinting off to the fountain at the middle of the marketplace. In that moment, and Heracles wasn't sure whether it was anything to do with the sisters, he had the sinking suspicion that they were being watched.

17

They hurried through the market place. Apollo followed closely behind Heracles. It felt slightly strange to Heracles that the market place was still so busy given it was several hours later in the day but tried to ignore that thought.

Heracles started to slow in his movements. Apollo followed suit and turned to him.

"Something wrong Heracles?" Apollo asked with concern in his voice.

"Maybe."

They continued on, at a slower pace now, less urgency in Heracles' forward motion. They spilled out into the centre of the market place and laid eyes on the fountain. It was a small but impactful attraction. Circular in shape, the market circling out around it. The fountain contained a low wall, at the perfect perching level for sitting and a low pool of water being recycled through its rudimentary plumbing system. The centre of the fountain contained a statue of the mayor of the city, Sisyphus, reading from a parchment of some sort and looking quizzical.   As Heracles was starting to suspect, Selene and Achilles were nowhere to be seen. But he was not worried.

Apollo was.

"Where are they? Do you think they've panicked and gone looking for us in the market?"

"Look around Apollo."

Apollo stopped for a moment, still confused but trying to see what Heracles was seeing. Heracles was hopeful he was projecting his calm to Apollo. Apollo looked around him at the fountain, then his gaze flew upwards to the sky. His expression then changed to one of understanding.

"The sun is still at its highest point," he said, before looking to the fountain again. "The shadow on the fountain wouldn't be falling like that if it were later on in the day. It's still the same time of day, same as when we entered the sister's hut, isn't it?"

Apollo was sharp as a tack. He gathered himself so quickly. Heracles was highly impressed at someone so fresh into The Alliance. The kid spoke so eloquently, and with his confidence growing, he would prove far smarter than Heracles in no time.

"Bingo. My guess is that the sisters had a few more tricks up their sleeve. Namely, a suspension of time. We're around the same time as when we went in, and still too early for Selene and Achilles to join us."

Heracles sighed in relief. This was all a little irritating, but ideal for them given the need for urgency. They had lost no time. They were still on track and with way more information than they had previously. Heracles was of course worried about the price they would pay for that information but they would cross that bridge when they came to it. For now, they were in a good position.

"Sit tight Apollo. They shouldn't be too much longer now."

Heracles sat himself down on the edge of the fountain and rested lazily, brushing his fingers into the water of the fountain to cool off in the hot sun, warm against his back as he caught his breath. His heartbeat slowing from the earlier worry. Apollo joined him, perching on the ledge with perfect posture.

"Let's figure out how we're going to find this Theseus character whilst we're at it."

18

Ten or so minutes later, Selene and Achilles

appeared from the crowd, ponchos and supplies neatly thrown around their shoulders. Selene waved at them both. Achilles looked slightly more relaxed than he had been before.

"Hey gang. Get what you were after?" Achilles said as he threw a few bits down onto the floor by Heracles' feet. "Pretty happy with our haul. Got some ponchos for both of us, some dried wood for torches and some bags to carry a few bits. Got some decent supplies as well. Patching up kits and a very decent whetstone to sharpen up my blade."

Selene concurred.

"Achilles was actually highly useful. Imagine my shock." she smiled. It was always welcome, given it was a rare occurrence with Selene in the short time Heracles had known her. Achilles reciprocated. He seemed to have calmed somewhat. Selene's influence no doubt.

Apollo chimed in.

"We…had an interesting time our end."

He looked at Heracles for confirmation that he was fine to entertain them with their escapades. Heracles nodded and Apollo began to recount the last few hours. Or in reality, the last few minutes.

19

Selene's expression had changed back to her usual dispassionate appearance.

"I'll be honest. I am both impressed and concerned. The information is excellent no doubt, but the price that comes with it…"

Heracles replied in hushed tones as not to attract attention, the four of them sitting closely together on the fountain.

"I know. I know. But it's a path we'll have to cross later Selene. We don't know what dangers we'll face in the Labyrinth, barring this Minotaur, and we'll need to be reactive. This is good for us. It sets us out onto the path and gets us moving forward."

"But one of us will have to sacrifice somethin…"

"Not one of us Selene, only me. None of you will go through this. It has to be me. You're all in this because of me. We'll see what the situation is like in the Labyrinth, and then act. That's all we can do."

Selene rescinded, reluctantly.

"Right, now that we're all up to date and we have our supplies, let's march on to Minos. We need to locate this Theseus character. And fast. I fear we're still in a race against time."

Heracles took his poncho out of the bag and held it under his arm. He pointed over in the direction of a street that headed for Minos.

"That's the way we're heading. We wait until we're out of sight of the crowd, further down that street over there, and then we swing these ponchos on. Hoods up and all. Wouldn't want anyone seeing us without the covers on when we enter Minos. We're not too far away from there now."

He stood up. His body clicking from his fatigue. The others followed suit. He turned back towards the street he had pointed to earlier and went to move, when he saw the path now blocked by a figure, shadowed in the light of the sun.

She spoke softly, but there was an undeniable undercurrent of authority.

"Sorry to bother you all. Do you mind if we have a little chat before you head off to Minos?"

20

The person before them was immaculately dressed. Wearing a tightly fitted black and blue armour plate on her chest, with a blue multi-headed beast painted directly onto the front. Her skirt hung from underneath her chest plate, to just above her knees, pleated, also in black and blue. She held no weapon that Heracles could see.

"Just a minute of your time please. My partner and I have a few questions."

Heracles glanced over his shoulder and saw who she was referring to. Another immaculately dressed warrior. Same chest plate, arms folded over his chest obscuring the beast, but Heracles could just see that it mirrored that of the person in front of him. He was a large and imposing man, bigger even than Achilles, and a lot older in age than all of them.

Heracles felt Achilles slowly move towards his sword. He grabbed down at his hand and stopped him, shaking his head at him slowly. He addressed the woman ahead of him.

"Not here. Too many people. Let's walk down that street a-ways and talk."

She nodded her approval and turned to the street, beckoning them to follow her. Her consort walked behind Selene, dictating the pace of the group ahead of him and ensuring they were sandwiched between the two of them in a line.

After a few minutes of walking Heracles signalled for her to stop. He was sure that they were far enough away from the market to go unnoticed and Heracles recalled that the road to the poorer side of town from the middle ground was relatively quiet when the market was buzzing with people.

"This is fine. We can talk freely now. I just don't want to cause a scene, if the conversation were to turn sour…"

"I don't intend it to, but that is wise, Heracles."

He baulked. Another that knew his name. They were making a bad habit of this today. So much for being inconspicuous.

"Talk. Now. Who are you?" he asked, no kindness in his voice now. Straight to the point. If anything were to happen, he felt more confident of not dragging any innocents into it, or at the very least being able to make a quick getaway.

She smiled. Her partner walked slowly past Selene and joined his partner by her side. They stood together.

Heracles was now convinced that they were wearing some sort of uniform. He wondered what bearing that would have on the conversation. He didn't recognise it but it did have undertones of the armour and uniform that The Alliance wore when in combat, but it was certainly nothing he had seen previously so wouldn't use that as a sign that they weren't hostile.

"This here is my partner, Hector," She pointed to the man by her side with both hands, presenting him like a trophy. "He doesn't speak much so I'll do the lion's share of the talking.

"I am Helene," She said proudly. "Of the Argonauts."

CHAPTER VII
THE LABYRINTH

1

Heracles was wary. Standing before him were two soldiers, clearly very prepared, who had gotten the drop on their foursome. Not only that, but they had engaged in polite conversation with them to reinforce the leverage they held over them. It was infuriating. They had tried to be careful, but the sisters of fate had thrown their day into chaos already and they had become careless. And now this.

Heracles glanced round at Apollo to his left. He was standing tall. Calm and composed. In that moment he looked like a real warrior. His confidence was growing by the hour, learning from each experience he had faced the last few days: his first day at the academy; his Rite ceremony; the attack on The Alliance; a meeting with The Fates; and now this. Heracles felt lifted by his ability to progress.

He turned to his left and looked upon Selene and Achilles. Selene, as she always appeared to be, was calm in the moment. Her hand resting firmly on her blade. Drawing its strength. It's serenity. Achilles, as Heracles had imagined, was ready to fly at both of them at a moment's notice. No hesitation. Whilst rash, he would prove a great fighter with the right guidance given to him. He was fearless. Far too proud of course, and cocksure in his abilities even after only drawing his sword so recently. He must've felt himself a formidable fighter even before he ever drew that blade, and Heracles was curious to see him in action. But he was fearless none the less.

Heracles, a half step forward from the others, was

calm on the surface, but frustrated underneath. They needed to be careful with these two. Heracles sensed great strength. He engaged in conversation with the pair, keeping a close eye on both their emotions and their stances. Always ready. Always analysing.

"So, what can we help you with?" Heracles started out slightly conversational, with a hint of sarcasm to his tone, in an attempt to keep it all relatively light and civil.

Helene smiled. Her partner did not. Hector, it appeared, was the strong and silent type.

"I'm glad to see manners are not lost. Why not introduce us to your friends first Heracles? We've kindly introduced ourselves."

Heracles was about to respond when Achilles spoke.

"Introduce ourselves to a couple of pirates? Not likely."

Heracles was unsure what Achilles was referring to but it seemed to land with Helene somewhat.

"We *prefer* treasure hunters. And you've quite the insight Mr...?"

Achilles was quick to avoid the question, simply scoffing before Selene joined the discussion.

"Tell us what you want and we'll play ball." she said, wise enough to not divulge information without first trying to gain the upper hand. Hector and Helene already knew of Heracles, and that was already too much.

Helene rolled her eyes. She was older than Heracles, but Hector looked a lot older still.

"Fine, fine. We're all friends here, no need to be so cold," She waved her hair out of her face delicately. Purposefully. "I'll be blunt. We have a pretty good idea of the mission you are currently on, and we want to help you. Our boss has a vested interest in the items you are searching for. What do you say?"

Straight to the point Heracles thought, and at the

mention of their mission he again tensed up. How did so many people know about the items they searched for when it was supposedly highly classified information?

Helene waited patiently, her arms now folded across her chest plate, much like Hector beside her. Heracles studied her. He had so many questions. How did they know about the items? How did they know they were looking for them? Who was pulling the strings? However, one thing was in their favour. They seemingly did not know where to start, and were, on the surface, unaware of the Labyrinth. If they could lose them here, they could continue on and lose their tail. They didn't need their help and they certainly couldn't trust others to join them.

Heracles was careful with his words. He would need to try to get a message to the others. Heracles also didn't want to confirm or deny anything with them at this stage. He casually dropped his hand to the handle of his blade as if he were leaning his arm lazily against it.

"Let's say we believe you. And that's a big *if.* What happens to the item once we find it? Are you hoping we'll turn it over to you?"

"Heracles, no!" Selene protested.

Heracles halted her. Helene responded quickly.

"Let's just say we're eager to help. I don't want to give up much information to you yet. We have our orders. We will help you get whatever item you are searching for. We can talk further then."

"Ok, say we were to strike a deal…"

Selene again protested. He turned to her with an angry façade.

"Look Selene, we can *close our eyes* to this deal all we want," he said, closing his eyes purposefully and tapping his sword handle to get his point across. "But ultimately we need all the help we can get. When I tell you to look the other way, you do so. Got it? I am the leader here, not you."

He hoped desperately that Selene would get his point. He turned back to Helene.

"Name your terms." he said, calmly.

"You arrogant son of a bitch!" Achilles had turned to him now. Showing his protest at his discussions. Heracles hoped he would get the hidden message in his words but he was head strong, dumb and stubborn as usual. Heracles ignored him.

"All of you. This is my decision. It's final."

He stared at Apollo, Selene, and Achilles in turn. Helene chuckled in the background.

"My word is law. When I say look the other way you do so? Am I making myself clear?"

He raised his voice further now. Forceful. Booming.

"Look the other way! NOW!"

Selene grabbed Apollo and Achilles and turned them fully around and away from Heracles. She had caught on. Thank the gods! Heracles flipped his thumb against the handle of his sword. It popped neatly up out of its sheath. A blinding light emanated from it, filling the area all around them with bright white light. Helene and Hector flung their arms up to their face to shield their eyes, recoiling at the light as it penetrated their retinas. Heracles grabbed at Selene in the light, who, he hoped, in turn was holding onto Achilles and Apollo.

He fully drew his sword. Lightning coiled and waved around the four of them. A circle of electricity ran in a circle around them. It shot up in a circular stream, engulfing all of them in a fantastic bright light.

And they were gone.

2

The light dissipated, revealing the four of them stood huddled together, still clutching each other's hands.

Achilles broke away and vomited into the dirt of the floor. Apollo broke away also but held his breakfast. Finally all of them took a step back away from each other. Heracles looked up. Ahead of them was the archway that defined the small walled entrance into Minos.

Sisyphus had erected this small wall, acting as a divider between the middle ground and the poor ground, as one of his first acts in office. It had no guards patrolling it or marshalling it. It was simply to show the divide between the poor and middle grounds' wealth and their position in society: a symbolic divide, ensuring the citizens knew their place. Heracles had always hated it. And Sisyphus for building it. There were several arches that ran across the border into the poorer part of the city. All acting as entrances and exits between the divides. Each one with a sign at the top, with varying names depending on the archway. This one read 'Minos'. They had arrived at their destination.

Heracles had never tried to teleport more than himself before, and it was hugely taxing on his body, but he had had no choice in that moment. He couldn't risk a fight with powerful adversaries, drawing unwanted attention to all of them, in a built up, populated area. Let alone risk injury before their already daunting and dangerous mission into the Labyrinth. Thankfully, he had pulled it off.

"What the hell was that?"

Achilles was examining his body intently, wiping his mouth of any sick that still remained. He was now patting down his arms for some reason, a look of horror on his face. Heracles found the look hilarious.

"Am I singed? I feel like I'm singed."

"You're not singed Achilles," Heracles said, stifling a laugh. "You were just a part of my teleportation technique. I will admit...I'd not tried it with more people than me before. Thanks for being the guinea pigs."

Achilles's jaw dropped. Clearly astonished at the

sheer lack of preparation of it all.

"Guinea pigs…you son of a…"

"Thanks Heracles. That was the right call. We couldn't afford to make a scene back there." Apollo said, interrupting Achilles swiftly. At least Apollo had his back. He nudged Achilles beside him as he spoke.

"Yeah, yeah…thanks," Achilles conceded, before continuing. "I will give you this though, you've got some moves. That teleport trick is damn fast. And that flash trick was impressive as well. Glad to see you're not just all bark."

He grinned. Heracles tried not to get carried away with Achilles warming to him but it was a step in the right direction.

"Thanks. It's all thanks to this baby," He tapped his sword like a proud father. "It grants me impressive speed. But…it's still untamed. I can't control it overly well even after years of practice. I'm still growing with it. That was definitely a gamble, but I am glad it came off."

"So this is Minos eh?" Selene said, giving the impression that she was ignoring all the slapping backs in congratulations, in favour of keeping everyone on track. Heracles didn't mind that one bit, welcoming it even.

"Yes, this is Minos. Where I grew up. It was the first thing that popped into my mind when attempting the teleport. I doubt those two back there will be far off our trail though so let's get moving."

Heracles stepped forward and through the entrance, beckoning the others to follow, and they talked as they walked, Heracles leading the way.

"We'll head into Minos, aptly nicknamed the Labyrinth of Minos. Sisyphus describes it as an 'above ground catacomb of alleyways and dead ends' to try and deter people from coming here from the middle and wealthy grounds. It's fine if you know it like I do but you wouldn't want to enter without prior knowledge of it. It'd be dark by the time you found your way out, likely sans your money pouch."

"So we're after some guy named Theseus then?" Achilles double checked. "Any idea what he looks like? Any leads from those crazy sisters?"

Apollo was quick to respond to Achilles.

"Not much information to go on to be honest. Only the fact that he is the grandson of the last person who was able to find and enter the Labyrinth," Apollo turned his head to Heracles as he walked. "Probably not wise to mention the Labyrinth too much though, right Heracles? People might start asking questions right back at us. Or think us somewhat mad."

"That sounds about right," Heracles agreed. "I say we keep the initial questioning centred around finding this Theseus character. Then, when we've found him, we can divulge a bit more to see if we can't find out what he knows."

He stopped in his tracks. "Ah, here we are."

They were standing before an alleyway. Unassuming at first, but Heracles saw the old tell-tale signs of the entrance to the above ground labyrinth. An old, crooked sign, resting on a cracking plank of wood buried into the ground, read 'The Labyrinth of Minos - Tourists turn back' in dark red writing. Not the most welcoming of signs but doing its job nicely as a result.

"Ponchos on gang. Keep your eye out for anyone keeping an eye on us. We need to be very aware of our surroundings in here. And don't fall behind, or it could be hours before we find you. There are many twists and turns and if you take the wrong one, Minos can seem like a creepy place in the dark."

With that he took a step forwards and marched forward into the alleyway.

3

The light of the dimming afternoon soon vanished

as they delved further.

The alleyways were relatively narrow at first, but as they took a few turns they grew wider and started to populate with several people. Some sat on stoops outside of boarded up homes. Some lay down behind beat-up metal bins. Their clothes were as Heracles remembered, and the ponchos they had purchased allowed them to fit right in. The cobble stones of the richer grounds were a mile away, replaced with trudged mud and dirt. The thatched roofs replaced by wooden boards crudely attached to the rooftops, slanted downwards. It was a far cry from the upper echelons of the city and stank of neglect.

They took more twists and turns. Delving deeper into the maze. Achilles dropped his breath to Heracles.

"This is where you grew up? No offence mate, but I can see why they call it 'The Dump'. I am already more lost than I have ever been. Bit of a shit hole, aint it?"

"None taken. But you'll see its charm soon enough. This is just the entrance. Everyone you see here around you is playing their role. Guarding the entrance. Keeping an eye on everyone who enters. Driving away any unwelcome guests. The fact that they aren't kicking us out of here bodes well for us. We'll be nearing the hub of it all soon."

Selene stole in. "So all of these people aren't homeless?"

"Don't get me wrong, there is desperate poverty here and these poor folk are sufferers of that, but they are being paid in food and warmth, fire and kindling and such, for keeping an eye on the entrance, and that keeps them surviving. The chiefs of Minos ensure they don't go without. Somehow. Most are happier here than they ever would be in other parts of the city and often come here when they see the corruption and greed outside of Minos."

"I never saw much of that in the city though?"

"Of course you didn't Achilles, you were nestled within it. And I know it's not your fault, but The Alliance always favoured your family and looked after you all, right? They don't afford that same luxury to a large amount of the population. Even less so here unfortunately. It's a sad moment when you realise one of the biggest failures of The Alliance. Sisyphus' influence is everywhere here, and he has crippled Minos."

Achilles sulked at that. He seemed to not have a retort though, which Heracles took as him accepting that Heracles was right.

They took more twists and turns. Heracles could hear the music and see some of the lights from the centre of Minos now. They were close.

"Can I hear…music?" Apollo said.

Heracles simply laughed and waved them all to hurry on. They turned the corner of the final alleyway to the centre, and Heracles heard an audible gasp from one of the team behind him.

They had come across the real Minos. The one full of life. Full of attraction. The real market of the city in all its glory. Before them was a magnificent sight. A big open space, surrounded by the same towering buildings as the rest of the alleyways they had seen, but with magnificent light all around them. Festoons hung from wall to wall in a plethora of colours. Sound was everywhere. Shouting and selling. Music and singing. Performers of every kind, trying to make their way in life. It was always Heracles' favourite part of returning home.

Selene stepped past Heracles and marvelled.

"It's so full of life! How?" she said, turning to Heracles now, searching for answers. "The poverty is clearly rife here. How is it so cheerful here? Are they blind to it all?"

Heracles chuckled.

"They aren't blind to it Selene. They are making the most of it. Imagine yourself in their situation. Living day to day and not knowing where your next meal is coming from. Would you wallow in your self-pity? Or would you band together as a community and make the best of a bad situation? If you have nothing, you have nothing to lose. And everything to gain."

Selene pondered this. Heracles left her to it and continued to look around. It had been some time since he was last here and it was still as full of life as he remembered. This would be the place to find what they were looking for. Minos was known for its information, being the hub in the know, but most wouldn't dare to enter the alleyways in search of it. If only they knew what was really going on here. Still, the mystique kept those that the community didn't want in here, out.

"Right gang. Let's stick together this time. After splitting up last time, and what happened, I doubt it's the right thing to do, especially in here."

Heracles moved forward. It was time to properly start the search for this Theseus character.

4

Heracles weaved and bobbed through the market place and its inhabitants, his band of fellow adventurers closely in tow. He was searching for one person in particular who he felt could help them in their search.

The locals called her 'The Oracle'. She knew most of what happened in Minos and was wise beyond her years. Heracles remembered her as a slightly older, battle hardened woman when he was a kid, so surely now she was sat back enjoying the retired life. Heracles highly doubted that, but it was a nice thought.

Heracles felt a tap at his shoulder. He whirled round and came face to face with nothing except a confused expression on Achilles's face.

"What the hell are you doing?" Achilles said, as

he looked around himself, paranoid now. Heracles stumbled over his words. Unsure now of whether he did feel anything.

"Uh, I…sorry, I don't really know. I thought I heard…"

A whisper shot through his mind. All sound around him escaped his ears except this light and low voice. It was soothing, but commanding.

"Welcome back Iphicles. Or is it now finally Heracles again? I sense you seek my help. Come, we need to talk. You know where to find me."

And suddenly Heracles did. He saw an alleyway leading off the market. One of many of course but this one was marked with two collapsed bins that were tinged with red paint. All they had to do was locate those and follow the path. He was sure of it. The Oracle had beckoned him.

He was shaken back to life by a forceful shove against his chest. The noise of the marketplace filled his ears once more and he was met with his three companions staring at him. Selene was slightly more forward and withdrawing her fist.

"Sorry. You were blank so thought it best to slap some sense back into you." Selene said, nonchalant as usual and with a remorseless look on her face.

"Thanks Selene. I guess," Heracles responded, absentmindedly scanning the area around him. "Got lost in my own thoughts for a second there, but I think I know where to go. We're looking for someone that can help us find this Theseus guy. An old acquaintance of mine. They call her 'The Oracle' around these parts, but I know her as Delphi. She'll know who we're after. She…she just spoke to me."

"And how the hell is that possible?" Achilles blurted out, always doubtful of that which he didn't understand.

"Just trust me ok. She has a power, like us. The knife she carries was one she drew many, many years ago and it grants her some sort of telepathy. She's ex-Alliance. If we can find an alleyway marked with red painted bins, then we're on the right track."

Apollo nodded. His gaze darted instantly around the marketplace. Selene lazily turned to look also, seemingly uninterested. Achilles began to unabashedly ask those around him if they had seen painted bins anywhere. Those he asked drew back from him instantly, clearly intimidated by his tone and his imposing frame. Heracles grabbed him and began to walk towards something he had spotted through one of the stalls.

Sure enough it was the bins in question. One stacked and crushed on top of the other, clearly marked with red paint. Heracles also noticed a small O shape under one of the markings. Pretty unimaginative, but whilst Delphi was always careful to avoid any unwanted guests, she was always available to those in need of help if they knew where to look.

Heracles recalled a time where he had been playing with several of his friends in one of the alleyways, many, many years ago, and someone had broken the window of one of their neighbours' houses with a rock. When they were asked about it, they all remained silent. Loyal to each other. Delphi of course knew exactly who it was. She happened upon the scene, with one of the parents asking her to help divulge who it was. Heracles clearly recalls her looking directly at Heracles, winking, and turning back to the parent. She told them it was none of the children. It must've been a bird or something. Heracles then saw a small shadow float quickly past his left foot, and as he slyly glanced up, he could see the small rock floating high above them and over the roof adjacent, out of sight. The children always liked Delphi after that day. First afraid of her musings, but then welcoming and curious of her powers of levitation and telepathy. Heracles also remembered Prometheus being present that day, and watching on from the corner of the alleyway, his back firmly rested against a wall. Smiling from ear to ear at what was unfolding in front of him.

It was a hard childhood growing up without parents, with only infrequent visits from Prometheus when he could get away from The Alliance HQ, but it was made all the warmer by the kindness of those around him, and the friends he made. He would always remember that.

Heracles was about to step down the alleyway when someone called out to him.

"Iphicles! Is that you?"

Heracles turned to find himself being chased down by a man, similar in age to himself. A rugged, but boyish, clean shaven face topped with short blond curly locks. He had a long cloak draped over his shoulders, which fell down to just over his calves, all brown and very dirty. The clothes he wore made it all the more confusing that his face was so clean cut and pristine. Heracles didn't mind noting that he was quite the handsome figure.

Heracles recognised him instantly. He had grown tall and well-built but at the heart of it all he was still clearly his old childhood friend. Heracles jogged over to meet him, throwing his arms around him in a strong bear hug.

"Daedalus! How long has it been?"

Daedalus held onto Heracles tightly for a moment and then drew back. His grin had soured somewhat but Heracles felt this was in jest.

"Too long you bastard. Stopped visiting us, didn't you! Too fancy down here versus your trashy Alliance?"

He laughed a hearty laugh. Heracles noticed Achilles scoff at the mention of The Alliance being trashy. Heracles dropped his voice a touch.

"Free time is at a premium in The Alliance I'm afraid. Do you mind not mentioning The Alliance again for me as well? We're on the down low to be honest with you."

"Say no more. Minos welcomes those who need

a place to lay low, very few questions asked. Business?"

Heracles trusted Daedalus with his life. He was a loyal and fierce friend growing up. He had always looked out for Heracles. Heracles always felt terrible for having to lie to him about his true identity. And for leaving him down here.

"Yup. We're in need of a chat with The Oracle. Tell you what, let us get to our business and we'll meet back here and catch up? Be great to reminisce with you."

Heracles, conscious of time, knew that was a lie and that they wouldn't be coming back after chatting to the Oracle. They needed to continue on their quest. A shame, but he couldn't bear to hurt his friend's feelings. He would have to leave him. Again.

A look of perplexity touched Daedalus' face.

"That's…a coincidence. I am also heading to see Delphi. She just called me, out of the blue. I've not spoke to her in a long time. Not a lot of people have. She's off the grid of late. Thought I'd best jump at this chance to see her though."

Heracles knew this was no coincidence, knowing Delphi. Daedalus must be of help in finding this Theseus character. Delphi didn't do coincidences.

"Is that right," Heracles said, a slight lace of sarcasm in his voice. "Well if you're joining, I'd best introduce you to the gang. Daedelus, meet Apollo, Achilles and Selene."

Daedalus shook each of their hands in turn, dropping a slightly mischievous kiss onto the cheek of Selene. Heracles expected her to punch him square in the face, but she blushed deeply, much to the amusement of Apollo.

"Charmed. Nice to meet you all. I'm Daedalus."

His smile beamed. Selene blushed again. Heracles grinned, happy that Selene had shown a touch of emotion at his undoubtedly handsome friend.

"Right then, shall we go?"

5

The group of them, now five in strength, proceed down the alleyway. It was unnaturally dark, even with the daylight creeping away as the day dragged on. It grew ever darker as they paced, the light ebbing around them.

A spark illuminated behind him. Apollo walked past Heracles with his thumb raised in the air and a flame sat neatly on top of the edge of his nail. Almost hovering over it.

"Ever seen one of those flint stones light a fire with a spark? Seems like it works for me too."

Although Apollo was facing forward leading the way, Heracles could hear the smile in his speech, proud of himself for trying something new and having it work for him. Daedalus leaned over to Heracles.

"Care to tell me how the hell he is doing that?"

Heracles often forgot that those in the lower runs of the city didn't often come into contact with those from The Alliance, and their powers. Heracles explained The Rite to Daedalus as they walked, glancing at his face in the dark to gauge his reaction, and keeping his voice relatively low to avoid prying ears. He explained that Delphi was part of a similar mould, able to draw powers from the Shield of Aegeus. Heracles could only see part of his face now as the alleyway, stretching ever longer it seemed, was growing very dark but he could make out the excitement of Daedelus as he spoke.

"Man, what I wouldn't give to get something like that in my hands."

It was getting really dark now around them, Apollo's light brightening as they walked as he added more height and strength to his flame. The sound of the market behind them had dimmed to a low murmur. It was eerily quiet. Heracles looked up and could see no sky. That was why it was so dark. Perhaps they were under some sort of cover? He suspected not, but it should not have been so dark in this alleyway. There was something peculiar about it all.

They marched on and, after several minutes more in the dark, Selene broke the silence.

"Apollo, put your flame out a second."

"Really? It's pitch black around us."

"Just do it, please."

Apollo did as she asked and quenched the flame between the two fingers he had dampened on his tongue. Darkness engulfed them. But, as Heracles' eyes adjusted, and as Selene had clearly assumed, he saw something up ahead. He strained his eyes to make out what it was.

It was a small blue circular light, hovering wondrously in the dark, and sat above what appeared to be a dark red door. The blue was beautiful in the night: a radiance emanating from it but lighting only the door itself. Nothing else around it. He wasn't sure how he hadn't been able to see it against Apollo's flame light but it was heartening to find an end to the alleyway.

"Good work Selene. Let's check it out." Heracles said, as he stepped forward towards the door, stumbling slightly in the dark as he bumped his legs on various unseen debris scattered on the floor. Heracles would have guessed that anyone who stumbled on this alleyway, except those who knew what was down here, would've turned back as soon as it started to get dark. The alleyway was strangely silent and the light above the door was working in mysterious ways. The fact that they couldn't see the sky at all now appeared to not be the cause of a cover, but more of an illusion.

"Shall we knock?" Daedalus spoke through the darkness, his smile resonating again in his voice.

Heracles nodded, before remembering that he likely couldn't see him and replying positively.

He drew his hand up to the door, mostly to check that it was still present on his body. He saw that it was, and rasped on the door, loudly, three times. On the third strike, the door slowly swung open, offering the five of them an invitation to enter. The entrance before them was as dark as everything else around them, but Heracles felt somewhat buoyed that Delphi surely waited patiently inside.

He hoped.

6

Inside the door, as they all shuffled slowly through, was a long corridor. Abnormally long. Seemingly endless before them. Heracles held the door open for all five of them to enter, and as he closed the door behind Achilles, the hallway shortened instantly, closing in on them and drawing another door close to the front of them.

Heracles heard Apollo cough slightly to muffle the small yelp he had made. The corridor shrinking had shocked Heracles also, but he had held his nerve.

The door in front of them sprung open now and, desperate to get out of the now tight hallway, Heracles stepped through. What greeted him on the other side was a relatively modest room. Half the room was in darkness, shrouded in a veil of artificial night.

What he could see in the room was a small stove, with a small fire burning inside of it. A small metal kettle rested on the top surface, with a run of thin steam escaping the spout in a twisted swirl. Whatever was boiling in the pot had an intoxicating aroma.

"Fancy a cuppa Heracles?"

A voice emanated from somewhere in the room. Heracles strained to see into the darkness and, as his eyes adjusted, a figure appeared, slumped into a low comfy looking chair. She peered back at him as the room slowly came to life, lights on the walls slowly turning on and showcasing the rest of the room in full. Around the figure were five other low chairs, of varying styles and sizes, ready to be sat in. Heracles recalled the meeting with the muses and thought the chairs were again no coincidence.

"Hello Delphi. It's been a long time." he said to the seated figure, her eyes firmly fixed upon him.

"My boy, that it has. That it has. Come join me. Daedalus, do you mind making our guests a pot of tea please?"

"Sure thing Delph," Daedalus's demeanour had changed instantly. Rather than the curious figure he had portrayed mere moments ago, he was now completely at home in his surroundings. "Five cups of delicious herbal tea coming right up." Curious.

Heracles turned back to Delphi. She was stood up now with her arms out stretched. Heracles walked over and embraced her. It was warm. Wonderfully so. He was so happy to just have somebody he recognised in both Daedalus and Delphi from his childhood, and it filled him with a sense of safety. If only for a moment.

Delphi was older now of course, after so many years. Her once purple hair greying at either side above the ears, with several grey hairs intertwining with fading purple on the long fringe that framed the right side of her face. She wore a wonderfully colourful top, defined by its purple frills on the shoulders and frills at the waist where it sat above her trousers. She looked in great health, even with her age having moved on. She wore the sneaky, knowing smile she always did.

She pulled Heracles away and rested her hand outstretched against both his arms and admired him.

"You've grown strong Heracles," she said, chuckling. "It's going to take some getting used to, calling you by your real name. Prometheus would've killed me if I'd let slip that I know your story."

Her face fell sullen.

"Prometheus. I miss him already Heracles, as I am sure you do. He was an exceptional man. He loved you deeply. I hope you know that."

Her eyes, slightly watery now, looked up towards Heracles. He felt the certainty in her voice, and it tore at him.

"I know. I miss him too." he offered her. Scant consolation but it was all he could muster in that moment. She wiped the tear from her eye before it could fall and turned to look at the others.

"Anyway, enough of that. It's lovely to meet you all. I am Delphi. Also known as the 'Oracle of Minos'. I am a telepath," She tapped the small knife in its sheath on her left hip. "This little beauty grants me the ability to speak with other minds. It also allows me to see a brief images within minds of those that I am with. No future sadly, although I sometimes feel a glimpse of it but it's always far too hazy for me to give any real direction to anyone."

She turned to Apollo.

"And you must be…Apollo. Wielder of flame and strong of heart. I see you well Apollo. You have a kind aura about you."

She held out her hand, and Apollo took it, as she guided him into the seat on her left. Heracles joined Apollo in sitting. Selene and Achilles patiently waited their judgement with great interest.

"Selene is it? I can feel your serenity even now without you ever touching that moonlit weapon of yours. I can see past that tough exterior though."

Delphi winked at Selene, who smiled back. A knowing nod to each other.

"And finally Achilles. Son of the famous Stratigos. He was a great man. A kind…"

She paused.

"…oh? Sorry, I see you don't speak of your father much. I won't either then. In you I sense great strength. *Great* strength. But an abundance of pride. Not a good combination my boy. You'll need to address that before you truly become something special."

She drew Selene and Achilles to their seats before turning to Daedalus at that final point. Achilles was visibility angry at the bashing she had given him over the others. He sat, frowning heavily. Daedalus brought the tea over and set each cup down on the small round coffee table in the middle of them all. He took a seat next to them; the wind of his movement blew the small run of steam emanating from the cup closest to him slightly.

Delphi began again.

"Daedalus hasn't been entirely truthful with you Heracles. Much like you haven't been with him. He knows about your heritage now. I brought him up to speed before I sent him out to greet you. I sensed you in the middle town market earlier today and made my preparations, although you disappeared off the grid for a moment there."

Heracles shot a look to Apollo, as he recalled their wondrous meeting with the three sisters.

"No matter. I know what you seek Heracles. You seek that damned Labyrinth." She paused, the word Labyrinth spewing out her mouth like poison. "You came to the right place though. There are few who know about it, let alone where to find it. And I know how to help you. Well, I know someone who can help you. You seek Theseus correct?"

Heracles sat forward in his chair now, the business at hand.

"Yes, desperately. We are conscious of time. There are forces searching for the Labyrinth too and I don't know how far off they are or when they will make their move."

She waved her hand to slow Heracles.

"Ok, ok, I get it. You know I'm not one for beating around the bush. You can talk to Theseus now and discuss the finer details."

She turned to look at a space past Daedalus.

Heracles looked past him to see what she was looking for. Another door perhaps. Was Theseus going to join us here?

Delphi let out a long laugh. It was a heart-warming laugh. As always.

"No, no, you look too far Heracles."

She pointed directly at Daedalus. He held his arms up either side of him, pointing to the sky.

"Ta-da."

7

"Wh..at?" Heracles baulked.

"When I said Daedalus hadn't been entirely truthful with you, I meant it Heracles. Daedalus has had to keep secrets from you just as you with him. He was in a surprisingly similar position. He couldn't afford people to know about his lineage either lest they use him to gain access to the Labyrinth. He is the grandson of Aegeus, the last seeker of the Labyrinth."

Heracles joined the other three in shock. Mostly at the revelation but also at how well this was falling into place for them. He didn't want to get complacent, but all was going well so far. Although he feared a fall may be yet to come as a result.

His mind moved to Daedalus actually being Theseus and questions flew into his mind. He went to open his mouth and Delphi halted him.

"I can sense the questions you have Heracles but maybe let Theseus talk for now."

Heracles nodded, staving off his urge to blurt out question after question, and sunk back into his chair. He motioned to Theseus to go ahead. Theseus nodded in return.

"Thanks…Heracles. Just getting used to that also," He chuckled to himself. "My birth name is Theseus. My mother sadly passed not long after my birth and my father was left to raise me alone. We had some fun those first few years. We lived in the middle ground and passed the days with my father telling me stories of my grandfather often. Every detail. You might think he would be against the idea of me ever going near the Labyrinth but he was as obsessed with it as my grandfather had been. He was going to go himself again one day. But that day never came."

Theseus paused, picking up the small mug in front of him and blowing gently on its rim to cool it. He drank a sip of his tea to compose himself, before continuing.

"It was around my tenth birthday. You remember me only coming to live here around a similar time to you? Well it's because people came after my father, looking for a way to find the Labyrinth. How they had found out about it, I don't know. They attacked us in our home. Dad spotted them coming and told me to hide. They wore robes which covered their faces and bodies so I have no idea who they were to this day. He fought bravely but they were far too strong for him."

"They left him for dead when they couldn't get the information out of him. I watched him die in my arms, much like he had watched my grandfather die in his. The last thing he said to me was to change my name and forget about the Labyrinth. I think he didn't want me to fall to the same fate as he and my grandfather had. But as with them, it's only spurred me on. I changed my name to Daedelus and escaped to here, where I've lived ever since. Delphi kindly looked out for me when she could. I've been waiting for a chance to tackle that goddamned Labyrinth. With the right people of course. And with this."

Theseus reached into the top of his shirt and pulled out a necklace. Attached to the end of it was a wondrous gem, sapphire blue sparkling against the light of the room.

"This is how my grandfather found the Labyrinth.

It calls to me. I can feel it. I've been searching for it, and I now know where to find it. This will guide us and I wouldn't mind betting get us access in there."

Heracles sensed an end to his speech and jumped in. "We've had confirmation of where it is also. We have it on good authority that it is just outside of the city walls. Sound about right?"

Theseus was slightly taken aback but nodded his approval.

"Bingo."

Heracles had questions now.

"So what else do you know about the Labyrinth? Do you know how we can best the Minotaur that lives in there?"

Theseus pondered for a second, his thumb and fore fingers resting neatly on his smooth chin.

"So that's its proper name is it. Dad just called it the bull. Sadly, I don't know anything more about it than the fact it is a monster beyond belief. My dad only mentioned grandfather coming across it as he searched the Labyrinth, and it ultimately costing him his life. Dad never said what he was searching for either, whether it was just treasure, or whether he was after something more special."

Heracles leaned forward in his chair. His mind awash with thoughts. Concerns. Plans.

"The hide of the Nemean Lion."

Heracles discussed his and Apollo's meeting with The Fates. A look of excitement and bewilderment rose in Theseus. Delphi was also interested but continued quietly listening.

"So you believed that these three were some sort of deity? Dad never mentioned any lion's hide." Theseus said.

"I don't know what they were, but there was certainly an immense power emanating from them. They were wise beyond belief and had insight into things that no one person could know. And when they spoke of the treasure the Labyrinth holds, there was no doubt they knew what they were talking about."

Theseus thought further. He looked around at all those present, except for Delphi. He looked somewhat doubtful now.

"You can all fight, right?" There was a slight apprehension in Theseus' voice as he spoke. "You're all willing to enter that Labyrinth knowing that it may well cost you your life? Could be plenty of things in there that could kill you, *especially* that Minotaur. Are you really that concerned with finding this lion's hide that you would risk it all? You gotta make sure you have a purpose in all of this or it'll be worth jack shit."

Theseus was questioning, gauging each of their reactions. Heracles remained quiet to let the others decide for themselves. He hadn't seen Theseus as serious as he was right now in all the time he had known him.

Achilles, of course, was the first to speak. He was leant back in his chair, somewhat casual for him.

"Thanks for the lecture but we're the ones coming to you remember. We're the ones pushing for this. We have our reasons," he leaned forward, his intensity rising now back to his usual self. "Want to know mine? I fight because I'm strong. I choose this path and have never been one to back away from a challenge. I joined The Alliance to fight, and to get stronger still, and you can be damn well sure we'll keep that lion's hide out of the hands of those intent on using it to kill others."

Achilles was on his feet now, standing tall against Theseus's seated position. Before Theseus had a chance to jump in and retort, Apollo was standing up.

"We all have cause to be here Theseus. I may not be the most confident of folk but I am here to fight with everything I have to ensure that these items don't end up in the hands of Tartarus, or anyone else hellbent on seeing this world crumble to dust. We can fight. And *will* fight."

"Well," Theseus attempted to interject but was

again cut short. Selene was up on her feet, more proactively than Heracles had seen her before. She had her arms folded over her chest and was not looking directly at Theseus.

"I go where these two bozo's go. If only to keep an eye on them and make sure they don't do anything stupid. I'm the glue that holds this group together."

Finally Heracles joined his gang of empowered fighters.

"We can fight Theseus. You can be sure of that. And will fight with everything we have."

He looked to Achilles, who nodded.

"We will fight anything that gets thrown at us. Together."

He turned to Apollo who mouthed something along the lines of 'damn right'. Heracles turned to Selene, and then finally back to Theseus.

"And we will find the Hide of the Nemean Lion and protect it with our lives, even if we come face to face with death itself."

Theseus remained motionless in his chair. He had his head pointed down, looking at his hands which are shaking slightly.

"You have our answer Theseus. Are we agreed?" Heracles said, still stood in a powerful stance with his cohorts.

Theseus slowly raised his head. A wry smile now beamed across his face. He placed his hands on either arm rest and leapt up. He swung his hand into Heracles' hand, releasing an almighty clap. They both grinned at one another.

"Well what the hell are we waiting for? Let's get on with it!" Theseus said, a look of pure excitement blinking wildly in his eyes.

8

Delphi rose from her chair. She dusted the crumbs from her lap, crumbled from the biscuit she was enjoying whilst sipping her tea quietly and relishing the back and forth between her guests.

"So, it seems you are ready to go then. I'm pleased. A word of warning before you do though. The Labyrinth will be no picnic. We have no idea what traps, enemies, and challenges lay in wait for you there. You must all work together if you are going to survive. This is no time for heroics. No time for pride. Work together or I fear that none of you will make it out of that Labyrinth alive."

The tone in the air turned sullen after the empowering rallying cry they had just experienced. Delphi was right to bring the tone down but it was still a damper. Heracles knew that they needed clarity of mind and thought to traverse this Labyrinth. They had gotten carried away slightly and a level mind was what was needed.

"Delphi is right," Heracles said, supporting her lowering of the tone. "We consult on everything. We work together. We look after one another inside the Labyrinth. We do that and we'll conquer anything that comes at us."

Delphi smiled at Heracles.

"You've grown into a fine man Heracles. Good luck and come back and see me after all of this is over. I should like to hear the tale in full."

They embraced. A strong and full hug, one of love and friendship.

The five of them said their goodbyes, and headed out into Minos once more, Theseus grabbing a pre-packed bag on the way. He was certainly prepared for this. Delphi had briefed him well with the insight she had.

Heracles noticed instantly that the alleyway they

traversed to get here was completely light when viewed from this side. He turned back and saw the alleyway dark once more, the small light resonating against the darkness. How had he not noticed that before? Had he not once turned back? Had none of them? He laughed to himself as they walked to the end of the alleyway and back out into the market area.

The market was still bustling but had died down somewhat with the hour growing late. It would be growing dark soon. Was it pertinent to rest up for the evening and tackle the Labyrinth in the morning or continue onwards now? He picked up with Theseus, who pondered for a while before replying.

"Well my thinking is that if we leave now, by the time we reach the Labyrinth, it will be dark which on the surface seems like we should wait. But when we enter the Labyrinth it is bound to be dark anyway, so the time of day will make little difference to us when in there. We can of course rest now but wouldn't it be more prudent to locate the Labyrinth and set up camp there? At least then we're at our destination and can tackle it once rested. Your call Heracles."

Heracles greatly appreciated the logical nature of Theseus. He had always been sharp as a kid, but mostly put it to use in making schemes. Now he was seemingly using it for the better, clearly laying out the options before them in a logical manner.

"What do we think gang? Are we ok to continue on to the Labyrinth?"

Heracles assessed them all and they all nodded to continue.

"I think it's wise to continue on until we find the Labyrinth. The adrenaline will carry us through for now." Selene was sharp also. She would be a great asset in the Labyrinth. Heracles had no doubt about that. She was calm and wise beyond her years. Albeit sarcastic and seemingly dry of compassion currently.

Each of those present had their strengths and faults of course, and Heracles hoped that by working together they could leverage the good over the bad.

"Alright we continue on and we will set up camp when we reach the Labyrinth, as long as all goes to plan. Where to Theseus?"

Theseus was arranging the items in his bag as Heracles talked. He looked up at being mentioned.

"We need to head out of the city slightly. I know a way out where we can avoid the main entrance to the city. That should avoid us being seen by those you don't want to be seen by. I would imagine word of your apparent murder of Ares will be spreading wider than The Alliance now Heracles."

Heracles felt a pang of homesickness before motioning to Theseus to keep his voice down. Theseus laughed, teasing him.

"Right, follow me and stay close. We don't want anyone lost in this Labyrinth before we even get to the real one, do we."

9

Theseus was quick footing it through the many twists and turns of Minos now. It was clear he knew the place like the back of his hand. There was no second thought. No pausing to check where they were. He was rapid, and the rest of them were following closely behind, conscious that, if they lost sight of him, they could be lost for many hours.

The nickname given to these alleyways of Minos, the Labyrinth, was an exaggeration of course. Yes, the buildings were very high in comparison to the rest of the city, with its open cobbled streets and smaller height houses, but the buildings in this area were built high at their conception to ensure they could be filled with as many of the poor as possible, in an attempt to hide the cities poverty. The alleyways were built slim to cram in more and more buildings and made difficult to navigate so that the poor stayed where they were, and to dissuade those with wealth against entering. It was a system that unfortunately worked quite well but was horrifying once you knew its true purpose.

Heracles wondered what the others thought of it, having grown up in the middle to high grounds of the city. It was not pleasant to look at most of the time but it had its charms, such as the central market place. When night descended, it did take a somewhat sombre turn, as the festivities died down and the alleyways became quiet, bringing out an almost sinister nature to the place. Although with Theseus as their guide, they had nothing to worry about, as they flew through alleyway after alleyway.

They exited the Labyrinth of Minos and come across an open courtyard, cobblestoned and rectangular in shape. Ahead of them was the entrance to the camp of Minos, labelled with a large sign to greet all those that approached it. Heracles had only brought himself to return to here once after the night so many years ago, where he fell to his knees at the sight of his father dead on the hard cold stone, covered in a deep dark blood. Prometheus and he had returned once a few years ago, just to get closure on the place. Heracles feeling the need to exercise some demons of the past. It was still heartbreakingly sore, even more so now after coming face to face with Tartarus.

This was Heracles' greatest secret. His inability to get over the death of his parents at Tartarus' hands on that hate filled night. He thought about it, always. It fuelled him. Revenge filling his lungs as he breathed in the area of the courtyard. He hid it well but knew that one day he would likely crack under the pressure of it all. He tried not to think about it, but it defined him somewhat. He prided himself on being kind and open to those around him, but he held a deep and insurmountable rage within himself that he could not quite control. He longed for revenge, and that was his hidden curse. Until he achieved it, he would not be whole. He would never be himself.

He was snapped away from his thoughts by a hand on his shoulder. Apollo was looking at him deeply. The others had walked on ahead, with Apollo dropping back to check on him. Heracles heard a muffled question, amid the dark thoughts that plagued his mind.

"I'm fine thanks Apollo, just some old memories of this place popping into my mind."

He smiled, forcing himself to do so. Apollo eased somewhat at that. He joined Apollo as they walked towards the entrance to the camp. Theseus was halted in front of it, looking upwards at the sign.

"The Camp of Minos. I hardly ever come here to be honest with you. Too many military folk for my liking," he said, before stopping himself and looking round at those present around him. "Ah sorry. No offence meant. Where we're heading is off to the left a bit anyway. A little secret exit out of the city I came across as a kid. Handy for venturing outside of the city without anyone knowing."

Theseus led them past the wooden spiked walls of the camp entrance, and they continued left to where the spikes headed backwards and joined with the walls of the city. He approached the city walls and placed his right hand upon them, feeling for something as he dragged it both left and right in one particular spot. He stopped his hand movements and pressed, hard. The stone he was touching slid away from his hand for a second before locking into place with a dull thud.

"There we are. Achilles, you look like a strong lad. Give me a hand, will you?"

Achilles scoffed, as he so often did, but this time Heracles heard a slight twang of smugness in his voice at being called upon. He approached Theseus, who pointed to a collection of stones, and motioned for him to push. They both laid their hands on the area, leaned into it, and drove forward. The stones gave way in one motion, all of them sliding in one clump away from the rest of the wall, and out. Heracles expected the wall to give way, but the clump moved away from the other stones neatly in a sliding motion. As it moved past the rest of the wall, Theseus and Achilles slid it to the right along the edge of the outside wall, and neatly tucked it to one side, creating an exit for them.

Theseus clapped his hands together, removing some of the gathered dust. Achilles followed suit.

"There we are. Didn't make this myself before you ask. I found it one day whilst messing about out here. One of the lads and I were rough housing around it and I slammed into this, moving it slightly. A gang of us kids managed to push it forward and out. It's a great little spot. Often wondered who put it here. Must be a remnant of the old wars, some sort of escape option. I don't really understand it but it allows us exit, so that's all that really matters to me!"

He stepped through, the others following him out into the open air of the outskirts of the city. As they all gathered in a line on the outside of the wall, they stopped and wondered at the sight before them.

Heracles had never been outside the walls, and he hazarded a guess that the others, barring Theseus, hadn't either as their looks told him as much.

Before them was an open, vast landscape filled with beauty. Directly ahead of them in the distance was a vast mountain range. Heracles had seen a few maps of the outside world in The Alliance's library and recognised it to be the Magnesia Mountains. A vast mountain range spanning miles and miles of terrain, and essentially dividing the land they lived on in two. The other side of those mountains he had only read about. And he would love to one day head over the mountains and traverse the land beyond.

To the right, far closer than the mountain range but still some distance away if walking, was a vast and blue lake, glistening in the lowering sun. Heracles had heard tales of it in his studies. The lake was known as Siren's Lake, and it apparently held untold secrets within its depths. It was frequented by many small boats throughout the day, fishing for their food and livelihood with the catch of the day being sold into the city. But none dared traverse the lake at night. It was known to be home of The Sirens. They were known to take the shape of one's true desires, to tempt people out into the lake and ultimately to their deaths, as they enticed them overboard and dragged them down into the dark depths. They, for some unknown reason, didn't come out during the day. Some speculated that they draw their power from the moonlight. All stories of course, but Heracles was coming to quickly realise that life outside of the Headquarters was full of strange and new things, some magical and some he would've never believed had he not witnessed them first hand. Namely the three sisters of fate.

The fields before them were littered with fabulously yellow plants, stretching as far as the eye could see and casting a golden glow against the green of the grasslands. Patterned throughout the field were tracks of both mud and stone, seemingly roads for access into and out of the city. Heracles was coming to realise more and more how restricted and cooped up he had been at The Alliance Headquarters. He understood the reasons of course, but he had been exposed to so little beauty and his eyes began to water at the scene before him.

He felt Selene place her hand lightly on his arm as they looked out. She dropped him a sweet smile. Heracles, as always, was surprised when she showed even the slightest bit of compassion as it apparently wasn't in her nature. Still, he felt closer to her, and to them all already, even after so little time together. It had been excitement enough so far, and he felt that the bond would only grow as they traversed the Labyrinth.

The Labyrinth. Heracles had lost himself in the scenery and now refocussed on the task at hand.

"So where to Theseus? Hopefully not too far of a trek?"

Theseus chuckled.

"Don't worry. We're not going mountain scaling. It's close. Follow me."

He turned and followed the walls of the city to the left, his hand trailing on the cold hard stone as he walked. Heracles doubted it was for any reason. He just looked somewhat comforted by it.

As the walls curved round the side, another wall came into view. It steadily appeared as they advanced forward, with Theseus taking out his amulet now. It flashed a brilliant blue, almost blinking against the dimming sun of the day. It seemed to have come to life. They must have neared their destination, especially given the information gathered from the sisters about the Labyrinth being directly under the city.

The wall came fully into view. It was simply that. A wall. An extension of the city, that jutted out in a straight line away from the city walls. Heracles approached. It was only maybe five metres in width, and maybe the same in height. He walked around it and saw that it was roughly three metres deep, before the fields surrounding the city began again. Simply a wall built out from the circular city walls. Totally out of place, and apparently totally useless. He returned to the others. He now saw, however that the amulet as an even fiercer blue, blinking rapidly as Theseus holds it aloft.

"Must be the place. This thing is going crazy. Vibrating," Theseus approached the wall and placed his hand against it. "Help me look for some kind of cavity. Something that we can potentially push the amulet into. A lock of some kind. I don't really know quite what we're looking for but we may as well look."

They did as he instructed. The day was rapidly drawing to a close now; the sun setting around them and the night drawing in. Heracles couldn't recall it changing so rapidly but put it down to the fact that they were so focussed on the task at hand and unaware of what was happening around them that it perhaps seemed quicker than it was.

He watched as Apollo placed his hands, and then his face, sweetly against the stone of the wall, almost trying to sense a heartbeat. But more likely trying to sense some wind coming through any cracks hiding an entrance.

Achilles was roughly slamming his fist against the wall, and then waiting for any hollow sounds to resonate back. An interesting tactic.

Selene was staring up into the sky, and Heracles noticed that the moon was forming high above them, replacing the sun as the keeper of the sky for the night. She radiated slightly as she watched, completely transfixed.

Heracles darted his eyes left and right. Up and down. Trying desperately to find the clue before night descended. Before he could make headway though, he saw a spark shine brightly from Apollo's hand out of the corner of his eye.

"Got something. Not sure what but it's a different look and feel to the rest of the wall."

Theseus walked over to Apollo and Apollo pointed out what he as referencing.

"Good eyes Apollo. This looks good."

Theseus held the amulet up to area and it was clearly resonating now. Almost uncontrollably. Theseus moved it closer to the wall, and as he did a thin blue beam shot out of the centre of the amulet and into a small groove in the wall. The stone around it lit up in an instant in a brilliant blue hue. The stone started to crack and crumble before them, forcing itself to pull away from the other stones. Layers of stone trudge both left and right, crumbling and creaking as they moved. Heracles had maybe seen some of the weapons at The Alliance produce powers such as the beam escaping from the amulet but had never seen a seemingly inanimate object produce anything of the sort.

A cold harsh wind escaped the wall as it parted. And an almighty stench. The stench of something that hadn't been opened in a long, long time. Darkness escaped also, matching the growing darkness of the night descending upon them.

The walls got as far as they were going to and creaked to a halt, locking into place with a low thud. Heracles marvelled at the sheer brilliance of it. The Labyrinth must have been ancient, but to have these sort of fantastical mechanisms to it was nothing short of incredible. Almost magical in their design. Automatic. Heracles had never seen anything like it. Dark magic was at play here, unlike anything he had seen back at HQ.

Theseus stepped forward slightly, walking past Apollo and half way into the darkness of the entrance. He looked up, silently and stared into it long and hard.

He then looked back to the others, his arms stretched out from his body. He offered a bow to them all and then stood back up strongly in his stance.

"Welcome, to the Labyrinth. Shall we?"

He turned, stepped forward, and vanished into the darkness.

10

Heracles motioned to the others and they followed Theseus into the entranceway.

As if reading Heracles' mind, Apollo raised the brightness from his flame and lit the room before them. They all entered and gathered inside. The room was far bigger than Heracles was expecting, plenty big enough to hold the five of them comfortably with lots of space around them to move around in. Completely juxtaposed to the wall they had entered into, much like the three sisters' home from earlier today. Heracles felt a similar supernatural weight heavy against his body.

As Selene crossed into the light, the walls behind them slowly started to creak closed.

"Last chance to back out." Theseus said. He was motioning to any of them to leave if they wanted to, as the wall neared its closed position but of course none of them moved an inch, watching as the wall became one again behind them with a clunking yawn.

Apollo had noticed stacks of wood tucked neatly into multiple triangle metal cones, bolted to the wall in various places around the room. He was lighting them one by one with his fire, illuminating the room fully as he reached the last one. With the darkness cleared, Heracles could see before them were two great stone doors, tall as the ceiling they stood under. Hugely impactful to Heracles' eyes. They were framed with thick spider's web, waving slightly against the wind squeezing through the slight gap between the wall and the doors' arch. Heracles watched as a thick black ball darted away from the centre of one of the webs as the light flickered against it.

Sat in the middle of the door was what they all feared was yet to come. The head of a snarling bull, complete with very real blood dropping sluggishly from its jaws. It looked almost fresh, and Heracles suspected this may be further proof of the dark magic in the place. Its eyes were firmly shut, the fur of its mane resting over them slightly. Hanging from its nose was a great golden ring which Theseus was approaching with an outstretched hand.

Heracles went to stop him, and then retracted. They had come this far. They needed to enter the Labyrinth at all costs and this was the only way to do so. They must plough forward.

Apollo lit a torch from his backpack and held it aloft for Theseus, radiating extra light directly onto the Minotaur's face for him to have a better view.

Theseus placed his hand on the nose piercing. Heracles and the others waited with bated breath but the head of the Minotaur did not move. He pulled at the ring, hard, and it swung upwards. He held it there for a second, his arm straining against the heavy weight of the ring, and then slammed it forward, producing a long and blaring bang that resonated throughout the room, bouncing off the walls around them. The sound was deafening and Heracles moved to cover his ears. Several of the others did the same. Only Theseus remained unmoved. Fully engaged with the process at hand.

The sound dissipated, leaving only silence as they waited for what would happen next.

After a moment of waiting, dust dislodged from the top of the door and crumbled down on top of Theseus' head. Heracles swore he saw the Minotaur move slightly in that moment, and Theseus must've sensed it also as he slowly stepped back away from the door.

The Minotaur's eyelids blinked open furiously, revealing its frightening eyes, bulging from their sockets in a horrid rage. Blood red eyes. Dark and deep. Full of fury. Hypnotic. The eyes stared, hard, at all of those present in the room. They darted quickly between each of them. The Minotaur's nose snarled and huffed, dust escaping the nostrils in short sharp blasts. More dark magic at play, but Heracles had the sinking suspicion that this door not only represented the danger inside, but that it also represented the beast itself. And by knocking to be let in, they had awoken the Minotaur from its slumber.

Still, the door did not move. The Minotaur simply stared on. Heracles felt Achilles move slightly behind him and the Minotaur's eyes widened, throwing themselves to Achilles's position.

Its mouth creaked open.

"WHO ATTEMPTS TO ENTER *MY* LABYRYNTH?"

All of them were taken aback as the beast roared before them. Achilles, with the Minotaur's eyes firmly locked onto him now, stepped forward.

"Open up you goddamned bull. We are here for the Hide of the Nemean Lion!" Achilles roared back at the Minotaur, attempting to match its ferocious volume.

The Minotaur considered him for a second before bellowing back, very much engaged in the shouting contest they were partaking in.

"BRAVE, *BOY*. STUPID, BUT BRAVE. YOU SEEK THE HIDE?" It said again, before laughter echoed all around them. "YOU SEEK *DEATH*."

"Listen here you nose ring wearing, bull headed piece of shi…"

Heracles was on him, his hand placed firmly across his mouth to stop the next part of the rant from escaping. Achilles turned to him furiously and Heracles stared him down as he held firm. The Minotaur thundered a rapturous laugh once more. A hysterically high pitched laugh, more akin to that of a human than that of the bull.

It settled itself.

"INSULTING ME AND STILL ASKING FOR ENTRY INTO THE LABYRINTH. WHAT FOOLISH PRIDE. IT'LL BE YOUR DOWNFALL, *BOY*."

Heracles held his grip on Achilles, feeling his rage. Theseus stepped forward towards the bull, as Apollo jogged over to Achilles to assist Heracles in keeping him contained.

"Beast! I am the grandson of Aegeus, the last adventurer you faced and he who took a part of your horn. I come to claim the rest of it…along with your head."

The Minotaur roared again, albeit this time its voice was clearly tinged with real fury.

"GRANDSON EH? OF THAT FOOL! MY

HORN STILL BURNS NOW, AFTER ALL THESE YEARS. I WOULD VERY MUCH LIKE TO KILL YOU IN HIS STEAD..."

The beast fell silent, pondering its next move. His eyes darted around the room again, studying his soon to be foes and hopefully his next meal. His eyes thinned and bulged, as he examined them, before he huffed mightily. His decision made.

"FINE. YOU MAY DIE AT MY HANDS, LONG BEFORE YOU EVER SET EYES ON *MY* TREASURE. I WELCOME THE HUNT OF WORTHY PREY AGAIN. ESPECIALLY SO MANY OF YOU."

A great grasping tongue escaped his mouth and licked his hair tangled lips. His tone was becoming somewhat sadomasochistic in nature.

"I YEARN TO FEEL THE WARM THRILL OF KILLING YOU ALL WITH MY AXE. RIPPING YOUR FLESH FROM YOUR BRITTLE BONES. CRUNCHING YOUR SKULLS AND BREAKING YOUR BODIES," The Minotaur paused, calming himself somewhat. "PREPARE YOURSELVES WELL. BRING ME AT LEAST A CHALLENGE. KNOCK THREE TIMES AND I WILL ALLOW YOU ENTRY. THE HUNT WILL SOON BEGIN."

And with that Minotaur was silent. Its eyes firmly shut and its head returned to a motionless state. Theseus moved to knock and Heracles stopped him swiftly.

"Theseus, wait. It's given us time to prepare. We should use it. Now we are inside here with your amulet still on you, we are no longer in danger of others getting access, and also in no danger of attack from within the Labyrinth. Give me a few hours. We can use this time well."

Theseus considered Heracles' words. He was clearly on edge and desperate to enter the Labyrinth, but he was also clearly full of adrenaline and knew that tiredness would come. Heracles extended his point.

"We train hard for a few hours. We rest hard. And then we tackle the Labyrinth, and the beast within, together. That is all I ask. Or I fear a terrible and swift death as our adrenaline ebbs and our energy wanes."

Theseus was clearly annoyed, and as annoyed as Heracles had ever seen him, but he conceded. He moved to the corner of the room, sat down on the cold hard floor, and leaned himself against a wall behind him. He beckoned to Heracles to get on with it as he shut his eyes in rest. Heracles turned to the other three.

"Watch closely, all of you."

11

Selene, Apollo, and Achilles looked at Heracles intently as Heracles drew his sword from its sheath. Its light radiated wonderfully in the darkened room even with Apollo's fire spread out across its walls.

Heracles held his sword aloft, pointed high at the ceiling of the room. He closed his eyes. Normally he wouldn't draw this process out, but he wanted to ensure the three of them didn't miss a second of it. He drew a great deal of power from his sword, less so than he usually would for this technique as he only needed it to last a short time. The sword electrified and pulsed in sequential bursts. He moved the power down through his body, allowing the current to flow throughout his whole being. Through his veins and into his heart. It pulsated around him, striking the ground, and sending small bits of dirt into the air before they were caught by the electricity and evaporated. He felt the electricity drown him, bathing him in power, resonating wildly.

He focussed.

With a great force of will, he forced the power residing in him back up through his sword and out of the tip. It shot skywards and when the beam of light reached its peak, it split off into five golden strands that arched, before descending back to the earth around Heracles. The strands flooded with light to meet one another, forming an umbrella arch around Heracles. The light from his body joined with the arches and Heracles was bathed completely, now knowing that he was obscured from the others sight. The light sat around him only for a moment, but that was always long enough to allow the change.

The light dispelled outwards and as Apollo, Selene, and Achilles raised their hands to their faces, open at the fingers to try to not miss anything whilst still shielding the light, they marvelled at Heracles. He was stood before them in his fantastic golden armour, that which he had called forth during his battle with his younger brother. Heracles had discovered that he could call forth this armour upon Prometheus's instruction. It had taken him time to reach a level of competence with his sword before Promo was then satisfied that he was ready to learn the technique.

Prometheus had created the technique himself. He had only discovered it towards the end of his career and felt it too temperamental to teach to anyone and everyone. He had taught it to only a handful of the current Stratigos – Atlas, Athena, and Gaia - and they had kept it as a hidden technique, afraid of its power in the wrong hands. Wise, Heracles thought, given the betrayals they had experienced of late.

He quickly steadied his mind and turned to the three recruits before him.

"Under normal circumstances, you wouldn't be anywhere near learning this technique, but needs must. We need to see if any of you can learn this ability and quickly. I am conscious that I've thrust you three into a very dangerous situation without giving you any of the training you should've had. If you can activate it, this ability will serve you well in the Labyrinth, but it comes at a risk. It gives you great strength and defence but will drain your stamina swiftly. This is a hidden technique of The Alliance, and you three are now privy to its existence. Keep it as such. We attempt to learn this together but know that you will likely not achieve it now, but we must try regardless. Then we rest for the battle ahead of us. You first Selene."

Selene, surprised at being called first and blissfully unaware of Heracles' faith in her intelligence and quick learning, stepped forward towards him.

"Draw your weapon Selene."

She complied, slowly slipping her sword from its sheath. It radiated calm and translucent light as it appeared. Heracles felt serenity wash over him again, as it had during her Rite ritual. He felt empowered by it, but in a different way to his own sword: a quiet confidence running through him. He had also been feeling that Selene's power had a strange and unknown quality to it. One he felt would assist her in her learning. He knew not how he knew, but he felt it somehow.

"Good Selene. Your sword is seeping a bit of power though. I'll help you control that as we go. It'll help you not release too much power too quickly and drain your energy. For now though, I want you to use that stream of leaking power and concentrate on releasing it into one point. Draw the power of your sword deep into your body first. It should feel like waves of energy flowing over and through your body, filling you with the power of your blade."

She held a look of puzzlement upon her face. Heracles grabbed his sword and stood by her side to walk her through the process again. Selene mirrored him at every step. She was sharp, focussed now. Watching his every movement and mirroring it perfectly. Heracles marvelled at her grace and ability to copy him exactly. He had never seen anything quite like it. As Heracles drew his sword up to the sky, emitting his radiant light, he stopped, letting it all fade, and watched on as Selene continued the process, rightly undeterred by Heracles' stopped movement. She was totally focussed on succeeding.

A pale white light emitted from her sword. Much less dramatic than Heracles' own transformation. Slower, more methodical but none the less, a pale moon light engulfed her and it wrapped around her body, snaking its way around her in a cylindrical fashion. She was gone, blocked from view by the fantastically inviting light. Heracles was completely and utterly captivated by it. His heart was racing and calm all at the same time. He had now stepped back somewhat to observe.

The light dissipated, slowly, revealing a magical sight. Selene stood, strong and straight, with her arm still raised to the ceiling. She slowly lowered it as a realisation dawned on Heracles that she had managed to pull this off at the first attempt, where it had taken him many, many attempts to get it even half right. Promo had been at the end of his tether by the end of his training, but Selene had managed it straight away. Heracles admired her sheer brilliance. There was something to her power, Heracles was sure of it. Something that allowed her to mirror that around her. She was a genius.

Her armour was simply magnificent! Her light blue chest plate was similar to Heracles' in that it had no arms but at each shoulder was a buckle in the shape of a crescent moon, both facing inwards to one another and holding in place a superbly draped cloak that fell down her back. She had a layered leather skirt protecting the top of her legs now, a light grey, and a hue was radiating across the top of every surface, much like it had been at her Rite, seemingly adding that extra layer of sharp protection.

Heracles stepped over to her.

"That's unbelievable Selene, to get it on your first try. You really are a prodigy. Prometheus thought as much. That is a demonstration of exceptional control over your power."

She beamed, caught herself, and returned to her usual cool demeanour.

"Thanks Heracles. Just a bit lucky I guess, but I do feel like this power of mine helps me…somehow. I…don't know how to put it, but when I was watching you going through the movements, my mind seemed to follow perfectly, and without much assistance my body moved on its own. I can't explain it."

"We'll work that out together as we go Selene. I felt it too. It took me many goes to master this. It's an incredible achievement. But know that the drawing of the armour can be taxing once it fades, so please limit yourself to activating it once more now before resting up for the battle ahead. You'll learn to don the armour for a longer period as you get comfortable with it also so be careful not to tax yourself too much now."

She beamed again at the mention of Heracles struggling, thankful at his humility, and then moved to another spot in the room to practise. Heracles turned to Achilles next. He stepped over to Heracles and stood side to side with him. He seemed less proud than usual and genuinely eager to learn. Heracles felt it is a step in the right direction. When it came to learning and growing, he sensed that Achilles was open to anything that would make him stronger.

Achilles attempted the activation of his armour for a long period without success, asking questions of Heracles frequently. Over two hours passed, and Achilles was getting rather frustrated, along with Heracles' fatigue slowly creeping in. He needed to go over this with Apollo also, and knew how long this training could take. It was not something that could be picked up so easily, which made Selene's successful activation all the more impressive. Achilles did seem to be picking it up quickly though. He had a lot of potential and was clearly somewhat of a prodigy himself.

"One more attempt with me showing you

Achilles and then I'll have to start with Apollo. You'll get it, keep at it for a while longer."

Achilles looked slightly annoyed, before closing his eyes and focussing his mind. They went over the movements together again and as they reached the pinnacle of the move, Heracles stepped back to watch closely.

The three cadets really were something, Heracles thought to himself as Achilles's armour flickered into existence for a moment, before evaporating from his body. In that moment, a bronze aura escaped from the tip of his sword in an arch and engulfed him in a bright chestnut colour. It as quick but with Heracles eyes he was able to capture everything about Achilles' armour.

Achilles's armour was different to that of Heracles and Selene. It is a real warriors' armour. A shining bronze helmet sat atop his head, with the plating arching above his eyes and falling either side, covering and protecting his nose and cheeks. The helmet was circular, with a tuft of thick, straight amber horse hair tufting out of the top in a straight line from just above his forehead, stretching back to the nape of his neck. His bronze chest plate stretched to his shoulders, where it then connected to two further plates on either arm that stretched to just above his elbows. There was no detail on the armour, being very simple in nature.

Heracles let out a sigh of relief, even as Achilles raged at himself. He was tiring now and the more they trained, the less time to rest there was, but this was important for them: it would give them an immeasurable boost before assaulting the Labyrinth. Achilles would don his armour fully soon, as surely the pressure of the Labyrinth would allow him to finally bring his armour forth properly. Heracles had no doubt about that.

"Incredible work Achilles. It's almost there. I saw your armour in all its glory, if only for a second. Hugely impressive my friend. Rest up for now. You'll get it in no time, trust me."

Achilles, clearly frustrated, and stubborn, went to argue with Heracles but he waved him away. Heracles repeated himself.

"It'll come Achilles, *trust* me."

Achilles rescinded, before nodding and walking over to a spot by Theseus to begin his rest.

Next up was Apollo. However, try as he might, and try they did over hours and many, many attempts, Apollo could not bring forth his armour. Heracles sensed that something was holding him back, his new power seemingly too unruly. Too raw. In fact, Heracles sensed he had the most powerful sword out of the three of them, but he was unable to control it in the way Selene, and Achilles, could. Unable to hone it. Use it as fuel. Every time Heracles thought he was close, the fire would spread too far and too hot, causing Heracles to swoop in and quell it. Apollo was growing more and more frustrated at the process as a result.

Apollo dropped to his knees on his final attempt. His head in his hands. Heracles approached him and placed his arm onto his shoulder. Achilles and Selene looked up from their makeshift beds, before falling back and into a light slumber. Theseus had been asleep for hours already. Immune to the booms and quakes in the room seemingly, two small pieces of fabric jammed roughly into his ears.

Heracles lowered his voice so that only Apollo could hear him. He wasn't going to like what he was about to say.

"Apollo, you need to rest now. I am sorry, but it'll come. It took me a while to get it also, and even then, it takes far more time to master. I can feel it in you. I was the same. We both have that raw power that is so difficult to tame. You have a role in the Labyrinth either way. I want you to assist Theseus and protect him when we're in there. Stay by his side. He is key to all of this."

Apollo looked up at Heracles and it nearly broke

his heart. Apollo was clearly furious. Not at Heracles, but at himself. He was frustrated and angry that he couldn't do what Selene, and to an extent Achilles, could do and it sat across his face. He nodded silently and went over to the others. Without saying a word, he set up his bed, lay down, and rolled over on to his side. Heracles caught Selene moving to comfort him but she thought better of it and turned back to her bed. Heracles followed suit and prepared to rest.

They would need all the rest they could get. The Labyrinth loomed ever closer.

12

Theseus was up first Heracles saw as his eyes lazily opened. He was staring intently at the Minotaur's head, desperate to speak to it again and ask it to open. Desperate to enter and begin their quest. Heracles also noticed that he had a long thick blade attached to his right side. A weapon he must've been carrying, and concealing, in his long thin backpack prior to this moment, for some reason.

He was clearly prepared but Heracles hadn't thought to ask him whether *he* could fight, back when he had asked all of them at Delphi's place. What an idiotic thing to miss, Heracles thought. He rose to his feet and approached Theseus, startling him slightly as he placed his hand on his shoulder.

"Are you ready for this? Sure you can use that?" he said nodding to the sword he held.

Theseus rolled his head back and laughed. The laughter aroused the others from their slumber as it echoed around the room.

"Don't worry about me. I may not be the strongest fighter there is, and that's why I am glad you lot are here, but I pride myself in my speed and cunning. I carry my grandfather's sword and I will use it to cut the

Minotaur's throat."

He strained to get the final word to release from his mouth, and as it did, it was tinged with hatred. He turned to the head of the Minotaur now, goading it intensely.

"Hear that you dumb beast? We are coming for you. We're ready when you are!"

The beast's eyes flew to life once more. A great puff of dust shooting from either nostril with enough power to blow a few small rocks on the floor loose from their resting place. Heracles noticed that the dust was marginally damp from the inside of the beasts' nose as a small bit hit his arm. More black magic.

"SO BE IT! I WILL AWAIT THEE IN THE LABYRINTH. COME."

The head fell lifeless once more. Theseus picked up the ring on the bulls' nose as it quieted and rasped three times, the loud boom of metal hitting metal reverberated around the room, jump starting the other three into life instantly. The doors the head was attached to boom loudly also and started to slowly creak open.

Theseus was poised, eager for the door to swing open so he could dive in. Heracles remained at his side, and without looking at him, he addressed him.

"Theseus, remember. We're in this together. We stick together. That's the best way of us succeeding in there. Don't forget that. Don't forget yourself, my old friend."

Theseus nodded beside him.

"I know, I know. I'm glad you're here Heracles."

Heracles nodded in return, his hand falling to his sword. A force of habit. Heracles spun round to the others.

"You ready?"

All three of them silently drew their weapons from their sheaths in unison and walked towards Heracles and Theseus, having quickly jammed their makeshift beds messily into their backpacks after Theseus's laughter had woken them.

The five of them stood side by side as the door finished its opening motion. The doors sighed a cold wind and stilled. Theseus drew in a deep breath and turned to Heracles one final time before entering. He was searching absently with his hand inside his satchel as he looked at Heracles. He drew from it an orb of red and white thread from his bag and held it in front of Heracles.

"My grandfather gave my father this, my father passing it down to me. It's how my grandfather made his way back out of the Labyrinth, despite all his grave injuries. Hence the red soaked into the white thread. My heart is telling me that the item we seek will be directly in the middle of this maze, and there will be many twists and turns that will help us to forget where we have been before. We use this to leave a trail and follow it back out," he said before stalling. "And should we fail, it will likely serve the next poor soul who dares to tackle this behemoth. Apollo, would you mind?"

Theseus was motioning to Apollo now, who reached into his bag and pulled out two large chunks of wood that Achilles had provided him with yesterday. He threw one to Theseus and kept one for himself. Selene did the same, drawing another bit of wood from her bag and throwing it to Achilles. Apollo snapped his fingers and the bits of wood exploded into life, fire brimming from the top part of the wood in a fiery blaze.

"Let's go." Theseus said to the rest of them as he walked through the door. Heracles turned to the others and moved for them to follow.

Selene sarcastically bowed with her right hand across her chest and her left arm outstretched, inviting Heracles to enter first. He did so gladly, following closely behind Theseus, with Apollo next, hurrying slightly to catch up with Theseus, followed by Selene, and finally Achilles at the rear.

13

The instant they crossed the threshold into the Labyrinth, the doors behind them slowly began to close.

Theseus pulled out the thread from his bag once more and moved to the door before it closed completely, holding a piece of the thread out in his hand. As the door closed, he flicked the thread into the gap, and held it in place until the door fully shut. He pulled at the thread and, when it didn't budge an inch, he walked backwards, drawing out a bit of the thread as he went. He tugged at it again, and when it didn't move for a second time, he turned around to face inwards into the Labyrinth, placing the thread back into his satchel with a tuft of it poking out underneath his dropped arm. Heracles could see that his plan was to have it slowly ebb out as he walked, so that he wouldn't have to concentrate on it too much as he traversed the maze. Clever.

Heracles looked around at the scene before him. Somehow, whilst they were in the previous room, they must've travelled underground, as a ceiling lay high above them now. Exceedingly high above them, and all around them were vastly tall walls of hardened stone, god knows how thick. Heracles felt the dark magic at play again. Possibly the entryway they stepped through was some sort of gateway down into the depths of the earth underneath the city. He wasn't convinced by it all, but felt that as good a guess as any, given the unusual things that had happened of late.

Before them, down a corridor of tall walls, lay their first hurdle. A cross roads. Right at the start of the Labyrinth, almost taunting them with how difficult a journey this would be. No signage. No gimmicks. Just a simple left or right choice.

Heracles approached the junction, carefully, poised. He stood at the fork and looked left. Nothing interesting except for another bend a few metres from where Heracles stood. He looked right and saw much the same. Both turns turned inwards further into the Labyrinth and both seemingly provided a forward moving option. He turned back to the others and gave his thoughts.

"Both ways look the same. I guess we could pick one and head down it for a ways. If we come to a dead end, we'll know we've gone the wrong way. It's not ideal but it's a lucky dip down here," he shrugged. "Any other ideas?"

Achilles stepped up to Heracles, and past him, placing his hands on the wall.

"We could give it bloody good clout with our combined strength and see if one of the walls caves? I don't know how thick it is. Looks pretty damn dense, but it's worth a try?"

"I'd be aware, Achilles, that there is a hulking great beast lurking in this Labyrinth that I don't really think we should be wanting to attract unless we absolutely have to." Selene's sharp tongue lashed at Achilles' for what she clearly thought was a stupid suggestion.

"Point taken, but it could be worth finding out whether it's a possibility at least, given how big and empty this place feels. It's giving me the serious creeps. I don't really want to spend a second longer here than we have to."

"In all honestly, it's not a bad idea Achilles, just maybe not the right one. Keep thinking."

Heracles absentmindedly joined into the debate as he motioned his head left, then right, then left.

"You're the boss, boss". Achilles remarked and Heracles grinned back at him. His caution for Heracles was subsiding a little with every passing moment. Happily so.

Theseus was staring straight upwards at the cavernous void above them.

"Blocked at the first hurdle eh? Is there any chance of us going upwards and taking a look?"

Theseus pointed upwards, and glanced sideways at Heracles, who considered this for a second.

"Well the Minotaur does know we're here already, and it's in our interest to scope out as much of the Labyrinth as we can. Even if only to get a sense of the scale of this place. I think it's worth a shot. Achilles was right in that it's worth trying something, even if it does end up attracting the beast. We'll have to face it sooner or later. The Fates have confirmed at least that much."

Heracles approached Achilles.

"Reckon you've got it in you to throw someone up onto the ledge of one of these walls?"

Achilles grinned, deeply. He held up his right arm, tensed his muscles and slapped his left hand against his bicep.

"You know it!" he said, smugly.

"Selene, fancy it? You've got the sharpest eye." Heracles offered.

Selene shrugged as if to say, 'why not' and suddenly ran at Achilles, who bumbled to get ready, unprepared for the quick action. He managed to correct himself just as she jumped, and as she landed in his outstretched hands, he forcibly pushing upwards, launching Selene high into the air. She overshot the top of the wall slightly but was able to correct herself and land daintily on top of it.

"These walls are way too thick. There goes your idea Achilles!" she shouted down at them. "I'll need some serious light up here also. It's as dark as night in here."

Apollo turned to Achilles to try and join her up there, but Heracles stopped him. He placed his hand against his sword and felt the familiar jolt of electricity.

"A little party trick for you Apollo. Cover your eyes for this first bit!"

Heracles winked at Theseus and balled his left fist up. He felt the electricity surge through his body, and down into his left arm. His fist started to vibrate and from within his hand expelled a long bolt of light, pulsating under the pressure of his clenched fist. Heracles, eager to expel the power before it did any damage to his hand, threw it high up into the sky above Selene. It climbed higher and higher, and once it reached its peak flight, it exploded with a wonder of light, flooding the Labyrinth's sky.

The light lingered in the air, before splitting into several beams and starting to descend.

"Now Selene!" Heracles called up to her. "Open your eyes and look around, quickly!"

The light remained for maybe a few seconds as it fell, enough to get a brief glance of their surroundings, before fading, returning them to the darkness of night, barring the flickering torchlight they held. Only silence remained. They waited for Selene's response.

A booming roar echoed towards them, bounding, and bouncing off of the walls and directly into their ears. It was a bone chilling roar, one that the magical head of the Minotaur was not capable of even remotely matching. This was it, the real beast of the Labyrinth, sounding both close and far away concurrently.

Heracles looked up at the wall, trying to get a glimpse of Selene. As he stared, a shadowy figure appeared in the air above him, descending rapidly. Achilles was past him in an instant and safely scooped Selene out of the air, placing her softly on the ground.

"Thanks big guy" Selene said as she patted Achilles on the top of his arm.

"Two things to report. One, this place is a damn sight bigger than I, or probably any of us, had imagined. It honestly seemed endless at first, but I managed to judge it a bit. It seems to be a big square, with what looks like a large room at its core, and seemingly *that,*" Selene pointed behind her at the entrance they had taken into the Labyrinth, "Is not the only entrance into this place. See that large archway over the entrance? I think I can make out three more of those on each side of the square…"

Worrying, Heracles thought to himself. Whilst multiple exits allowed for multiple escape routes out of the Labyrinth place, it all also offered several ways in. Selene continued.

"Two, I managed to get a view of the centre, and whilst it's a while off, it's achievable. It's a big square right at the heart of the Labyrinth and, as you thought Heracles, we'll just have to keep checking we're on the right track as we go. We head right at this fork it seems."

Selene shrugged her arms, apparently annoyed that was all the information she could gather. Heracles thought differently.

"That helps us massively Selene, well done. We'll just need to keep going and aim for the centre, checking where we are periodically It's not ideal, but it's the best plan we've got. I doubt the Minotaur could tell our exact location from all that blinding light, and if we move swiftly, this tactic may serve us well as we go."

The others nodded, and Heracles hoped they hadn't heard the uncertainty in his voice when describing the Minotaur.

"Let's be prepared for anything. Selene, lead on."

As they moved, Heracles could hear Achilles letting Selene know of his surprise at how easy it had been to propel her upwards, like she was lighter than the air itself. Heracles also heard the dull thud of, assumedly, Selene's fist crunching against Achilles arm as she hit him. Finally, he heard her whisper a thanks.

14

They needed to be quick and cover as much ground as they could, whilst also being cautious to the many secrets and deadly temptations the Labyrinth might hold. Not an easy task with a band of five who barely knew each other, let alone with a team mostly of rookies.

Selene was swiftly guiding the group along, judging which way to turn based on her quick glance of the Labyrinth from above. Heracles and Theseus were next, keeping close to each other, Heracles with a fear for Theseus' safety. Apollo followed, heeding Heracles' words, and also keeping a close eye on Theseus, with Achilles checking the rear, turning around often to check that they weren't being followed, or at risk of attack.

Every twenty minutes or so, which felt like an eternity in the dank, dark palace of solitude, they would send Selene up onto the top of the walls around them to check their positioning. She suggested they remained on track and were slowly eating away at the Labyrinth with every moment that passed. They were buoyed every time she checked, with even Selene allowing for a chirpier tune to her voice as they made more progress through the Labyrinth.

Heracles' feelings dropped as they turned the next corner, however, with Selene skidding to a halt, and Heracles able to stop just before he crashed heavily into her. They had come across a long, thin, corridor. One littered with long, vertical, rectangular slits in the walls on either side, with no sense of how deep they were and stretching along its entire length. At the end, Heracles could see another crossroad choice. Left, or right.

Achilles, adjusting himself after knocking into Apollo ahead of him, drew himself level with the others. The five of them could just, barely, stand in a line together in the width of the corridor.

"Did you not see this coming on your last look up top Selene?"

"No…not at all. Which worries me, and the walls here seem to be exceptionally higher than what we've experienced before."

"The magic of the Labyrinth." Theseus muttered to himself. Achilles nudged him, seemingly to get him to speak up so that everyone could hear his thoughts.

"...Sorry. My father mentioned the powers the Labyrinth holds within its walls. The power it has over people. Apparently, my Grandfather had always theorised about it, and dad said that when he was holding him in his arms as he died, he seemed nonsensical at times, spluttering gibberish in between clarity. Gibberish about the 'voices in the Labyrinth' and the 'changing shape of the walls'."

He paused, perhaps hurt at the thought of his grandfather's death.

"Maybe you can't see everything from above Selene, or, maybe, the Labyrinth doesn't want you to." Theseus finished.

"I've yet to find one reason to believe in any of this crazy supernatural shit." Achilles said, his patience waning somewhat. "It's just a series of stone walls. There has to be logic to it. We keep going and eventually we hit the centre. Easy."

He stepped forward past the others and walked forward confidently into the hallway. From his left, several dark shadows shot out of one of the long slits in the wall and flew through the air. Even Heracles had a hard time keeping up with them, but he instinctively reached out to grab Achilles none the less, pulling him back just before the shadows fly through him. Achilles faltered back and fell flat onto his arse, bounding off the ground as he landed.

He looked up, and drew his hand up to his face, wiping the edge of his nose. Heracles watched as he put his hand down to examine it, opening it to reveal a trail of blood. His nose had a thick, but not deep looking, cut running across it.

"Wha...what the hell was that?" he spluttered, still tapping his fingers on his nose and checking to see how much blood there was.

"Arrows. Several of them shooting out of those slits in the walls." Heracles offered, throwing Achilles a look of 'I told you not to be an idiot, didn't I?'.

Theseus was kneeling beside Achilles now, helping him to his feet.

"Traps. I thought it might come to this. I guess we didn't all expect it to be just the Minotaur we'd have to face, right?"

Achilles rose to his feet, a little shaken at the last thirty seconds. His pride hit a little. He brushed himself off, layers of dust falling sweepingly from his backside.

"So what now?" he asked, mainly at Heracles and Theseus.

Heracles surveyed the scene. Over was certainly not possible. Heracles had a suspicious feeling that the same strange enchantments making the walls look far higher in this spot would keep them from reaching the top. Every time he looked up, they seemed to grow higher and higher as a feeling of vertigo crept over him. Under was also out of the question. Whilst the ground had felt a little soft in some parts of the Labyrinth so far, this area felt rock solid and impenetrable.

The trap seemed to be designed around attacking it head on. So through seemed to be the only choice. But how would they traverse the arrows? If all the slits produced arrows then it was a hell of a lot of danger to avoid. That's if they all produced arrows. They could well have different dangers hidden within each slit.

Heracles glanced at the others. They were all in deep thought also, none more so than Selene. Heracles could almost hear her brain whirring. Surprisingly though, it was Apollo who stepped up first with his thoughts on the trap.

"So. We've got maybe ten slits either side spanning this slim corridor. I doubt up and over will be possible," he said, slamming his foot on the floor, coming to the same conclusion that Heracles had about the ground. "The floor is rock hard. So *through* is our course. Do we think it's possible to draw the arrows out somehow? Send down a decoy that sets everything off and then we hurry behind it?"

Not a bad idea Heracles thought. There was the question of whether the source of the arrows was enchanted also and, as a result, limitless in their number. It was clearly a deterrent to stop anyone venturing further into the Labyrinth, so they must be on the right track direction wise.

Selene jumped into the discussion before Heracles could share his thoughts.

"Apollo, I have a theory. Can you send a wave of fire down the corridor? Sorry, I know you're new to your power but it looks like we can try a few things out from a safe distance, here."

Apollo nodded, scratched his chin, and mimed an upwards slash motion down the corridor with his arms. He thought about it further and then repeated the motion.

"Think I might have something for us. Worth a try." he said, stepping forward slightly, but not as far as Achilles was when he was tagged by the flurry of arrows. He steadied himself, taking a deep inwards breath. Heracles sensed that he was still somewhat sore from their armour training but he was composed now, and Heracles felt the determination radiating from him. And the heat of his powers.

He began.

CHAPTER VIII
TRIALS IN THE DEEP I: THE SUN

1

Apollo was nervous.

His mind was filled with flashbacks to his training with Heracles. His failure. He tried hard not to let it rest on his mind but he couldn't shift it. Selene, and to an extent Achilles, had been successful in their attempts and Apollo felt somewhat feeble by comparison. It had always been this way for him. Always second best. Always in the shadow of his sister. The golden child of the family. Miss Perfect.

He didn't hate his sister. Far from it. He thought of himself as a loving and compassionate person generally and really did love his sister dearly. But she had always been one step ahead of him in everything. Always. And it was *hard* to love her. She was not the nicest of people.

He knew he shouldn't dwell on these feelings, so insignificant in the grand scheme of things, but he had tried over the years to drop them without any success. Every time he thought he was past it, he would hear news from his step-mother and father about Artemis' accomplishments. Her triumphs in her endeavours, whether it was over-achieving in her school studies, in sports, or during her time at The Alliance as she climbed ever higher through the ranks. Her crowning achievement was becoming a member of the fabled Stratigos.

Something not even his parents thought she would reach, even with all their faith in her abilities and intelligence.

Their thoughts about Apollo differed vastly. Apollo felt as if nothing he achieved in life would ever measure up to their stratospheric standards. That he was never enough. That they didn't even see him.

He had told no one about this over the years of course. In other's eyes he was the brother to Artemis. The great Artemis. They must've assumed he was happy and content with that.

He wasn't.

He didn't crave adoration. Or fame. Or fortune. Far from it. He only wanted to be noticed by those he cared for. And for all his efforts, they simply didn't reciprocate. His parents only had eyes for Artemis, and Artemis only had eyes for success. It was why he had hidden his family ties when attempting The Alliance's entry trials. It may have helped if those marking knew about his sister. It may have hindered. But he couldn't face the questioning again. The comparisons between him and his sister.

The test before him was one he must pass. One he must assist his new found friends with. To show them his worth, and to be noticed by them. During their short time together, Apollo had grown to enjoy their company. He felt something between them. He couldn't explain it but he felt a connection. A bond. And he would do anything to keep that. He already felt welcome in the group, especially so by Heracles, but wondered how long it would last. His confidence in people, and himself, had never been high.

But he would prove his worth right here and now.

Apollo surveyed the scene before him. Can't go over. Can't go under. Only through. What was he missing? What was the trick to it all? There was always a trick. Some sort of gimmick or failsafe to traps.

When they were younger, Artemis would always

set traps for him. He would fall for them time and time again. They called her The Huntress for a reason. She was master of the bow, and a master hunter. But he would only fall for the same trap once. He learned from his mistakes. His failures.

What could he liken this trap to? What did he feel was its weaknesses?

The slits in the walls might be able to be blocked somehow, but with what? There was nothing around him. No major debris, only small stones crumbled from the walls of the Labyrinth, lying on the floor.

No, that wasn't the solution.

Could he use his new found powers somehow? He hadn't tried them out much of course barring the armour training, having only received them recently, but the best kind of training was practical and he could always try a few things out whilst in this truly awful place.

As his thoughts weaved, his mind wandered to the conversation happening around him, and Selene's analysis of the situation. She addressed him directly, just as he was focussing entirely on them.

"Apollo, I have a theory. Can you send a wave of fire down the corridor? Sorry, I know you're new to your power like most of us but we can try as much as we want."

She was on the same wavelength as him. That was refreshing and reassuring for him. It was nice to know that she was having the same thought processes given her clear intellect and analytical skills.

"Think I might have something for us…"

Apollo thought he might be able to somehow trigger the arrows and test their number by sending a run of fire directly down the centre of the corridor. He touched his sword and fire instantly burned through him. He had felt somehow buoyed by his new found powers since he received them. They spread through him like a forest fire, filling him with the confidence he had always sorely lacked. They had filled out his body somewhat as well, a nice perk, and he generally felt stronger. If he could have more faith in himself, perhaps he could conquer this power and master it, in time.

He concentrated, feeling the heat move into his chest, before spreading equally down both arms. As he did, the fire became visible on the outside of his body, concentrated and burning red hot.

Apollo swung his arms forward, one after the other, hurtling two lines of fire down the centre of the corridor, slicing the air vertically like fiery razor sharp blades. As they traversed the small space, they activated the traps. Swift arrows darted out of each of the slits in the walls in turn, activating as the fire went past their range. As the arrows hit Apollo's flames, they fizzled out and only escaped the other side as they passed through in small puffs of dust. The arrows were thankfully not invincible but they were seemingly endless; continuing to shoot out from the walls after the fire had passed, only halting after a few seconds of inactivity around them.

Apollo smiled. This was still good. His power was the right choice to get them through this first test of their group, and he was secretly overjoyed, the tiny smile on his face hiding the sheer amount of joy rising inside of him. He might well be able to help the team here.

He bellowed the fire once more, this time much closer to each wall, and closed his eyes firmly shut. He concentrated. Focussed. His mind filled with fire at the moment of focus and he imagined the fire before him; stationary now, blowing slightly in the wind periodically rushing through the Labyrinth. As he slowly opened his eyes, the fire remained stationary still, blocking the path of the arrows on either side and creating a pathway of fire down the corridor, allowing passage through. The arrows continued to fire continuously, but they were unable to penetrate the fire Apollo had cast.

Apollo spun round quickly to the others and beckoned them forward. "I won't be able to hold this for long! We need to go!"

The others were off in a flash, knowing that there was no time for acknowledgments for now. Apollo was already straining to keep the fire stationary in place and it surely showed across his face. His powers were new to him, and the sheer fact that he had been able to pull this off this time was dumb, blind luck. He knew that. And he would hone his powers as he pushed forward, but for now he was content with the service he was providing.

As Achilles ran past him, at the end of the group, Apollo turned and sprinted forward. As he moved, the fire behind him dissipated in sequence; his concentration breaking under the force of control he had exerted.

He picked up the pace, following behind Achilles and growing ever more worried that the fire might evaporate completely and render the others in grave danger. The fire was ebbing, and as Apollo looked behind him, the arrows filled the corridor in a black blur, crossing paths with one another and completely obscuring where they had run from.

Fortunately, Theseus had made it to the other side now, followed by Selene in quick succession. The fire was closing in behind him, but he felt that as long as the others could make it through he would be happy with that. He kept his concentration as well as he could, his body aching under the pressure of maintaining the stationary fire, weaving, and waning against the walls of the corridor.

He could hold it for only a moment longer.

Heracles passed through. And finally Achilles, his head glancing back at Apollo now. He halted, leaned forward, and put out an outstretched arm, clearly seeing the fatigue on Apollo's face. Apollo desperately reached for it as the first arrows hit his legs now, the fire vanishing instantly around him.

Apollo grabbed Achilles hand and he felt the strength of his compatriot drag his body through the air and out of imminent danger. At the same time, Apollo felt hot piercing metal hit his lower body, puncturing him in several places. He hit the floor with a hard thud, just to the left of Achilles; Achilles facing the corridor now, having pulled back hard and landed onto his backside, much like he had done at the start of the corridor.

Apollo raised himself up slightly and tilted his head back to look. The arrows were no more but there was a crimson mist of blood in the space Apollo had just vacated, mixing seamlessly with the settling dust hanging in the air.

2

Apollo glanced down to find two small circular holes through the calf in his left leg, and two holes through the thigh in his right leg. His lower half was badly slashed from several other arrows which had narrowly missed going through his body. His legs were torn, and red. Apollo could feel a different fire running through his lower half; one of pain, but he pushed it out of his mind. He turned back to face the others, who were approaching him now. They were all safe. He was thankful for that. He didn't care about the state he was in. His primary concern was their safety. Heracles had trusted him and invited him along on this journey. The least he could do was help keep him alive and see him succeed in his quest.

Achilles was kneeling beside him now, helping him to a sitting position and being overly careful of his legs.

"'Pollo mate, that was brilliant. You got us through that. But your legs…"

Apollo looked up at him, projecting a smile on his face to quell any concern he might have about him.

"It's fine Achilles, honestly. I'm fine. I'll be alright. I am just glad everyone is ok."

Heracles patted him on the back as Selene was surveying his legs, a look of concern strewn across her face.

Heracles looked him up and down.

"Apollo, well done. That was hugely brave. Thanks for getting us through." Heracles diverted his gaze to Apollo's legs and Selene hovered her hands over the wounds. Apollo could feel the calm transfer to him slightly, and the pain eased somewhat.

"Can you walk do you think?" Heracles said.

Apollo raised his right leg and placed it on the ground, whipping his body up into a crouched position. The pain came searing back, worse than before. He grimaced but continued raising his body until he was standing, with Heracles and Achilles either side of him helping him up.

The pain was excruciating but he attempted to hide it from the others.

"I'm ok to continue. I'll be a sitting duck here if the Minotaur happens upon us, and we need to push forward. If I slow you down then continue on ahead of me."

"That's not going to happen," Achilles said, forceful with his words. "You're with us 'til the end 'Pollo. We go on together."

"Achilles is right, we'll help you all the way." Theseus was kinder in his approach to Apollo but stern enough to drop any thought of Apollo falling behind.

Selene reached into her bag and drew out a spare top she had with her. She ripped the sleeves off of each side and then again ripped them into thin strips. She dropped down to Apollo's legs and went to bandage them up. Apollo halted her with a soft hand.

"Bear with me a second."

Apollo radiated fire in his hand. The fire bloomed into a circle in his palm. He ran the hand over each of the wounds in turn and, at the first, let out a stifled yell through gritted teeth. The pain was the worst yet. But as he moved to the next, the fire had done its job, cauterising the wound, and stopping the flow of blood. He continued through all of the wounds, growling intensely at each one. At the final one he let out a heavy, heavy breath. But the worst was done. He motioned kindly to Selene for her to bandage up the wounds and hopefully keep them closed.

Apollo noticed Theseus moving in his peripheral. He turned to him to see him pacing the end of the corridor. Left and right. Checking which way they should go next. The walls of the corridor were still high, unendingly so, and Apollo had a sinking suspicion they would be unable to use Selene's birds eye view from here on out. It was down to them to decide and back their decision on which route to follow. The magic of the Labyrinth that Theseus mentioned perhaps.

As he finished his thought, the Minotaur's roar echoed back at them, much shriller and fiercer than any shout Apollo had produced. It was much louder than before, and that didn't bode well. The Minotaur was closer, and more ferocious in its call. It must've heard Apollo's anguish. Careless of him, he thinks about himself.

One test down, but Apollo feared that, in his weakened state, it paled in comparison to that of the Minotaur. The trial had succeeded in its intended purpose, he thought.

It had weakened the group.

CHAPTER VIII
TRIALS IN THE DEEP II: THE MOON

1

Selene stood up as the roar of the Minotaur echoed around them. The sound was deep, and cut through Selene's whole body, vibrating her very core. She hated that sound. It filled her with a great deal of fear. The fake Minotaur, roaring at them, as its head sat atop the door leading into the Labyrinth, she could handle. But the real thing was astronomically worse. The danger was very real now, and she was ill prepared, and sick to her stomach.

She had only been in The Alliance for a day when everything had started to unravel.

Confidence had never been a problem for her growing up. She was always confident in herself and her strengths: whether it was her keen intellect, that others had praised many times; or her calm in any given situation. She prided herself on her ability to remain focussed at all times, before analysing and acting accordingly. Those were her strengths as she knew them from a young age. Playing to them was also a skill. Using them. Honing them. It was ultimately what had gained her a place in The Alliance and helped her to begin her training.

But then the first day had unravelled everything.

Everything was seemingly going well, at first. She had drawn an incredible weapon. One that filled her with even more calm and confidence. One that filled her with a serene quality, like a calm ocean breeze rushing against her face; her body awash with warm, light waves of water washing over her skin. It was infectious and she could feel others around her benefitting from her power. It was perfect for her, complementing her persona.

That had made her smile, if only inwardly. Although she possessed all the confidence in the world, she remained stoic through it all, afraid to show emotion to anyone. She had been burned too many times before. She had been close to friends in the past and they had simply tossed her aside when they had felt like it. It had hurt her, deeply and she thought beyond repair, and even though she felt close to this group now after such a short time, she wouldn't allow herself to tread that path again. They would leave her behind. Everyone always did.

Then the attack had happened. She had remained calm and composed, as she always did, analysing the situation and helping those around her. But even as she did so, people continued to die. She couldn't help anyone. She also couldn't help herself. Those attacking The Alliance that day were clearly far more trained than she, and she felt it instantly. Her new powers were untrained. She used them little during that defence, using her base fighting skills instead. She didn't know *how* to use them in a way that would help those around her yet. Her greatest shame.

Then she had the misfortune to come face to face with a foe that she had no hope of defeating.

She knew it instantly. She could feel their aura. The capability to kill in an instant, and it had shaken her to her core, much like the Minotaur's cries did. She was willing to put everything into fighting them but after a single moment, it was over. They had flashed towards her with unparalleled speed, their hooded clothes obscuring them entirety, and slashed her to ribbons. But they hadn't killed her. The other hooded figure had stopped them from doing so, even as all of her new companions fell to their deaths around her. It felt like the other assailant had taken pity on her.

And then she had found out that it was Hermes who had crippled her so. One of The Alliance's very own Stratigos. And that it was Heracles' brother that had stopped Hermes from killing her. She couldn't bring herself to tell Heracles that. A shame gripping her tightly at her failure to protect any of those around her. And for being spared above the others.

Following that, she had continued with a façade. A fake confidence. She had, for the first time in her life, felt no real faith in herself. She had felt somewhat empty.

That was until Heracles stepped forward towards her and showed her how to draw out her armour.

She had felt his *spirit* as he showed her how it was done. It was radiant. Exceptionally bright and welcoming. A confidence lay there that even Heracles probably wasn't aware of. Selene felt his heart and it filled her with her own confidence again. He, who had told them stories of all the hardships he had experienced in his life up until that point. He, who was ostracised from The Alliance he loved deeply. He, who was venturing out on a quest that would surely cause him untold pain and expose him to innumerable dangers, and would've done so alone had Apollo, Achilles and she not accompanied him.

She felt drawn towards him, and to the mission they were now embarking on. She would do anything to help him in his quest.

She had donned her armour first time as a result, seemingly able to copy Heracles' movement completely. She couldn't vocalise properly to those around her at the time, but it had felt like her power had taken over her, guiding her in achieving her goal, and she felt Heracles' had brought that quality to the surface. Come what may, she would help Heracles succeed at all costs.

She drew her mind back to the present. Theseus was looking upwards at the walls and noting their height now. Selene thought that she wouldn't be able to hop up there for a better view anymore. That would make everything a damn sight harder in this dark pit of despair, and Selene feared the Minotaur was edging ever closer to their position. They would have to be quick footed now and continue on against the alchemy at play within the Labyrinth.

"We need to move. That Minotaur sounds a damn sight closer than he was a few hours ago, and we can ill afford to be caught off guard against it, especially with Apollo injured." She offered the group.

Heracles nodded at her. It filled her with even more strength.

"Agreed. We need to get moving. Selene, any suggestions on left or right from your memory of the Labyrinth's layout?"

She considered for a moment. From her last memory they were edging left somewhat, so they would need to edge right again to get the route on track for the centre of the Labyrinth. It would be tricky to calculate but she believed in herself again now and her ability to recall the rough route. The picture of the labyrinth, much as the picture of her armour before drawing it out had been, rested in her mind.

"Leave it to me. We head right from here."

She set off, and the others followed. Apollo was in the middle of the pack and as Selene glanced at him, she could see his pain. But he was ploughing forward regardless, surprisingly quick footed for someone with his injuries. He was tough, but where he was readily able to express his emotions, she knew Apollo didn't have confidence in himself or his abilities. Selene recognised this in him immediately, where she had felt the same loss of confidence in herself recently.

Theseus broke her train of thought as he shouted beside Apollo. "Be ready for any further traps as you go. We don't know what else the Labyrinth will throw at us from here on in. I doubt it's finished playing with us."

"I'm on it!" she called back at him.

She didn't know anything about this Theseus character. He seemed charming enough, and had felt herself blush on occasion when he spoke, and he was driven in his goal, but Selene was still slightly untrustworthy of him at this stage for some unknown reason. It was good to be standoffish of new people she thought. And even though she was growing in trust for Apollo and Achilles already, she was still apprehensive. That was in her nature, given her past rejections, and Theseus would need to prove himself worthy of her trust. As Heracles had worked hard to do.

They were travelling faster than before now. That was good. They couldn't stay in here forever. The quicker they could get in, get what they came for, and get back out again the better. The Labyrinth had a strange feeling about it. One that was moving inside the atmosphere. Scheming. Dark. Dank.

They ran around corner after corner. Selene tracking the movement and route to the centre of the Labyrinth in her mind. She couldn't be completely sure they were heading the right course but she believed they were from the picture firmly painted in her mind still. The walls around them remained high now so a look from above was still out of the question. Her belief was confirmed when they came flying around a corner and she screeched to a halt at the sight before her. She turned to the others as she stopped and shouted for them to stop also. Had she not done so; she could've careened over the cavern stretching out ahead of her.

The room before them was as wide as it was long. It was the largest room they had come across so far. But it had no floor whatsoever. Nothing but a seemingly endless pit lay before them. One that was expelling no air whatsoever, and one that held the haunting presence of death. The air felt heavy to the touch.

Selene's mind was suddenly filled with dark thoughts. Thoughts of jumping head first into the pit. Ending it all. Here and now. She simply couldn't shake the thoughts from her mind. They were warming to her now. She was calmed by the thought of jumping. The thought of having peace. Thoughts of her past came rushing into her mind. Friends deserting her. Her father being too busy with work to pay her any attention. The Alliance shunning her, much as they had done Heracles. All of the bad things in her life flashed before her eyes, but for some reason they felt many miles away, of no harm to her now. It was amazingly comforting. The pit called for her, for her to join them in the darkness below. The pit would keep her safe. Safe from any more pain and rejection.

Selene moved her foot forward to walk over the edge towards her now welcomed death.

2

She was grabbed by the hand and pulled back forcefully, her left leg swinging over the chasm and off the ground before she caught her footing again.

She fell into a pair of arms and came to her senses. She looked up and saw Heracles. She was toppled over onto him from the force of him pulling her back. His face full of concern. His voice soft but powerful.

"What the hell are you doing Selene? You could've been killed!" he said to her, his face a picture of concern.

She mumbled a reply and then cleared her throat, replying properly.

"I...sorry...my mind was telling me to do it.

To…jump in. I'm ok now. Sorry."

Heracles scooped her up off of him and stood them both up, and away from the edge.

"I can sense something here as well. Something dark. Evil. It's the Labyrinth trying to manipulate us. It seems like the traps here aren't only going to be physical."

Selene had almost lost herself in that moment. Almost given in to the cavernous pit before them. Driven herself forward and right over the edge before her. She could feel it feeding on any self-doubt inside of her. Hungry for it. Drawing it out of her and down into the dark depths, now unsatisfied with its latest meal.

Selene approached the end, this time waving off Heracles who was keeping a close eye on her, and peered into the darkness. She could feel the others watching her from behind and mumbling some thoughts on how they would get across. Selene ignored them and placed her hand on her sword. She drew it slowly from its sheath, holding the sword by the handle with both hands, the blade now facing down towards the pit.

She closed her eyes and focussed her mind. She could feel a power bubbling away, speaking to her that this was the right way to progress. A voice the polar opposite of the one she had heard emanating from the pit. This was the voice of her weapon. And of her heart. All of her surroundings melted away as she concentrated deeply. She was in complete control of her mind and had blocked out all other sounds, all other thoughts. Her sword's power resonated through her completely, filling her with calm and confidence.

She imagined herself stood in a circular room. Stone walls ran around the outside, closing her in. Protecting her. She stood in the middle of the room. Above her was the light of the moon, streaming down from the open roof and surrounding her. Filling her. Emanating around her fully. She felt warm, light. Filled with a purpose and a drive that she had been slightly lacking as she first happened upon the pit. She felt as if she could accomplish anything.

She also felt the pit reach out to her. Coaxing her to step out and down to her death once more. Goading her. Telling her she was worthless. That she would never have anyone close to her, no one to love. She would die alone in the pit, and no one would care or mourn her. It was a harsher voice than it had been previous. Totally desperate now in its address.

"Why don't you join us down here? It's warm and full of new friends for you. We'll protect you Selene. Jump. We'll catch you."

This time was different. Selene heard the attacks of the pit but let them float away on the wind, picturing a dark mass attacking her bubble of solitude and bouncing off furiously. Blocking all the thoughts from entering and messing with her way of thinking. She was confident and focussed. And ready.

She heard protests as she stepped forward, but rather than falling to her inevitable death, her foot landed on something solid. A wafer thin silver disk had appeared before her, solid under her foot and floating in the air above the pit, stopping her from falling forward and down into the dark. She felt the pit cry in anguish. Beaten. She had sensed that the way to beat this task was to overwhelm it with positivity and confidence. Beat it at its' own game and push forward with no fear. No doubts.

She opened her eyes and called back to the others.

"Have no fear, no doubts in your mind! It's what the darkness wants. It craves it. Is fuelled by it. Clear your minds!"

She extended the range of the circle in her mind. She felt Heracles enter, followed by Theseus and then finally Apollo and Achilles. She would protect them. Keep them confident. Keep them calm.

She could feel some hesitation from Apollo. She reached out her mind to his and projected her calm, feeling him accept it willingly and watching him step forward along with her. They moved as a team, and as they moved, the same silver circular disk appeared under all of their feet as they walked, mirroring their steps, and providing a platform to walk safely upon. Before they knew it, they were safely over the other side.

Theseus was looking dumbfounded over to the darkness they had just traversed.

"Wha...? How did you do that?" Theseus enquired.

"I…just felt it. Much as I imagine you did Apollo on the first task we faced. I felt that this was a test for me if that makes any sense."

The others were thanking her in turn. Selene turned to Apollo who was last to thank her. She lowered her voice to him alone.

"Apollo. I felt your thoughts just now. You have nothing to fear. We're in this together. We can give each other the confidence to succeed."

Apollo looked initially taken aback but then smiled sweetly. He nodded in solidarity to her whilst remaining silent, recognising that he was not quite there yet, but that he would try. And that was enough for Selene. She felt comforted in the knowledge that she had company in her thoughts and fears.

Heracles stepped forward towards Selene.

"Those powers of yours…are you understanding them more? What they can do?"

Selene pondered this for a second, her mind filling with a small explanation to assist her.

"Medusa called me the Moon, didn't she? I feel like this power involves some sort of mirroring, created by the gleam of the moonlight. Projecting images into my mind, helping me to copy techniques or retain information. Seems like I can create these disks of moonlight that are solid enough to walk on, and that I can project calm on to myself and others. I don't truly understand it all but I will continue to test it Heracles. Might be useful for defence perhaps, but I really don't know yet."

"It's a hell of a start though Selene. You have our thanks." Heracles was warm to her, and she bathed in it.

Heracles then called to the others.

"We need to move forward now everyone. We may well have cracked the back of this gods damned Labyrinth, but there is the biggest test still to come."

He paused, looking between each of them. Selene could feel his leadership qualities shining brightly before her. She felt instantly empowered by him.

"Keep aware. Be ready. Let's go."

CHAPTER VIII
TRIALS IN THE DEEP III: THE BLADE

1

Achilles was pissed off.

All it took for him to reach this level of annoyance lately was a tiny push. He had been so angry. So frustrated.

He was feeling more and more annoyed at himself for accepting this mission and taking himself away from The Alliance. He was going places. He knew he could've made something for himself back at HQ. Climbed the ranks. Becoming better than his father ever was. He felt it deep within his core. But now he was stuck and lost in this goddamned Labyrinth with this gaggle of outcasts. It infuriated him. Had he stayed at The Alliance, he would've had the chance of being a star.

He knew what he is capable of. He just hadn't had the chance to showcase it yet. Selene and Apollo, who he did hold a liking for, had jumped at the chance to stand out in this team: Apollo with his show of fire control back at that goddamned arrow corridor; and Selene with her calm and cool head in that giant cavern situation they found themselves in a few hours ago.

They had taken a *lot* of turns since then, with Selene still at the front of the group and directing everyone, and it had left Achilles with time to think. Time to stew. Why had they acted in those situations and why had he not. He felt himself wanting to but he had acted slower than both of them and before he knew it, they were taking things into their own hands. Grabbing the situation by the scruff of its neck and wrestling it into their favour.

It sat on Achilles' mind now. He had been silent since they left the cavernous pit, ignoring any conversation. It was petty, sure, but he knew he was the best fighter here. *He* knew that. *They* knew that. He was a proud individual and he had taken a knock to that pride now. A chink in his shining armour. It was bad enough that Selene had managed to succeed in her armour training much quicker than him. At least he had the satisfaction of Apollo failing. He *hated* feeling that way towards Apollo but it just served to confirm his own superiority over him. There was no shame in Apollo accepting that. Understanding that. But he seemingly didn't.

"Achilles…"

He also couldn't shake the darkness he had felt following the last room. And he didn't really feel like that at all did he? He didn't hate any of them, did he? He felt so conflicted in himself.

The vast black vacuum had reached out to him. Engaged with him. Filled his mind with dark, terrible thoughts. Showed him visions of blood. Visions of injury. Visions of death. His mind had embraced it fully and that worried him. His anger and his pride he could handle, but those dark thoughts were taking him to a dark place. He had welcomed them at the time. Until Selene had used her calming influence to wash the thoughts away of course. For a short while. Which had pissed him off even more.

He felt the darkness held a grip over him in that moment, and that was the most worrying thing about this whole situation. Not the fact the others were seemingly unaware of his greatness and potential. Or the fact that he hadn't been able to demonstrate that yet. It was the ease at which his heart had opened up to the darkness. Had almost grabbed at it, yearning for its power and influence. Was every thought he was thinking now drenched in the darkness of the labyrinth? Clouding and filling his mind? Did he really *feel* any of the thoughts he had been having over the recent chunk of time?

He didn't know. And that was the most worrying thing of all.

"Achilles? ...Achilles?"

He felt an arm on his shoulder now. How long had it been there? Had he been so deep in his thoughts that he was completely unaware of its presence? He snapped back to reality and looked at the owner of the hand. It was Theseus. He had seemingly dropped off from the rest of the group to join him at the rear.

"You ok big man?" Theseus' asked him, his voice soft. Caring. It both warmed and sickened Achilles. His heart wrestling with the right feeling.

He grunted in response, then felt the innate need to properly address Theseus. His mind was so torn at that moment. The worry crept back into his mind.

"Yeah...thanks. I'm ok. Just wrestling with a few thoughts at the moment." Achilles sighed as he spoke.

'He looks to pity you.' the darkness said as it crept into his mind once more.

Theseus smiled at him. He seemed so comfortable with his feelings. He owned them. He was confident, yet cool. Sharp, yet open. Out of everyone he had met and interacted with over the last few days of his time inside and out of The Alliance, Theseus was the one he warmed to the quickest, even without much conversation or interaction. Achilles was jealous of the way he held himself. His manner. And it only made him like him more. Achilles felt that Theseus appreciated his strength and potential somehow. Maybe as somebody who wasn't apparently as strong himself on the surface, he could see and appreciate Achilles' strength.

"I know how you feel Achilles. This place...it's filled with darkness. And I don't just mean aesthetically. I feel a horrid presence radiating all around this place. I hear whispers on the wind that blows steadily through the corridors. Murmurs from around corners. Thoughts congesting my mind," Theseus paused. "It's eating me up."

Achilles felt a twang of thanks run through his body. So it wasn't just him struggling with the pull of the dark. He liked Theseus more in that moment.

"Appreciate you saying that Theseus. I...I've been having thoughts in the dark also. Unpleasant ones. It's really messing with me at the moment."

Theseus raised his arm and slapped Achilles on the back, holding his hand in place for a moment as he spoke.

"You're not alone here. We'll keep an eye on each other. Deal?"

Achilles felt another light, warm feeling flood through him, letting himself force a smile. The dark thoughts he had been having washed away whilst he talked to Theseus. He felt somehow stronger in his presence. A weight lifted slightly from his shoulders.

"Agreed. I've got your back. I can handle anything this Labyrinth throws at me. Stick with me and you'll be fine."

Theseus showed a slight expression on his face at the last part. Maybe Achilles' tone was slightly condescending but Achilles ignored it and moved forward with Theseus, picking up their pace somewhat to catch up with the others. Selene was slowing now somewhat in front of them. Second guessing herself perhaps, Achilles thought.

She stopped completely as they turned a corner and happened upon yet another choice, but this time the Labyrinth split into several directions. One directly forward, one to the left and one to the right. She was darting her head towards all options as she analysed.

Achilles felt the heat rise up in him again at her leading the group.

He stepped forward in his frustration.

"Time's up Selene. We're going left."

Selene moved to question Achilles and he waved her off. It was his time now.

"The more time we spend in here, the more tired we'll get. We need to make some quick decisions. I feel good about turning left. Trust me ok?"

He was off and running at a canter before anyone could even respond to his question.

2

He hardly heard the objections of the others as he moved and didn't much care if they followed him. Before he knew it, he was out of earshot and moving quickly down the corridors, following the flow of the Labyrinth, skating round corners, and ploughing forward. The darkness crept into his mind again, telling him what a good job he was doing with the directions. What a good decision he had made.

As he neared the end of the corridor he was in, an almighty gust of wind, much stronger than the others, dashed through the Labyrinth and hit him hard, holding him in place slightly as it passed. His clothes fought against the gust as it hit him. As he cleared his eyes of the dust contained within the wind, he saw several bits of debris on the floor that had appeared towards the end of the corridor, just before the next turn. He headed towards them, and as he bent down for closer inspection, he saw what they were.

Bones.

Brutally cracked and disconnected bones, with bits of flesh still clinging to the surface, the rest having been apparently torn clean off. A small run of them had scattered across the hallway. He couldn't make out what the bones were from as he twisted and turned one in his hands.

'Bones? Down here?' he thought to himself, confused as to the fresh flesh also.

A thought popped into Achilles' mind as he rose to his feet. A smell hit his nose and he instantly knew what was ahead of him.

"The minotaur has been given food." he said aloud as he darted forward. He turned the corner and entered the next room, swiftly surveying the scene. The room was as wide as it was long. It was a surprisingly large room, and Achilles understood the concentration of the wind and its strength in that moment, given the tiny corridor it had to escape into from the room.

The room was edged with light, with fiery torches sat neatly in golden holders in numerous places on all four walls, adding a flickering light to the room, and casting small shadows on the places the light couldn't quite touch.

With the aid of the light, Achilles could see that the room was filled with bones and carcasses. Some somewhat fresh, some seemingly there for a long period of time, withering and decaying in piles scattered around the room, and on the floor, in random order. He could see clothing draped on many of the carcasses. Ripped and shredded. Tattered remains, pounded into the dust of the floor. The bodies seemed to have been either pierced or slashed.

Right at the back of the room crouched a hulking great figure, towering over a pile of remains. Achilles could hear the teeth crash against the bone, gnawing and grinding away, whilst snarls escaped its mouth as it ate. Its back was mighty. Dark brown hair lined the tops of its shoulders and continued in an arch down the middle of its back, halting around its midriff. A blood red sash circled its waist, and a layer of cloth hung down, swaying against the top of the floor like a poorly constructed brush, thankfully covering the great beasts' arse from Achilles' view. Its crouched legs were powerful looking bulls' legs, the same dark brown hair covering them, thick and mangled with blood and small bits of flesh. The torso was of a gigantic man, and the legs were that of a beast. A blood curdling combination.

To the floor on the beasts' right was the biggest axe Achilles had ever seen: a giant silver axe head, with mightily sharp looking edges, rested on a thick brown handle.

Its head was crunched over the prey it was devouring, and Achilles' view of it was disrupted, but he felt he would be seeing it soon.

Surely enough, his wish was granted as he took a further step into the room, when the beast turned its head slowly to see who had disturbed it. A shadow grew over the side of its face as it moved, but Achilles could see it for what it was. A mighty bulls' head, much like the one sat upon the door into the Labyrinth, but seeing it first hand was something of a new and haunting experience. Its horns jutted from either side, with thick bone at the base before narrowing slightly into the tip which curled upwards. They both looked razor sharp. Its nose was clipped with a large golden ring which sat just above its top lip. The rows of its teeth were clearly visible as its jaw hung open, breathing heavily into the air, drool hanging lazily out of the corner of its mouth. Its endlessly muscular chest was layered with thick grizzly hair.

Achilles gathered himself. Shaking the fear from his legs and making them move forward slowly. He drew his sword from its sheath as the beast continued to slowly rotate round. Its nose bellowed hot white smoke into the air as its rage clearly escalated.

The dark voice crept into his mind once more. *'Face the beast alone'* it said. *'You have the strength to fell it with ease'.*

He sent his sword into the sky and called forth his armour instantly. He found it much easier in that moment, having nearly drawn it before when training with Heracles. The adrenaline from the situation he faced grew inside of him. Fuelling him. He stood tall and ready for the beast.

The Minotaur turned fully around and with its mighty tree trunk arms on its knees, pushed itself up to full height. The Minotaur towered over Achilles, and casted a dark shadow around him, but he did not waver.

This was his moment. And his moment alone.

The beast raised its arms to either side, threw back its jaw and roared deeply into the musty air of the Labyrinth. The wind that escalated from its surroundings was powerful. It flooded the floor of the room, moving bones and bits of body though the air with ease as they landed around Achilles, skidding across the dusty floor.

"SO YOU HAVE COME! EXCELLENT. THE BODIES SENT DOWN HERE BY THAT FOOL SYSYPHUS FILL MY EMPTY STOMACH BUT DO NOT QUENCH MY THIRST FOR BLOOD."

The Minotaur paused, its beady red eyes focussed solely on Achilles now.

"WILL YOU PROVIDE ME CHALLENGE, *BOY*?"

3

Achilles felt the anger burn inside of him, rising up and out into his response.

"Will you give *me* a challenge, beast!?"

The Minotaur threw back his head and laughed. The laugh was deep and rough, full of both hatred and joy at the same time. Achilles, tired of the standoff, lowered himself and darted at the Minotaur, launching himself into the air with his sword outstretched: his armour blaring against the reflection of torch flames littered around the room. He blocked all other thoughts and sounds from his mind. The dark voices remained but he pushed them aside. This was his moment, and his alone. He would kill this beast where it stood. This would be his greatest moment.

Achilles came face to face with the beast. Their eyes locked in perpetual intensity in that moment.

The beast swept its right arm up to its face to block Achilles as he attacked, clearly sensing Achilles' target trajectory. Achilles slashed with all of his might and the sword cut down into the Minotaur's right arm an inch deep before it stopped dead. Achilles pulled it swiftly from the arm, slicing neatly backwards out of the fur. Blood spirted in an arch out of the beast, and splashed against Achilles' face. He felt the warmth against his skin. The blood stank, but he remained focussed. The Minotaur released a furious roar, more powerful and incensed than the last and the scream resonated through Achilles core, vibrating his bones.

It swiped at Achilles, its arms wide and muscular. It was surprisingly swift for something so large and Achilles struggled to move out of the way in time, as he ducked and rolled across the ground in a forward roll, quickly flipping round and back onto his feet as he moved to safety.

However, the beast was on him again in a flash, flailing now but in a methodical way. Achilles dodged left and right and under the blows, the beasts' boulder sized fists wailing and pounding into the ground as they narrowly missed their target. The beast grew ever more infuriated as Achilles managed to land several gashes on to the beast's body. The Minotaur's blood, now sat on Achilles's sword, splattered lightly against the dust, and mixed in with it in spirals around them as they fought.

The Minotaur finally caught a hold of Achilles as a dark thought clouded his judgement, and it batted him away with a huge force, Achilles crashing to the floor with a thump and sliding in the dust away from the beast. He watched as it turned, and swooped low to gather its mighty axe. It glistened against the torch light in the room and was magnificently silver. Glaringly so. The beast clutched the wooden handle fiercely and turned once again to Achilles.

"LET'S SEE HOW YOU DO NOW, BOY." It said, goading him. Achilles felt his body heat rise in anger at the pure gall of this god dammed *cow*. The darkness taunted him again. *'He is winning Achilles. He is beating you.'*

The Minotaur seemed unmoved by its wounds. Achilles had put a lot of strength behind the strikes he had landed, and even though he had landed some good hits and damaged the beast somewhat, its body held firm. The beasts' hide was tough like leather, and it was draining Achilles quickly in his attempts to pierce the thick, rough skin.

Achilles considered his options as the beast slowly walked towards him. Analysing the beast with every motion it made. Assessing what its weaknesses might be.

He heard the cries of his compatriots from behind him then. Some muffled nonsense about him stopping as they arrived upon the scene. He didn't hear them. This was it. He thought he could beat the Minotaur for speed now after clashing with it several times. He needed to go for the chest, avoiding the arms as he went, and plunge his sword right into its heart. It was a large enough target. The Minotaur's chest looked to be the most exposed area, open to an attack.

He needed to see what power this sword held. The others had drawn their powers to the surface under pressure and whilst theirs were obvious to see, Achilles was unsure of his, having never witnessed his father in battle. He regretted not making Heracles aware of that earlier. He felt stronger since drawing it, but not exponentially so as he fought the Minotaur. But there must be a hidden power he was not drawing out yet. He didn't need Heracles to figure it all out. He didn't need anyone. He would find that power here and now, in this next and final strike. He would prove his worth to everyone around him and make them rue the day they ever doubted his strength.

The darkness fell over his sight once more, and he struggled to push it away. He placed all of his strength into his legs and propelled himself forward through the air. His body low to the ground and flying towards the Minotaur with a powerful leap, his sword held in both hands in front of him.

The Minotaur's right arm swiped at him sluggishly, slower than he had been now he held the heavy axe in his hand. Achilles dodged under it easily and propelled himself upwards towards its chest. His blade closing in on its target. He felt his pride rise. His triumphant moment closing in.

The blade pierced the skin a fraction before he felt the weight of a building slam against his right side, knocking every last bit of breath out of him, sending him crashing to the ground and ripping his left arm to shreds, the magical armour fading instantly around him. Had it over stretched its use? Had he used it for too long a period? His mind muddled, the pain excruciating, and his eyes focussed on the Minotaur a moment before it landed on top of him, the axe digging into the ground to the left of his neck and the handle of the axe resting heavily against his wind pipe.

Both his arms were pinned under the weight of the beast. It breathed heavily against his face. Its stench was unbearable, its breath rancid, as it breathed deeply against him.

The mouth of the beast curled into a smile.

"THE GAME" it snarled into Achilles clenched face, getting closer and closer to him, as he fought in vain against the beast' grasp, "IS OVER, BOY."

A lump of warm drool dripped into Achilles eyes, blinding him momentarily, his arms unable to move to wipe it clear. His throat constricted under the weight of the axe.

This was it.

He had been foolish. He realised that now, and far too late. The dark voices had left his mind of course, and he realised he had been played like a fool; goaded into all of this by the Labyrinth's dark mystical magic. Persuaded to fight the beast alone, when he was not ready to do so. Typical. Another failure to add to the list. But at least this time he wouldn't have to live long enough to see the judging faces. The looks of disappointment. Those around him would simply forget all about him. The boy pretending to be a man. The one man army who couldn't even defeat a lone beast. Pathetic. He would die here, and they would carry on without him.

At this thought, he suddenly realised that his throat was free. He felt the breath of the beast move away from him quickly, Achilles' eyes still closed shut under the thick and heavy drool.

The beast was drawing back to attack, he thought to himself. It must be. One final drop of the beasts' powerful axe and it would all be over. He hoped it would be quick. He couldn't stand the thought of his body being torn apart by the very beast he was convinced he would defeat alone. He imagined his decapitated head bounce across the floor and the beast laughing at the sight.

He waited expectantly. But nothing came.

He realised in that moment that the weight of the monster was no longer upon him, his body only feeling a shadow of the former weight. He drew his arms swiftly up to eyes, and rubbed the drool off, flicking it neatly to the side of him.

Before him was the Minotaur, a few paces away from him, standing tall and immeasurably mad. He was bellowing. His rage streaming from his pores in a hot mist. A sword was wedged into the side of his neck. Deep. Blood strained from the wound and seeped down the

Minotaur's chest, knotting its fur further.

It was Theseus's sword. It was stuck hard and fast as the Minotaur tried to yank it from its body. It bellowed again. Pure frustration and fury escaped its jaws as it was unable to remove the blade. As the Minotaur removed its hand from Theseus' sword, and as Achilles' eyes adjusted from removing the drool, he now saw Theseus himself, clutched in the left arm of the Minotaur with its heavy fist curled around the majority of his body. He was somewhat limp, the life being drained from him as the fist clenched around him still, the rage undoubtedly pulsating through the Minotaur's blood.

As Theseus's head bobbed back, Achilles could see an almighty gash running from the middle of his forehead down to the top of his mouth. His left eye was completely gone, covered in a congealing dark red blood.

CHAPTER VIII
TRIALS IN THE DEEP IV: THE LION

1

Heracles watched as Achilles drove at the beast. He heard Selene cry from behind him, Apollo close behind with a shout of his own. Both imploring him to stop. To come back and regroup. He heard none of it. Or he chose to ignore their cries of anguish.

Heracles noticed several gashes on the beast, including a nasty slice to its arm, and several on its torso, sticky and wet with fresh blood. Achilles had clearly been able to damage it slightly on his own. Impressive. But the beast's hide looked to be exceedingly thick. And the fact that Achilles sword could only do this amount of damage was worrying to Heracles.

Achilles was fast, dodging under one of the beast's muscular arms and driving forward towards the beast's chest. He was clearly strong.

But the Minotaur was stronger. As Achilles was about to drive his sword into the heart of the Minotaur, Heracles saw a wry smile run across the beasts' face as it's arm batted Achilles away with ease. The thing was surprisingly swift for its size. It moved with grace: years of trawling the Labyrinth no doubt leaving it with untold strength in those bulls' legs of his.

It all happened so fast.

The Minotaur was on top of Achilles in and instant. Its mouth gaping as it boomed at Achilles. Taunting him. Telling him it was all over. It was going for the kill: its axe weighing heavily against Achilles' neck, slowly crushing his ability to breathe,

Heracles dropped his weight into his legs, but before he could move, he sensed a flash beside him. It was Theseus, flying through the air now. He was indeed swift, as he had told him before they entered this stinking cesspit. His grandfather's sword was outstretched in front of him, and he made no sound in his movement. Swift and quiet.

He crashed into the beast, the sheer force of his speed, and the trajectory into its top half, ensuring he was able to topple it over and off Achilles' somewhat limp body. He had wedged his grandfather's sword deep into the Minotaur's neck, but the beast was back up and wailing at him promptly, filled with pure hatred for Theseus now.

Something was wrong. As Theseus was rolling around, trying to dodge the creature's mighty swings, his speed was stifled by both his hands being up to against his face. The beast caught him as a result, crashing down upon him and slamming him hard into the dirt. Theseus tried to rise to his feet but Heracles now saw what troubled him. A large gash ran down one side of his face, over and through his left eye, which was seemingly anything but an eye now. Blood was pouring from him, but still he attempted to stand. The beast had caught him straight and true.

He was sluggish in his movement and the beast caught him again as he tried to dive at his grandfather's sword, the blood clearly rushing from Theseus's head and clouding his judgement and clarity. One of the beast's horns was caked in blood, seemingly the cause of Theseus's anguish.

Heracles motioned to Selene and Apollo, Selene

with her armour donned now, to move to Achilles and check he was ok. Heracles sensed death in the air, and with his armour also firmly surrounding his body now, he made his move.

2

Heracles needed to relay some strategy to the others despite the grave and disadvantaged situation before them.

He would need all the help he could get from Apollo, Selene, and that damned fool Achilles. They needed to end this fight as quickly as they could, before they sustained even greater injuries. The longer they fought, the more fatigued they would become and the Minotaur looked to have tired little in the time it had fought both Achilles and Theseus. It only grew in rage and strength. With Apollo's injuries from the arrows, Achilles' wounds from his lone initial fight with the Minotaur, and with Theseus missing an eye now, they were in declining strength as a team.

Achilles had been an absolute fool. He had not only abandoned the others to push on alone but had also engaged with the very beast they had been wary of the entire time they had been in this catacomb. His pride had not only been his own downfall, but it had also now cost Theseus dearly and, most likely, permanently.

Heracles shook his head, for now ridding his mind of Achilles and his recent actions. He needed to get Theseus out of the clutches of the beast, and fast. He scooped low, placing the edge of his blade against the dirt before quickly dragging it forwards in an upwards arc. Electricity crackled and shot along the ground towards the Minotaur, running along the dirt like a lit path of spilled alcohol. Heracles was conscious of hurting Theseus but felt the best way to halt any momentum of the beast was to connect his electricity with it quickly, aiming primarily for its legs.

The Minotaur turned its head in time to find the bolt just reaching its leg. Heracles' lightning was too fast for it. It struck him, and it was clear when the bolt was running through the beast's body as its whole being tensed up instantly, straightening its body upwards. Theseus let out a cry as the beast's hand tightened around him but then its grip sprang open, dropping Theseus heavily to the floor.

The Minotaur turned on Heracles instantly as the current dissipated from its body, its red eyes glaring. The current having only a momentary effect on the beast, seemingly not penetrating enough into its bodily current.

"Apollo! Head for the next corridor with Theseus and Selene! Achilles, with me!" Heracles said towards the team. They needed to restrict its movement, its mighty swings, and stomps, as much as they could. The corridor would allow them to flank it from either side. The others needed to get behind the beast so that Heracles and Achilles could drive it into the confined space as best they could.

Apollo nodded and ran towards Theseus, now a balled up wreck on the floor, scooped him up and ran towards the corridor with Selene, glancing backwards constantly as he went. The beast's focus was solely on Heracles now. That was good. Achilles joined Heracles at his side, and Heracles turned to him, dropping the pleasantries from his words.

"Follow *my* lead." Heracles said sternly. Achilles nodded sheepishly, remaining silent.

The beast took one step closer, moving into a stance of a charging bull before them, and roared powerfully.

"NO MATTER HOW MANY OF YOU ANTS THERE ARE, I WILL CRUSH AND KILL YOU *ALL.*"

Its rage was building to its peak. That was good

for them. The more the beast inside clouded the human's clarity, the more they could manipulate it. Heracles lowered his voice to Achilles as the beast continued to roar and stomp its right leg against the ground, running it across the floor in deep cuts into the dirt.

"Drive it back towards Apollo. We're going to pincer it in the corridor and hit it with everything we've got."

Achilles nodded, shaking off any fear he was holding onto, before shooting his sword upwards towards the sky. His armour came to him, but his face showed that it was weakened considerably and that he would struggle to maintain it. Heracles doubted it would last long at all.

"When I've given it enough volts, drive it back as hard as you can Achilles. I'll try to keep the volts out of you but if you feel it, bear with it."

Achilles nodded back to Heracles as the beast roared a final time before driving its s axe into the ground, locking it in place, and ploughing forward towards them in a charge, its head lowered and its horns like spears before it. Heracles charged forward, Achilles right at his side.

Heracles ran his sword against the ground as he ran forwards, slicing upwards through the air again but this time continuing the movement and shooting multiple runs of electricity at the beast. Achilles jumped and landed hard on the ground as the beast was trying to dodge the bolts, sending a tremor through the earth, and knocking the beasts balance slightly. Clever, Heracles thought to himself as the bolts hit their target and the beast again tensed, its legs locked at the current running through its veins. All of the bolts made their mark and the current was far more effective than before, rendering the beast stalled in its motion.

As it fell forward, Achilles hit the beast's left arm and dug his sword into it, pushing with all his might, with the arm of the beast tucking tidily into its own chest as he drove forward. Heracles did the same on the right arm and kept the current flowing through the Minotaur. Heracles's blade dug deeper into the beast than Achilles' blade, having coated it in a thin white hot run of lightning, deathly sharp. He checked to see if Achilles was feeling the current, and he certainly seemed to be, but he was gritting through it, seemingly eager to atone for his previous actions.

As they pushed upwards and forward. The Minotaur edged backwards, sliding across the dusty floor. The beast was heavy, but with the two of them pushing they were able to get the beast slightly off balance and moving backwards. They heaved, and pushed outwards together, with the beast toppling backwards and into the corridor ahead of them, crashing to the floor on its backside and rumbling the earth beneath it.

"Apollo, create a wall around us!" Heracles called out, somewhat frantic in his instructions now but in control of the situation. In control and quelling any rage bubbling inside of him.

Apollo complied and conjured a ring of fire that sparked in a circle from either foot, hitting both walls beside himself and travelling to just behind Heracles and Achilles, where it met and closed. They were now trapped in together with the rampaging beast, hopefully to their advantage. The corridor was narrow and would restrict the beast's swings of its deadly axe.

Almost to confirm Heracles' thoughts, the beast went to let out a swing of its fists but the corridor blocked its movement and it clattered against the hard surface, catching the fire as it struck it. The Minotaur yelled in frustration, shaking its fists free of the fire that had caught on its fur.

"Apollo keep that guard up! Selene go for its legs! Achilles with me on its body!"

Heracles' imagined it would be all Apollo could do to keep this barrier up and prayed he could cope with the strain on his body with the wounds he had sustained.

Selene made her move, sliding through the dirt and slashing at the legs of the Minotaur. It buckled and kneeled on one leg, its bloodied calves dropping to the floor. Selene had also managed to cut deeper into the beasts hide, her sword emitting the blue hue of before, seemingly sharp to the touch.

Heracles and Achilles rushed in. Achilles's sword drove into the beast's chest, slightly left of his intended target of its heart. Heracles drove forward as it swung its arm down from above its head. He was caught slightly in the air, but managed to correct himself by grabbing Theseus' sword. Heracles tugged at it as he moved past, ripping the sword from its hold, and slicing a large chunk of skin and bone as he moved, blood oozing from the open wound now left in the beasts' neck. Heracles landed comfortably before wheeling around for another attack but his body tensed before he could move. His powers were drained more than he thought at the exertion of the past day.

The beast lowered its head, and bashed Selene out of the way hard against one of the walls, before charging at Achilles. Even after the onslaught, its injuries were either nothing to it or its rage and adrenaline were fuelling it beyond limitation.

Achilles was stranded in the corridor and all he could do was take the brunt of the attack, the Minotaur's horn driving into his shoulder and wedging there before shaking and smashing Achilles directly into and through the fire behind him, out of sight: his cries of pain muffled as he passed through Apollo's flames.

The beast turned on Heracles and he dodged well, avoiding multiple swipes from the beast. Both he and the beast were tiring now, and their speed was slowing. Much as the Minotaur could not go all out in this corridor, Heracles was in the same boat and his lightning powers were limited in this tight space. He had thought that between them, he, Achilles, and Selene could overpower the beast quickly and effectively and tire it, but he hadn't factored in the sheer endurance and intensity of the Minotaur, even with the gaping hole currently at its neck.

He needed to get close and touch the bull, to fill it with intense heat and light. It was a gamble but it was his only choice now without Achilles or Selene to back him up. He moved in closely and avoided several swipes of horn and fist to place his hand squarely onto the chest of the Minotaur. He put all of the power he had left into one final attack and summoned a fury of lightning into the beast's body. Light escaped from the beast's mouth as it roared upwards, and again from the gash in its neck, burning the edges and escaping white hot light. Both Heracles and the Minotaur were engulfed in a bolt of light descending from the sky above, the bolt aching and straining against the heat and power flooding through it.

Heracles felt the beast wane and weaken as the lightning scarred the area around them both and the smell of burning flesh hung in the air. The number of volts running through the beast was astronomical and no man could survive this much punishment. The beast was simply mythical in its power and endurance.

The Minotaur's eyes flashed open and its hand caught and clutched Heracles, the air slowly ebbing out of him as the Minotaur squeezed: despite the damage the lightning was doing to its body, content with dying together with Heracles and squeezing the life out him.

Heracles tried to call out to Apollo, desperate for help, but the grip around his body was paramount and trapped his voice in his throat. Dragging the air out of him, his face swelled and swam. Spots appeared before his eyes. His arms locked by his sides, he struggled with all his might but the lightning attack they were both engulfed within started to fade, the beast sapping his strength with its iron grip.

The lightning dissipated and Heracles looked at

the beast before him. The beasts flesh was burned and smoking from the previous attack, melted and bloody in several locations, and its hide was finally highly damaged. The gape in its neck grew ever bigger, and deeper. But still it stood. Still it fought.

The Minotaur towered over him, laughing maniacally and heavily panting, hot droll and blood dripping from his mouth onto Heracles' face, hungry from the fight. Heracles felt himself fading. The drooled blood continued to drip onto his face and he heard the distant crack of several of his ribs as they popped under the weight of the bull.

He faded once, before flooding back into reality, the grip slightly weakening against his body. The drool continued to drop. But this time it felt heavier. Hotter.

He managed to force his eyes open and saw the dumbfounded look on the face of the beast. Its eyes rolled back into its head and its body waned, rocking slightly back and forth in the corridor. Perched atop the beast's shoulders was Theseus, blood still streaming from his face and onto his clothes. His grandfather's blade embedded deep within the Minotaur's cranium.

The beasts' eyes lolled back into view momentarily and, as it let Heracles drop to the floor, it looked him dead in the eyes with pure understanding. Its eyes were both alive and dead all at once. It knew that this was the last sight it would see.

Theseus fell sideways off the beast, leaving the sword lodged firmly in its skull as he collapsed from his injuries. Heracles' mind swam again as he watched the beast falter and fall to its knees. Its eyes were now firmly closed, blood pooling around its face and covering it in a gruesome sea of red.

The last thing Heracles felt was being dragged backwards and away from the beast. The last thing he saw was the beast's body burst into red, hot flames.

And then he swam into darkness.

CHAPTER IX
ACHILLES' HEEL

1

Heracles was rocked gently awake. He opened his eyes sluggishly and saw Selene over him, flitting her eyes between his face and body, assumedly checking for any damage.

"I'm fine Selene, honestly." he assured her as he leaned over to one side to push his body up to a seated position. He repressed the urge he felt to vomit.

He rubbed his eyes heavily. He was absolutely exhausted in that moment. His ribs ached from the breaks, his body was damaged, his legs ached, and he was simply drained from the use of his powers in a live combat situation – one he had not had experience in at all.

He surveyed the scene before him. Selene was nodding and moving away from him now, standing up and walking over to Apollo, who was hovering over Theseus. He was sat on the dusty floor with his back against the corridor wall. He was slumped over, unconscious. Hopefully only unconscious, Heracles thought as a pang of worry shot through him. Heracles could only see one side of his face: the side of the face with the almighty wound delivered by the Minotaur. And in a lot of ways, Achilles. He could see that the wound had been cauterised by Apollo, as best he could, but there would undoubtedly be a terrible scar running down his face after all of this, and where his eye was completely gone, a life with half of his eyesight would be his to live. His boyish good looks would be forever marred by the curse of the Labyrinth.

Heracles moved his glance over to the other side of the corridor, and saw Achilles, his back also against one of the walls with his legs bunched up to his chest, his head slumped into the gap, hidden, and his arms tightly wound around his knees. Heracles felt torn. He knew that the boy was the cause of Theseus's injury, a simple truth he would need to carry with him for the rest of his life, but he was clearly hurting. He knew what he had done. Would that be punishment enough? Ultimately it was not Heracles' place to decide. Theseus would have to forgive him or not, and that would be the say on the matter. But if he found Achilles not learning from this grave mistake, he would bear down on him with the fury of the gods.

Heracles also knew the Labyrinth held a dark and deeply disturbing magic, and Achilles had seemed haunted and different somehow whilst in here. Clouded in some way.

Past the corridor, and back into the room Achilles had first engaged the beast, Heracles could see a large lump heaped on the floor: its large back pointing up to the sky, and its mighty bull head face down in the dirt. Its back was still smoking from Apollo's fire, Heracles last recollection of the events before passing out, and wisps of smoke were rising into the air before disappearing in the slight breeze endlessly flowing through the Labyrinth.

The Minotaur had been bested, lying dead and cold on the dusty floor. Even so, Heracles had an innate urge to go over and check the beast was definitely dead. He clambered to his feet, shook on them momentarily before catching his balance, and then moved forward. His body felt like it had been hit by a falling tree. He moved lazily at first, but his movement came back to him relatively quickly. That was good. They still had progress to make through the Labyrinth and he could ill afford to falter here.

He approached the beast. Cautiously. The fur on its back was mostly gone now. Only torrid scorch marks remained, hot and waxy against the beasts' back, some parts worse than others, but it showcased how thick the beasts' hide was. Even if Apollo had hit it with all the force of his fire, Heracles thought it would've been little help. The beast would've likely brushed it off without a second thought at Apollo's current level of skill and power, but where it was likely dying anyway, it had succumbed to the flames. The blade lodged into its head had clearly done the damage. Theseus hadn't retrieved it yet, most likely because he was currently unconscious. Its neck was also gruesome from where Heracles had ripped Theseus' sword clean out it from during the fight.

The sword looked stuck. Hard. Theseus had clearly driven it into the beasts' thick skull with all his might, and his grandfather's sword had held true. It had pierced right into the beasts' brain and ended its fury once and for all. Heracles felt that had Theseus not acted when he did, and he had no idea how he had mustered the strength in the state he was in, Heracles would've been lying on the floor himself. Cold and lifeless. He was hugely thankful to Theseus for that and felt their bond grow at the heroic act.

Apollo appeared by his side as he analysed the Minotaur's corpse.

"How's Theseus doing?" Heracles asked without looking at Apollo, curious of his saviour's state.

"He's...alive at least. His eye is gone. I've cauterised it as best I can, and thank the gods he was unconscious as I did so. Selene seems confident he'll live. She has calmed his breathing and he is stable. He has several broken ribs," Apollo looked to Heracles as he said this as he touched his own broken ribs carefully. "But we've done our best to pop things back in where we could. Selene knows her stuff."

Heracles nodded. Apollo would become a fine right hand man. The battle would do his confidence wonders once he got over the initial shock, and he was always learning and growing. Gleaning information where he could. It would serve him well, and Selene was quickly proving herself immeasurably crucial to the team.

"And you and Selene? Are you ok?"

"Mostly. We'll be fine, just beaten up. Fatigued. But we can finish," Apollo replied, his voice sure enough. "I think Selene was shaken by it all. The beast was mighty. My fire hardly touched it even when it was dying anyway. It was only when the beast fell that it finally took hold, and I let it burn the thing as long as I could to make sure it was definitely dead."

Heracles agreed wholeheartedly and was thankful they were both alright.

"And Achilles?" Heracles asked, trying to hide his anger at the kid.

Apollo stalled on his answer. He was clearly angry at Achilles for his actions also. Rightly so, Heracles thought to himself.

"He's fine. Looks like he heals quickly on the outside. Internally I'd imagine he's fighting a much fiercer battle."

"I'd imagine he is. Leave him fight," Heracles said before he caught himself. He could feel his blood slightly boiling over, and he quelled it quickly. "We'll give him time Apollo, that's what he needs. He knows what he has cost Theseus."

He looked at Achilles, still slumped in his ball against the wall.

"Leave it to me. For now, gather Selene and Theseus. I know we're suffering but we need to find this Lion's Hide and get the hell out of here. Make sure Theseus' thread is still trailing also…and you may need to carry him from here on out. Sorry. And take this."

Heracles placed his hand on the sword wedged deep into the skull of the Minotaur and wrenched at it. After a titanic effort it wrenched out of the beast, its head pulling upwards as it did so before falling back to the earth in a dull thud. Heracles handed the sword to Apollo who sighed slightly, in recognition rather than aggravation. Apollo turned on his heels and returned to Selene and Theseus, wiping the sword against his torn trousers as he did so to clean it somewhat.

Heracles drew his sword, remembering The Fates words now clearly forming in his mind. He couldn't remember the exact phrasing but words formed in his mind, nonetheless.

A willing sacrifice made to escape the Labyrinth.
Return the horns of the beast to The Fates.
Face them again when all items are gathered together.

The beasts head was mammoth and Heracles didn't think it was worth carrying the whole damn thing about with them, so thankfully The Fates had only requested the horns. Still, they were *big*. They would need to be carried by two people. One each. He went to work, cutting deeply around each of the horns and prying it from the Minotaur's thick skull. It was not easy but eventually he was able to pry them free. He dusted the creamy base of the horns on the floor and covered it in dust to mask the blood. The smell was atrocious.

He turned. His next task ahead of him. Heracles walked over to Achilles and kneeled beside him.

2

Heracles considered his next move carefully, silently crouching by Achilles for a moment before opening his mouth.

"Achilles." His voice was calm, holding back the contempt he sadly felt for the boy now. Achilles raised his head from his makeshift shelter and looked at Heracles. His eyes were red, irritated. The boy looked a shadow of his confident self: his self-belief whittled away. He was clearly hurting. Heracles's contempt faded as he remembered he was just a kid, albeit a brash and idiotic one.

"Achilles, I'll be brief as I know you're hurting. You've fucked up. You know that. The worst thing you could've done was abandon the team and you've now seen the cost. Theseus is forever affected by your actions."

Achilles didn't break his gaze with Heracles. He simply nodded in acceptance, his eyes watering slightly. It was an interesting sight, seeing this once bold and proud warrior reduced to a hunkered pile on the floor. Heracles rested his arm on his shoulder, his offering of an olive branch.

"Ultimately it's Theseus that decides your fate. I've said my piece, but for now, your team needs you as we finish this and get the hell out of this place. Do that, not for yourself, but for those who need you. Put your pride aside and join us. Let's finish this, together, Achilles."

Heracles said no more. He simply pushed against his knees, rose to his feet, and joined Selene and Apollo, with Theseus placed over his shoulder, who were now walking down the corridor.

Heracles didn't look back but he heard Achilles wait for a moment before rising to his feet and following closely behind them.

3

They didn't need to travel far to find what they were looking for.

As Heracles turned another corner, several after the corridor they had fought the Minotaur in, he found a series of brightly coloured gems and golden trinkets littering the floor in front of him – thrown along the floor as if they had been trudged through. The gems ranged in size and shape: some buried in the dust of the Labyrinth floor; others stacked on top of each other messily. Heracles dared not touch them. They were there for a singular prize only. He told the others the same. He, perhaps over cautiously, feared retribution should they take anything they didn't initially seek in the Labyrinth. They would only serve to weight them down anyway.

As if to confirm his suspicions that the items strewn across the floor had been trudged through and scattered, they turned into a hallway leading into what had to be the centre of the Labyrinth.

Before them lay a vast room, filled with pile after pile of wealth and wonder. The room was clearly the den of the Minotaur. The other room must've been where it feasted, with this being its place of rest. Heracles was still perplexed about what, or whom, the bones in the feasting area belonged to.

The room was well lit, much like the feeding room of the beast, with torches on all its walls. Towards the back of the room was a large throne that had been fashioned out of the pile of gold and jewels, wriggled into in the shape of the formidable beast.

The fates had mentioned the mass of other items that had been stored in here over the years but Heracles had been doubtful when they hadn't encountered anything else throughout the rest of the catacombs. He wasn't doubtful now. There was enough here to make any city in the land *the* formidable powerhouse of wealth. And it looked as if the Minotaur had hoarded it all into this one place, guarding it. Heracles had heard tales of mythical beasts coveting treasures: it seemed the Minotaur was not exempt from that trait.

"Sisyphus," Achilles said, breaking the silence in the room. Heracles turned to him, confused at the mention of the city's mayor. "The Minotaur mentioned something about Sisyphus sending people down into the Labyrinth to feed the beast when I first engaged w…". He stopped, remembering his past actions.

"Go on Achilles." Heracles encouraged, keen to hear where this was going.

"I don't know what it all means but Sisyphus somehow knows about this place. The Minotaur said that Sisyphus has been sending people down here to their death. The bones prove that. They were…human."

Heracles didn't want to accept it but he knew Achilles was right. The bones and carcasses had undoubtedly been human, and the scattered clothing was indeed proof of that. Heracles proposed that the Minotaur had been catching these 'guests' wherever they were in the Labyrinth, bringing them back to the feasting room. The rest of the Labyrinth hadn't had any bones or carcasses to speak of. It made some sense in Heracles' head as he ran through the facts over and over.

"If that's the case, then this Labyrinth is less of a secret than we thought. But it begs the question why Sisyphus hasn't tried to get at the wealth down here. Maybe he just thought it would be safe here if he ever needed it." Heracles said aloud.

"Or he wasn't able to get at it." Selene offered. She was right of course. This would become a piece of a bigger puzzle if Sisyphus was involved and actually sending people down here to feed the Minotaur. Maybe he was trying to soften the beast to himself, in order to get access to the treasures lying within the Labyrinth? There could be any number of possibilities. There may come a time when they would be able to confront him about it, but Heracles thought it mattered little currently.

"That's a worrying thought, but we need to focus on finding the Nemean Lion's hide now. Apollo, Achilles, split up and check as many piles as you can. I don't know exactly what the hide will look like but anything you find that you think might be the one, grab it and bring it over here."

He remembered his previous thought.

"But be *careful*. We don't know what traps there

might be, or whether we can mess with the other treasure, but I feel that as long as we are looking for the hide itself, we'll be safe. No grounds for that, just a feeling, so be careful."

"On it." Apollo offered Heracles. Achilles nodded in silence, reverting back to his quiet state. They both turned and pointed to where the other was heading, Achilles splitting off to search as Apollo placed Theseus on the ground softly by Selene, before heading off himself to search.

"Selene, I want you to keep trying to bring Theseus round please. You know your stuff, and I desperately need your help here."

Selene nodded in confirmation, and lowered herself to Theseus, attempting to bring him round. She then turned to Heracles with a smile on her face. "Thank you, Heracles, that really means a lot."

Heracles smiled back sweetly. "No, thank you. We make a great team." With that, Heracles turned back to the room.

Apollo was over to the left hand side of the room, digging deep into the piles and examining various items. Achilles was slowly ebbing away at a pile to his right. Leaving Heracles the middle, namely the area surrounding the throne of the beast. He approached it. Cautiously. The stench of the beast radiated in the air again as he closed in on it. The thick, dense smell of something that had been down here for untold years, steadily growing more beastly with every passing day. He lay his hand on the throne, and then forced his hand inside, grabbing at small golden idols, tiny jewels, large jewels. He pulled them out and dropped them on the ground behind him. The throne wavered as Heracles removed elements of its structure, before it folded and lost its shape. Heracles wondered how on earth the beast sat in the throne without it collapsing. Or perhaps, he pondered, it was just for show. A homage to the beast from itself.

The throne toppled, jewels and gold flowing over one another like a mini waterfall escaping down the side of a cliff. As they dispersed, a small bit of fur became visible to the left of the middle of the pile. Heracles considered it. He needed to be cautious but equally they couldn't leave this place without the hide of the Nemean Lion, so he gambled. He moved the jewels and gold aside with a flat hand, brushing at the pile in a circular motion. The fur started to display more of itself.

It was a wonderful blonde, bright in the torch light. Whatever beast it belonged to must have been magnificent to look at. Heracles felt a touch of wonder run through his body as he forced his hand towards the fur, a strange feeling pulsing through the air around him. His hand landed on the fur, and he grabbed a tight hold of it before pulling. The jewels flowed off the fur as it emerged, scattering on the floor around Heracles. He pulled it fully out of its hiding spot and held it aloft in front of him, much as he would were he admiring a winner's trophy.

This was it. He could feel it within both his heart and head. It was truly a special item. The fur was cut in a relatively jagged way. Whoever had managed to skin the hide of the beast this fur had belonged to did so at great struggle and difficulty. But they had managed it.

Heracles draped it over his right arm. The fur was smooth to the touch as Heracles ran his hand across it. As he did so, his fingers parted to allow the fur to brush against his fingers and for him to really enjoy the feel of the item. The long hair of the beast sat beautifully against the hide itself. If Heracles were to believe that this hide had been taken from a lion, it must've been the most legendary of beasts. He imagined whoever had fought it had been through a great and illustrious battle, and that this was the spoils of victory.

Shaking off his wonder, he moved to check the item was indeed what he thought it was. He hated the thought of doing what he was about to do, but he had to know for sure. Even if it wasn't the item they sought and he then ruined the wondrous hide beyond repair.

He lay the hide on the ground. Strangely the dust simply sat against the hide, not contaminating it, or covering it in any way. A strange phenomenon to behold. Heracles drew his sword and flashed a brilliant jolt around the edge of the blade. It enhanced it, giving it an extra edge of sharpness. His fatigue showed once more at drawing further power out of his sword, and he clenched slightly, but he continued, nonetheless. He had to know for sure. He placed his blade to the side of the hide, pressed down firmly and slashed across it in a swift movement. He knew the sharpness of his enhanced blade. Had seen it cut deep into that damn Minotaur. But as he examined the hide before him, there wasn't a single scratch. No cut hairs. No sign of damage whatsoever.

He tried again. And again. Slicing at the hide in several different directions and with great force. But to no avail. The hide before him was seemingly impenetrable. That confirmed it for Heracles. This was indeed the item of lore they had been searching for.

4

Heracles turned around and walked back to the others, who had no doubt stopped searching after witnessing Heracles slashing furiously at the item on the floor before him.

"There's not an ounce of doubt in my mind that this is the die we've been searching for."

Selene placed her hand onto the fur of the lion as it was draped over Heracles shoulder. Heracles noted how light the hide was as it sat on him. Light enough for him to easily forget it was there after prolonged wear, he thought to himself.

"It's so soft," She said. "It's magnificent."

Heracles agreed, it was indeed a magnificent thing. A special item. The first of three they must gather. This one had come at great cost already, and an almighty challenge lay ahead of them. Heracles thought that it would only get harder and more dangerous from here, but even still, the next obstacle they had to surmount was getting out of this hellhole.

"So, time to get out of here is it?" a gruff voice offered from the left of Heracles.

Heracles saw that Theseus was now sat up slightly as he looked past Selene. She had succeeded in rousing him, but he looked awful, pale, beaten, his eye hidden by a stretch of cloth that Selene had tied around his head. Heracles walked over to him and patted him on the back, softly.

"Welcome back. Good to have you with us still."

"Thanks for avoiding asking whether I am ok. I couldn't be doing with pity right now. I am sure I look absolutely top notch anyway." He winked as he said the last part of his sentence. A blink now Heracles guessed, before pushing the dark commentary from his mind. At least Theseus was in good spirits.

"Of course. We're just glad you've come to. Can you stand?"

"I think so. Only one way to find out."

Heracles helped Theseus to his feet. He stumbled slightly and then steadied himself, his legs still a little bit weak. His strength was clearly hugely sapped at this point, but Heracles felt his determination and knew he would walk out of here on his own come hell or high water.

Theseus drew his glance to Achilles, who was sheepishly watching him and Heracles in their exchange.

"Achilles. Come here." Theseus called out and Achilles, his manner definitely drained of his natural confidence, walked over to him.

Theseus stared at him at first through his remaining eye, saying nothing. Heracles was prepared to stop Theseus if he were to do something stupid. Even though he had every right to do so. He raised his hand, and Achilles flinched slightly as it came up from his waist. Instead of a clenched fist, as Heracles had expected given the circumstances, it was an outstretched hand, open at the palm.

Achilles was clearly surprised. He would've surely welcomed some retaliation from Theseus given his actions. But not this. Heracles felt the same. Theseus was clearly a bigger man than he.

Theseus shrugged. "Take it Achilles. It is what it is. There's nothing either of us can do about it now. Let's move forward. We killed that goddamned bull and have what we came for. We're all still kicking, and that's all that matters."

He wagged his hand slightly, inviting Achilles to take it again. He did so, and as they locked hands, Heracles saw the confidence rise back in Achilles. Forgiveness could be a powerful thing. Theseus had remarkably kept the team connected with that huge gesture and Heracles was thankful of that. Achilles would now have time to atone, and he had no doubt that he would do all in his power to do that following Theseus' gesture.

Apollo walked over to Theseus and handed him the ball of yarn he had been looking after for him.

"I believe this belongs to you Theseus. Good to have you back." Apollo's voice was kind. Heracles felt the team had maybe had doubts about Theseus at the start of all of this but felt it no more. The simple act of saving one's life could do wonders for trust. He had proved his strength of will.

Theseus thanked him in return. "It's time to get the hell out of here. Back the way we came, following this yarn closely. Let's hope it's held up."

Heracles nodded in agreement.

"Be prepared for anything. Let's get the hell out of here."

5

The five of them trudged back through the Labyrinth together. Their stamina waned, drained at the hard fought battle with the Minotaur and tests they had overcome in the dark. Even with their fatigue, the return journey to the door they entered in was still somewhat easier than their journey towards the centre of the Labyrinth. They knew what to expect now and the traps they had faced on their way here had seemingly stopped for some reason. Perhaps the Labyrinth knew it was bested and was granting them safe passage? Heracles hoped so. They could ill afford any more surprises.

They made it past the feeding room of the Minotaur, still walking carefully past the charred corpse of the beast, with Apollo kicking it again to make sure it was indeed dead. Its head sans horns, with both tucked messily in Heracles and Selene's packs,.

They made it past the room of despair, as Selene had so fondly named it, and found the floor present this time. Selene mentioned the voices she had heard again but only because they were no longer calling out to her, seemingly defeated. Achilles grunted at her mention of the voices, but he remained quiet still, not himself at all.

They were even able to traverse the arrow room with little effort, with the arrows no longer shooting perilously out of the slits in the walls. Apollo was highly cautious even then and was ready to act should he find any change in the dynamic of the corridor. But it didn't change.

Everything was quiet now. Still. An eerie silence ran through the Labyrinth, and even the breeze that had followed them throughout much of their journey inwards into the Labyrinth was gone now. Replaced with stagnant dust. It also felt darker, their small lamps the only light source for them now on their return journey.

The journey was still taxing on their bodies.

Theseus was not at anywhere near his best, and he often stumbled as he walked, with whoever was nearest to him at the time catching him or offering him some assistance. He was stubborn but in a kind way, taking any help he was offered, but only to a point. Selene seemed drained, her usual icy barbs few and far between. Achilles remained silent and Apollo was deep in thought, the damage to his legs painful now Heracles imagined, as his adrenaline ebbed.

Heracles felt their pain. It had been a daunting task, and the darkness of the Labyrinth only served to drain them further. He was physically and mentally drained having used his powers more in this time than he had ever done during his time at The Alliance. Mostly because training had to be reserved for the dead of night, when he was already tired from his day job. This had been a great test for all of them. And they had all come together to conquer it, even with Achilles's rash actions.

They turned the final corner, the thread getting bigger and bigger in Theseus hands as it coiled back into its original circular form. Where they expected to see the door they had entered into the Labyrinth from, they now only saw a flat wall. No opening. No markings. No exit.

"What the hell is this?" Selene said, worry in her voice. "Have we made a wrong turn?"

"Can't have. The thread is undamaged. It's led us all the way back here. This is definitely where we entered, but I can't tell you why there is no exit. The thread is still in the wall where the door used to be also." Theseus said, offering Selene little consolation.

He stepped forward and placed his hands on the door just above the thread, feeling for any signs of exit. He placed his head against it, likely feeling for any breeze but he shook his head in disbelief.

"Nothing." he said as he turned back to the others, shrugging in his usual fashion.

As he started to walk towards the others, a

booming voice rang out around them, seemingly from everywhere but also driving directly into Heracles's ears as it clattered around the walls of the Labyrinth, bounding, and echoing to monstrous effect. It was deafening.

"DENIED."

It was not the voice of the Minotaur. A new voice he had not heard before. Maybe it was the Labyrinth itself. The master of traps. The setter of tasks within the underground halls. The keeper of the treasure they sought. It seemed farfetched but Heracles had sensed a presence in here other than the Minotaur since they arrived, as if the Labyrinth were somehow alive.

"It's the same voice as the one I heard when I nearly stepped into the pit." Selene was quivering slightly as she talked and Heracles could hardly blame her. The voice was weighty, powerful, and apparently everywhere at once. It repeated itself, after no answer from the team was forthcoming, adding a slight change to its words.

"EXIT DENIED."

Heracles offered it up an answer in the form of a question.

"What do you want from us?" he shouted. He knew the answer of course. His mind wandered back to the conversation with The Fates, feeling like a lifetime ago now. He recalled the list he had running through his mind earlier.

A willing sacrifice made to escape the Labyrinth.
Return the horns of the beast to The Fates.
Face them again when all items are gathered together.

It was the moment he had feared. All that they had sacrificed to get here was not enough. Theseus' giving his eye would not be deemed a willing sacrifice it seemed, so Heracles assumed it didn't count towards anything that the Labyrinth wanted. It wished to wound them further still.

The Labyrinth merely repeated itself, as if confirming Heracles' trail of thought further.

"EXIT DENIED."

Heracles stepped forward to level with Theseus, who had halted on his return to the group and simply turned round to face the door. The door of course wasn't where the sound was coming from but it was as good an area as any to focus on.

"You seek a willing sacrifice from us, don't you?" Heracles calls out into the void.

Silence followed for a few seconds before the Labyrinth replied, this time with a simpler response. Heracles also felt a cackle echo around the single word.

"YES."

6

Heracles turned to the others. Apollo had a forlorn look on his face, already knowing what was coming. Achilles was slightly away from the group at the back, still solemn.

"The Fates spoke of a cost for each of the information they provided," Heracles explained to the group. "The first of which was Labyrinth requiring a 'willing sacrifice' made in order for us to be granted exit from its depths, as the voice is asking for now."

Heracles paused to gauge the look on the others' faces. They were listening intently. Fearless, even in light of the subject. Heracles was proud of all of them in that moment.

"The second cost was bringing The Fates the horns of the Minotaur. That we are at least halfway there with. Finally, the third cost was that I returned to them when we had gathered all fabled items into our possession to face them again."

He paused again, looking down at the dirt for a

second to gather himself and then looked back at all of them.

"Whatever we sacrifice, we have to hope it's enough."

Heracles addressed the Labyrinth once more.

"Labyrinth! Do you seek death as a toll?"

The Labyrinth was silent again, mulling over its response, before answering.

"DEATH IS TOO EASY A PRICE. WE SEEK THAT WHICH WILL LEAVE YOU INCOMPLETE. BROKEN. A SHADOW. LEAVING YOU WITH A HALF LIFE"

The Labyrinth boomed and was then silent once more. Heracles considered its response carefully, out loud so that the others could join in his thought process.

"My understanding is that the sacrifice needs to be of something one of us holds dear, something which will weaken us further, and permanently. I can feel the darkness of that voice. The evil. It wants us to leave this place less than when we entered. It wants a sacrifice for the Hide of the Nemean Lion."

As Heracles finished his thought, a heavy breeze suddenly rushed round the corner and brushed into and past them, as if to confirm Heracles' suspicions.

"So what are we to do here? How can we possibly decide who makes this sacrifice? And what sacrifice?" Selene asked the group, a look of dread upon her face.

"I want no arguments here. I will be the one to make the sacrifice." Heracles said sternly.

Apollo went to interrupt, and Heracles was firm with him.

"No Apollo, you know as well as I do why it has to be me. I will be the one to make the sacrifice. You have all sacrificed far too much already down here, and this is my burden to bear with the path Gaia has set me on. I am grateful to you all for joining me and I cannot ask this of any of you."

Theseus was calm, knowing that he wouldn't change Heracles' mind on this one.

"...What will you sacrifice?"

"That is what I need to decide. It needs to be something that will affect me in an immeasurable way. Weaken me permanently. I fear that my speed is what they want. Without it, I am weakened considerably. The way to that sacrifice is through my legs."

The other's went to protest once more and Heracles waved them away. They argued amongst themselves as Heracles tried to gain order.

"It's the only way," He said again, sterner still than before. "The Labyrinth requires a sacrifice. We need to get the hell out of here. Theseus, you have already sacrificed so much. Apollo, Selene, Achilles, you have your whole lives ahead of you and you need to go on with this mission, even if I...cannot."

Apollo was past him in a flash, fiery red flames whirling around both of his arms. He launched a huge blast at the wall before them. When he saw that the impact had caused no damage whatsoever, maybe just a slight scorch mark, he wildly fired fire at the wall in a fury.

Selene was behind him swiftly, her sword drawn. She pointed her sword at the wall and a beam of pure white escaped the tip and flew towards the wall, pouring to either side as it hit its mark. The two of them were desperate to stop the inevitable. It was admirable but the lack of damage caused to the wall was apparent.

The Labyrinth would have what it craved.

"No."

Heracles turned to his right to find Achilles addressing him, finally breaking his silence.

"What did you say Achilles?"

"I said *no*, Heracles."

Apollo and Selene had waned in their attacks, distressed at the lack of impact any of their attacks have had. They turned to hear Achilles addressing Heracles now, confusion on their faces.

"Achilles, what…" Heracles went to question Achilles but he was cut off swiftly.

"It shouldn't be you who makes the sacrifice. You're the leader here. You're the one Gaia chose for all of this. She clearly trusts you for the mission above all else. There is no way you cannot push forward at full strength. It cannot be you."

Achilles looked over to Theseus now, seemingly blocking out Heracles' arguments. Heracles stared at Achilles, taken aback by his interjection and unsure of himself in that moment, and he hesitated. A grave mistake.

"Theseus. I give this gladly after the pain I've caused you. The pride I held was too great. I am truly sorry what I have done to you."

He turned his face to Heracles, looked deeply at him, before then looking back at Theseus. "An eye for an eye."

He paused, taking a deep breath. Before Heracles could react, even given his great speed, Achilles had drawn his sword with his weaker left arm.

He held it out in front of him and sliced through his wrist, cutting his hand clean off with one fell swoop.

7

"Achilles!" Apollo and Selene called out simultaneously, rushing over to him as he fell to his knees, clutching his cleanly dismembered wrist into his left armpit.

Heracles stood in shock at what he had just witnessed. It was not often he was left completely off guard but this was one of those occasions. Everything seemed to go in slow motion now. Theseus remained static alongside Heracles. Apollo ignited a ring of fire in his hand, which sat an inch or so off the palm and flickered into life. He pressed it to Achilles's outstretched wrist. Achilles was deathly pale now. He was clearly in immeasurable pain but tried to keep his face as stoic as he could, trying desperately not to show his pain to them. He plainly had no regrets at his actions, however.

Heracles finally moved, Theseus moving beside him also and crouching beside Apollo, with Heracles standing by Selene a step away from them both so as to not crowd them.

"Achilles…why? We were square. I forgave you wholeheartedly. Why would you go so far?" Theseus said, his tone both questioning and kind. Angry but concerned.

Achilles's voice carried not a hint of weakness, or anything resembling someone who had just cut their own hand from their body.

"We were not square." Achilles whimpered, shaking from the pain. "You lost your eye, and with it half your sight. I couldn't live with what I had taken from you, no matter what you said. It would've eaten me up inside. I am so, so sorry for everything."

Tears fell from Achilles's eyes. He made no attempt to wipe them away, wearing them proudly upon his face.

"I always thought I was stronger on my own. Not needing the help of anyone else. Looking at your faces back there after fighting that goddamned Minotaur tells me I was a fool. I'll do whatever I can for you all from here on in. You have my word. With this, we can hopefully leave this place and never have to come back."

Theseus leaned forward to Achilles. He placed his hand on the right side of his face.

"Valour comes from how we respond to our mistakes Achilles. How we address our faults. Whilst I will never understand what you have just done here today, I am thankful to you with all my heart for your sacrifice."

Heracles watched as the two reconciled. Both less as people physically than when they entered, but now so much more. A darkness formed around Heracles now, shadows forming on his face. Several ripples of electricity jumped around his body, jagged and electric blue. Heracles looked upwards and shouted into the void. His rage paramount. Overflowing. Unable to contain it any longer.

"Are you happy Labyrinth!? Are you satisfied? He's just a kid!"

This time the Labyrinth boomed back instantly, with a truly sadistic laugh. Heracles saw Selene shiver slightly in his peripheral view. Heracles' rage intensified. If this wasn't enough to grant them exit from this festering pit of a place then he was going to truly lose control of himself and throw everything he had at the walls of the Labyrinth. He feared the white light forming in front of his eyes and losing himself in his rage. Heracles had felt that the team had had the run of luck until this moment in time, but now two of his team were irrevocably injured.

Heracles was about to explode against the Labyrinth when the laughter quelled. It addressed the group of five.

"YOUR PAYMENT IS MADE. LEAVE NOW AND NEVER RETURN."

The door the five of them entered the Labyrinth through appeared before them, fading back into existence, before coming to life and scraping slowly open. Air entered the Labyrinth in a gust as the door creaked and groaned. The ball of thread fell from the door as it opened. The panels of the door finally came to rest at either side, presenting them with their exit from the Labyrinth.

Heracles' rage subsided, but he still retained a level of high stress. He noticed the look of concern on the other's faces and ignored them. They had not seen him lose his cool before, and Heracles was mortified to have lost himself as he did, if only slightly, but Theseus and Achilles had sustained irrevocable damage in these halls, and Selene and Apollo had seen dangerous and haunting things that a rookie at The Alliance should never have to see. The anger Heracles held was for himself now, having subjected all four of them to this torment, for his own needs and for that of the mission.

In that moment, he decided that he would go on alone after ensuring their safe return to the city. It was the only way. He could not subject them to further pain no matter how much they had impressed him, all of them, down in the depths of this god damned Labyrinth. It was simply inhumane.

"Achilles," Heracles said softly as he crouched beside him. "I hate to do this, but can you go on?"

"Of course." Achilles replied without hesitation. Heracles sensed a change in him somehow. He supposed a decision such as slicing off your own hand to atone for causing pain to another would do that to anyone. He rose to his feet with the assistance of Apollo and readied himself, holding his sword loosely in his left hand to get used to its weight again.

Heracles looked round at all of them in turn. Their bodies were badly broken and bloodied, especially Achilles and Theseus. Their aura had diminished somewhat, their adrenaline the only thing carrying them through, but still they rallied. Heracles couldn't be prouder of all of them in that moment. They had tracked down the Hide of the Nemean Lion, surmounted the seemingly impossible task of traversing the Labyrinth and defeated the toughest foe they had all ever faced in the Minotaur. They were truly greats in Heracles' eyes.

It was time to leave.

Heracles beckoned them all forward, and the five complied, stepping through the same door they came in, as it closed with a groan behind them.

8

Heracles considered resting in the room they had trained in before entering the Labyrinth, before moving the thought from his mind. He needed to get the team back to the city, drop Theseus off back in Minos and then allow Apollo, Selene, and Achilles their passage back to The Alliance.

Heracles felt truly awful for Achilles, after his sacrifice. He would need to work harder than ever to even get back to close to where he was, let alone progress through the ranks of the Alliance as he had planned. His talent and potential was knocked immeasurably. It was all Heracles could do to get him back to The Alliance and into their care. The resilience he had seen from the kid told him that he would learn to use that sword in his left arm. And he would get past this, after a long road to recovery.

They pushed forward and exited out into the world. Time was lost to them in the Labyrinth and as they exited out it was night-time around them, much as when they had entered. Heracles felt they may well have spent two days down in that stinking hell hole. No wonder they were so exhausted, having only slept a rough sleep once during their time down there. The fact they had managed that feat in, seemingly, a day or two was remarkable and a credit to them all.

"The moon is fuller. Looks like we were down there for two nights at least." Selene said as if to confirm Heracles' train of thought, albeit with a much more thoughtful process.

Two days. Confirmation of the exhaustion they all felt. They were in desperate need of some rest and treatment.

"Let's get back to Minos, we can rest then before we head out again." Apollo said, moving forward towards the entrance back into the city and motioning to the others to follow. They did so. Heracles noted his leadership qualities once more. He was a hugely likeable ally.

Heracles didn't mention his new plan of the return of Selene, Apollo, and Achilles to The Alliance. He would wait for Theseus' return to his home before sending them all back to The Alliance to rest, regroup and report back to Gaia before he set out into the world to continue the mission alone.

9

One by one they shuffled through the stone entrance and back into the city. They were all exhausted but Heracles felt the feeling of togetherness radiating throughout the group, empowering them. It ran through them like a calming wind.

Get to Minos and rest, Heracles thought to himself. He could then think about next steps after that. He needed his strength back, and the others even more so. He had never faced a challenge quite like the labyrinth before but at least he had been trained well by The Alliance, and by Prometheus. But the others? Their bodies had all received untold stress, and their minds would be wailing. It would take them a few days to get over the bodily damage but the mind can take some time to heal still. This would be the making or breaking of them all.

They rounded the corner of the Minos training camp, sighting the entrance into the alleyways of Minos.

Heracles couldn't wait to get out into the world and not have to hear the word Labyrinth again for some time. He was sick of it now after a childhood spent in Minos and several days in the Labyrinth below the city. It was enough for anyone to be sick of the word.

They made their way across the courtyard, Heracles leading the group, and deep in his own thoughts as usual. The entrance to Minos grew closer and closer. Theseus tried to throw some life into his tired and beaten body by offering up some good thoughts.

"We are so close I can almost feel the warmth of my bed. It calls to me!"

He motioned his hands in an exaggerated movement.

"Oh bed! How I have missed you!"

The others chuckled. Heracles felt somewhat sad in that moment that he would have to leave his old friend again. But it was for the best. He could never bring back his eyesight but he had helped him avenge his grandfather and that was hopefully enough. It must be an overwhelmingly emotional time for Theseus now, and he had earned his rest.

Apollo mimed himself stepping into an upright bed and whipping the covers over himself, a look of smug glee on his face as he rolled side to side in the air.

Selene laughed heartily as she walked. She also mimed a large yawn, and then snored loudly. Even Achilles, in his broken state, laughed. The bond between them was growing with each passing moment. Heracles again thought it would be a shame to lose it but needs must.

As they all chuckled to each other, a cloud of dust abruptly swirled on the ground ahead of them as they neared the entrance to Minos. The dust raised off of the floor slightly and grew out from a small circle to one much larger. Heracles halted the others with an outstretched arm as he spotted it.

Instantly, three cylinders of smoke shot down out of the air, slamming into the dusty ground. The smoke dispersed and three hooded figures now stood before the weary adventurers.

The central hooded figure lifted back its hood and cackled. The most beautiful person Heracles had ever seen stood before them, almost glowing in the moonlight above her.

"Is this a bad time?" she asked nonchalantly.

10

Heracles placed his hand to his sword and lowered his body slightly in preparation. This was bad. They were in no shape to engage with anyone in a fight, let along members of Tartarus, judging by their robes.

The figure before him continued to cackle, her long silvery hair waving in the wind caused by their appearance. She brushed the hair out of her face as it caught against her nose. She looked older than Heracles, her hair suggesting so, and her eyes had a cold hard stare even with her cackling mouth wagging continuously.

"My, my. What a gaggle of giggling pricks we have gathered here. Weaklings. You all look like you've been through the ringer. I assume we've caught you at the worst possible time. Quite the coincidence, don't you think?"

She was no longer cackling. Her forehead had dipped forward and her eyes sparkled a fantastic blood red.

"We *really* don't have the time nor the patience for this. You three are a part of Tartarus I presume?" Heracles's voice was strong in that moment, even with the great dread he felt throughout his body, and his prevailing injuries.

The look on the face of the figure before them deepened.

"Tut, tut. So impatient. Just like your brother."

Heracles anger rose again, his blood boiling far quicker than usual. "Cut the foreplay. Who are you and what do you want with us?"

She cackled again.

"He's got a mouth on him this one," she said as she motioned to the hooded figures either side of her.

"Hades *will* be pleased. Now then Heracles. We can be civil with *you* at least." She winked, one of her deep red eyes blinking in and out of view.

"We are indeed Tartarus, and you can call me Eros. I have a lovely little nickname, as all the Generals of Tartarus have, that you can call me if you prefer. 'Desire'."

She was all smiles again now, her mood switching from deathly serious, to humorous, and back in an instant. She turned to the person standing to her right. They nodded and pulled back their hood.

Heracles recognised the person before him immediately, having spoken to him on many an occasion and hearing everything about him from Demeter over the years. Anyone from The Alliance would recognise the once aspiring Stratigos, turned newly revealed traitor. His pitch black hair swept from his forehead over the top of his head, sitting neatly at the nape of his neck, as always. His handsome face darker now, perhaps some guilt remaining from his betrayal perhaps, but Heracles doubted it. It was more likely that he was now showing his true face. One that even over the course of a few days, had the look of wickedness about it now.

Heracles blood continued to boil. He was fighting back the urge to fly forward and rip that fucking smirk right from his face. The rage he felt in the Labyrinth not quelled it seemed.

"Nyx, you conniving *bastard*." Heracles said.

Nyx continued to silently smirk at Heracles. He never was one for words and now, more than ever, it infuriated Heracles. He was about to address him again when the person to the left of Eros removed his hood also. A full set of traitors lay before them. Heracles was at tipping point now with his anger bubbling ferociously.

"And Pontus..."

"Heracles. Nice to see you too."

The fake easy going persona of Pontus ran through now, the façade continuing even after his revelation as a traitor. Ever the perfect candidate for the Stratigos. Ever the golden boy. The strongest person outside of the Stratigos and the likeliest of candidates for the promotion before the attack on The Alliance. His short, clipped hair looked almost black in the moonlight, hiding the dark blue hue it actually had. His face was far brighter than Nyx, almost gleeful in seeing those before him.

Heracles, through gritted teeth, addressed them both, turning his head slowly between them and ignoring Eros for now. She didn't seem to mind, her smile showing that she was enjoying the exchange of words.

"You two have got a *lot* of nerve showing your faces here." Heracles growled at them.

"Are you not enjoying our little reunion Heracles? I'm surprised they let someone of *your* rank out of The Alliance. I would've loved to have seen Demeter on your little mission instead. Watching her die by my hands would be quite the thrill."

Heracles stalled, Pontus' words hitting him like an arrow to his chest. They knew of the mission. And the death threat on Demeter had pushed Heracles to his tipping point.

Eros, seeing his distress, pounced.

"Oh? You didn't think we'd come here by chance, did you? How idiotic. We come to you at your most vulnerable. It's called strategy. Did they not teach you that at that precious Alliance of yours?"

She cackled again. It cut Heracles like a hot knife through butter.

"Now, to business. We've come for whatever item it is you've found in the Labyrinth. Sisyphus was kind enough to tell us all about it after some…persuasion," She mimed her thumb running across her neck from right to left in a slicing motion. "Hades would very much like that item for himself, and we are tasked with delivering it to him."

That name again. Hades. Heracles didn't recall ever hearing it before, but it may prove an insight into the hierarchy of Tartarus, but he was done with talking. He had had enough in that moment. His anger tipped over into a boiling rage, his sword drawn in an instant. He felt his strength flood back to him, the rage fuelling him. Feeding him. His body was very much moving on his own now, but the white mist had not descended over his eyes fully yet. That was good. He retained some control of his actions even with his rage paramount.

He had to finish this quickly. The others were in no condition to fight and if the rage encompassed him, it could endanger the others.

He disappeared from sight, a small circle of dirt flickering from where he once stood. He reappeared again behind Nyx, and before he could act and spin round fully, a flash of blood sprayed from his chest and upwards into the air. Nyx fell to once knee in shock, clutching his chest heavily, his hand dropping to his sword. Heracles saw it all in slow motion. He turned and sliced the sheath of the sword, and as it dropped lazily to the floor before Heracles, he kicked it away from them both. All before the bastard could move more than a few inches.

Heracles felt a pang in his lower back as he moved, the exertion of this speed after all his body had faced paining him beyond belief, but he needed to protect the others now. Or they would all die here.

Heracles was gone again, as he watched Pontus turn to Nyx as he crumbled. Eros' remained stationary.

He rounded behind Pontus and appeared back to back with him. Their backs touched for an instant, and Heracles whispered to Pontus as the blood spurted in a diagonal angle from the right side of his chest. Pontus had been able to move slightly out of the way of the full attack, and Heracles was impressed with his speed of movement even as his body slowed and he leaned forward to hold the gash in his chest. He was no match for Heracles' speed but he could ill afford Pontus to draw his sword. He feared his powers hugely.

Heracles turned to Eros, her gaze still forward, looking over at the others still. He disappeared again, desperate to finish this off before his body collapsed from the strain.

He appeared point blank in front of her and swiped his sword diagonally down upon her, with all of his speed and might. A thunderous bolt of lightning escaped his sword sideways in and arc as he met his target, the noise rumbling through the air magnificently, and cracking against her.

He could feel his sword stuck firmly. The light of the lightning faded, and his eyes cleared. Before him was Eros, an outstretched hand held aloft in front of her, holding Heracles sword with ease as it twitched and reverberated in her hand against the force Heracles was exerting. Her eyes fell upon Heracles. Blood red and thirsty. A wry grin spreading across her face.

Heracles suddenly felt all of his strength drain out of his body as he stared deep into those eyes. She rendered him completely motionless, held firmly in place by a single hand, and Heracles felt in that moment that she was way above his level.

She drew his sword towards herself further still, Heracles feeling her pull his face towards hers. She passed his face and stopped at his ear, whispering softly into it.

"You feel it don't you Heracles," she said, somewhat seductively. "Your wants, your needs fading. Your desires growing dim. That is my power you see. I can render you harmless. A fly caught in a spider's web. My desire far outstretches your own."

Heracles felt the tip of a blade slowly enter his stomach, piercing the skin and filling his belly with hot fresh pain.

Suddenly, all he saw around him was fiery light and Heracles was ripped back from Eros' grasp. Apollo was beside him now, tumbled on the floor from the weight of both Heracles and his force of pull. Before them, stood tall, was Selene: her sword drawn in front of her and a brilliant glow around her, a beam of moonlight radiating from the moon above, filling her with strength.

"We need to get out of here!" Selene screamed at them all. "We're in no condition to fight here!"

Selene was right of course, but Heracles felt that Eros wouldn't let them leave without getting what she wanted, and even then, he felt the cold touch of death in the air. She wanted the item Heracles held in his pack, and their lives on top for good measure. She was stronger than all of them in their weakened state.

As he gathered his thoughts, a tide of water flew at Selene. She manoeuvred her arms in a flowing wave and the mighty tide of water crashed to halt against a white wall before her, splashing hard against the barrier. Pontus held his sword outstretched, controlling the water, and pushing Selene back. His nickname had been 'The Ocean' at The Alliance and for good reason. He could manipulate water at will: a gift from the Shield of Aegis and Medusa. Whilst he could multiply and manipulate water, Heracles had heard tell he couldn't create it. Water was escaping from underneath his cloak, perhaps hiding several containers of water underneath.

Eros appeared to one side of the wall of light, which was now struggling against the weight of Pontus' attack, and approached Selene. Selene's legs continued to wobble where she stood against the pressure of Pontus' power. Heracles had no idea how Selene was halting the water before them but it was saving them all, and Heracles felt her sword's power in that moment and recorded the moonlight in his mind.

Heracles noticed Nyx sluggishly getting back to his feet, aiming to gather his sword.

Apollo drove at Eros as she approached Selene, with his sword outstretched in front of him now, flames bursting from his sword in a sharp arch above the edge of the blade and down to the handle. Eros smirked again and drew her sword. Heracles only just caught it with his eye before Apollo was flung back towards him, crashing into him on the ground once more.

In that moment, Selene buckled under the weight of the water and was herself thrown back, crashing against the dirt, before sliding to a halt, grazing the side of her body as she landed. She looked defeated in that moment, putting all of her power into stopping Pontus with her newly acquired powers. Apollo also looked exhausted, the use of his powers having drained him considerably, but still he tried to rally. Achilles was rising to his feet also, clutching his sword shakily in his left hand, trying desperately to clutch it properly.

Even with the team at full strength, Heracles feared that they would have difficulty against the three before them. Nyx and Pontus they could likely take, in a five on two scenario and with great difficulty, but Eros seemed leagues above them. If this was what Tartarus had in their arsenal then the inevitable battle between them and The Alliance would be fierce. As the team were now, they had no hope of defeating her. They were simply too early and too damaged on their journey to face an opponent of such power. After all they had been through, this may well be it. Heracles himself felt drained of all power. Something about Eros had sapped all of the strength he had left within him.

After all they had faced together these short few days: The ferocious fight against the outwardly insurmountable Minotaur; overcoming the trials of the Labyrinth; Theseus and Achilles' life changing injuries; and their acquisition of the Hide of the Nemean Lion. Perhaps all for nothing. If they succumbed to this now, the hide would be lost to Tartarus and they would continue to search for the other two items without challenge from this group of newly acquainted adventurers.

Heracles rage snapped at the thought. It boiled over completely and he was lost to the white light before him.

11

Heracles was flying forwards towards Eros once more.

He had experienced the white light descend only three times over the years. Prometheus had been able to stop him on two occasions where his rage had consumed him, Heracles was unable to recall why he had let his anger slip so far on those occasions. The most recent time was against his brother and in all those moments, Heracles had lost himself, only able to think simple thoughts with no control over his actions or desires. But always, as the great white light descended over his eyes, he felt immeasurably powerful.

He was simply a passenger in own body. The price paid for the power that this form granted him. His blood boiling over and his lust for battle was overwhelmingly insatiable. It was so against his usual character, but the rage had always been there hidden deep within him. It was starting to rise out more and more of late. That was the most worrying thought for Heracles. He was a slave to the light now and try as he might he could not stop it. He prayed that he injured none of his comrades in his blind rage. They were already running thin on health as it was.

He felt Eros's emotion now in that moment. It had changed into worry.

Their swords clashed at blinding speed and Heracles could feel himself closer to matching Eros' power, at the cost of his seeping sanity. He feared being lost in his rage permanently if he didn't stop it somehow. But he had no control over his body and feared it was impossible to stop the decent. Eros was exceptionally skilled with her sword. Even with Heracles' immense speed, heightened tenfold in his rage, she was able to deflect Heracles' attacks to a degree. A true sign of her strength, even if she was acting worried now and was completely on the defensive.

Heracles could feel his strength growing further and further. Metal clashed, sparks flew, and the dust around them seemed to sit in the air, still to the action and lost in time.

Heracles' power rose still. He could feel Eros' unknown power trying to sap his strength as it had done so before, but the more she sapped Heracles' energy, the more power took its place. Eros stepped back against the sustained pressure, her face grimacing under the onslaught of slashes and strikes. She was being driven back now. Heracles hoped the others behind him were able to get away from here. For them to understand that he was out of control. He hoped that Apollo, Selene, Theseus, and Achilles had enough sense to carry on to the alleyways before them and get the hell out of the area before they got caught in the cross fire.

As the thought of the others crossed his mind, he had an image form of Nyx and Pontus making their move, starting to walk towards the others with their weapons raised and their faces awash with wicked smiles. If what he was imagining was true, they were capitalising on the situation as Heracles engaged with Eros.

Heracles was about to fade completely now, his mind filled with overbearing light and his head throbbing with pain.

"Enough!" Eros screamed at him, and he stopped dead, all of the strength again draining from his body instantly. Heracles could feel her inside his mind now, wriggling and probing. She was manipulating him and had brought him out of his rage with her power, her sword weaving and whirling in her hands in hypnotic fashion.

Heracles was still no longer in control of his mind

or body. The anger was gone, replaced with a sense of helplessness. He was at the complete mercy of Eros as she stepped back towards him, slowly driving him back. Her face was a picture of her own rage now.

Heracles could hear the others engaged in a fight behind him: the outcome of the fighting unclear as he was unable to move to them. To help them. To even turn around to check they were ok. It was infuriating and he felt utterly helpless against 'Desire'. She had some sort of hold over him. A power within her blade that was being used on him in this moment. He felt glad that his rage hadn't hurt anyone else, but the all-consuming rage was sadly the only chance he had against her, and that chance was gone.

He was resigned to his fate and watched as Eros drove her sword forward directly at his chest. He would fall here, without any chance of retaliation. He felt robbed. He felt frustrated at everything, but more so, his inability to protect those around him. He had always longed for the chance to prove himself at The Alliance for so many years and even with his wish granted, he still couldn't realise his potential. That was the real failure here and others would pay for it alongside him.

The sword drove hard towards him and Heracles closed his eyes to the pain.

He remembered the Hide of the Nemean Lion too late now, as it rested in his bag. Why hadn't he drawn it around him, using the power of the impenetrable hide. Did he fear the unknown of the item?

He waited for his final moment.
But it didn't come.

12

A clang echoed out across the courtyard, reverberating the sound of metal against metal through the air. A heavy breeze emanated from the area where Heracles should have been stabbed clean through by Eros' sword. He withdrew slightly at the strength of the wind.

Heracles opened his eyes to find Eros standing before him, her sword held firmly in place by two small dagger blades that were reaching around Heracles's body. They were hung low, inches from him, and if they hadn't stopped the blades trajectory he would surely be dead now.

A look of fury was spreading across Eros' face, her control of the situation lost in that moment. Eros' sword vibrated and grinded against the daggers, trying to force her sword further onwards to its target, but to no avail. The twin blades pushed up strongly and Eros was knocked upwards into the air and off her feet. She tumbled to the floor some yards away from Heracles and skidded in the dirt. She spun round on her knees quickly and stared at the figure behind Heracles, her rage growing and pouring from her face in a hot, red blush.

The figure started to walk past Heracles now and was once again immaculately dressed, as she was at their first meeting.

Helene. She turned to Heracles as she walked to Eros, who was rescinding slightly now and scuffling back on her knees. She threw a serious look at Heracles, before turning back to Eros.

"Nice to see you again, old friend. A shame we meet under such negative circumstances," She smiled as she continued to walk forwards. "A bit beat up, aren't we?"

Eros's rage was tipping over, much as Heracles had. Her face continued to flush a scarlet red.

"Don't you dare speak to me! You are lower than dirt to me! You BITCH."

Helene tutted audibly multiple times.

"Now Eros, is that anyway to treat me after all these years? *He* mentioned he'd heard you were part of Tartarus now, but I'd hoped you'd know better than that."

Eros was on her feet, sword in front of her now, screaming at Helene, incensed at her words.

"You're no friend of mine! I severed all my ties a long time ago, and you are no different! Stop interfering or I will *kill* you where you stand." Eros was spitting everywhere.

Heracles heard Helene smile through her words. "You can try."

Eros flew at Helene and they engaged once more, Helene matching Eros in her skill, with a calm beauty. They were more than an even match for each other, Eros's strange power seemingly having little effect over Helene, where it had crippled Heracles. He turned to the others now, as the thought of Pontus and Nyx returned to his mind.

He saw another familiar fighter engaged with not one, but both of the assailants, and fending them off well. Hector was a powerful looking man. His grizzled beard sat atop his square chin, the white hair glistening in the sunlight of the courtyard, seemingly withered with his older age, and containing only a few black hairs now. He was attacking solely with a shield, using it to both block any oncoming attacks, swinging it with magnificent ease, and then using it for attack as well, forcing it vigorously forward against Nyx and Pontus's swords and driving them backwards. He fought with his left fist also, blocking incoming attacks and smashing his large fist against the faces of his attackers, without any caution that Heracles could see.

Three of the four others were fighting alongside him, Apollo and Selene supporting with the majority of the fight, and Achilles keeping Theseus safe. Theseus was still not in any condition to fight in that moment but cheered the others on vigorously.

Eros and Helene halted, Eros saying something to Helene which Heracles didn't quite hear. Or perhaps she was saying it to Nyx and Pontus, as they ejected out of their fight and landed beside Eros, somehow hearing her over the clashes and clangs of their fiery battle. Out of breath, Eros tried to catch it as Nyx and Pontus gathered themselves.

Heracles glanced round and saw the others with their eye's fixed solely on Eros, Nyx, and Pontus, watching for their next move, and in great anticipation.

Helene stepped slowly back to Heracles now, and he rose to his feet beside her, still very wary but mightily glad for her assistance. Without her and Hector he, and most likely the others, would be dead and the hide would be lost to Eros and Tartarus. The others moved closely to Hector in a similar manner; cautious but appreciative.

Eros looked at Helene with the same disdain she had held on her face since her arrival, and also threw a horrid glance towards Hector. Nyx and Pontus tried to portray a strong demeanour beside her, puffing out their chests and standing straight upwards, but Heracles felt they were betrayed by their large gasps for air into their lungs.

Eros mumbled something under her breath that Heracles again didn't catch. Helene seemingly didn't either as she shouted from beside him.

"Speak up Eros, you've gone quiet all of a sudden."

This maddened Eros further, a completely different person to the calm and controlled one Heracles and the others had encountered minutes earlier.

"I *said* that I am going to kill you with my bare hands Helene. Mark my words. I will personally end your life."

"I'm right here Eros. Go ahead and try." Helene said confidently, now in complete control over the situation.

Eros scoffed, her rage falling from her face as she somehow gained some semblance of control over herself.

"Fine, you win this one. We'll stand off for now, but just know that you and that goddamned fool of a boss cannot protect him Helene. Sooner or later Tartarus will end his worthless life and possess that item he carries. It is inevitable."

With that, she exploded into a swirl of black smoke and was gone, returned to where she came from.

Nyx and Pontus stood for a moment longer, Pontus staring directly at Heracles now.

"We'll see you *real* soon Heracles."

"Looking forward to it, you rat bastard." Heracles retorted quickly and powerfully.

Pontus laughed as the smoke engulfed him and Nyx, and they were gone, only a swirl of wind blowing the dust around where they stood remaining, circulating in the air before slowly falling to the earth below.

The courtyard was silent once more.

13

Heracles' legs buckled and he fell to the ground, landing hard on his knees and putting his hands out in front of him to catch himself from falling fully forward. He was at his limit now, exhausted from the last few days: the attack on The Alliance and the emotional trauma of Prometheus' untimely death; the Labyrinth and all of its tests and challenges; the recent brush with Tartarus. His mind was empty. His body was drained. He was in serious need of some rest.

He felt a hand drop to his shoulder. He stiffened up, remembering the potential danger that Helene and Hector poised them, but given their recent acts he was conflicted. He allowed the hand to rest there, even though his body tensed. He couldn't fight them as well.

"Heracles. Hopefully, this goes some way to offering you our trust." Helene said, and he strained to rise his upper body to address her.

"Thank you both," he managed. He almost sighed

it out of his mouth. "We were in a dangerous position there. I thank you on behalf of us all."

Helene nodded, and Heracles watched as Hector walked over to join her, silent as always.

"Glad we found you, after your little light show gave us the slip," She gave a scolding look to Heracles at mentioning that moment. "I understand your lack of trust, I really do, but we could've helped you sooner. Maybe our approach in the market wasn't as welcoming as we thought..."

Heracles thought this to be true given the nature of their first meeting and how uneasy they had all felt.

"Our initial meeting wasn't the warmest Helene. Why help us? What's in it for you?"

Helene smiled sweetly. A genuine smile and it instantly made him feel a little less apprehensive.

"The pirate thing, as your comrade so eloquently put it during our initial conversation, is just a cover for us. It's how we're able to go about our actual business. A rumour that we spread ourselves."

She turned to Hector, seemingly to check he agreed to what she was about to say. He bowed silently for her to continue.

"Our group is called the Argonauts. The truth is that we're on the same side. Many of us are ex-Alliance."

Selene let out a small breath at this revelation. Nothing melodramatic but an acknowledgment that this was unexpected. Heracles agreed. He hadn't expected her to say that.

"*Ex*-Alliance? So you were kicked out like Heracles?" Achilles offered, his demeanour noticeably a lot less aggressive since the Labyrinth, being more curious now.

"Voluntarily ex-Alliance. Way before I joined, our group followed both our leaders out of the door twenty odd years ago. We have never repaired the relationship with The Alliance following that but we both share the same goal: a support of keeping these three fabled items from the wrong hands. With whatever item you found, they are now no longer fabled."

"Who are these leaders? Eros mentioned them as well." Heracles enquired.

"Our captain is called Jason, and he is, and always has been, the right hand man of our true leader - the ex-Stratigos, and co-founder of The Alliance, Poseidon."

No wonder they wanted to help them. After Poseidon had reached out to him just before he left The Alliance and shown him that vision, he felt that they were destined to meet some day. He felt him calling out to him: a small voice in his head every so often offering encouragement and guidance. Not actual words but a feeling. A strange, strange feeling.

"He's been helping The Alliance in secret since he left. He's always been loyal to The Alliance. Poseidon is too proud to offer his support outright. We've been working in the shadows ever since, trying to support where we can in the fight against Tartarus, and in search of the items of lore. We had heard there was an item in the Labyrinth but thought it safe with The Alliance being in such close proximity. We were…wrong. Tartarus no longer care who they attack, or when. They have grown strong."

She paused, to allow the others to get their minds around what she was saying, before continuing.

"In any case, we think we've found the location of another of the fabled items. We want you to help us with the search. Poseidon holds great hope for you Heracles, and Jason follows his lead. We're here to guide you to them in order to discuss the finer details."

She looked around at the others present and her face lightened a bit from the intense conversation they were having.

"But first I feel we rest. You all look terrible; I am sorry to say. Then we can talk details."

"Agreed." Heracles said, as his legs continued to wobble underneath him, desperate to get out of the open after the commotion they have caused. God know who they had woken up, and who were watching them now, scared for their lives after the fight that just took place around them. How no one from The Alliance had come down upon them since they left was anyone's guess.

"We know just the place."

14

Heracles rapped on the door. It creaked open, as mysteriously as before, with no one operating it. At least this time he could be safe in the knowledge that this was a secure space for them to finally rest.

They walked through the corridor and entered into Delphi's lounge. She stood there waiting for them, a tray of tea readily available on the counter with some sweets off to the right hand side in a bowl. Theseus jogged lightly past Heracles and embraced Delphi. It was a strong and weary hug. She embraced him back with passion. A motherly bond had clearly formed there over the years they had spent together and it was a joy to see them so close.

Delphi held Theseus at arm's length and surveyed him. Heracles walked over to the tea, and as he glanced, he could see that Delphi was of course gazing at Theseus' lost eye.

"Oh Theseus. I am so sorry that I didn't see this coming."

"Would it have changed anything Delph? I think not. I was always going to join this lot in the Labyrinth as soon as they walked through our door, and the outcome would've surely followed through either way, had I known about it or not. You know that as well as any of us."

Delphi nodded. "It's still difficult to see you like this. Wounded to such a degree."

Theseus smiled that sweet, charming smile of his.

"Its fine, we'll patch it all up…likely literally…and I'll get on with it. I'll have to."

"Well let's get to it. It looks absolutely awful." She grimaced away from Theseus in jest and smiled, but Heracles thought there was some realness to her gesture. Delphi turned to the others.

"My dear friends. I am sure you need a well-deserved rest. Why not rest here this eve' and we can talk tomorrow about what you plan to do next. Help yourself to tea. There are plenty of beds on the second floor for all of you. The place is deceptively large and has housed many a poor soul in my time here. Sleep well."

She turned, before turning quickly back to them as a thought crossed her mind.

"And welcome to my new guests. Don't try anything whilst you're here please."

She winked and turned to leave with Theseus. Theseus walked with his arm raised over his head and his palm outstretched to offer a goodnight without looking back. Heracles turned back to the table in front of him and poured six teas. He then sat in an empty seat and motioned for the others to join him. In turn, they did so.

"Sorry, I know we are all exhausted and you all have done exceptionally well, but there are a few things I would like to discuss with you all and hope to give you the night to mull them over a bit. Then we can finally turn in for some well-earned rest."

Heracles picked up his cup of tea and blew on it. A small wisp of hot smoke puffed forward as he did so. He took a heavy sip, placed it back down and cleared his throat.

He began.

15

"What!?" Apollo questioned, enraged by what Heracles had just suggested to them. "You cannot be serious. After all we've been through?"

"This is some kind of bullshit Heracles." Selene offered in her calm and collected way, her face stoic and set.

Achilles remained silent, deep in thought as he often had been since their departure from the Labyrinth. Helene and Hector also sat silently, knowing that this conversation was not yet for them. They happily sipped their tea and watched on.

"Apollo, I know that this won't be what you want to hear, but it is the right thing for all of you."

"That's a crock of shit and you know it." Apollo snapped back. Heracles hadn't seen Apollo like it before. "We've come all this way with you. Challenge after challenge we've shown that we're capable. Yes, we've had serious casualties but we're alive and here with you. You must see that. We're with you Heracles."

"Apollo is right," Selene said, offering Apollo some support. "We're in this together and there is no going back. We'd never feel the same at The Alliance after all of this.".

They aren't understanding, Heracles thought. They were stubborn. Much like he could be. But he could not afford anymore injuries to them. He cared for them too much now, even after such a short time together.

"Don't you get it?" Heracles said firmly. "I couldn't handle seeing any of you get horrifically wounded, or even worse, on this crusade. Or whatever it is we're on. I care for you all, and it would be a tragedy beyond me. You're not understanding how I feel about you all."

Heracles was forward in his chair now, almost

pleading to them. Selene and Apollo considered it for a moment before Apollo leaned forward to join Heracles in his stance. Achilles remained out of the conversation and silent.

"Look Heracles. We get it. We understand. I care for you all as well. When people have been through the things we have over the last few days, it naturally creates a bond. But that's the exact reason why we can't break it. We're in this together, whether you like it or not. And we're here with you, until the end."

Apollo looked at Selene and she nodded firmly.

"You're being selfish Heracles. Albeit in your kind way." Apollo finished.

Heracles' frustration rose. They were not listening to him. He went to speak when he was cut off.

"Heracles."

Achilles finally offered his words to the group after quietly contemplating and listening intently to them all from his chair.

"I will stay behind. The others will carry on with you. I will deliver the horns of the Minotaur to the Fates, and I will report back to Gaia."

He paused, lifting up the arm that once attached to his sword hand. He then dropped it, realising his missing hand, before raising his left arm up to his eye line.

"I need to learn how to fight with this arm now. I know that with training I can learn to adapt to this set back. I need The Alliance for that. I won't be a burden to you all as I re-train. But you must know that Selene and Apollo are with you fully, and without them you will not succeed in any of this. I know that now. And when I am ready I will re-join you. I'm with you completely also. But for now, this is what I can do for the team. Let me do it."

Heracles was stunned by Achilles words. His calmness. His level-headed approach. It was years away from the Achilles he knew when they had first met. Coming out the back of a serious failure could do that to someone, he supposed. Before he could reply though, another interjection prevented him.

"If we may interject here," Helene offered. "This seems like the right opportunity for us also to engage with The Alliance also. Poseidon won't like it, but Jason tasked us with making peace here if we got the chance and whilst our primary focus was assisting you, we now have an opportunity to also go to The Alliance with Achilles here."

Heracles had questions, of course.

"But we can't all go to The Alliance Helene. I am banished from there. I cannot go back, and I will not wait."

"I will report with Achilles and accompany him."

Hector had creaked forward slightly in his chair, his large frame struggling in the small chair he had chosen. His silence finally broken. Apollo muttered something to Selene about his surprise that he could actually talk. Heracles thought he was quite the articulate fellow. Surprising.

"I will assist Achilles with confronting these 'Fates' he speaks of. I will assist him with his report to Gaia, before then journeying by myself to meet you all at our own HQ when our business is concluded."

Heracles moved to talk again but was cut off once more. He was getting pretty tired of everyone doing so.

"No. That's it settled Heracles. Hector will accompany Achilles and offer his assistance before re-joining us down the road. I will then accompany you all and take you to Jason and Poseidon. End of conversation." Helene was stern now. Heracles felt he was losing this conversation, and fast.

"Well that's settled then," Selene said as she got up from the table. "Achilles, we'll welcome you back with open arms when you're ready." She softly kissed him on the cheek before walking towards the stairs at the back of the room.

"Sele..." Heracles stuttered.

"Agreed. Sounds like a plan. I'll see you all in the morning ready for when we depart." Apollo was also up and walking towards the stairs. No looking back or hesitation in sight. Heracles' protests went unheard.

"Agreed, we are settled then. Let us retire Hector. We can talk through the finer details quickly upstairs."

They both retired, leaving Achilles and Heracles alone at the table, Heracles with a look of complete loss on his face at the scene that had just unfolded.

Achilles offered him a return to the conversation.

"Heracles, it's for the best. We're with you. I get that now. I will help anyway that I can but for now, this is all I can do for you. I can be your eyes and ears at The Alliance, and as a friend on the inside."

He looked deeply at Heracles.

"For all you have given me these past few days, it is the least I can do. My pride will never get the best of me again. You can be damn sure of that. And I will join you all when I can. You can be damn sure of that as well."

Achilles was highly serious in that moment.

"Let us do this. Please."

Heracles let out a large sigh, took one final sip of his tea and considered. This had all happened so fast and the others seemed so sure of it that Heracles honestly thought he had no chance of bringing them around to his side of thinking. His options as he saw them were either leaving in the dead of night without anyone seeing him, or, conceding and letting this move forward. He conceded.

"Thank you, Achilles. I mean that."

Heracles reached down by his side to his bag and pulled one of the Minotaur horns from his bag. He handed it over to Achilles in what felt like some sort of ritual gifting.

"Selene has the other one so grab it from her in the morning. Don't take any shit from The Fates. And be careful. The Alliance may well have been compromised and the only person you can trust right now is Gaia. And my long-time friends Atlas and Demeter. They will keep an eye on things with you if you invest your trust in them."

Heracles paused, and looked around the room before returning his eyes to Achilles.

"Also, keep an eye on Hector as well. I hope everything Helene has said is true, and I do believe it is, but just be wary ok?"

Achilles nodded.

"Agreed. And take care of yourself. I wish you all the luck in the world. And if you need me, I'll be there."

"Deal."

They both moved their left arms forward in a swing, locking hands in a strong embrace.

The plan was set in motion, and Heracles hoped to the gods that it was the right plan of action.

16

Achilles retired for the evening.

Heracles sat alone in the room. Alone with his thoughts. Alone with his successes. Alone with his failures.

He went over the last few days events in detail in his mind, analysing where he could've, and should've, done better for those around him. He had to improve, not only his strength, his cunning, his strategies, but also his leadership and his protection of those around him. He had to learn to control the fury that resided within him. Control it and use it to its full extent. He also needed to hone his use of his lightning powers astronomically. Only then would he be able to challenge Tartarus and fight them on equal ground. If Eros was any indication of how strong they were then they were in for a serious battle in the future, and Heracles and his team needed to be exceptionally well prepared for that.

He also thought about Helene, and her skill in defending them all from Eros. Her strength in battle. How Eros' power seemingly didn't affect Helene. She would be an excellent companion in their journey to track down Poseidon.

Poseidon…

Heracles had many questions for him. The items of lore and his knowledge of them. His relationship with The Alliance. His relationship with his parents. He would spare nothing in his quest for answers. And his quest for revenge on those who killed his parents. He would achieve his goal at any cost. But he would not drag the others into that. That was his burden to bear. And he would bear it alone when the time came. For now though he would accept the help of the others in his search for the items of lore.

He finished off the rest of his tea, grimacing at the coldness of it now, and placed it down onto the table.

He headed for the stairs. He would sleep well that night, knowing that it would surely be his last good sleep for a long, long time.

17

Heracles was woken up by Selene, nudging him gently with her hand as he slept. He woke easily, feeling sore but refreshed. He quickly pulled the covers up across more of his body, before turning to her, not quite catching her first words as he lazily came round.

She was sterner the second time, annoyed that he hadn't heard her.

"I *said,* it's time for breakfast. Come on."

As straight as ever, and Heracles enjoyed that about her really. At least there was no underlying messages in her words. They were clear cut, and he liked that about

Selene.

"Gotcha. Two minutes."

Selene nodded at his reply, and headed off downstairs.

Heracles set about packing up his things and getting dressed. He surveyed his ripped clothes and thought the first thing they needed to do before they set off was to hit the market, straighten up their current attire, and purchase some new kit and rations. They had given themselves a bit of time, and Heracles didn't think Tartarus would try and attack again after failing last time out.

He finished off getting ready and headed downstairs. The rest of them were sitting at the table now, Achilles with a fresh bandage on his stump, wrapped expertly. Theseus was also freshly dressed, with a leather patch over his eye which someone had fashioned for him, likely Delphi. It suited him well as it happened, adding a bit of mystery to his boyish good looks that in fact increased his handsomeness, much to the jealously of Heracles.

He caught Heracles looking at him and smiled.

"Admiring the new face accessory, are we?"

Heracles snorted.

"Well, it is in prime position on your face. But seriously, it looks great Theseus. Suits you."

"Thanks mate." Theseus said with a slight sadness in his voice, still getting used to it all but making jokes to make himself feel fine about it. That was the Theseus that Heracles remembered the most.

"Heracles." Helene called to him from her chair, as she lazily brushed the crumbs of her bread from her mouth. Heracles walked over and joined her.

"I have a question if I may?"

So formal.

"Shoot." Heracles responded, trying desperately to make the conversation casual.

"Why didn't you attempt to use the hide you

found in the Labyrinth during the fight with Eros? You were in desperate need of something to assist you against her but it didn't cross your mind?"

Heracles, his bag upstairs with the hide tucked away in, thought back. He also noted to himself not to leave such an important item off his person. Ever. He would not fail in that again.

He hadn't even considered using the hide against Eros until the point where Helene had saved him. It scared him to be honest. It was such an unknown that he dared not mess with it until he could figure it all out.

He decided to be straight with Helene.

"I guess I was a bit apprehensive about messing with it until I truly understood it. Such a unique item could hold untold curses or hexes, and I couldn't afford to risk that, no matter how grave the situation."

"Wise. We will see what Poseidon thinks of it all when we see him. He'll have some insight I am sure."

She gathered her thoughts.

"My second point considers Eros."

Heracles thought this might be coming. Eros and Helene knew each other and Eros seemed to back off instantly upon seeing Helene.

"I know you'll ask so I will give an explanation. I will be brief, but Eros and I knew each other many years ago. We grew up together. We were both looked down upon by the other kids for some reason. We didn't fit in at all. Bullied. Chased. Beaten. We became close, but where I was able to move past the torment and change my path, Eros succumbed to it. She lost herself in the pain and went down a dark, dark path."

She paused, the memory clearly painful to her.

"Frequent wrong turns over the years led her to an assassin's life. She fell in with Tartarus a number of years ago it seems, and they granted her that power you bared witness to. Poseidon had witnessed it first hand in a chance encounter with Tartarus recently. She almost got the drop on him. Her power only affects men you see. She has control over your gender, but none over women. Still, she is strong and I am fortunate she cannot affect my mind. That is how I was able to push her back as I did."

She paused again, keeping her gaze on Heracles as she spoke.

"She is one of five generals of Tartarus, and Poseidon gauges her as the weakest of the five. The Generals of Tartarus are monsters. We'll have our work cut out if we are to go toe to toe with them as we are. This is where I hope to have Poseidon and Jason come in."

"Do you think they'll be able to help?"

"Undoubtedly Heracles. And they will explain all when we meet with them."

She finished her breakfast, eating it politely whenever she was waiting for Heracles's reply to avoid speaking with her mouth full. Heracles had been doing the same.

She stood.

"I think it's time to go if we're all ready. Say your goodbyes to Achilles and we'll be off."

She was formal, but warm. A strange combination, akin to that of a teacher.

18

Heracles watched as Achilles and Apollo embraced strongly. Apollo said something to Achilles, and he broke slightly. He nodded, and mouthed an apology that Heracles saw clearly. Hopefully, Apollo had cooled his anger towards Achilles' actions in the Labyrinth.

Achilles hugged Selene. It was a warm hug, and unusual for Selene but Heracles could feel the friendship there. A bond grown even over a short few days. There was something in being part of the same class of pupils, and The Alliance was much the same in that regard.

Theseus and Achilles simply bumped fists. Unbelievably, no animosity between them. Both with losses, and both just moving on with it all. Theseus said his goodbyes and wished him luck. He said one more thing before disappearing upstairs for something.

Now Achilles turned to Heracles, and they strongly embraced. They said their goodbyes at each other's ears.

"Take care of yourself Achilles. Thank you for doing this. An important part of the mission that we couldn't do without. Stay safe out there and keep your wits about you."

"No problem. Good luck with everything, and I will be here whenever you need me, Heracles."

They parted, locked fists, as they did last night, and their goodbyes were said. Hector, silent again now, bowed at all of them in turn.

"Make sure you contact us when you've finished at The Alliance Hector. Jason will want an update from you as well." Helene said as she reached into her bag and handed Hector what looked like a large shard of glass. "You know what to do. I'll be waiting."

He nodded, and they saluted to each other. It reminded Heracles of the salute of The Alliance, with a twist.

Heracles turned to Delphi. "Thank you for everything Delph. We appreciate it more than you know."

She smiled and hugged him tightly.

"You take care of yourself Heracles. Long travels and hardships await you I am 'fraid to say. But I know you'll overcome all that lies before you, my boy."

She pulled away, before going in for another cuddle, her arms barely wrapping around him. How things had changed since he was a kid growing up in Minos.

Heracles addressed everyone before they departed.

He felt the need to say something before they went their separate ways.

"I thank you all for all the help you've given and good luck in your respective missions. We will meet again, and I look forward to that day with a heavy heart as we leave. Gods-speed."

Everyone in the room looked at him, and saluted back in their own unique way; whether it was the salute of The Alliance from Selene, Achilles, and Apollo; the unique salute of Hector and Helene; the wink and wave of Delphi; or the strange overtly sarcastic diagonal slash Theseus made with his arm, imitating The Alliance's salute poorly. Despite all his jokes, Theseus looked terribly sad at being left behind. A pang of guilt ran through Heracles in that moment but he was better off here.

Heracles feared it would be a while before they saw each other again but he put the thought to the back of his mind as he, Apollo, Selene, and Helene left Delphi's home, heading out into Minos once more.

CHAPTER X
ASCENSION

1

Having spent some time in the market, gathering additional supplies for the trip, the four of them then reached Theseus' secret stone exit out of the walls of the city, thinking it best not to draw any further attention to themselves, especially after their altercation in the courtyard outside Minos. They had been lucky that those who heard it had not come out in their droves for fear of their own safety. They wore their cloaks around them for cover.

Achilles had mentioned that he and Hector would head to The Alliance after heading to The Fates to update them. Hopefully with that, Heracles and co would have time to get on their way without The Alliance trying to head after them, if they decided they wanted the Hide of the Nemean Lion in their possession, instead of with Heracles now. It should buy them some time at least.

"Helene, how far a trip is it to your Headquarters? A while off I'd imagine." Heracles enquired as they shuffled through the exit and out into the open air.

"Correct. Our own HQ is about a week's flight from here so we'd best get moving."

"A week's *flight*?" Apollo enquired, instantly hesitant.

Helene shot him a look of annoyance at having to repeat herself.

"Yes, a week's flight. Don't make me repeat myself Apollo," A scolding for the young lad from the older woman. Apollo retreated to walk next to Selene.

"How do you think we got here? We have a façade of being sky pirates to uphold you know. The flight takes time, as we have to go a specific route to our Headquarters to avoid flying into any…trouble."

She turned her attention back to Heracles.

"Our ship is a walk away, hidden at the Siren's Lake: Poseidon's favourite haunt when at The Alliance. He loved teasing the Sirens whenever he could."

She pointed right to Siren's Lake: the lake that Heracles had spotted before entering the Labyrinth. So he would get to go there after all.

They walked out further into the grasslands.

"The Sirens are real then…" Heracles murmured to himself, too quietly apparently, as Selene spoke over the top of him to Helene.

"That's our destination then? Tell me Helene, do you think you can help us locate the other two items of lore? You've been searching for them too, right?"

Helene nodded.

"We have yes. It's been an arduous task. One that has led us to many a dead end over many years. I am glad that the Labyrinth wasn't misplaced information after the trouble it caused us to get it, and you are very fortunate to have met with those 'Fates'. I don't quite believe any of the mystical bullshit, but it's good that they pointed you in the right direction."

She formed quotation marks in the air as she said the words 'mystical bullshit', much to Apollo's annoyance. He scrunched his face sulkily.

"You weren't there Helene. I promise you that they were the real deal. They *knew* things."

"Fine. Think what you will. I get it. I've seen many unusual things in my time with the Argonauts so I'll leave it at that, but I will say you were highly fortunate and that these things can often be explained simply. Anyway, Jason thinks he has another of the three items pinned down this time. Mostly as two of our strongest members have not returned from the place where they sought it."

She paused, clearly hurt by the mention of her missing comrades.

"No matter though, we march on. I will tell you more on the ride to our headquarters."

"Which is where exactly?" Apollo said, still nervous at the thought of flying.

"You'll see."

As she spoke, Heracles heard a shout from behind them. He whirled round to check who was following them and was pleasantly surprised to see a familiar face running towards them.

2

Theseus was bounding towards them like an excited puppy, waving his arms furiously over his head. He had a pack on his back, filled with gods know what.

He reached the four of them and leaned over, panting frantically as he rested his arms against his thighs.

"…Been…trying to…catch-up." he breathed, heavily, trying desperately to catch his breath.

"Hey Theseus." Selene offered nonchalantly as only she could.

"What are you doing here Theseus? Did we leave something behind?" Heracles enquired, confused as to his presence.

"Yes, you dolt…me!"

He composed himself for a second before rising to his normal posture.

"I'm coming with you guys." he said, offering the group a handsome and cheeky smile.

"Uhh…" Helene said, unsure of what to say, and assumedly apprehensive about too many people joining them. It was the first time Heracles had heard her stumble on her words. Heracles cut her off before she could catch herself, seeing a chance to have Theseus be a part of his life again and welcoming it gladly.

"Great news! The more the merrier right Helene?"

Heracles turned to her and smiled. She was clearly annoyed but gave in relatively quickly. She breathed an audible and melodramatic sigh.

"Fine. Fine. But he's the last one, you hear me Heracles? We need to push forward."

Heracles nodded and turned to Theseus. He swung his arm around his shoulder, clutching his old friend and dragged him forward to continue their march towards Siren's Lake, ensuring that he grabbed the side opposite to the eye patch so that Theseus could look at him properly.

He lowered his voice so that Helene couldn't hear him.

"But seriously, you're sure about this? After the Labyrinth?"

Theseus smiled sweetly.

"Absolutely. Inside the Labyrinth I felt more alive than I ever have. I am forever in your', and your' friends, debt for helping me avenge my family, and for that I will gladly follow you into any battle Heracles. I mean that."

He looked at Heracles with sincerity in his eyes. Heracles could feel his spirit, his vigour, and he knew that the group would need that in spades on this journey. He was thankful to have Theseus on board, forgetting all of his apprehension at him joining them from a few hours prior.

"That sounds great Theseus. It really, really does."

3

They continued onwards, Helene leading the way

and very much deep in her own thoughts, with Heracles desperate to know the inner workings of her mind.

Heracles and Theseus walked side by side, reminiscing about the old days, a chance they hadn't had yet given all that had happened over the last few days. It was a welcome change of pace for them and Heracles intended to enjoy it. As they walked through one of the fields, Heracles ran his outstretched arm across the tall blades of grass subconsciously, just happy to be outside in the open and outside of the city.

Selene and Apollo were bringing up the rear. Heracles overheard something about Achilles whilst they talked, and hoped he was ok. He had grown following the Labyrinth, and it would serve him and The Alliance exceptionally well. He hoped for great things from Achilles and saw no reason why he wouldn't grab the opportunity firmly with both hands.

Heracles baulked at his choice of phrasing before his mind drifted back to The Alliance. He would miss it of course, but his adventures out in the open world were too strong a calling. He had always longed for adventure and felt that the Labyrinth was both a success and failure for him. He had to grow. Learn more about his powers. And seek to revenge his parents after all these years.

He had so many fond memories of The Alliance. He had really had some great days there, especially with Demeter, who he would miss deeply. But he would see her again, and his old friend Atlas, eventually reporting back to Gaia with good news of their successes. He hoped. And with Achilles there, The Alliance was gaining another strong and important member, now experienced in live combat, albeit in need of re-learning his sword skills with his left hand and exploring exactly what powers his father's sword contained. Achilles would just need to be careful and watch out for any further traitors in The Alliance. Heracles did not believe that they were yet free of those who wished to do them harm, from both inside and outside the organisation.

And of course Ares and Hermes were still missing.

Either way, he would look back on it fondly, and though he missed Prometheus more than he would ever be able to articulate, he had been his friend and mentor for many years and he would always treasure that and be happy in that knowledge.

He took one long look back at Athenaeus before Theseus snapped his mind back to the present as he continued regaling him with stories of what he had missed when he left Minos many years ago.

4

They had been walking for what had seemed several hours. He hadn't realised that it would take so long to get to Siren's Lake but did recall those journeying there daily doing so mostly on horseback, which would exponentially cut down the travelling time. At least his time with Theseus was making it all go quicker.

Heracles stopped and grabbed some water out of his backpack, slurping vigorously as he attempted to quench his thirst. Helene stopped also, noticing Heracles stop, and the others follow her lead.

They were nearing the end of the plains heading towards the lake now and were a short distance from their destination and Helene's flying transport, which Heracles was secretly hugely excited for.

He didn't know anyone who had flown before. It was such a rare occurrence in their city, and the only time he had ever even seen an airship was when an unknown visitor came to The Alliance years ago. She had been dressed in a long satin clock, and Heracles had only caught a brief glimpse of her face, still vaguely remembering it. He hadn't recognised her then, but now felt a sneaking suspicion in the back of his mind as he thought back. Had he now seen her somewhere? He tried to rack his brain for the information but it wasn't forthcoming.

He felt Selene tap him lightly on the arm. His face must've been showing signs of a frown as he chased the thought. He waved her off with an absent smile.

He had it! He had seen the woman once before, recently, as a part of Poseidon's vision. One of those at the round table, that he hadn't recognised at the time. Of course it was her. How could he have forgotten that? Strange. But he knew nothing further about her, apart from that she had access to an airship and Gaia was very pleased to see her at the time of her arrival.

No point in dwelling on it now, Heracles thought to himself, and he packed his water pouch back into his bag.

"Not much farther now everyone." Helene offered them as a dangling carrot to reinvigorate their weary legs.

"Keep up." she added as a throwaway comment and it slightly derailed her previous sentence. No matter, Heracles thought. They would get used to Helene. She was a keen fighter and the language of the blade spoke volumes to fighters such as them.

They marched on.

Apollo came to the side of Heracles as they walked, and Theseus, getting the hint, dropped back to Selene. Heracles watched as she blushed deeply, before throwing Heracles the most scathing glance. He turned away sheepishly to speak to Apollo, who was walking beside him now.

"What's on your mind Apollo?" he asked.

Apollo shuffled his feet as he walked and held his head low before replying, his confidence waning again in that moment.

"A couple of things really. Uh...would be up for teaching me how to activate my armour again?"

"Absolutely Apollo, I had the exact same thought."

Heracles really meant that. He had seen the look on Apollo's face when he couldn't activate it in the short time he had to learn, and how he had felt less than the others in the Labyrinth. But he secretly felt that Apollo had the most potential out of all of them.

"We'll see what Helene's airship is like and then if it suits, we can use the time we have travelling to practice further. We'll look at as many things as we can with the time we have."

Apollo nodded.

"That brings me to my second question...I *hate* heights. Is this thing gonna be safe?"

Heracles laughed before noticing the look on Apollo's face, and apologised through a mouth holding back laughter.

"Sorry, I didn't mean to be cruel. I am sure it'll be fine. Helene and Hector likely use it for their travelling a lot so it's *got* to be safe."

Apollo pondered this and then nodded further. Seemingly satisfied but still with a hint of nervousness on his face.

"Last quick thing..."

"Ask away Apollo, we're a team now. No need to sit on any questions you have."

"Ok, thanks Heracles. I've...been thinking about all of this and, we're not likely to be back at Athenaeus for a while are we?"

"What makes you say that?" Heracles enquired, even when he felt the same way.

"It just feels like the other two items, if what Helene said is anything to go by, are going to take some serious time to find and, as we're all in on this, there is no going back without them, right?"

Heracles considered this for a second.

"You're right, there's no going back now. We

either succeed or die trying. That's the path we follow. Having second thoughts?"

"No, no. Honestly. Not at all, but I just wanted to voice my mind. I...I've never been great at that, so it feels nice to be able to have someone to talk to about everything."

Heracles clasped Apollo on the back. He was really starting to like the kid.

"We'll do it Apollo. Trust me."

5

The lake before them was vast. Heracles had never seen it up close before. Saying that, he had never been permitted by Promo to even leave the city lest he get carried off into his oblivion by unknown assailants (Prometheus' words, not his).

This was new. Exciting. And he was sharing it with many whom were in the same boat as him. Those that hadn't been afforded the opportunity to leave Athenaeus. It was rare for anyone to leave once they had settled there, unless they were sent out to forage as part of their work.

The stories about the cities past the mountains were legendary. A vast land filled with the unknown. Heracles had heard stories of it being an unlawful land in places. Of cities of great and mysterious technology. And cities of pure debauchery. But most of all, he had heard of the freedom. Heracles was most excited about that, and that was why he held a slight jealousy for Helene, who was clearly a traveller of the world.

"Helene?"

Helene turned to Heracles as she walked ahead of him, dropping her pace to join him and Apollo.

"Yes?" she offered, in her formal way.

"Are the stories about the lands beyond the

Magnesia Mountains true?"

"Depends what stories you've heard Heracles. There are many."

That mostly confirmed Heracles question without the need for follow-up he thought, but he continued regardless.

"I heard tales at The Alliance of some unruly lands beyond the border of the mountain range. Some incredible cities. New technology. Where everyone was free to do what they wanted, for better or worse."

"You're not wrong. I always find myself a little bored coming over to Arcadia, but it is at least lawful. Mostly full of good people. Hellas is fraught with both good and evil, a constant struggle between those that harm and those that heal. Filled with frightening beasts. Cities of great size and technological advancements. Airships fly high above all of it. Kings and queens of the sky, just like us Argonauts. It feels so *alive* to me. So full of possibility."

Heracles felt her passion come out finally. It was a nice feeling, and one that warmed her, pulling her away from her formal shell for a second.

"I would imagine that you will all love it, having been relatively shackled your whole life. Hellas will allow you to fly. To break free. For better or worse, as you put it so eloquently."

Heracles' experienced a rush of excitement in that moment. It was palpable. The stories of the land across the mountains, Hellas, were seemingly true and he couldn't wait to see it with his own eyes.. Adventure lay ahead, and whilst he would always have a fondness for his side of the mountain, in Arcadia, he felt the call of Hellas now more than ever.

"I will say this though," Helene said, interrupting Heracles' thoughts of grandeur. "What you had, and I mean *had*, here was safety above all else. Crossing the border before us strips you of that. Poseidon knows all about you Heracles. He discovered you had survived all those years ago, where others did not. He felt your presence but felt safe in the knowledge that you would be protected in Arcadia. In Athenaeus. That you would follow the call of The Alliance one day, and that they would offer shelter for you. He left you there for good reason."

She paused. Heracles was focussed on her completely, shocked at this latest revelation and the level of information she held on him.

"But Tartarus are mobilising again. The recent attack on The Alliance proves that. Poseidon realised their movement too late. You are lucky that Hector and I were already in Arcadia…on business…when Poseidon contacted us about it all. They will come for you again Heracles. We don't know why, but they will come. Especially so now that you carry that lion's hide with you. And considering they now know that you wield your father's sword."

Helene darted her eyes down at the backpack Heracles was carrying, before darting her gaze back to Heracles' sword.

"You must always be ready. This isn't some family outing, as I am sure you are acutely aware."

She turned back to face forward. Her formal shell now fully returned and sat snuggly around her exterior. She stepped forward quickly and walked alone once more.

Heracles remained alone with his thoughts, and he could feel that Apollo knew this is what he wanted and remained silent for him to process it all. Poseidon knew a lot it seemed and had deeper connections to him than he realised. He had to meet him and ask the multitude of questions now circulating his mind, whirling in furious circles.

Poseidon might be the key to the information he lacked on his parents, and of that fateful night so many years ago where they were brutally disposed of. That which Prometheus was either unsure of, or not willing to share with Heracles. He would not make the mistake of waiting to enquire further with Poseidon. He would get all the information he required there and then when they met.

His mind continued to whirr as he remained marching forward. The lake within touching distance before him.

6

"Right, hold up here." Helene said to the gaggle of people behind her, all of them rounding to a halt together in a small group, the excitement building. Barring Apollo who was as distressed as ever at the thought of flying.

They were at the edge of the lake now.

The lake was glistening in the morning sun, its water clear at the shore before darkening considerably as it stretched out into the lake. It really was beautiful and Heracles wondered what secrets it held in its depths.

Helene stepped forward towards the water's edge now.

"So what now Helene?" Heracles said as she simply stared out to the lake.

"Now, you watch."

She drew something from her pack. It looked similar to the remote control Gaia had used during the vision Poseidon had shown him.

Heracles watched on, completely impatient, a rarity for him, as Helene stalled in her movements. He shot Theseus a look, with him offering his famous shrug, walking forward to stand beside Heracles. Apollo joined them, with Selene also following suit. Selene with a look of wild excitement on her face now, one which Heracles had rarely seen from her.

"What's up with you?" Heracles enquired. Her

eyes were wild.

"I...I *love* the thought of being able to fly...I can feel we're close and I just cannot *wait*!"

Heracles was slightly taken aback by her sudden change in character.

"Uh, this is a new look for you Selene." Theseus said to her.

She turned her head sharply towards Theseus, blushing slightly as she always did when she spoke or looked at him.

"No, no...it...it's a good thing! Honest!" Theseus said, stumbling over his words and backtracking.

She seemed content with his backtracking and went back to her wild looks towards Helene, waiting for her to show even a little bit of the airship.

Helen finally moved her second hand up to the device in her hand, quickly checking behind her and at the surrounding area to see if they were indeed alone. Satisfied, she turned back to the lake and rotated one of the dials on the remote.

An area of water on the surface of the lake bubbled before them, only slightly, before a rumble was heard, rising in volume as whatever was in the lake came towards the surface. Heracles nerves rose at the unknown but were matched by his excitement.

The water rumbled and bubbled harder and faster, more furiously with every second that passed, the volume of it all becoming very, very noisy. The bubbling continued to grow in size, more and more metres apart now in diameter. Waves formed and crashed against each other on the once peaceful lake surface.

Heracles then clocked that something was starting to protrude from the water before them, edging out quickly now and forming into a marvellous sight.

Water cascaded from around the shape, crashing back to the surface of the lake. Heracles could only marvel at what was happening, and imagined that the others were also completely focussed on the sight before them. As the object emerged from the lake completely, it hovered in place, heading slowly towards them before resting just above the surface of the lake. Heracles glanced round and noticed Helene smiling beside them, likely due to seeing the shock on all of their faces, as the object came to a halt just before them and hovered in place.

Before them lingered a magnificent airship.

7

"Ladies and gentlemen. I give you our airship." Helene said before pausing to look fondly at the magnificent machine before them.

"I give you, The Argo."

It was simply a wonderful sight. The airship Heracles had seen before was both at a distance and surrounded by many people, so he wasn't able to get a good look at it from where he was stood. This, however, was right in front of him. Up close and personal and a marvel of technology he didn't fully understand. The previous airship he had seen was maybe fancier, and a lot bigger but this was still unbelievably impressive in its own right. And it looked *fast*.

The airship was long and thin, with a sharp cylinder of wood at the front, sharp at the edge, which faced them and had a propeller attached to it. Either side of the propeller, painted onto the ships' helm, were two large white eyes. As Heracles walked to his left to get a better look at it all, he saw that it had the body of a boat, which Heracles found fascinating, as he could not yet imagine how this thing could fly. But fly it surely would.

The majority of The Argo was made out of wood, finished beautifully, with trims of long golden strips of metal adorning the lower part of the airship, the middle of the airship and the trim towards the deck. It was a mix of brown and gold, beautifully painted and decorated with interesting patterns of old. Heracles recognised the style of design from the pillars of The Alliance, namely Hephaestus' workshop. Jutting out of either side of the ship towards the front were two thin masts, facing horizontally, that had propellers protruding out of the top of them up towards the sky. The same masts also jutted out in the middle of the ship, and toward the back.

In the middle of what he could only assume was the deck of the ship, he could just make out, another mast, this time vertical, with another propeller on top of it. The same structure was in the middle of the decking, again toward the back. Seemingly all of this combined to make the wonderful contraption fly up and into the air.

Heracles felt his heart racing again. The excitement building once more.

"Shall we go?" Helene said, again so formally. So unaware, or nonplussed, about the sheer astonishment everyone else was going through. Straight and to the point, so as to not waste any more time. Heracles thought it best to just go with it, and he looked at everyone in turn to check they were ok to go forward. They all nodded back, even though Apollo's reaction was a little slow and reluctant.

"Ok, great." Helene said as she turned to The Argo and pressed another button on her device. A set of steps appeared out of the bottom of the boat, seamlessly appearing from the wood, and revealing a way up and into the hull of the ship. She ascended, turning slightly to the others, and beckoning for them to follow.

Heracles ascended and stepped up and out onto the decking of the ship after several steps. It was wonderfully finished. As a boat it was magnificent. As an airship it was wondrous!

The decking had some sort of a cabin towards the back. No doubt the captain's quarters, and likely reserved for Helene whilst she commanded the ship, and for Jason whenever he was on board. Towards the front of the ship was the helm, ready for Helene to steer The Argo on their journey. Heracles was looking forward to seeing how it all worked. It was all very exciting.

Selene was frantically jogging around the deck now, her excitement overflowing, letting out little squeals as she moved around. Apollo was against the edge of the ship holding on for dear life, even with them not yet moving, and looking deathly pale, noticeable on his amber skin as it tightened against the strain of his hands, gripping onto the side of the ship.

Heracles went to say something but then thought better of it. Better to let him concentrate on not throwing up his breakfast at this point.

Heracles called for Theseus to join him towards the front of the ship. He was placing his bag into a box with a latch on it, just to make sure it was secure during the flight. The box looked to be built directly into the ship's frame and highly secure. Theseus threw his bag over as he walked, and Heracles placed it in there also.

"What do you think? Bet you didn't factor this into your future, did you?" Heracles said to Theseus, interested in what he was making of all of this.

Theseus laughed heartily.

"You're not wrong, my friend. What a few days. Between this and the Labyrinth though, I'd gladly choose the sky and the wonders it holds."

"Well you're about to find out what it's like up there Theseus." Helene said from behind them. She was now stood strongly at the helm, smiling.

"Are you ready to go Heracles?"

The ultimate question. One he wasn't quite ready for but must answer anyway. They had come this far. The only way was forward now. And what better way to get there than by flying in this wondrous airship.

"We're ready when you are Helene." he offered back.

She nodded and sent Heracles a smile. "Grab onto something then. It'll be a bumpy ride as we take off."

She flicked a switch with her foot, and the propellers slowly started to buzz into life, whirring above their heads and to the sides of the ship's hull. Both Heracles and Theseus grabbed on to the side of the ship, and Heracles glanced over to the Apollo and Selene to check they were ok and doing the same. Apollo hadn't moved of course, and was still clinging on for dear life, but Selene had now joined him by his side, one of her hands on the side of the ship to steady herself and one on the smalls of Apollo's back. The look on her face was still wild with excitement.

The propellers quickened rapidly, spinning faster and faster now. They became a blur, but the noise was surprisingly minimal given the speed at which they were rotating.

Heracles felt himself slip a little on the decking as the airship sprung upwards slightly, as Helene took control of the airship.

Helene stalled, quickly looking to all of them and checking they were ok before nodding to herself. Helene shouted over at them all.

"Here…we…go!"

She grunted and pulled back heavily on the helm.

The airship rocketed skyward forcefully, Heracles holding tightly onto the railing as it did so, desperately clinging on now and following Apollo's lead. He was right in thinking it was fast.

He glanced at Apollo who had his eyes firmly shut, his face crunched into a mess of skin, and his hands grasping at the ship as hard as he could. Heracles laughed through the force of the wind against his face. He let out a loud shout at the top of his lungs. Theseus joined in the shouting, as a release of adrenaline, screaming into the afternoon sky.

The airship shot upwards and into the heavens

above them, piercing through the low lying cloud in the air. Darkness fell around them for a moment before they burst out the other side and glided effortlessly into the open blue air.

The airship hung in the air for a moment and Heracles shouted to the others.

"One week of travelling lies ahead of us team! Now the real training begins!" he bellowed, thinking it time to get the others used to their powers, with the assistance of both Helene and Theseus. They would need the time afforded to them, and they would use it wisely.

Helene stalled for a second longer, just to check that Heracles was finished. He nodded to her and Helene slammed forward on the helm.

The ship propelled swiftly forward, sending them upwards and onwards towards Hellas.

Towards The Argonauts' Headquarters.

Towards Freedom, and, towards their destiny

Printed in Great Britain
by Amazon